Plea of Insanity

JILLIANE HOFFMAN

PENGUIN BOOKS

PENGUIN BOOKS

Published by the Penguin Group
Penguin Books Ltd, 80 Strand, London WC2R ORL, England
Penguin Group (USA) Inc., 375 Hudson Street, New York, New York 10014, USA
Penguin Group (Canada), 90 Eglinton Avenue East, Suite 700, Toronto, Ontario, Canada M4P 2Y3
(a division of Pearson Penguin Canada Inc.)
Penguin Ireland, 25 St Stephen's Green, Dublin 2, Ireland
(a division of Penguin Books Ltd)
Penguin Group (Australia), 250 Camberwell Road, Camberwell, Victoria 3124, Australia
(a division of Pearson Australia Group Pty Ltd)
Penguin Books India Pvt Ltd, 11 Community Centre, Panchsheel Park, New Delhi – 110 017, India
Penguin Group (NZ), 67 Apollo Drive, Rosedale, Auckland 0632, New Zealand
(a division of Pearson New Zealand Ltd)
Penguin Books (South Africa) (Pty) Ltd, 24 Sturdee Avenue, Rosebank, Johannesburg 2196, South Africa

Penguin Books Ltd, Registered Offices: 80 Strand, London WC2R ORL, England

www.penguin.com

First published by Michael Joseph 2007
Published in Penguin Books 2007
Reissued in this edition 2012

... Capote, copyright
... rtz. Reprinted by
... Schwartz.
... the P. J. Kavanagh,
... Reprinted by

ISBN: 978-0-718-19373-7

www.greenpenguin.co.uk

MIX
Paper from
responsible sources
FSC
www.fsc.org
FSC™ C018179

Penguin Books is committed to a sustainable
future for our business, our readers and our planet.
This book is made from Forest Stewardship
Council™ certified paper.

For Rich, Amanda and Katarina –
my beautiful, daily inspirations.

And for those who face the world when reality goes missing,
may you find peace, tolerance, understanding and a cure.

Where does one go from a world of insanity?
Somewhere on the other side of despair.

                                    T. S. Eliot

Prologue

Georgia Adams finished off the rest of the coffee in her oversized 'Some Bunny Loves You' mug, sat back in her chair at her desk and closed her eyes. At a quarter to five in the morning, even four cups of hot caffeine wasn't keeping them open anymore, and she drifted into a crazy dream almost immediately, right there, at her desk. She'd been on midnights for almost a week now, but her body clock still hadn't adjusted to owl's hours. Georgia hated working nights, but because of the baby she had no choice. Roofs didn't get tarred at night, so Randy had to work days, they needed the money, and day care wasn't – and would never be – an option for her. No matter how much her overachieving, workaholic mother-in-law insisted it should be.

The beep sounded suddenly and loudly in Georgia's ear, startling her awake with a familiar rush of adrenaline. She sat up in the chair and reached for the button to open the line. 'Police and fire,' she said in the programmed, calm monotone that the department had taught her as she rubbed the dream out of her eyes. 'What's your emergency?'

The dead hum of silence buzzed the line.

'This is the nine-one-one operator,' Georgia repeated. 'Is there an emergency?'

Silence again.

'This is the nine-one-one operator. Do you have an emergency?' Georgia asked once more. She was a bit irritated now. Maybe she shouldn't have drifted off, but being woken up by either a drunk or a prankster was starting to tick her off.

'Help us,' a small, far-off voice finally said.

Georgia rolled her chair closer to the three-screen console in front of her. 'Okay, I can help you,' she replied calmly. Her fingers hovered over the CAD keyboard, the Computer Assisted Dispatch system. When she typed in a particular signal number, the computer would automatically dispatch the right response, either fire rescue or police. She didn't know what she had just yet, what button to push. 'What's your name, hon? Can you speak up?' she asked, adjusting the volume on her headset when there was no response. ''Cause I can barely hear you.' Unfamiliar, prickly goose-bumps suddenly erupted across her body, raising the tiny hairs on the back of her neck. She'd been an emergency operator for a long time – too long, maybe – but the one thing she wasn't usually was affected. She'd listened before while husbands beat their wives, road rage erupted into gunshots, and women had babies on their kitchen floors. But there was something in *this* voice. Something that was not right. Something that inexplicably *affected* her.

'Help us . . . please.'

So small, so distant, so unsure. *Like a child.*

An address accompanied the telephone number that stared back at her from her Positron screen, the public-safety phone system that automatically tracked incoming calls on the emergency line. On the PowerMap monitor, a small, one-dimensional computer-generated house appeared on a map on a block lined with other computer-generated houses. She could see that the call was coming from a residence.

'I'm going to help you, honey,' Georgia replied calmly. 'I need you to stay on the line and tell me exactly what's happened.'

'I think he's coming back,' said the whisper in between short, labored pants.

2

'Who's coming? Are you hurt? What's your name?' *Identify with them, Georgia. Keep them on the line, whatever you do, girl. Get details, if possible.*

'I think he's coming back,' the voice repeated, breaking as it started to cry now.

'Who's that? Has someone been hurt? Do you need an ambulance?' It was getting harder to maintain the monotone. Georgia looked at the computer-house, flashing helplessly at her on the screen. *What the hell was happening in there?*

And then, abruptly, the tears stopped with a sucked-in sniffle. 'Uh-oh. No, no, no. Sshh, sshh, shhh . . .' Silence filled the line once again.

Maybe this is just a prank, Georgia told herself. *Maybe it's just a kid messing around.* She'd fielded dozens and dozens of pranks in her career – most of them being made at sleepovers with giggly adolescents whose parents never taught them that dialing 911 wasn't some kind of a joke.

A soft thud sounded in the background. Georgia hesitated for just a moment and then started again. 'Hello? Hello? Are you still there?' She stood up in her seat to signal her supervisor so he could pick up the line and listen, but he was away from his cubicle, which was clear across the room. In fact, dozens of cubicles were empty on the floor. Oddly enough, the hours between 3 p.m. and midnight were the busiest for emergency dispatchers – rush-hour accidents, people getting home from work all stressed and taking it out on their family and friends. The graveyard shift was supposed to be the quiet one. 'Hello? Is there someone on the line?' Georgia demanded. 'Is there anyone there? This is the emergency operator.'

'No, no,' said the broken whisper, starting to cry once more. 'Oh, no, no, no, please . . .'

Then the line went dead.

Georgia stared at the screen in front of her, her heart beating fast. The house continued to flash at her, glowing ghostly white in the dark seclusion of her cubby.

She never worked midnights again.

'Dad, the world is getting dark now. I can feel it more and more . . .'

'Son of Sam' David Berkowitz, in a letter to his father, dated one month before his first murder, November 1975

I

The old Spanish house sat back away from the street, nestled behind lush tropical foliage and towering palms. Halloween decorations dotted a manicured front lawn, where a six-foot-tall, black-hooded Grim Reaper waited menacingly to scare trick-or-treaters from a flower bed filled with impatiens. Home-made ghosts with magic-markered black eyes dangled from the branches of an oak tree, twisting and turning in the gusty breeze that had come in overnight, courtesy of an early-season cold front. In the fast-fading moonlight they glowed an odd, bright white. Somewhere up the block a dog barked, as night yawned into morning.

The short whoop of a police siren broke the sleepy pre-dawn quiet as it turned onto Sorolla Avenue from Granada. Coral Gables PO Pete Colonna ignored the long driveway and instead pulled the cruiser over at the curb. Stepping out of the car, he surveyed the house for a moment and then made his way up the winding brick walkway to the front door, past scattered sticks of sidewalk chalk and an abandoned tricycle. When he spotted the little bike with silver racing stripes he moved a little faster. He rang the bell and pounded on an impressive oak front door. He could hear the loud chimes inside, but no one answered.

'8362, Gables,' Pete said into his shoulder mike.

'Go ahead, 8362.'

'10-97 at nine-eight-five Sorolla. There's no response.'

'Stand by, 8362.' After a moment the dispatcher with the Coral Gables PD came back on. 'Bell South has checked the line. It's open, but there's no conversation. They're not getting an answer.'

'I don't hear any ringing from inside.'

As Pete looked the front door up and down, the voice of his sergeant crackled to life on the radio pack. '8362, this is 998. Go to channel two.' Channel two was the talk-around channel, where they could speak without going through dispatch.

Pete switched over. 'Go ahead, Sarge.'

'What have you got?' asked his sergeant.

'I'm checking the residence,' Pete said as he moved about the front yard. 'There's no broken windows or evidence of a break-in that I can see, but . . .' he hesitated.

'Yeah?'

'Something don't feel right, Sarge.'

There was a pause. 'Alright. Trust your gut. I'll come now, then.'

'I'm gonna take the door.'

'The hell you are. Stand down. Wait for me,' his sergeant said sternly.

Pete looked through shrubbery that hid a black iron fence and back gate. Forgotten toys drifted lazily across a still pool. 'Kids live here,' he said. Pete's wife was pregnant. In just a few weeks he would have two little ones of his own.

'Wait for me. Don't go in there alone, Colonna. You may find a confused homeowner with a shotgun in his hand that didn't hear the doorbell. 10-23 for back-up. I'm there in five.'

Pete clicked back over to dispatch. His sergeant's voice radioed in. '998 is 10-51 to 8362's location from the University of Miami. Five-minute ETA.'

Pete walked back around to the front of the house where he spotted the tricycle again. Mounted next to the front door he noticed a hand-carved 'Welcome Home' plaque. An uneasy, anxious feeling began to spread through his chest.

It seemed like a lifetime, and definitely more than five minutes, before he heard the squad car pull down the residential street and up to the curb. Sergeant Demos was a large man, and with just weeks to go before his retirement party, things moved at a considerably slower pace for him. It took more than a few moments for him to get out of the car and lumber up the walk.

'Still nothing, Colonna?' he asked.

'Nah, Sarge. No sign of life.'

'The hang-up was a kid, right? Could be a prank,' Demos said, scratching at his lumpy, bald head. 'Great. Everyone's in bed except for junior. Kid's sweating it out right now, watching us from behind Bugs Bunny curtains,' he finished, looking up at the dark windows above.

Pete shook his head. 'Line's alive, but there's no ringing. No one's answering the door. I got a feeling.'

'You and your feelings. I got a feeling you're looking for some OT, what with all the reports you'll be writing.' The sergeant used his asp to bang on the door. 'Police! Anybody home?' After a moment, he looked at Pete again. 'Any history on the house?'

'Not that I know of. Dispatch didn't say and I know I ain't been here before,' he said, looking around at the stately homes that lined the block. 'Nice 'hood.'

'Don't let the address fool you, Junior. O.J. lived in Beverly Hills.'

'Actually, I think it was Brentwood.'

'Same damn difference. The point I was trying to make was domestics happen everywhere. You'd do good to remember that.' Demos sighed. 'A little kid? Alright. Minimal damage. Take the pane. The City's paying for it, so don't go nuts.'

Using his flashlight, Pete broke out one pane of the frosted, etched glass that framed the front door, reached in and unlocked the lock. The scream of an ear-piercing alarm sounded when the door opened.

'Well, if everyone was sleeping, they ain't no more,' shouted his sergeant. 'Give it a second.' They stood together on the front stoop with the door wide open, but no one appeared.

Dispatch came back on the radio. '8362, 998. Be advised we have ADT on the line. We have an audible alarm at your location.'

'10-4,' said Demos, '998 and 8362 have made entry through the front door. Has the homeowner called in for nine-one-one response?'

'Negative, 998. Still no answer on the line.'

The sergeant nodded at Pete. 'Alright. Let's go in.'

'Coral Gables Police! Is everyone okay in here?' Pete yelled into the dark house. He pulled his Glock and stepped inside, his sergeant breathing heavy behind him. Shards of glass from the windowpane crunched under his feet.

Twenty-foot ceilings loomed over a beautifully decorated formal living room. A staircase zigzagged up a sidewall and an ornate iron railing stretched across an overhead balcony. Past the balcony and down the upstairs hallway Pete could see a light was on. 'Police!' he yelled again, competing with the scream of the alarm.

They moved quickly through the first-floor rooms. Laundry sat piled on a washing machine and toys cluttered the family room. In the kitchen, cleaned baby bottles were lined up neatly next to the sink on paper towels.

The alarm suddenly stopped. Dispatch had probably told ADT that officers were at the location. Now the house seemed too large and too quiet. Pete thought of the baby bottles and a feeling of pure panic squeezed his chest.

'Coral Gables Police!' Demos yelled. Still nothing.

Pete ran for the stairs. Behind him he could hear the labored breathing of his sergeant as he tried to keep up – the jingle of the cumbersome equipment belt under the sarge's well-endowed belly, the heavy clicking of his heels on the stone steps. Retirement probably seemed a lifetime away at that moment.

At the top landing, Pete's feet touched padded carpet. Light spilled softly into the hallway from a back room whose door was partly closed. It grew brighter and brighter as he made his way down the hall. Family pictures smiled at him from every angle. All the other hall doors were shut tight.

'Anything?' called Demos, still on the stairs.

Pete moved down the hall toward the open door. Like in a movie under the hand of an artful director, select pieces of the room slowly came into view. Colorful butterflies danced across a bright purple wall. A Hello Kitty mirror. A wall plaque that spelled out EMMA. The edge of a Disney Princess comforter. 'Kid's room,' he called out.

'What the fuck did you step in?' Demos asked suddenly.

Pete looked down. Behind him in the faint light he saw the dark smear of footprints where he had just walked. Red drops spotted the pink carpet before him that led into what was obviously a little girl's room.

'Jesus Christ!' the sergeant said, answering his own question.

Suddenly Pete wanted to stop. He didn't want to see anymore. A sick, unfamiliar feeling churned his stomach and sweat dribbled off his forehead. For instinctively he knew that what he was about to witness was something he would probably spend the rest of his life trying to forget. He took a deep breath and pressed his head against the wall, his firearm out before him at the ready. His hands shook and he thought for a moment of his wife and the two perfect, innocent babies he had not yet met. From the sonogram he knew they were both girls. Madison and McKenzie were going to be their names. 'Police!' he shouted again, struggling to hide the slight tremble in his voice.

Then he entered the room and completely fell apart.

The scream of sirens exploded throughout the county, their deafening, high-pitched wails growing louder as they seemingly closed in from every direction on Sorolla. A blur of police cruisers, both marked and unmarked, raced down the sleepy street, until within minutes, the entire block was ablaze in blue and red flashing lights. Uniformed officers with the Coral Gables and Miami-Dade police departments crawled over the lawns and sidewalks, jabbering into their handhelds simultaneously, and the fading night air was electrified with the crackle of static and police jargon. Neighbors, most still dressed in their pajamas, began to slowly seep out of their homes and gather in small clumps on the sidewalk, staring from a comfortable distance at the exploding scene down the block. Clutching their robes in modesty and against a brisk wind, they chatted nervously among themselves, half-listening to each other as they craned their necks to watch the frenzied commotion unfold in front of the home of Dr David Marquette and his pretty wife, Jennifer. Some finally made their way down the block, where wooden police horses and yellow crime-scene tape held them back off the sidewalk. A Channel Ten news van pulled up across the street, followed by one from Channel Seven. And more police cars.

Sergeant Ralph Demos sat in the majestic living room on the floral-print couch, the stone staircase with its ornate railing looming high above him. He wiped his head with a paper towel, but the perspiration just would not stop. He wished at that moment that he hadn't quit smoking ten years back. Or drinking. Cops, it seemed, were everywhere and still coming. Upstairs, half a dozen uniforms stood guard outside the bedroom doors while Crime Scene techs with Miami-Dade PD snapped their photos. Bright flashes of light exploded in the hallway above him.

'Looks like they're bringing the County in,' said Carlos Sanchez, a road sergeant with Coral Gables, as he watched another crime-scene tech in a MDPD windbreaker walk past and head upstairs. 'I saw Steve Brill head into the kitchen before. He's with Persons,' Sanchez said, looking past the hallway that led to the kitchen where detectives were now interviewing Pete Colonna. 'But I bet Miami-Dade's gonna send Homicide.' The Persons Crime Squad was the Coral Gables detective unit that handled crimes against persons, like robbery or sexual assault. The Gables didn't have a Homicide Squad. 'I heard Brill can be a prick, but only if you're sleeping with him,' the sergeant said lightly.

'Don't know him,' murmured Demos, unable to take his eyes off the stairs. Every time the flashbulb would flash, the camera would make a loud, high-pitched hum that softly faded off. Fingerprint techs had begun their handiwork in the front hall, and fine black soot covered everything. To Ralph Demos, the air tasted heavy and bitter on his tongue; a taste he feared might never go away. In the kitchen he could hear the detectives talking with Pete Colonna, who was still crying.

'You okay there, Ralph?' Sanchez asked with a frown. 'You want me to get one of them EMTs down here to take a look at you?'

'Poor kid,' said Ralph, running a trembling hand over his sweaty head and looking back toward the kitchen. 'He saw it first. I mean, I knew it was gonna be bad when I saw all that blood, but he's only been on the force, what? A year?'

'His wife's due with their first,' said Sanchez, shaking his head. 'I think that's why it hit him hard.'

'Twins. I know. I just heard.'

'Pete'll be okay. Psych will take care of him if he needs it.'

'He will. Christ, he will. He wanted to take the door when he first got on scene. I told him to stand down and wait. Maybe it would've made a difference . . .' Demos's voice tapered off and Sanchez said nothing.

Two men wearing blue windbreakers that read MIAMI-DADE COUNTY MEDICAL EXAMINER'S OFFICE in bright white letters walked through the front door. With a somber nod they headed back up the stairs. The ME himself was already on scene. Ralph watched them go up.

'Who found the father?' asked Sanchez, forcing his friend back to the living room.

'Me,' Ralph said softly. 'Is he gonna make it?'

'Don't know. He looked pretty fucked up. They're taking him to Ryder.' Ryder Trauma Center was a part of the University of Miami's Jackson Memorial Hospital in downtown Miami.

'Goddamn,' Ralph mumbled and shook his head. 'Anybody else?'

Sanchez said nothing again, just looked at the floor.

Ralph fought back the tears. 'A whole family,' he said. 'What kind of animal would do this shit? What kind of world are we living in?'

Sanchez waited a moment, watching big Ralph Demos wipe buckets of sweat off his pale head. He looked like he was gonna drop. 'You gonna be okay, Ralph?'

'Me? I'm outta here in a few weeks. Hell, maybe now I'll go tomorrow. But Colonna, see, he's just started, Carlos. He's got to deal with this shit for another twenty-four if he wants to go out on eighty percent.' Ralph paused and wiped his head again. A white flash exploded from the hall upstairs and the familiar hum softly faded off. The shuffle of footsteps sounded again on the stone steps above him.

'God, this job sucks,' was all Carlos Sanchez could think of to say as big Ralph began to cry. Then he watched in silence as the two men in the ME windbreakers carried the first of the small black body bags downstairs and out the front door.

'But I don't want to go among mad people,' Alice remarked.

'Oh, you can't help that,' said the Cat. 'We're all mad here. I'm mad. You're mad.'

'How do you know I'm mad?' said Alice.

'You must be,' said the Cat, 'or you wouldn't have come here.'

Lewis Carroll, *Alice's Adventures in Wonderland*

3

Miami-Dade Assistant State Attorney Julia Valenciano stood at the State's podium in courtroom 4–10 – a 74-page trial calendar before her and four boxes of felony cases stacked at her feet – and she panicked. She nibbled at the inside of her cheek and stared in disbelief at the yellow Witness Availability Sheet in her hand that Mario, her Victim/ Witness Coordinator, had prepared for her late last Friday.

'State?' grumbled the judge from the bench, obviously waiting for an answer. It was one Julia really didn't want to give him. The Honorable Leonard Farley was already in a mood more foul than usual. She closed her eyes for a second and wished she were somewhere else. Like Hawaii.

It was Monday morning and the packed courtroom bustled around her. Even though printed signs everywhere warned 'No talking, no children, no cellphones!' the air buzzed with the hushed whispers of the victims, witnesses, family members, and out-of-custody defendants that filled the rows of benches behind her. To her right, a long line of irritated, toe-tapping defense attorneys snaked its way behind the defense podium and through the small wooden pass-through gate that led into the gallery. Most had several clients on calendars throughout the courthouse, which meant they were going to be late for somebody's courtroom this morning, but no one wanted to be late for Judge Farley, so everyone came to 4–10 first. Behind her, a similar line had formed for prosecutors at the State's podium. She could almost hear both sides' collective sigh of impatience as she fumbled through the file marked *State vs. Powers.*

Corrections opened the door to the jury room at that moment, and a line of disheveled-looking defendants – fresh from the Dade County Jail across the street – made their way into the jury box, their wrists all chained together, like a surreal string of paper-doll cutouts.

'Am I speaking?' the judge asked, exasperated, looking around as Corrections settled the defendants into seats in the box. He still had not gotten his answer. His eyes fell on Jefferson, the bailiff. 'Can *you* hear me?' he asked. A nervous Jefferson nodded.

'Judge,' Julia began slowly, 'we seem to have a problem.' Scrawled across the computer-generated Witness Availability Sheet, in Mario's barely legible handwriting, were the words, 'Victim uncooperative. Refuses to come in now – MG.' Julia could've sworn those words were not there on Friday when she'd prepped the Monday-morning calendar until eight o'clock at night.

'I don't have any problems, State,' said Judge Farley, leaning back in his chair, his dark blue eyes crinkling to slits. He smelled blood and it made him happy.

Each of the twenty felony division judges that worked in Miami's downtown Richard Gerstein Criminal Justice Building had three Assistant State Attorneys (ASAs), three Public Defenders (PDs), and two Division Chiefs (DCs) – one for each side – assigned to their courtroom. 'A' prosecutors and 'A' PDs handled first-degree felonies; 'B's handled second-degrees; and 'C's worked the bottom-feeder third-degrees, like simple burglaries and grand thefts. Division Chiefs supervised the letters and handled 'no-name' homicides – those murders that didn't grab headlines or get snatched up by prosecutors in specialized divisions like Major

Crimes, Domestics, Organized Crime, Career Criminal, or Narcotics. It was just the luck of the felony-assignment draw for Julia Valenciano that she'd been picked to be the B in Judge Leonard Farley's division, better known around the courthouse as Siberia.

Julia had been a prosecutor going on three years now, and for a good part of those three years, she'd have to say that she'd been blessed with some pretty good divisions and nice judges. Even in County Court – where she'd first started out in misdemeanor crimes and criminal traffic before moving offices across the street to felonies and Circuit – the judges had at least been respectful. Maybe they weren't all learned scholars, but straight out of law school herself then, she'd had a lot to learn about the Rules of Evidence, too. Then the honeymoon had ended, reality had set in, and for the past long, four months, she'd been stuck here in Siberia with no end in sight.

It wasn't just that her judge was difficult; he was impossible. On good days they still did not like each other – a fact which was not all that surprising, because Farley didn't like anyone, and he particularly didn't like women – but it was definitely stressful. She supposed life could be easier for her if she did what most prosecutors in his division did: nothing. Simply let the judge have his tantrums, and object just loud enough for the court reporter to hear when he made a ruling that was outrageous or just completely wrong. Let the State Attorney's Legal Division decide what messes they wanted to clean up on appeal. But, unfortunately, Julia wasn't the type who could just do nothing. So every day became a battle. And Farley wasn't going anywhere anytime soon. As a sitting retired judge, he couldn't even be booted off the bench by a zealous opponent or an outraged public at the polls. Only the Chief Judge – his brother-in-law – could move him. And until he died, the best Julia could hope for would be to move her way up and out of Siberia to an A-spot in someone else's division, or pray for an assignment to a specialized unit. Neither of which was going to happen right at this particular moment.

Farley tapped his pen loudly on the bench. The packed courtroom now sensed trouble, and the light chaotic buzz peppered to a stop. Suddenly everyone was very interested in what the judge had to say. Probably because he wasn't going to be saying it to them.

'*I* seem to have the problem, then, Your Honor,' Julia said, clearing her throat. She finally looked up. 'Apparently, my victim on Powers is now unavailable.'

'But you announced ready for trial on this on Thursday.' A deep frown sliced across the judge's already wrinkle-crowded face, forcing his white, wiry Albert Einstein eyebrows together.

'I did, Your Honor. You see, my availability sheet at that time said the victim was ready, but since then she's apparently indicated a reluctance to go forward. I'm going to need to have her personally subpoenaed—'

'That should have been done already.'

'Judge, we set Powers as number twelve for trial today. If you could just reset this till later in the week, we can go forward on Ivaroni or Singer this morning. I'm definitely ready to go on those. I can then have—'

'You announced ready, State. That meant you were ready for trial. I'm not resetting this. You're either ready or you're not. If you're not, I'm dismissing.'

The Public Defender, Scott Andrews, smiled at the defense podium. One less case on his docket, and the chances of the State re-filing an Aggravated Battery without a victim were pretty much non-existent.

Julia felt everyone watching her. From the corner of her eye she spotted the defendant, Letray Powers, in the box, a big gold grin on his pockmarked face. He raised a chained hand and high-fived the inmate seated next to him. Sporting at least 250 pounds on his six-foot frame, his muscles showed even through the baggy orange jail jumpsuit that he wore. Julia looked down at the pink arrest form, and remembered how Letray had taken a razor blade to his pregnant girlfriend's face. Her jaw clenched. *Here we go again,* she thought, and looked back up at Farley. 'Then the State is ready for trial, Your Honor,' she announced, almost defiantly.

'Did I just hear you right?' asked the judge, sitting up straight in his throne. 'No victim and you're telling me you're still going forward?'

'Judge, Mr Powers has a lengthy history of violence, including priors for Resisting, Aggravated Battery and Aggravated Assault with a Firearm, not to mention three arrests in the past for domestic battery. He viciously attacked his girlfriend with a razor blade because she looked in the direction of another man in Winn-Dixie. His five-months-pregnant girlfriend, I might add. It took sixty-two stitches to sew her face back together.'

'And now she doesn't think it's important enough to come in.'

'She's a domestic violence victim, Judge.'

'She's an absentee victim, Ms Valenciano. And I don't have the time to coddle her. I've got a very busy docket.' *That* had to be the understatement of the year.

'If Your Honor refuses to grant the State a continuance so that I can personally subpoena Ms Johnson, rather than see this case dismissed, I have no choice but to go forward without her testimony.'

'And just how are you going to do that, State?' The judge was more than mad now. He was furious. Domestic violence was a prickly topic. It was not good press in a crowded courtroom for him to look this insensitive.

She swallowed. 'I don't need the victim, Your Honor.'

'That's a first for me, Ms Valenciano. Didn't they teach you corpus delicti in law school? The body of your crime doesn't want to come in.'

'Witnesses can testify about her injuries.'

'Who's gonna tell me how she got them? Did anyone see her getting attacked?'

'Her statements to the police—'

'Are hearsay,' cut in the PD. The judge glared at him, too.

'Are admissible for the truth of their content as an excited utterance,' finished Julia.

In the law, people were thought to be more honest than usual when acting under the stress of certain situations, and so any statements they made during or immediately after the stressful event to other people were thus admissible in trial. Excited utterance, as it was known, was a recognized exception to the hearsay rule, which generally prohibited the in-court use of any statement made outside of court when that statement was being used to prove 'the truth of the matter asserted'. Being sliced to ribbons by a maniac with a razor blade qualified as a stressful event, Julia thought. Maybe it was a stretch to try a case without a victim who wanted to prosecute on just an excited utterance, but the hell she was gonna let the bastard high-five it right out of here with a smile while the judge yelled his goodbyes to him in her face.

'Don't play coy with me, Ms Valenciano. I won't indulge moot-court trial antics in my courtroom,' Farley bellowed.

'I have no intention of doing that, Judge.'

'Then you damn well better be ready to pick a jury.'

'I am, Your Honor.'

The judge glared at her for a long moment and the courtroom stayed disturbingly quiet. 'You want a trial? Nine o'clock tomorrow, then. I'll see you back here.' The PD opened his mouth, but the judge cut him off with a wave of his hand. 'Don't bother, Mr Andrews. Ms Valenciano says we're ready even without her victim, so we're ready. Be here tomorrow and let's see what she does. Ivonne,' he said to the court clerk who sat at a desk below the bench, 'set over the rest of Ms Valenciano's trials to print on Wednesday's calendar. Powers won't take us long.' He shook his pen at Julia. 'If you waste my time with this, State,' he cautioned loudly, 'you'll have more to worry about than double jeopardy, so I strongly suggest you use the next twenty-three hours to find your victim.'

Julia stepped back away from the podium and gathered her boxes as the ASA behind her from Economic Crimes called up his case. Her blood was racing, so hard that she could hear it pound in her ears, and her hands shook. A light buzz started up again in the crowd, and she felt the eyes of her colleagues upon her. All she wanted was to get out of the courtroom and scream.

'Don't let him push your buttons,' her Division Chief, Karyn Seminara, said cautiously under her breath as she helped Julia load her file boxes onto a collapsible metal cart.

Julia looked up and took a deep breath before she said something she knew she would later regret. Her DC never pushed anyone's buttons. Laid-back and completely non-confrontational, Farley probably thought pretty Karyn Seminara the ideal woman, but for the fact that she occasionally opened her mouth and actually said something. She'd been his DC for over a year now, either because someone upstairs thought mild-mannered, compliant Karyn could best handle the judge and his crazy temper-tantrums, or, as was more likely the case the way Julia figured it, she'd really pissed someone upstairs off. While she and Karyn had become what some would call friends over the past four months, it was definitely a cautious friendship, forged over semi-mandatory Friday-night happy hours and *après court* cups of *café con leche*. Cautious, because her DC wanted to be friends with everyone – particularly anyone in her division – and as Julia's Uncle Jimmy had warned her the day she'd landed her first job stuffing Boston Kremes down at the local Dunkin' Donuts, she knew that 'Friends don't make for good bosses and bosses don't make for good friends.'

Julia exhaled the breath and stared at her DC. It wasn't hard to see the disappointment in Karyn's half-smile, nor was it hard to figure out why it was there. 'If I say what I'm thinking right now, Karyn,' she replied in a low voice, 'Farley will sit me in the box next to my defendant, so I'd better just shut up.'

'He's not going to change, Julia. And you're not going to change him. But from the shade of red you made his head turn, he just might leave the bench on a stretcher one of these days,' Karyn replied with a sardonic smile and a shake of her head. 'You're a good lawyer, honey, but are you really going to try this case without a victim?'

'I have no choice.'

'She does. She's not here.'

'If I have to try it without her, I will.'

'And the point of that is?'

Julia looked over at the box where Letray Powers sat with a smile, like the cat who ate the canary. 'He's gonna do it again to her if he gets out. Only next time maybe he'll go for the throat.'

'I hate to be the bearer of bad news, but you know the judge is right. Investigations won't find her because she doesn't want to be found, Julia. All you're going to accomplish here is to piss the judge off some more and have double jeopardy prevent you from re-trying if your victim ever does see the light and wants to prosecute. Why don't you just let Farley dismiss and then hand this case off to Domestics and let them try and re-file without a victim?'

In the four months that Julia had been in the division, she'd yet to see her DC actually go to trial. Even a simple hearing was a rare occasion. As Karyn saw it, every case had a problem, every victim an agenda, every defendant an excuse. So for her, everything was negotiable, including murder. Sometimes at bargain-basement pleas that fell way below statutory guidelines.

'Domestics will be in the same situation as me, only worse,' Julia finally said, as she turned her attention back to the file cart. 'Look at that guy, Karyn. If he walks, he's heading straight back home.'

Karyn rolled her eyes. 'You can't solve all the world's problems, Julia. Jesus, I hate domestics. They should keep them all in DCU and out of division. You know, you've got some set, girlfriend.'

'Thank you,' Julia replied, snapping the bicycle strap across her file boxes.

'Apparently I'm not the only one who's noticed, either.' Her DC's voice lowered once again and her face tightened. 'Listen, while you were duking it out with Farley, Charley Rifkin dropped by the courtroom.'

Charley Rifkin was the Division Chief of Major Crimes and the State Attorney's right-hand man. Julia immediately felt her palms go sweaty. *Uh-oh.* 'And?' she asked, hoping her voice still sounded strong.

'And he wants you in his office in ten minutes. And, Julia,' Karyn called out with a flip of her cool blonde bob and another half-smile of disappointment as Julia made her way to the gallery swing-door, 'he didn't look happy.'

4

Damn. Nothing good ever came from a Monday. Julia dragged the rickety cart stacked with trial boxes behind her down the handicapped ramp in back of the courthouse and hurried across Thirteenth to the Graham Building, home of the State Attorney's Office. A gusty tropical breeze threatened to Marilyn Monroe her skirt right in front of the steel-barred windows of DCJ and the two leering Sabrett sausage vendors gathered on the corner, and she cursed herself for picking out the one suit in her closet without a tailored hemline.

She knew Karyn thought she was being overzealous and combative. And her judge was mad at her – again. She had just a day to prepare for a trial she really wasn't prepared to have, with a judge, a DC, a defense attorney, and even a victim who didn't want her to have it. Now, just when she thought the day couldn't get any shittier, the Chief of Major Crimes was demanding to see her in his office.

In the food chain of the State Attorney's Office, Major Crimes was right up there with administration, and its chief, Charley Rifkin, definitely had more than just the ear of the State Attorney – he'd also been the man's golf partner for the past ten years, and his campaign manager a decade or so before that. Being summoned to Rifkin's office was not a normal happening for anyone, and especially not a B, unless, of course, he'd observed something in court that he didn't like. Or, Julia thought nervously as she nibbled a fingernail and watched her file boxes pass through the

Graham Building's metal detector, had a judge or another attorney call him about a problem.

Major Crimes was the specialized trial division that handled explosive media cases, complex homicides, and all death-penalty cases. Each of the ten or so elite attorneys assigned to the division had more than a dozen years of prosecutorial experience, which – thanks to dismal salaries and a high burn-out rate – was practically a lifetime in an office where most people didn't stay ten seconds past their three-year commitments. There was no doubt that Major Crimes attorneys were good at what they did, and there was also no doubt that most of them knew it. Their presence in a courtroom could instantly command the respect of the judge, the attention of the jury and the envy of the defense bar. It also could, and usually did, intimidate the hell out of a lot of the pit prosecutors in division, especially if whatever lurid, high-profile case they were appearing on had attracted a camera crew and a few eager reporters to the back of the courtroom. And it wasn't just the newborns – new Cs fresh from Juvi or County Court – who lost it, either. Julia had witnessed even seasoned As and DCs develop a sudden, uncomfortable stutter when a Major Crimes prosecutor strode into the gallery and asked to call a case up on calendar.

She uselessly hit the lit lobby elevator button again, and waded back into the waiting crowd of uniforms, attorneys and assorted interesting persons that were headed upstairs. Even though it probably wouldn't have deterred her from pressing forward on Powers this morning if she'd known that Charley Rifkin was standing behind her taking notes, she still wanted to kick herself for not knowing that he was.

Other than an occasional elevator sighting and seeing him speak at an office voir dire training session one afternoon some months back, Julia had never actually met the Division

Chief of Major Crimes before. In fact, while she'd been to the second floor maybe a zillion times over her two years in felonies to either see Career Criminal about getting a plea offer on a habitual offender, or visit the offices of other division attorneys, she'd never once even been through the secured access doors that led to the Major Crimes Unit. The Hallowed Hall. It wasn't that her identification card wouldn't open the door; it was just that there'd never been any need. None of her cases ever involved issues that appealed to Major Crimes – like a famous defendant, a celebrity victim or a brutal serial killer. And as for socializing, for the most part, attorneys in specialized units did not interact or hang out with the younger pit prosecutors in division. Like Julia supposed it was in every corporate workplace, there existed at the SAO an invisible and unspoken social and economic caste system among its workers: administration dined with administration, senior trial attorneys lunched with senior trial attorneys, support staff noshed with support staff. And in their five minutes of free time, pit prosecutors shared *croquetas*, PB&Js, and the morning's courtroom war stories with other pit prosecutors, either at their desks or over at the courthouse cafeteria across the street.

She got off on two with a guy who she figured for either a drug dealer or a plain-clothes City of Miami narc in need of a shower. The tattooed head of a King Cobra slithered out of the collar of his T-shirt, bearing its fangs in a wicked grin as it arched its back and aimed for the jugular. Its owner smiled at her like he knew her, before disappearing down the hall that led to Career Criminal. She hesitantly smiled back and hoped he was a narc.

Her own office was up on three, but she decided it might be better to head straight over to Chief Rifkin's office first, thinking that maybe if the man actually *saw* the four enormous trial boxes on her cart, he'd remember just what carrying a caseload of 102 B felonies was like before he ripped into her for taking on her judge with a doomed domestic. She stopped at the door marked Major Crimes, wiped her palms on her skirt, took a deep breath, and slid her card through the security access. It clicked open and she entered a long, lowlit, empty hallway, painted – like the rest of the State Attorney's Office – the most depressing shade of pasty gray.

Immediately, the air changed. That was the first thing Julia noticed. The second was the collective blank stares of the eight Major Crimes secretaries whose lair she'd landed in when the depressing hallway abruptly ended. A fluorescent-lit maze of Formica and plexiglas cubbies, and there she was, standing dumb-faced right in the middle of it, like a kid whose waterslide had unexpectedly dumped him into the deep end of the pool. Conversation didn't just softly die down – it dropped dead in mid-sentence.

'Hello,' Julia began, trying her best at a big smile. Since no one looked away, she addressed them all. 'I'm looking for Charley Rifkin's office?'

'Is he expecting you?' one of the faces asked, an older woman with a sour expression and droopy, doughy cheeks. Somebody cracked gum.

Julia glanced down. On the desk in front of droopy cheeks was a plaque with a plastic manicured index finger that bobbled back and forth. It read *Don't Mess With Grandma*. 'I think so,' Julia answered slowly. 'My DC told me that Mr Rifkin wanted to see me.'

'Oh,' said Grandma. Her face slid down until it looked like it would just melt into her neck. 'You're the one from Judge Farley's division.'

That couldn't be good. 'That's me,' Julia replied, and casually dried her hands on her skirt again. Unfortunately, she'd inherited the sweaty-palm gene from her mother – a career curse. She still tried to hold on to the smile, but it was fading quick.

Grandma picked up the phone, hit a number, and turned away. 'She's here,' was all she said. Then she looked back at Julia, and motioned down the hall with a nod of her head. Her doughy throat jiggled like a turkey's. 'Two-oh-seven. Take the hallway to the second corridor and make a right. Last office on the left.'

5

She felt the stares of the secretaries silently follow her as she walked past them, like moving pairs of eyes in paintings that decorated the halls of a haunted mansion. The walk to the corner definitely seemed a lot longer than it looked, and she was all too happy to be out of direct staring range as she rounded the second corridor and entered another long hallway, this one lined with closed office doors, each adorned with the engraved nameplate of the resident lawyer inside – most of whom, she was realizing, she'd never met, and some of whom she'd never even heard of. Apparently, no one in Major Crimes was particularly social. Not that it was a constant party up on three, but among division prosecutors, office doors always seemed to be open, and attorneys wandered in and out of each other's claustrophobic offices all day long to ask for advice on a case, bitch about a PD, chat up the weekend, or gulp down a quick shot of *café cubano* – hot, liquid, Cuban adrenaline – made fresh at three every afternoon by her best friend, Dayanara Vega, the B in Judge Stalder's division. On Julia's floor there was a sense of camaraderie in the pasty gray halls. Here, on what was known as 'The Power Floor', she just felt shut out from the rest of the world.

Next to the door marked 207, was the nameplate, 'Charles August Rifkin, Division Chief'. The three cups of coffee and bowl of Lucky Charms she'd had for breakfast suddenly began to threaten mutiny, and she prayed her stomach wouldn't start making any weird noises. Inside, she could hear Chief Rifkin talking in a low voice, his words muffled. She hoped he was on the phone, because an audience was the last thing she needed this morning. She wiped her hands one last time on her skirt and tapped on the door. There was a brief silence before she heard someone say, 'Come in.'

'Hi,' she answered cheerfully as she pushed open the door. The file cart she was trying to negotiate behind her nailed the metal doorframe with a loud thud.

'Leave that outside,' commanded another voice from somewhere on the other side of the door. One she immediately thought she recognized.

She nodded with a wince, backed out of the room, and pushed the cart up against the hall wall. She blew out a slow, steady breath before stepping back inside. The door closed softly behind her, but it wasn't Charley Rifkin who'd shut it, because he was sitting right there in front of her, in a high-back leather chair behind an oversized wooden desk, wearing what looked a lot like a scowl. The door-shutter moved from behind her to one of the two small red leather side chairs positioned in front of the desk and motioned for her to take a seat in the other.

Yes, the day could get worse.

'Good morning, Julia,' said the Assistant Division Chief of Major Crimes, Richard 'Rick' Bellido, looking cool and reserved in a conservative black Hugo Boss suit, crisp white dress shirt and gray silk tie. The gray in the tie accentuated the vibrant silver strands sprinkled throughout his otherwise jet-black, wavy hair, but in a flattering way. She stared at him for what felt like an incredibly long moment, but he didn't smile. He didn't nod. He didn't wink. God, he didn't even blink. Julia couldn't help but think that even the most talented psychic would be hard-pressed to guess at that moment that the two of them had slept together for the first time only three short nights ago. Even she was now doubting the memory.

'I saw you in court today,' Rifkin began. 'You like to test old Farley, do you?' Before she could reply, he turned to Rick and said flatly, 'She's going to trial on a domestic with no victim. Lenny had a fit.'

'Nothing unusual there,' Rick replied with a shrug as he sat down himself.

'How long have you been in his division?' asked the Chief, tapping his hand impatiently against his coffee mug. His wedding ring made a soft, distracting *tink, tink, tink* against the ceramic.

'About four months,' Julia answered. Four months, one week and one day, to be exact. Four months too long, she wanted to say. She sat up straight in her chair and got ready to defend herself, ticking off invisible bullet points in her head. 'He was going to dismiss—'

Rifkin cut her off. 'That's not why you're here.'

She wasn't sure if the invisible weight actually moved off of, or onto, her chest. With an almost ceremonious wave of his hand, Rifkin motioned to Rick, and the scowl seemed to deepen. She felt her cheeks go hot and she knew they were probably glowing like Rudolph's nose – another genetic curse from her mother, this one the result of being half Irish and fair-skinned. *Oh God. Please, please, please don't let this be about the State's policy on dating in the office . . .*

'There was a family murdered in Coral Gables over the weekend,' Rick began. 'I'm assuming you've heard.'

She let out the breath she'd subconsciously been holding, so hard and so fast it sounded like a sigh. 'Yeah, yeah, of course I've heard. It's been all over the news. A mom and her kids, right?' The horrible story had taken up the first five minutes of the news last night, and another five this morning, and made today's front page in both the *Miami Herald* and the *Sun Sentinel*. A whole family in ritzy Coral Gables apparently the victim of some psycho intruder. Other than the names of the victims and the fact that it was a homicide scene, she'd noticed that the news didn't have much to really report, though. The only people offering up long-winded, on-camera opinions were the chatty neighbors – everyone important was being very tight-lipped. The press, meanwhile, was having a field day whipping up fears of a late-night-serial-killer-type madman, cautioning every-one to lock their doors and windows and call police if they notice any strange behavior. In Miami, Julia knew that vague warning was sure to have the 911 lines ringing off the hook.

'Jennifer Marquette and her three children, Emma, Danny and Sophie, all under the age of seven, murdered in their beds. The little one, Sophie, was only a baby. Just a few weeks old, in fact,' Rick said, with a shake of his head as he tapped his Montblanc thoughtfully on the top of a yellow legal pad that had appeared on his lap. 'It's pretty bad.'

'Only dad's alive. He's over at Ryder Trauma,' Rifkin remarked.

'That's what I heard on the news,' Julia said. 'He's a doctor, right? Is he going to make it?'

Grandma opened the door at that moment. Apparently no one messed with her, because she didn't even knock first. 'Ruth Solly's headed over to court, Charley. She needs those files.'

'Okay, okay. Let me get with her before she goes,' Rifkin said, rising, his coffee cup in hand. 'Excuse me, I'll be back in a minute.' He headed out of the office with Grandma teetering close behind, in a pair of black stilettos and a skirt that was shorter than anything Julia could remember her own cookie-baking grandmother ever wearing.

Okay. *Now* she was confused. Apparently, this little *tête-à-tête* wasn't about Judge Farley or her combative attitude or her taking Letray Powers to trial tomorrow morning. She didn't know the name Marquette and she couldn't think of any connection she might have with the weekend massacre in Coral Gables, other than maybe one of her 102 defendants was being investigated as a possible suspect. And thank God, as far as she could tell, it wasn't about the SAO policy on sexual harassment and sleeping with one's superiors in the office. But five minutes into a conversation was still a long time to go without knowing if she should be floating a few résumés on Monster.com, so she decided to ask the incredibly awkward question that she didn't want to ask when she figured Grandma and her boss had cleared listening distance. 'Do you know why I'm here?' she asked quietly.

Rick nodded. 'I was the on-call this weekend.'

'Oh,' she replied, unsure if his response was being offered as an explanation for why he hadn't called her since Friday night, or actually an answer to the question. She suddenly remembered the last time they'd been together, his mouth on hers in the shower, his hands on places she shouldn't have let them go. She felt her cheeks start to grow warm again, and she looked away for a moment, finding a gray spot on the gray carpet to concentrate on. 'Where in the Gables was it?' she managed to ask, hoping her voice didn't betray her thoughts.

'Off Sorolla, near UM. Oh, I forgot,' he added with a touch of an amused smile, when she finally did look back up and caught his dark-chocolate eyes watching her, 'you're not from around these-here parts.'

It was no use. She lit up like Bozo at a birthday party.

Her shower was in Hollywood, a twenty-mile trip north of Miami.

'Sorolla and Granada, to be exact,' he continued when she didn't respond. 'It's in the older section of the Gables. A lot of expensive historic homes and mansions. Course nowadays, I don't think you can touch a trailer in Leisure City for less than six figures, so expensive is a relative term.'

'Is it going to be your case?'

'Hell yeah. I was at the scene all day yesterday.'

'What department's handling it?' she asked.

'John Latarrino's Metro Homicide. Steve Brill's working it for the Gables. You know them?'

The Miami-Dade PD used to be the Metro-Dade PD before they renamed both the county and the police department Miami-Dade more than a few years back. But even though the letterhead was different, for many old-timers in law enforcement the name change simply hadn't stuck. Even though he was only forty-five, with over twenty years in the office as a prosecutor, Richard Bellido was definitely an old-timer.

Julia shook her head. 'No, I don't think so,' she answered. Of course she didn't know them. She suddenly felt very young and very out of her league in the conversation, and not just because of her age. Senior trial attorneys and DCs knew all of the homicide cops in each department by name, because they worked with them all the time. It was a pretty small, macabre sort of clique. And given the hard, emotionally draining nature of the cases they worked, she knew that for many prosecutors and homicide cops working relationships oftentimes developed into tight, personal friendships that existed outside the office and after the clock struck five, at happy hours and family barbecues and kids' weddings. Julia didn't have any of those kinds of friendships yet herself.

Most of the time she didn't even recognize the names on the bottom of the arrest form.

'I've worked with Lat before,' Rick said. 'He's good. Brill's a character, though. You know, the Gables doesn't get many murders.'

'They don't let them in,' she mused.

'Very good,' he said, with another hint of a smile.

'Why would the Gables need the County's help?'

'As I said, they don't get many murders. In fact, their department doesn't even have a Homicide Squad, just a Persons. Metro has the experience and the manpower. They also have the lab.'

Strike one, not knowing that Coral Gables lacked an actual homicide detective. She cleared her throat. 'So, do you know what happened?'

'We're still trying to piece it together,' he replied, glancing over at the door, obviously waiting for his boss to come back in.

'Are there any suspects?'

Rifkin returned at that moment with a full, steaming cup of coffee, but no Grandma. 'I see you tried a DUI Manslaughter last month in front of Farley,' he said to Julia as he slid back behind his desk. 'Have you handled any other homicides?'

'No,' she replied. 'My A, Ellie Roussos, passed that down to me because I did DUI when I was in County.'

'Misdemeanors?' Rifkin asked, incredulously.

Julia shifted uncomfortably in her seat. 'Yes. That's what we handled in County Court.'

'Misdemeanors,' he said again. 'What'd your jury come back with?'

'Guilty as charged.'

'And what did Farley actually give him?'

She cleared her throat again. 'Two years and a lecture.'

Rifkin shot Rick a look, leaned back in his chair, and began impatiently tapping away on his coffee mug again.

'It was the defendant's first offense,' she added defensively, because she thought she had to. She suddenly felt very conspicuous, like a bug trapped under the burning rays of a kid's magnifying glass. Any direction she ran in offered no cover.

The *tink tink tinking* ticked off the seconds like a sledgehammer and no one said anything. Then, finally, just as she had begun to think maybe she should have another lawyer in the room with her, Rick leaned in closer, his elbows resting on his knees and his hands clasped in front of him, like a coach about to call a play. 'To answer your question from before, Julia,' he began in a low, excited voice, 'we do have a suspect in the Gables killings.'

'In fact, I just got the call from Joe Marchionne over at Metro. Our suspect's out of surgery,' Rifkin added with a snort. 'Looks like he's going to make it after all.'

Rick shook his head, but his intense, dark eyes remained locked on Julia's. 'That's why you've been asked here this morning, Julia,' he said after a moment had passed. 'That's why I wanted to see you. I want you to help me nail the sick bastard who murdered his wife and kids last Saturday night.'

6

Julia said nothing. She couldn't. If her brain was making all the right turns through all the right neurons to jump to all the right conclusions, she was being asked to second-seat a murder prosecution. *A Major Crimes murder prosecution.*

'Your judge might not be a fan, but your trial stats are definitely impressive, Julia,' Rick continued. 'Thirty-six juries picked in the past fourteen months; thirty-four convictions. I've heard some really good things about you at the Chiefs' Meetings from your DC. You're not afraid to work hard and stay late, and I know that you're a team player. I like how you have the balls to push difficult cases to trial – even today's no-victim domestic – and what's really impressive is that you've actually got the skills to back you up once you get before a jury, a talent that most attorneys in this office, frankly, just don't have. And, perhaps, the most important accomplishment of yours to date,' he said with a light chuckle, 'is that you've managed to bury yourself so deep under Len Farley's leathered skin, that there's a rumor he's finally thinking of leaving the bench. I believe you've had him try more cases in the past four months than he has in the entire two decades he's sat as a Circuit Court judge.'

Rick paused for a moment. 'I'm going to level with you, Julia. I've got a really brutal crime scene, four dead bodies, and a young, rising-star surgeon playing the role of father, husband and, right now, prime suspect. I can see that this case will be a time-eater, that it will get complicated, and that it will probably grab and hold headlines. It's going to take time, and a hell of a lot of commitment to work it up right. So I want whoever gets to sit second chair to be in on it with me from the very beginning, before Crime Scene mops up the last of the bloodstains and the cleaning crew wipes the print dust off the furniture. Charley and I have been tossing around some names this morning,' he said, casting a cautious glance across the desk before continuing, 'but everyone has their own caseloads here, with cases just as big, bad and time-consuming. And so,' he finished, leaning back in his chair, 'I thought about you. I think you'd be a good choice.'

She tried her best to hold it back, but the cheesy Miss America, 'Oh my God, I can't believe this is happening to me!' smile slipped out anyway. 'Thank you,' she said softly.

'Charley?' Rick asked.

Charley Rifkin sat forward in the high-back, carefully placing the coffee mug back down on his desk. His thin, bony fingers toyed with a wayward paperclip that had escaped its caddy. 'Rick Bellido apparently has a lot of faith in you, young lady,' he remarked after a long moment had passed, but the frown, Julia noticed, had still not left his face. 'It's your case, so I suppose in the end it will be your call, Rick. But,' he said, depositing the paperclip back into the caddy and turning both his chair and his full attention to Julia, 'I'm going to be honest here, Ms Valenciano. It's not just that I'm concerned about you falling behind in division work if you were to second-seat this case, because that goes without saying. And, of course, if that ever did happen, I'm sure your DC would be up here bitching in my one ear, and your judge would be on the phone chewing the other. As you well know, I supervise this division. The cases up here, they are assigned by me, and I wanted to make it clear, that even though the decision may ultimately be Rick's to make on what trial partner he wants to pick to try his cases with, in the end, those cases, they are *my* responsibility. Now while I'm confident that Richard Bellido, with over twenty years' experience in this office and seventeen death-penalty convictions under his belt, is more than qualified to work a quadruple homicide with the media breathing down his neck and a slew of high-paid defense lawyers up his ass, I'm not so sure that this is the murder case I want you cutting your baby teeth on.'

Ouch. Julia felt her stomach suck in, as if she'd been punched, and the smile instantly disappeared. She knew that there was nothing she could say right then and there that would help convince Charley Rifkin she was competent without sounding desperate, so she didn't even try. She also knew that if she looked directly into the man's hard blue eyes, she might start to well up – just the reaction she figured he was waiting for – so she looked past him and focused, instead, on the shellacked diploma from Stanford Law mounted behind his head and, for the second time that morning, thought of mai tais in Maui.

'Come on, Charley,' Rick protested, his voice suddenly rising to just below an angry shout. 'That's just bullshit! Other pit prosecutors, including a few As that I can remember, have tried cases with attorneys in this division, and no one has given a damn before, including you. I don't like my judgment being second-guessed here.'

'The stakes are a lot higher on this one, Rick. At this point, this is a death case. We're talking three little kiddies bludgeoned and stabbed in their sleep by their daddy. Assuming everything at the end of the day still points to premeditation and no mitigating circumstances, you're looking at four counts of murder one and a three-ring circus whipping up outside the courthouse. If Dr David Marquette becomes the next Scott Peterson *du jour* – which he has the face for and the crime to match – the press will be camping out in both your backyards until Corrections finally sticks the needle in.' He looked back over at Julia, obviously disappointed. 'She's never even tried a homicide outside of a DUI manslaughter, but you're now gonna possibly have her death-qualify a twelve-person jury with you?'

Rifkin's stinging words hung heavy in the air. Rick stood up and slapped both hands on the desk. 'I think it's shrewd for us to put a woman at the table, Charley,' he said sharply. 'If this does go that far, a jury's going to want to see someone young and pretty and feminine representing a young, pretty, dead mommy and her kids.'

'You want a woman?' Rifkin asked. 'Why not bring in Karyn Seminara? She's a DC who can at least offer you some experience. Lisa Valentine? Priscilla Stroze? I can keep going, if you want.'

'Because I've seen Julia in court. Have you? I had a hearing before Farley last month and I actually caught her giving an opening. She can give the victims a voice, Charley, a face – not just a particular number of years on a résumé. She can keep it human, and she can keep a jury in that room. Especially when things get dull and dry and it's all about forensics, fingerprints and DNA and everyone wants to take a little nap after lunch. Look, in her three years in this office she's had more than her fair share of trials – even more than the fair share of a few As and DCs combined – and not counting two hung juries, she's got a perfect conviction rate to date. Not too shabby, I think. Besides,' he added, his eyes not yet releasing the Division Chief's as he sat back slowly in his seat, 'you might be surprised to find, Charley, that Julia's got some pretty sharp teeth. And like me, she's not afraid to use them.'

Charley Rifkin stared back for a long moment, then held his hands up defensively. 'Like I said, Rick, it's your case. Pick who you want, but don't fuck it up on me. I like to think that after twenty-seven years in this office, I can smell the bad ones – the headaches that come back to haunt you. That come back to haunt this office. This one, I gotta tell you, I think it stinks, Rick. Like the perfect storm, it's got all the ingredients brewing for high profile. A fuck-up on that can follow you around for the rest of your career.' His eyes narrowed. 'Remember that, Ricky. Remember that.'

Rick nodded, as he smoothed a wrinkle from his suit jacket. 'I appreciate the warning, Charley.' Then he turned to Julia. 'Of course, we may be getting way ahead of ourselves. After all this, I don't even know if Julia's gonna want to try this case with me.'

She had yet to take her eyes off the diploma, not wanting to interject herself any further into the scary little King-Kong-Godzilla-go-round that had gone down right in front of her. Even if it was true that opportunities like this knocked only once, Julia now wasn't so sure she wanted to open the door, for fear it might just slam back in her face and catch a few fingers in the process. Maybe she wasn't competent enough to try a murder yet. Maybe she still did have her baby teeth, and everyone would see her struggling to learn the ropes on the eleven o'clock news, like Charley Rifkin was predicting.

Just a few years ago, Julia Anne Valenciano, Esquire, could never have imagined she would be sitting in this seat. She wasn't someone who'd always had a burning desire to become a prosecutor, or a judge, or even a lawyer, for that matter. There were no attorneys in her family, no pals whose parents were lawyers. In fact, most of her friends from Great Kills, the Staten Island neighborhood in New York where she mostly grew up, never even went on to college. But even though no one in her family had a college degree, her not getting one was never an option. So after toiling and commuting away four years at Rutgers University in neighboring New Jersey for a liberal arts degree – only to find after graduating that there was no such thing as a career in liberal arts – she'd drifted into law school when the grace period on her student loans was up and a friend told her some of the absurd salaries that lawyers in New York City made. The problem was, she unfortunately discovered *after* Georgetown had cashed her tuition check, the fields of law that actually paid those absurd salaries made her sleepy, and criminal law was the only class that had truly fascinated her in four long years of night school. Then, in her last semester, and literally only days away from officially throwing out her waitressing shoes and selling her soul on the dotted line to one of the boring Washington DC corporate law firms she detested, she took a trial advocacy class and was instantly and completely hooked on the courtroom. From there it wasn't too hard to make that leap into *Law & Order* on Wednesday nights and the role of prosecutor.

She'd picked Miami because they'd offered, and because, besides having plenty of crime, they'd been the only DA's office able to enclose with their offer letter a colorful city guide filled with pictures of happy, tan, bikini-clad residents apparently all commuting to work on jet skis and yachts. Of course, the two biggest and warmest and most insistent reasons of all to head down south were her Aunt Nora and Uncle Jimmy, who had homesteaded their condo in Fort Lauderdale years ago. A couple of months into her three-year commitment as an ASA, she'd realized that what was supposed to be a short-term stint at the government's expense to gain courtroom experience, would actually become her career. Her calling, if you wanted to get all mushy about it. The pay was crummy and the hours were long. There were few weekends she wasn't in front of her computer, and few nights that she left the office before six or seven – later if she was in trial. But no matter the complaints – from ornery judges and unethical defense lawyers to unco-operative, apathetic witnesses and thankless victims – at the end of most days she still felt as though she'd made a difference, however small, in someone else's life. And some-times, when she put a *really* bad guy behind bars, she knew that the difference she made might actually have been one of life or death, even if she never got credit for it. As a prosecutor, she had the power to change the often cruel world around her, and trying supermarket slip and falls just didn't seem so important anymore, no matter how much money she could potentially make.

Now she was being given the chance to take her career to another level. It was an opportunity she knew most prosecutors in her office would never be offered, an oppor-tunity that only an hour ago she would never have hesitated to take. Only now she was unsure of herself. Trying her first murder was one thing; trying her first murder in front of a bunch of cameras, skeptical colleagues and an administration that she knew was waiting to watch her fall was another. Then Julia thought of something else just as troubling. Though she didn't believe their recently escalated friendship was the reason Rick Bellido was asking her to second-seat, maybe that thinking was just plain naïve. And while she was confident that no one inside or outside the office knew about, or even suspected, their relationship – or whatever it was they were in right now – if it continued, chances were someone would eventually figure it out. Gossip ran reck-lessly and purposefully through the State Attorney's Office, like a match on the trail of gasoline. What then? What would people speculate was the real reason she was second-seating a Major Crimes case? Or worse, she thought suddenly, *what if it ended?* And even worse than that, *what if it ended badly?* Then what? A million questions screamed for answers in her head; a million doubts demanded instant resolution. And all the while, she felt both men watching her, waiting for a decision, like a bad reality show, as the seconds slowly ticked by. *Your fear of failure, Julia, should never be greater than your fear of regret*, another wise maxim espoused by her wise Uncle Jimmy. Uncle Jimmy, the garbage man from Great Kills who could have been a philosopher. What would he tell her to do now? God, she didn't want to fail and she certainly didn't want to fail so publicly, but she sure as hell didn't want to look back and see the now very obvious fork in the winding road of her career. The fork, she could hear herself saying over and over again, that she should have taken. She drew a deep mental breath. *Screw Rifkin and his opinion. She could do this. Right?*

'I understand your concerns, Mr Rifkin,' she said, finally moving her eyes off the diploma and looking the Major Crimes Division Chief right in the eye. 'But I would most definitely welcome the opportunity to second-seat this case.'

Rick smiled. 'Great,' he said, rising and walking back toward the door to open it. 'Drop off your files, then, and meet me down in the lobby in ten minutes. I want to take you over to the crime scene.' Rifkin notably said nothing.

She felt the Lucky Charms churn once again, but nodded expectantly, as if she'd already cleared the rest of the day's calendar. No time like the present to get her feet not just wet, but completely soaked, she supposed. No time to change her mind. She followed Rick over to the door, thanked both men again, and walked out into the hall to get her cart.

When she heard the door shut behind her with a click she finally exhaled the real breath she'd been holding, even though she knew that the conversation back inside was probably far from over.

7

She practically threw the cart up against the wall of her office, next to a tall, overgrown stack of dispo boxes – pesky final case dispositions that she had yet to get to – grabbed her purse from the desk drawer, stepped over another stack and hurried back out the door. She hollered an informative, 'I'll be back!' to her secretary, Thelma – who was busy watching *The Jerry Springer Show* on a portable TV/radio stuck up under her desk and who didn't really care where she was going or when she'd be back anyway – and then headed down the hall, hastily trying to retouch her lip gloss and check her cellphone for messages as she did. It wasn't even eleven yet and a lot of attorneys were still stuck in court across the street – their doors open and offices empty – but as she rounded the corner past the secretary for Judge Stalder's division, she spotted her best friend, Dayanara, at her desk on the phone.

'Oh good, you're here,' Julia said in a hushed voice as she rushed in the door, stuffed the cell and the lip gloss back in her purse, and grabbed the *Herald* off the top of Day's perfectly stacked in-box. The room, as always, smelled of lemon Pledge, Windex and Cuban coffee. There were no dispos on Dayanara's floor, no files waiting to be put away on her file cabinet – just a clock radio, a Tupperwared bag of Pilon coffee and a bottle of Dial hand sanitizer. Even on the small side table where she brewed *café cubano* for twenty every afternoon, there was nary an expresso bean or a sugar grain in sight. If the two of them hadn't been such good friends for such a long time, Julia might have allowed Dayanara's obsessive-compulsive disorder to make her feel inadequate, but aside from being insanely jealous that Day was in a normal judge's division, there was no competition between them. 'Can I borrow this?' she whispered, heading back for the door without really waiting for an answer.

'Hold on a moment, sir,' Day said and let the phone slip down into her neck. 'I haven't read the funnies yet. Don't crinkle it.'

'Not a problem,' Julia said, backing out with a quick wave. 'Sorry to interrupt.'

'Are we doing lunch?'

'Can't. Not today.'

'Are you in trial?'

'Tomorrow. Want to try a domestic on an excited utterance with me?'

'Hmmm . . . no. Thanks for asking. Where are you off to, then?'

'I'll tell you later!' Julia called out behind her as she made her way down the hall to the security door that led out to the elevator bay, 'but you won't believe it when I do!'

NO SUSPECTS IN GABLES MASSACRE blared the front-page headline in her hands. She hadn't had the time to actually read the article this morning before heading out to work, but now every detail mattered – every name, every title, was important to know and remember and catalogue away in her brain. She looked anxiously around the elevator bay and nodded with a checked smile at a couple of prosecutors waiting with her to go down.

Her eyes flew across the page: Jennifer Leigh Marquette, age thirty-two. Emma Louise Marquette, age six. Daniel Elan Marquette, age three. Sophie Marie Marquette, age six weeks. A small, grainy black and white picture of a smiling Jennifer ran under the headline, but even though the picture was bad, Julia could still see she'd been a pretty woman with a sweet, infectious grin that took over her entire face. It was funny how the press always seemed to find the absolute happiest-looking photos of murder victims to print alongside stories of their violent deaths.

> . . . found early Sunday morning by police responding to a 911 call . . . brutally slain at their four-bedroom home in a quiet, upscale section of Coral Gables . . . veteran police chief Elias Vasquez refused to release further details . . . described the crime scene as 'one of the most disturbing' he'd ever visited . . . watched as Miami-Dade Crime Scene techs removed items from the home all day . . . no suspects have been identified . . . pending the notification of New Jersey relatives . . . services have not yet been scheduled . . .

A strange, icy chill ran through her as she reached the bold-faced subhead a little further down the page.

PHYSICIAN DAD STILL CRITICAL; COMMUNITY, HOSPITAL PRAY FOR RECOVERY

Dr David Alain Marquette, age thirty-four. Another grainy picture smiled softly back at her, obviously a professional headshot. He was young, so maybe it was a med-school graduation photo. Disquietingly normal by all appearances, it was not the crazed Charlie Manson mug she might have expected, given what she knew the man was soon to be charged with. In fact, like his wife, David Marquette, too, was good-looking, with an all-American type of boyish charm that came across even in a snapshot. Their children must have been beautiful, she thought without really thinking. Another chill raced down her spine.

> . . . discovered near death inside the home
> . . . to undergo emergency surgery this morn-
> ing . . . no further details on his condition
> were available . . . young, orthopedic sur-
> geon from Chicago with a growing practice
> on Miami Beach . . . operated out of Mount
> Sinai Hospital . . . some famous clients in the
> sporting world, including Florida Marlins
> pitching phenom . . . loving father and hus-
> band . . . many friends and colleagues still in
> shock . . . relatives brace for another possible
> funeral . . .

She stuffed the paper into her purse as the doors opened onto the crowded lobby and made a mental note to buy Day another one.

Rick was already there waiting, chatting with the Division Chief of Narcotics and Pete Walsh, the office's only employment lawyer. 'Ready?' he asked, jingling his keys in his hand as she walked up. 'We'll take my car. I'm right here in the main lot.'

'Sounds good,' she said, feeling the eyes of the other two men follow them as they headed out the door together. She'd have to get used to the funny looks and raised eyebrows, she supposed, if they were going to work together. The match had been lit – the rumors would be next.

'Do you have to be back for court?' he asked as they stepped outside.

'No. I have nothing on this afternoon,' she replied.

'Good. I'm not sure how long we'll be. We may even take a run over to the ME's later,' he said, crossing the lot to where a shiny black BMW 525i sat. He clicked the alarm and held open the passenger door for her. 'So, are you ready for your first homicide?'

A disturbing image suddenly popped into Julia's head. *We're talking three little kiddies bludgeoned and stabbed in their sleep by their daddy.* 'Are the bodies still there?' she asked hesitantly as she stepped inside the car. 'At the scene?'

Another amused look crossed his face. 'I hope not. They'd be pretty ripe by now, Julia. They were found yesterday,' he replied, shutting the door.

'Oh yeah,' she said to no one but herself in the empty car. Strike two. Officially on the case less than twenty minutes and she already sounded like a moron.

He climbed in the front seat and looked at her with concern before turning on the engine. 'Why? Would it bother you?'

Hell yeah, she wanted to say. *Four dead bodies and a blood-splattered house might freak me out, yes, when the biggest scene I've been to so far is a DUI roadblock on the 4th of July.* But, of course, she didn't. 'No,' she answered with a shake of her head. 'I just wanted to prepare myself if they were.'

Richard Bellido fascinated her, impressed her, intrigued her, scared her. Long before she'd actually met the man, she'd heard of his reputation. Everyone who practiced criminal law in Miami had. He was arguably the office's best litigator, earning his coveted spot in Major Crimes after less than seven years in the office, and was rumored to be in line one day for even greater things than the prestigious title of the unit's Division Chief. He'd tried some of the most notorious, heinous murders in Miami history, including, most recently, Ronnie Sikes, the Jekyll/Hyde Miami-Dade police detective who'd fed what remained of his unfaithful wife to his backyard kiddie pool full of pet piranhas. Courted throughout the years by several different US Attorneys in Miami, Rick had turned down more than one chance to become an esteemed federal prosecutor, choosing, as the stories went, to try murders instead of plumped-up racketeering violations. But it wasn't just his intimidating trial skills that had the US Attorneys still asking him out and the Governor searching for his name on judicial nominating appointment lists. Tall, dark and handsome with a spicy Cuban twist, his age and experience, ethnic good looks and last name were an asset to any law enforcement office with a South Florida constituency.

Whether it was his reputation or his imposing, well-tailored presence that commandeered a courtroom when he pushed open its doors, Julia still wasn't quite sure, but she'd been in enough of them before enough judges over the past two years in felonies to have seen it happen herself. And she'd felt it happen herself, too. Normally she didn't let people impress her, but like a TV evangelist, or a smooth-talking politician, Rick Bellido just had this mesmerizing, authoritative, commanding way about him. What he said to a judge was often taken as gospel; what he asked of a jury was usually done. His days in the division pits long over, his colleagues now were all Major Crimes prosecutors, specialized unit Division Chiefs, local politicians, police chiefs, and high-paid, big-name defense attorneys. And so Julia had been more than just a little surprised when he'd sat down next to her in court a few weeks ago and struck up a conversation while he waited for a defendant to be brought over from the jail. Surprised and flattered. And, even though he was seventeen years older – or maybe *because* he was seventeen years older – definitely attracted. Casual cups of coffee had turned into a couple of off-campus lunches on Miami Beach and then finally, unexpectedly, Friday night. She hadn't heard from him since, which made this, their first moment alone, all the more awkward. Even though there were so many things to discuss, she had no idea what to say right now, so she opted for nothing and looked out the passenger window.

'Don't let Charley get to you,' he said, breaking the silence after they'd pulled out of the parking lot and onto 14th Street. 'He just likes you to know who's in charge. He does it to everyone.'

Somehow she doubted that, but it was still nice to hear. 'I'll try to remember that,' she said softly.

More awkward silence.

'I didn't pick you because of us,' he said finally, as the car pulled up to a light. 'Let's get that elephant out of the way right now.' He turned to look at her, leaning an elbow on the console and taking off his Ray-Bans. 'I meant what I said back there. I like what I see in the courtroom, Julia. You've definitely got talent and that intrigues me. You've got this kind of gritty, rebellious, "take no shit" attitude, which reminds me a little of C. J. Townsend, a prosecutor who used to be with our office. When this came up, I thought of you. I think,' he paused for a second. 'Well, I think you can make things interesting.' He smiled. The crinkle of crow's feet softened and warmed his otherwise intense brown eyes. 'And I like interesting.'

'Thank you,' was the best she could manage, returning the smile herself.

'Of course, what happened the other night was fun, too.

And I definitely think we should do that again,' he said, lowering his voice to just above a whisper. Without warning, he leaned over and kissed her on the lips, his hand finding its way through the tangle of her thick, long, dark waves to the back of her neck, wrapping around it and pulling her closer. She remembered Friday night, the water from the shower spilling off his muscular back like a waterfall, those warm, experienced hands in complete control of her body, shampooing her hair, then running over her shoulders, rubbing the rich lather all over her skin. The moment felt a little forbidden, a little embarrassing, totally exciting, just as it had then, and she kissed him back, her tongue finding his, her fingers running underneath his jacket, tracing the crisp starch lines in his dress shirt. The beep of a horn pulled them both back to the present.

'I'll do my best,' she said softly, touching a finger to her lips. 'That I can promise you.'

He slipped his sunglasses back on. 'Good,' he said with another smile, as the car pulled away from the green light. It was all he needed to say.

8

'Crime Scene has already videoed,' Rick said as the Beamer pulled up in front of a pretty mint-green house with beautiful carved oak and etched glass double front doors. Yellow crime-scene tape crisscrossed one of the doors, blue roofing tarp covered a missing glass panel. Under an expansive overhang, a couple of MDPD uniforms stood guard, chatting. Above them, a witch, dressed in a flowing black gown and neon purple striped socks, had crashed head-on into the stucco. Two obvious undercover cars – a Chevy Impala and a Ford Taurus – blocked an MDPD Crime Scene van into the driveway, and police cruisers from both Coral Gables and Miami-Dade PD dotted the perimeter of the corner house. Across the street, Julia spotted a blue Channel Seven news van, its forty-foot satellite antenna artfully dodging not just telephone lines, but the towering, old eucalyptus and ficus trees that shaded the stately block.

'So you'll get to see what it looked like yesterday when the uniforms went in and before the techs trampled over everything important,' Rick continued, looking past her at the house himself. It's always good to visit the actual scene, no matter what the crime. That's not always practical, I know, but a scene never looks the same in pictures or on video as it does in person. It's like going to a hotel, you know? The room's either better or worse than what you'd expected when you looked at the brochure or went on the website. Plus, when you get your detectives on the stand and they're describing a scene, you can *see* it. You know what the house smells like; how you could hear the neighbors upstairs arguing. There's even a taste peculiar to each crime scene. Then you can take what you've seen and tasted and heard and felt and you can tell the story to the jury the way it needs to be told, with the detail it needs to be told in.'

In the front yard, tiny, handmade ghosts danced in the thinning branches of an oak tree. As Rick talked, Julia watched them spin and twist in the breeze. On the neat front lawn, she could see a tricycle, a slip-and-slide, an oversized bouncy ball stuck in the bushes. The green canvas top of an elaborate wood swing set peeked over a black iron fence that ran alongside the house. Behind the fence was probably a pool full of even more toys. Toys that would never be used again. A strange, uncomfortable, *heavy* feeling settled in her stomach, like she'd swallowed an entire jar of peanut butter and it had gotten stuck on the way down. It was hard to imagine this Norman Rockwell house was a crime scene. It was really hard to imagine just what might be waiting inside that would still warrant the presence of so many police officers . . .

Besides the sudden shock of nerves that had turned her Lucky Charms to rubber cement, Julia felt a little ashamed, too. She'd never worked what Charley Rifkin would call a 'real' homicide before, but she still knew how they were investigated. Everything personal, anything private, inside that house was now subject to unlimited inspection by complete strangers. That meant drawers would be picked over, the tiniest of boxes opened, notes read, closets pilfered. And even though she'd never met young Jennifer Leigh, who was only four years older than herself, she still knew that there were things in that pretty mint house of hers that she'd never intended for anyone to see or read or hear. Ever. Because every woman had something – love letters, racy

Saturday-night lingerie, pictures, a revealing journal. Now dozens of hands would be rifling through those special somethings – Julia's included – touching them, photographing them, commenting on them, interpreting them. Perhaps what was most ironic, she thought grimly, was that even when the case did finally end – however that ending might come to pass – those private special somethings would still forever be stored away in some evidence locker, administratively categorized under Florida law as a very public record. She made a mental note to clean out her own cluttered closets when she got home tonight.

'Ready?' Rick asked, turning off the engine.

A sudden, hard *thwack* on the driver's side window made her jump in her skin. Standing outside Rick's window, in a slightly rumpled blue suit and a dress shirt the color of chewed Bazooka bubblegum, with microphone in hand, was Channel Seven field reporter Edward 'Teddy' Brennan. Julia recognized him from the *Trauma News at Ten*, although she thought he looked smaller in person than he did on TV. And, thanks to the metrosexual wonders of make-up, a lot tanner, too.

'Hey there! Teddy Brennan, Channel Seven News,' he yelled. 'Can I talk with you?'

Behind Brennan stood Willie Nelson with a big, expensive camera on his shoulder. Sporting a foot-long faded yellow-white beard and matching braid down his back, unfashionably ripped jeans and a *Dark Side Of The Moon* T-shirt that looked like it probably came from the 1973 Pink Floyd concert tour of the same name, the only thing missing was the guitar.

'I should have figured he'd still be lurking around,' Rick grumbled. 'Watch yourself around this guy, Julia. Brennan's a shit. I'll handle all the press on this,' he warned in a low voice, opening his door. It wasn't a date, so she immediately opened hers and stepped out.

'Mr Bellido, is this officially your case now?' Brennan asked, following Rick as he walked past the police barricades and onto the sidewalk. 'Can you identify any suspects for us yet? Your office looking at making an arrest sometime soon? Should people be worried there's a murderer on the loose? How about warning the anxious public with a description, some details, maybe?'

'Alright, step back,' said one of the uniforms who had walked across the lawn. He pointed at Brennan and his roadie. 'Behind the horse. That's what it's there for, guys.'

Brennan ignored him, and, as if he'd just gotten a great idea, practically ran back behind the car over to where Julia stood on the grass. 'Are you with the State Attorney's, too?' he asked.

Taken off guard, she nodded.

Like a shark to chum, the questions hit hard and fast. 'How'd they die in there, huh? Is it true they were mutilated? Is this a ritual killing? What about the father? Have you guys questioned him? Is he gonna die, too? Why doesn't your office want to make a statement on this?'

Julia turned away toward the house, and quickly followed Rick up the brick walk, careful to keep her eyes on anyone and anything but Teddy Brennan. Just the nod had probably given him too much. She knew she had a crappy poker face – heaven forbid it was a look from her that silently confirmed to the media that David Marquette was not just a suspect, but *the* suspect. *Damn.* Hopefully Charley Rifkin and the State Attorney himself wouldn't see her nodding dumbly on the ten o'clock news. On the marigold-lined path before her she spotted what remained of a colorful chalk hopscotch board, its playing pieces of rocks and bottle caps still deliberately scattered inside the numbered boxes, as if the game was still in play. Next to it, someone had scribbled 'Emma Luvs Tiler Stamm' inside a lopsided heart. Someone else had tried to scratch out 'Emma' and write 'Vicki'. She stepped over the marigolds and walked on the lawn.

'This isn't a press conference, Mr Brennan,' Rick called out behind him as he opened the front door and he and Julia stepped into a huge marble foyer. 'When I want to hold one, I'll let you know.' The door closed behind them with a thud.

'Scumbag,' Rick said under his breath as they stepped down into an enormous living room. Voices could be heard down one of the halls that shot off the living room. 'Latarrino?' he called out, disappearing down one of them.

She stood there in awe. She'd never been in such a big house. Such a perfect house. A stunning stone staircase, wrapped in a decorative wrought-iron railing, hugged a two-story faux-painted wall. The floor was a polished marble with square Brazilian cherry wood inlays. Expensive knick-knacks lined the shelves of an ornate curio cabinet and family pictures dotted an oversized buffet table. But for the thin coating of black dust that covered the glass coffee table and window sills, everything looked *Architectural Digest* perfect. At least from where she stood. The same foreboding, uneasy feeling she'd experienced in the car was back with a vengeance. It was like a horror movie. Any moment now she was going to find out why people were leaving the theater screaming.

'You coming?' Rick called out, walking back in.

She nodded. Something crunched under her feet.

'Careful. Uniforms had to break the window to gain entry when they responded. I guess it hasn't all been cleaned up. Don't slip.'

She followed Rick into what looked like a busy, cluttered all-white kitchen. The latest decorator gadgets and appliances crammed marble countertops, as did miscellaneous baskets of kitchen junk, and stacks of cookbooks and cooking magazines. Jennifer must have been quite the chef – or at least liked to look like she was. Julia herself had trouble boiling water. Next to the sink she saw that cleaned baby bottles had been carefully laid out on paper towels, dishes for the morning left to dry in the dish rack. A morning that never came, she thought somberly. The always-happy Wiggles smiled at her from atop a pile of children's books on the breakfast bar, next to a stack of clear evidence bags and red evidence tape and the smallest baseball mitt she'd ever seen; a Wiffle ball and plastic bat sat on the bar stool below. Standing around the kitchen's island, with their backs all to her, were two guys in MDPD CRIME SCENE polo shirts, another uniform, and what looked like a plain-clothes detective, the sleeves of his dress shirt rolled up to the elbows, a Glock holstered to his hip. A set of legs stuck out from a cabinet underneath the island's sink.

'He's having trouble with the trap,' said the plain-clothes with a chuckle as Rick walked up. 'Like you need a degree in fucking rocket science to be a plumber. Yo, Satty, you want me to call Roto-Rooter to help you do your goddamned job?'

'Fuck you, Brill,' said a voice from under the sink.

'Hey, guys . . .' Rick said, his voice trailing off in a not-so-subtle way. He nodded behind him in Julia's direction. 'You want to watch yourselves?'

'Whoa, excuse me,' said the plain-clothes, turning around. Short and stocky with an extra-full handlebar mustache, he had a conspicuous, perfectly round bald spot in the back of his head that made Julia think of the dead patch of lawn left behind when you put a kiddie pool away at the end of the summer. He looked her up and down with what was either a half-smile of approval or a smirk of disappointment. She couldn't tell which. 'Didn't realize you brought company with you, Ricky.'

'Steve Brill, this is Julia Valenciano. She's working this with me. Julia, Steve's a detective with the Gables.'

'Are you interning?' asked Brill.

'She's a prosecutor, you ass,' Rick shot back.

'Whoops, I'm sorry,' said the detective, raising his hands up. 'I'm just gonna shut up now.'

'Finally,' said the voice under the sink.

'You got it?' asked Brill.

'No, I don't got it. But you're finally gonna shut up.' The room snickered.

'That's it. I'm calling in a plumber, you incompetent—' Brill looked over at Julia again, hesitated, then finished his thought,'—jerk.' The next two seconds passed in awkward silence. She turned away, pretending to look out the sliding glass doors that led to a tropical backyard and the pool. And more uniforms.

Julia now knew what it must have felt like to be the first female sportscaster let into the men's locker room. She wasn't just the sole woman on this scene – a fact she was already acutely aware of – but she was also at least ten years younger than everyone else in the room, and, to put the icing on the cake, she was a lawyer. There were women in law enforcement – lots, in fact – but no matter what the person keeping track of the quotas in the front office might say, it was still a boys club. And if they could, most of those club members would gladly hang a 'No Girls Allowed!' sign on their station doors if the federal government would just let them. Then there was the fact that she was an attorney. Just because cops and prosecutors worked the same side of a case didn't always make them the best of friends. It was well known around any courthouse that cops didn't like lawyers. While ASAs had more redeeming qualities than their defense counterparts, they also had the unfortunate job of breaking bad news. *So sorry, but the career criminal you stopped with the stolen goods on his front seat who gave a full confession will be going home today because something went wrong.* Wrong with the stop, the search, the evidence, the confession, the ID, the law. And no one liked the bearer of bad news, especially when the bearer bore the ultimate power to drop charges. Top it off with a substantial age gap and pre-file conferences could get downright hostile.

'What are you guys doing?' asked Rick when no one said anything.

'Cleaning out the asshole's sewer line – what the hell do ya think we're doing? We're taking the traps.' He looked back over at Julia. 'Oh shit. Sorry for the language. Again.'

She shook her head. 'That's okay. Please, don't worry about me.'

'Speaking of sewers,' said the legs with what sounded like a laugh.

'Keep at it, Satty,' Brill said, giving the leg closest to him a half-hearted kick. 'And don't forget your day job, now.'

'Never. Besides,' the legs said with a final grunt, 'I got it. Hand me a bag.'

'Where's Latarrino?' asked Rick, looking around.

'Yeah, I'm happy to see you, too, Ricky. Thanks for exchanging pleasantries,' Brill quipped. 'Lat's upstairs. Master bedroom, I think.'

'You're looking good, Steve,' Rick said, slapping the detective's shoulder. 'The Rogaine looks like it's working.'

'That's better,' replied the detective with a laugh.

'Okay, Julia, let's head up,' said Rick, turning to her. 'That's where the bodies were found. Let me show you what we got.'

'Hey, Ricky, can we arrest this asshole yet?' called out Brill.

'Soon,' Rick yelled back from the living room. 'Let's see what the dad of the year has to say when the anesthesia wears off. And besides, I'm not picking up the tab he's running over at Ryder, Steve.' The state of Florida was ultimately responsible for providing medical care to any person in their custody. Arresting David Marquette now might make for a nice lead-in on the five o'clock news, but it also potentially could mean footing the bill for his surgery and hospital stay. In a setting where an aspirin cost upwards of twelve bucks a dose, that could amount to a pretty outrageous sum. One that Julia figured the taxpayers of Miami-Dade County probably wouldn't like to hear they'd be shouldering.

'Oh shit,' she heard Brill say to the guys in the kitchen. 'I did it again.'

'My kid makes you pay him a dollar if you say a curse word,' someone said.

'He must make a fortune off your fucking mouth, Ed,' joked another.

'College fund's paid off.'

Everyone laughed.

'"Are you an intern?" You're a fucking idiot, Brill,' said Satty.

'What? I think I have suits older than her.'

'I could see that,' someone said. 'Maybe you should think about getting a piece.'

'Fuck you, too, Burke,' said Brill. 'I ain't wearing no

67

toupee.' Then he yelled out, 'Hey, Julie, sorry about the language.'

'No problem,' Julia replied, with a sigh she made sure no one else could hear as she followed Rick up the stairs.

9

She hadn't even made it to the top step when she saw the large squares conspicuously missing from the beige shag carpeting. It was obvious that Crime Scene wasn't through yet: plastic evidence markers that looked like tiny white easels with black numbers on them had been placed in the spots where the carpet had been cut out and impounded. A strong chemical smell lingered in the air, but Julia couldn't quite place it. It smelled kind of like cleaning solution, but not just your ordinary household Mr Clean and Clorox scent. It smelled nursing-home clean, like antiseptic and death.

'Two sets of bloody footprints were found here,' Rick said, stopping in the hallway. 'One looks like it was from the responding uniform who unwittingly stepped in blood and then trailed it into the last room on the left. That's the little girl's room. The six-year-old, Emma Louise.'

Julia's eyes followed the path of phantom footsteps down a pale yellow hall to where they stopped just outside of a closed white door. Family pictures crowded the walls. Someone had scribbled in different colored crayons on the bottom of the door – someone who couldn't have been more than two or three feet tall.

'The other set we think is from the father,' Rick continued. 'But the scene got pretty chaotic when the officers initially found the bodies; there was a lot of blood and a lot of people. The suspect prints looked smeared somehow, and it doesn't help that it's shag carpeting. The long, cut piles don't hold prints as well as, say, a tightly looped Berber.

The warrant let us clean out Marquette's shoe closet, so we'll test all of them, even the slippers and flip-flops. If we don't get anywhere with that, I'd like to do a print and cast impression of his foot, but we'll need a separate warrant for that.'

'I wouldn't think you'd need a warrant to search the victim's own home,' Julia said out loud, her eyes moving away from the crayoned door and over the smiling photos. A beaming, sandy-haired Jennifer and a baby. A little girl with no front teeth in front of a Christmas tree and a fake fireplace. A baby boy swaddled in blue. The professional headshot of David Marquette from the morning paper.

'Think again,' he said, shooting her a look. 'A dead body might give you exigent circumstances to get in the house, secure the premises and wait for the ME, but it doesn't give you the right to do a full search, even if the victim, or in this case, victims, lived there, too. I've had even hotshot veteran cops somehow forget they need a warrant when they respond to a homicide. They see "dead body" and that's all they need.'

Strike three. *If you don't know something, it's better just to keep your mouth shut and let people maybe think you're stupid, than open it up and confirm it.* Another Uncle Jimmyism she should have remembered sooner.

Instead of heading down the hall that led to Emma's room, Rick instead turned and walked down another hall that T-boned the balcony and staircase. A set of closed double doors waited at the end. And more phantom foot-steps. 'Let's start in what we believe so far to be the order of the murders. This is the master bedroom,' he said, slipping on a pair of latex gloves he had pulled from his pocket. He handed her a pair. 'Even though Crime Scene has been through the upstairs already for prints, if you touch anything, use gloves. I hope you're not squeamish,' he said, opening the door. 'This is where the mother was found.'

Julia swallowed hard and tried to brace herself for something she was suddenly no longer sure she wanted to see. It was one thing to sit around and talk about a crime scene, discuss the position of the bodies, the entry and exit wounds, and the clinical cause of death; it was another to walk among ghosts down bloodstained halls. She had an urge to turn around, just walk quickly down the stairs, out of this creepy, perfect house and back to the car, back to the office, back home. Take her scolding from Charley Rifkin, kiss her budding relationship with Rick Bellido goodbye if she had to, chalk this overwhelming *bad* feeling that was slowly sucking the air out of the room up to inexperience. Just don't look anymore. Don't see it. Don't open the door, Julia. *Don't make it real again.*

But it was too late for that.

Dark red splashes of blood ran up arctic-white walls, splattering into countless tiny droplets on the ceiling. White evidence tape marked where blood and other body fluids had presumably dripped or pooled onto a dark mahogany wood floor. Above an antique sleigh bed, an elaborately framed wedding portrait of a smiling David and Jennifer looked down upon a stripped, bare mattress, stained, like the walls around it, a rich, dark red. Blood had seeped through the thin pillow-top, leaving a zigzagging level line on the side of the bed that looked a couple of inches deep in places. Julia's eyes returned to the happy, oblivious picture taken what must have been only a few short years ago. Blood had sprayed up onto the glass, coagulating and then freezing in time as it dripped back down, like drops of paint stuck forever onto a dry wall.

The ghosts were crying tears of blood, the silenced shrieks

71

of the dead playing over and over again in her head, like the violent crescendo of music in a horror film. That's when Julia realized she'd just walked into the part where everyone starts screaming.

'The body was found, as you can guess, on the bed,' Rick said, looking around the room. 'Crime Scene cleaned it up somewhat and the bedding has been impounded. The bloodstain analyst from Metro was here yesterday and again this morning. As you can see, we have spatter on the head-board and on the walls, traveling at a high enough velocity to actually hit an eight-foot ceiling. I don't know how much you know about bloodstain pattern interpretation, but a hell of a lot of force is needed on impact to generate that type of distal trajectory. The spray pattern starts here and travels up,' he said, moving over to the bloody mattress and motioning to the wall next to the nightstand, 'indi-cating Jennifer Marquette was lying flat when she was first struck. The shower of drops on the ceiling are satellite spatters, most likely the result of an arterial spurt when he hit the aorta or jugular. She was probably sleeping when it happened.'

Probably sleeping. 'What was the actual cause of death?' Julia asked softly, still staring at the mattress. The stain impression was only on one side of the king-size bed, in the general shape of a person. She didn't need crime-scene photos to see Jennifer Marquette's beautiful, twisted face, her eyes, open and vacant, staring dully up at the ceiling. Even if they were closed when she took her last breath, Julia already knew many of the macabre secrets death held in store. One of which was once the heart stops beating and the body shuts down, the eyelids involuntarily opened back up, staying that way until a mortician finally superglued them down in the basement of some funeral home.

We're so sorry.
So very sorry, Julia.
You shouldn't have to see her this way.
Not you . . .
She shut her eyes tight against the horror that lay right there in front of her, but even in darkness she could still see the bright yellow rosebuds and delicate pink ribbon that trimmed the nightgown's sleeve, the pool of glossy red blood that slowly, surely seeped across the floor. And her eyes, those beautiful deep-green eyes, open and forever terrified . . .

'Blunt force to the head with an unknown object and multiple stab wounds,' Rick replied.

'Thirty-seven in all,' said a deep voice behind Julia, pulling her thoughts off the bed, and making her jump in her skin for the second time that morning. Julia turned to a scruffy-faced guy in his mid-thirties, a white dress shirt and Tommy Bahama swordfish tie paired with old jeans and new Nikes. With light-blue eyes, dark-blond hair that definitely went past his collar, and well-tanned skin, he looked a little like a surfer who reluctantly had had to get a real job. A gold detective's badge hung around his neck.

'Just the man we were looking for,' Rick said. 'Julia, Detective John Latarrino, Miami-Dade Homicide. Lat, this is Julia Valenciano. She's a prosecutor in our office. She'll be working this with me.'

Latarrino nodded. 'Nice to meet you.'

'She's already met Steve Brill downstairs.'

'I'm sorry,' Latarrino replied.

'I was just showing her the scene. This is our first stop. Anything new?'

'Just got the preliminary autopsy report back this morning. Speaking of which, what happened to you last night, Bellido?'

'I had another engagement. One I couldn't get out of. I called over this morning, but Neilson wasn't in yet. I talked to Torie. She gave me a brief rundown.' Rick looked at Julia and explained the players. 'Joe Neilson's the Chief Medical Examiner. He did the autopsies late yesterday. Torie's Neilson's assistant.'

'So you know most of it, then,' Lat said. 'Blunt trauma to the head probably knocked her unconscious. At least that's what we're hoping. Impact on the side of the skull slammed her brain against the other side, resulting in a large hematoma and massive bleeding. Counted thirty-seven stab wounds to the chest and neck. At least three went through to the mattress.'

'That's one angry sonofabitch,' said Rick with a low whistle, running a hand through his hair.

'Angry is probably an understatement. As you said, one hit the aorta, another the jugular and that was it.' Latarrino shook his head. 'Jennifer Marquette celebrated her thirty-second birthday just last week. Boys found a couple of old "Happy Birthday Mom!" balloons in the trash. Pretty lady, too. She was found here, face-up on the bed, wearing just a nightshirt, which was ripped open, and a pair of panties. But no other evidence of sexual assault. Neilson did do a rape kit. It's not back yet, but the black light picked up what looked like semen.'

'Oh shit,' said Rick. 'Torie didn't mention that on the phone. Where?'

'On the shirt. Non-motile. No way to tell how old. We're

doing DNA. Hopefully it's hubby's. If not . . .' He didn't bother completing the thought. 'We think he surprised her here. There was nothing under the fingernails, no sign of a struggle in the room. No evidence the body had been moved. As you said, she was probably sleeping, he came in, hit her upside the head, made it look like a rape attempt and then went at her with a kitchen knife.'

'Have you found the weapons?' asked Julia, taking a few steps forward, physically distancing herself from the scene behind her. She didn't want to turn around again, or look into the mirror that was directly behind Detective Latarrino, mounted above a neat marble-top dresser dotted with more family pictures. The air continued to slowly seep out of the suddenly freezing-cold room, and she struggled not to gasp for more. *Keep it clinical. Stay focused on the words. Stay here, in the room. Don't let yourself go away again.*

'We did find a baseball bat in a closet in the boy's room. No blood on it that we can see, but the timeline works that he could've cleaned it up. The lab can check for microscopic blood, hair or fiber, if he left any behind.'

'What about the knife?' she asked.

'We think that'll be the one the docs removed from Marquette's stomach. We also seized every knife we could find downstairs. Pattern testing can compare Mrs Marquette's wounds to the knives we seized and see what matches. Neilson says it looks like a straight blade that attacked her and the children because he saw no tears consistent with a jagged edge, but that's the best he can do at this point. The knife the docs recovered was a Henckels boning knife. Straight blade, seven inches.'

'You guys can do the pattern testing, right?' asked Rick. 'Or do we have to send it out to the Feds?'

'Nah, we have our own pattern guy at the crime lab. John

Holt. Worst case is we use FDLE's lab in Orlando if we have to. Keep the Fibbies out of this. Although,' he said, looking around the bedroom, 'no Fed's gonna make a name for themselves in here, so it's not something that would appeal to them, even if they did have jurisdiction. Brill's taking the traps to see if there's blood in the drains that Marquette maybe tried to rinse off, although we found bleach under the upstairs and downstairs sinks, so there's a chance we might not find shit if the guy knew what he was doing with a bottle of Clorax. Rigor had not begun yet, so time of death, based on temperature, lividity and stomach contents was sometime between one and five a.m., when uniforms responded and found her.'

'That's the best Neilson can do?' asked Rick, exasperated.

'That's it. You must have pissed him off before with that charming personality of yours, Bellido, because he says to tell you that he's not a miracle worker, so don't ask him for the second hand on time of death.'

'Fuck him,' Rick grumbled. It was obvious the comment was not made in jest. 'Excuse me,' he said to Julia.

'From what we found out so far, looks like the husband was supposed to be at some American Medical Association conference in Orlando. We have verbal confirmation that Dr David Marquette was booked at the Marriott World Center through today. The front-desk manager got a bit nervous when I said the words "homicide investigation", so Theresa's readying subpoenas for the records.'

'Don't let them touch that room, Lat!' barked Rick.

John Latarrino was the same height as Rick Bellido, but somehow looked a lot bigger. He held his hand up. 'I've already done the warrant. You can look it over be-fore Orlando PD takes it to the judge for a signature this afternoon. See, unlike all those other hotshot veteran cops you've had to show the ropes to, Bellido, I know when I need to go to the bathroom and when I need a warrant.' He smiled at Rick and cracked his gum.

An uncomfortable moment passed. 'That wasn't directed at you,' Rick replied.

'Of course not.'

The tension broke with the ring of a phone. 'I gotta take this,' Rick said, unhooking his cell from his belt and moving into the master bathroom.

'Alright, then,' Latarrino said with a sigh of impatience, looking at his watch. Julia could tell there was a strained history between the two men, but it was too early to say just whose fault that history was. After waiting about thirty seconds, the detective turned and headed out of the bedroom and back out into the hall. 'Bellido's already had his tour, so follow me, Ms Prosecutor, and let's get this over with,' he called out behind him. 'It only gets worse from here on out, so prepare yourself.'

'Did you listen to the nine-eleven tape yet?' Latarrino asked once they were out in the hall.

'No,' said Julia, shaking her head as she caught up with him. 'I only know that units responded to a nine-one-one, but I don't know the contents of the call.'

'Okay, then, let me fill you in. Coral Gables PD received a call on their emergency line at 4:47 a.m. from what sounded like a child. We assume it was six-year-old Emma, although she never gave a name. She asked for help, told the operator that someone was coming. The line went dead before the conversation ended. But there was some muffling on the final seconds of tape. Digital enhancement of that audio and we can hear a man's voice calling out the name Emma, followed by our crying caller saying, "No, Daddy!" Based on the timing of that call, we believe that the father had already killed the wife, left the master bedroom, and then walked down this hall here, probably making some of the prints we took up on the way. We'll know more about whose blood is whose and whose blood is where when the DNA's back. Right now the sequence of events is pretty much just theory. Then we figure he entered either the infant's room or the little boy's room. At some point Emma was awakened, probably saw what happened or what was happening to her brother or sister, took the cordless from the charger in the hall and went back into her own room, where she hid and placed the call to nine-eleven. That's when the dad came in and found her, calling out her name because she wasn't in bed like she was supposed to be. When he finds her, she calls out, "No, Daddy!" and he hangs up the line.'

Latarrino stopped at the first closed door off the main hallway. He frowned and rubbed his eyes. 'Like Jennifer, Danny was found in his bed. God willing, the little guy never knew what hit him. Just went to sleep with a kiss from Mommy and never woke up,' he said as he pushed open the door.

Julia held her breath again. Racecars zoomed across blue and red striped wallpaper; tiny Matchbox cars lined white shelves. Set up off to the side of the room on the wood floor was a loop-de-loop Hot Wheels racetrack with a long line of cars and trucks backed up on plastic yellow connecting tracks. A toddler bed in the shape of a red racecar was pushed up against a far wall. The bedding was gone – long since stripped and bagged.

'This looks clean,' she said right away, her eyes fixated on the tiny bed. 'Cleaner than the other bedroom.'

'We had spatter, but because of the red wallpaper and the fact that Crime Scene actually did clean up in here, it's definitely nowhere near the scene we had in the master. Cause of death was blunt trauma to the head. Several stab wounds to the torso, but not much bleeding into surrounding tissue, so Neilson says they were made post-mortem, which is another reason it wasn't as bloody. No spurting or gushing because the heart wasn't pumping anymore. My take? This guy wasn't as angry with junior as he was with his wife. He showed restraint, if that makes any sense.'

'It does,' she said softly.

'It also makes him out to be more of a monster in my mind. Bastard pulled the covers back up and tucked the kid in again before he tiptoed out to find his daughter,' Latarrino said as he walked back toward the doorway.

'Why isn't the mattress stained, like the mother's?' she asked, following him out into the hall.

'You're pretty observant. For a lawyer,' he said with a smile that was hard to read as he closed the door quietly behind them. 'Rubber sheets. The little guy was still in training.'

God, she needed to get the hell out of here. Even for just a few minutes, even just to step outside and suck in some fresh air, instead of this stale, heavy, cold substance that now filled every room. *There's even a taste peculiar to each crime scene.* And she *could* taste it – heavy and acidic and bitter on her tongue. A taste your throat never forgets; a smell you simply file away into some dark alcove of your brain until something makes you remember it all over again. But Julia knew that even a request for a quick bathroom break at this point would be interpreted as a sign of weakness, especially by this detective and definitely by the crew downstairs, so she said nothing as she followed Latarrino to the door at the far end of the hall – the one with all the crayon scribbles. He stood there with his hand on the knob, long enough for her to realize he really didn't want to open it.

'This is Emma's room,' he said, finally, pushing open the door. 'We found her in the corner, behind a storage box of Barbie dolls and a Hello Kitty chair.'

Even though her Barbies had been seized and the Hello Kitty chair impounded, Julia immediately knew what corner it was little Emma had run and hid from her daddy in. Her blood matted the pink carpet and splattered the lilac walls, painting an eerie final picture. The story she had so desperately begun to tell to a stranger on the telephone, its ending now left to be translated into words by a specialist in bloodstain pattern analysis.

Julia could no longer maintain the cool, distant persona

of a prosecutor. She sucked in a breath as her imagination took over, placing the tiny, frightened figure in the scene. The dead were screaming once more in her head, and she could feel the jolt of adrenaline in her own body, the terror that seized Emma's heart when her father finally found her hiding spot. And then, the sinking, shocking feeling of betrayal when she saw the knife in his hand, knowing exactly what he was going to do with it before it came down on her, but still not believing it as it did. Still loving him even then. She covered her ears with her latex-gloved hands and turned away from the sight.

Latarrino looked taken aback by her reaction. 'God, this job sucks,' he said quietly. He drifted over to the bare picture window that looked out upon the backyard. Glassy-eyed stuffed doggies and bears sat on a custom-made pink checkered window cushion. 'It really does, ya know? Nothing ever preps you for this. No matter how many scenes you've been to or stories you've heard.' He paused. Outside, uniforms chatted and laughed in the sunshine out by the pool. The soft sound of their voices drifted up and into the room, filling the void of strained, reflective silence. 'You never want to get this call,' he said finally, exhaling a deep breath. Then he turned back to face her, immediately frowning. 'Enough, let's get you out of here. You don't look so good.'

The truth was, she didn't feel so good either. She fought down a wave of nausea. 'There's still the baby's room,' she said weakly, wiping away the sweat that had gathered on her upper lip with the back of her hand. The latex from the glove pulled on her skin, and she could taste its chalky bitterness on her lips. She felt incredibly lightheaded, and could only hope that if she did go down, she'd at least stay unconscious long enough for the ambulance to pull out of the driveway.

'Ain't nothing you need to see in there, Ms Prosecutor. Just a pretty nursery,' Latarrino said softly, taking her gently by the elbow and leading her back to the hallway. 'He only suffocated that one.'

12

She sat on the edge of the toilet-bowl lid, her forehead pressed up against the cool marble window sill, a warm breeze from the open window blowing on the wet wad of toilet paper she had packed on the back of her neck.

'Is it passing?' Latarrino asked, looking awkwardly around the bathroom.

'Yes,' she said into the wall, swallowing one last good gulp of air. 'I'm fine now, thank you. I think maybe I'm coming down with something.'

'Oh. Okay.'

She hoped her legs wouldn't twitch when she stood. Or at least that he wouldn't see them twitch. 'I can see the rest of the house now,' she said, looking up.

'You're still a little pale. I think you should stay down for another minute or two. You know, this happens all the time,' Latarrino said with a shrug. 'It's a tough scene, even with the bodies gone.'

She decided not to say anything. And she didn't get up.

'If you don't mind me asking, how'd you get on this case?' he asked, leaning up against the sink, hands in his pockets. 'I mean, I haven't seen you before at the State Attorney's, and I know that Bellido's definitely keeping this one in Major Crimes. Plus, he's not the type to share the glory. So are you a lateral hire from a different SAO, or have they been hiding you up in Legal?' Legal was the specialized division of brains at the SAO that assisted trial attorneys with the more complex legal questions and appeal issues.

Julia sat up stiffly, feeling the prickly hairs rise defiantly on the back of her neck. 'I'm in Judge Farley's division. Rick Bellido and Charley Rifkin asked me to be second seat on this case this morning.' Not entirely true, but Rifkin was there when the decision was made.

He nodded. 'I've had a few cases go in front of Farley. He's so friggin' old, I think everyone has. Is he still an asshole?'

She caught herself smiling. The pricklies died down just a little. 'Yes. And like a bottle of cheap wine, rest assured he's only gotten worse with age.'

'I thought wine got better with age.'

'The cheap ones turn to vinegar.'

Latarrino shrugged. 'I'm a beer drinker myself. I thought Karyn Seminara was the DC in Farley's.'

'She is.'

'Oh. Then who are you? The A?'

Her back arched once again. 'I'm the B.'

'The B? Wow,' he said with a low whistle, 'you must really be something special, then. I've worked with Bellido. He's got high standards for everyone, and like I said, I don't remember him sharing the limelight.' He looked at her, but differently for a second, as if he had just figured something out. Call her cynical, but that something, Julia figured, was probably that she was a woman, and *ergo* must have used her feminine wares to climb the company ladder.

The rush of defiance and pride eradicated the nausea and rejuvenated her. She rose from the toilet seat, took the soggy, bunched-up paper wad off her neck, flushed it down the toilet, and closed the window. 'Why does everyone think it's him?' she asked, smoothing her skirt and quickly changing the subject. 'The dad, David Marquette. Why is everyone so sure it's him?'

'Well, for one, units arrived within about six minutes of

the call and gained entry within another twenty. The alarm was still set. No one else was found in the house, and there was no evidence of a break-in.'

'Why did it take them so long to enter?'

'Good question. One I'm sure the boys will be asking themselves for a long time to come. They thought it was a prank, there were no previous domestics at the residence, no sign of trouble outside. Hindsight's always twenty-twenty, Counselor.'

'Oh,' she said, pausing. She didn't want to sound like an idiot again and say the wrong thing, yet she couldn't help but think of the case of JonBenét Ramsey, the six-year-old from Boulder, Colorado who was taken from her bed and murdered in her home Christmas night, 1996, with her parents and brother sleeping just down the hall. The police and district attorney had instantly focused on the parents, but the murder was never solved. The Ramsey detectives were criticized for having tunnel vision, theorizing that while police focused solely on Mom and Dad, critical evidence was destroyed, other leads ignored, and the real killer long gone and on the loose. 'Could a killer have gotten in some other way, without setting off the alarm?' she asked. 'Through an open window, perhaps? Maybe the screens weren't wired . . .'

'Now you're playing defense attorney.'

'Someone's going to.'

'There were no other signs of forced entry. The father was supposed to be speaking at some medical conference three hundred miles away, and he shows up here. He's the sole survivor in a scene out of a horror movie. He's got a knife stuck in his gut, but even though that sounds really bad, he surprisingly has relatively minor injuries when the rest of his family went through a bloodbath. We're pretty sure that when we dig, we'll find out some other interesting info. We always do.'

'Like a girlfriend?'

'Or girlfriends. Domestic strife. Money problems.'

'Insurance policies . . .'

'Now you're thinking on the right side of the law, Ms Prosecutor.'

'Please, call me Julia.' She paused again. 'So it was a suicide attempt?'

'Maybe. Murder and attempted suicide. Wouldn't be the first. I'm thinking maybe it was supposed to be just a murder. The suicide attempt came after he realized his daughter had called the cops on him and he was running out of time with an alibi that was still some three hundred miles away.'

'Where was he found?' she asked.

Latarrino looked around the bathroom. 'Right here.'

She followed his stare to a corner of the slate-tiled bathroom next to a glass-enclosed shower.

'Crime Scene cleaned it up. Shower was still wet. He was unconscious and naked, nothing but a towel beside him on the floor.'

'What were his actual injuries? I know he had to have surgery.'

'A collapsed lung and a carefully placed abdominal stab wound. Lots of blood. Could have been fatal, I suppose, but it wasn't. A pulmonary embolism he threw last night was what required emergency surgery.'

'Sounds serious.'

'He'll be fine.'

'And you obviously think the wounds are self-inflicted?'

'Definitely. They're too neat for what went on in this house.'

She paused again. 'What I don't understand is why. If suicide was an afterthought, like you're thinking, why would he do this to his family? To his wife? His kids? Jesus Christ, to a little baby? I mean, the man's a doctor . . .'

'Don't let the MD blind you, Counselor. There have been plenty of cold-blooded murderers throughout history that were smart enough to go to college. Matter of fact, the smarter they are, the more likely it is they might get away with it.'

'Fine. I'll try not to let his profession impress me. But you said it, Detective Latarrino, that's not just a crime scene in there – that's a bloodbath.'

'Let us finish the investigation. Maybe we'll find you your why. But I have some bad news for you, *Julia*,' he said, making sure he emphasized her name. 'Welcome to the Big Time, where there's not always an answer that makes sense. That's why the law doesn't make us prove why. Look, people are messed up, and sometimes they just snap. Especially in domestics. I'm sure I'm not the first to point out for you that fine line that exists between love and hate. When someone crosses it, nothing's gonna prep you for what he or she is capable of. Nothing.'

She could hear the clatter of kitchen noises even behind the closed swing doors, the friendly, mindless table-chatter all around her. The warm smells of fried bacon and freshly cooked waffles and brewing coffee filled the air. Sunday-morning sounds and smells that were normally so comforting were now anything but. The ordinariness of everyone else's morning made her want to scream.

'Some people are just not made right, Julia,' Uncle Jimmy said quietly while Aunt Nora cried softly in the booth seat next to him. 'Only God knows why they do what they do. It's best for all of us not to try and understand, ya know? Because we won't. We can't, ya know? It's too horrible to think somebody could . . . It's all just too awful to be real . . .'

His thoughts broke off as Rosey, their waitress, approached the table to tell them the daily specials.

The room suddenly felt like it was shrinking, the grisly information collapsing in on her, like heavy bricks in a wall. She took a deep breath and pushed the pieces of paralyzing memories out of her head, focusing instead on trying to count to ten. Her lungs felt as if they were being slowly shrink-wrapped, and her heart began to race. *Deep breath and get to five. Deep breath and get to six.* It had been years since she'd had a panic attack. *Please, God, not a full-fledged one now.* What she had to do was stay focused. Recognize what was happening to her and get out. 'Well I hope you can dig up that interesting info, Detective Latarrino,' she said slowly, her breath catching. 'Because a jury's going to want to know why, too. I wouldn't want us to later be accused of tunnel vision.'

The detective seemed mercifully oblivious, his back to her as he looked around the bathroom. 'So don't say the word JonBenét and I won't hear it. Trust me, no one here wants to fuck this up. Especially me. Assuming David Marquette wants to talk, we're gonna try. Just as soon as the docs at Ryder give us the green light. No one is looking for the easy way out. By the way, Julia,' he said, turning back to face her, 'call me Lat, please. Or John. Anything but Detective Latarrino. Save that for the stand.'

She nodded. She felt her heartbeat slowly returning to normal, her lungs expand, breaking the shrink-wrap, filling finally with air. She continued to count off numbers in her head, adding one more to each count as she clenched and unclenched her fists and pretended to still look around the room. 'Ready?' she asked when a few more moments had passed, in a voice she thought sounded smooth and steady.

'After you,' he replied, eyeing her carefully. Then he finally opened the door.

13

'There you are,' Rick said, as he came up the last stair. 'I was just looking for you two. Everything okay?' he asked, frowning when he saw Julia. Obviously she was still a little pale.

'Yeah,' replied Lat before Julia could answer. 'I was just showing her where we found the father.'

'Did you see the rest of the house?' Rick asked.

'Yeah. Detective, um, Lat,' she replied, correcting herself, 'Lat was showing me the kids' rooms. It's been . . . tough.'

'Just wait till you see the video. Alright, let's head back to the office, then,' Rick replied, looking at his watch. 'I wanted to head over to see Neilson, but I just got the call that I'm having a late-afternoon status report before Judge Gilbert on a motion to suppress.'

Julia looked at her own watch. It was already 2:45. She suddenly remembered the trial that she never should have forgotten. The one Farley had set for the morning, the one with all the witnesses she hadn't told Mario to call. Mario, her Victim/Witness Coordinator who left precisely at four, immediately followed by her secretary, Thelma, who wouldn't call anybody for her anyway. *Damn.* She wanted to slap herself upside the head. She'd been in such a hurry and such a state of shock when she'd rushed out of the office. Now she thought of all the work that had to be done between now and 9 a.m. tomorrow. 'I've got to get back, too, Rick. I've got that trial to prep for,' she said, dry-mouthing two Tylenol she pulled from the depths of her purse to calm down the stress headache that was already in full swing. The two men began to talk about other cases and people that Julia knew nothing about. She feigned interest for a moment then stepped away, moving over to the pale yellow wall that held all the family pictures she'd first seen when she came up the stairs.

An old black and white photo of someone's grandma and grandpa. A little boy she now knew had to be Danny, his tiny hands clutching a couple of Hot Wheels racecars.

Pictures were such funny things, she thought, as her eyes slowly trolled the smiling faces – faces that were becoming more real for her with every passing second. Snapshots were only a single split-second caught in time, but for most people they were meant to capture so much more than just a moment. A night out. A whole vacation. Life with a new baby. A time in college. The high-school years.

Emma Louise dressed as a winged fairy on Halloween one year. A very pregnant Jennifer wearing a Santa hat. David, holding Danny and Emma at Disney, fireworks erupting over their heads, a luminescent, purplish-pink Cinderella's castle the perfect backdrop to the perfect vacation.

The smiles all looked so real, but in this case they couldn't be, could they? If all these veteran detectives were right, how could such a monster – a man who would later go on to butcher his family one by one in the middle of the night – how could he stand there next to them all and smile like he really meant it? Like he really loved them? The truth was, she knew he couldn't.

David Alain Marquette. Class of 1994, Northwestern University, Feinberg School of Medicine.

Definitely handsome, with well-defined cheekbones, tousled light-blond hair and an easygoing smile, David

Marquette had a soft, round, well-scrubbed face that would surely make a patient feel at ease. Particularly women, Julia thought for some reason. And the lightest, most unusual gray eyes she'd ever seen. Eyes that seemed to transcend the glossy photo paper, as if they were staring right at her. His boyish good looks made him seem instantly trustworthy, which was definitely unsettling. Evil, she thought, should somehow look hideous. '*Ya gotta be trusted by the people that ya lie to,*' Uncle Jimmy had said once. '*That's what makes a really good liar really good.*'

'Alright,' Rick said, heading back over to the stairs. 'We're out of here. Ready, Julia?'

She nodded. They hadn't made it to the stairs when the Nextel at Latarrino's side chirped to life. 'Lat? You there? Come in.' Steve Brill's voice, complete with its distinctively guttural New York accent, echoed through the hall.

'Yeah, Steve, go ahead,' Lat said into the phone, but leaving it on speaker.

'Are you still upstairs?'

'Yeah. Try walking up a flight next time. It might do wonders on that beer belly.'

'Fuck you, you steroid-loving piece of crap. Oh shit. Are you still with Bellido and that prosecutor chick?'

'They're right here. Want to say a quick hello? Or should I just send a tech over to extract that foot from your mouth?'

'Maybe you should come down, then, 'cause I just can't say this without a little color,' Brill said, sounding annoyed.

'What's that?'

'The motherfucker just woke up.'

14

Julia sat back in her chair at her desk, exhaled a deep breath, and stared at the phone in her hand. It was still yelling at her.

'Don't fuckin' tell me that I gots to come down there! I don't gots to do nuthin'! And let me tell you, lady, nobody's done shit for me since Letray cut me up. Now you wanna talk all nice and be my friend?'

'What is it that you'd like me to do for you, Pamela?' Julia asked through gritted teeth, still trying her best to sound patient and understanding. 'I kept him behind bars for you for the past four months, that's what I did. Now to keep him there, you've got to come to court tomorrow.'

Pamela Johnson finally stopped yelling. There was a long pause before she spoke again in a much more hesitant voice. 'What if I don't want him to stay in jail no mo'?'

Julia closed her eyes. 'Pamela, he took a razor blade to your face.'

'I got chil'ren. One jus' born.'

'We can help you find shelter.'

'Bullshit!' The yelling was back. 'That's what I mean, y'all don't do shit for me. I need food, lady. My kids need ta eat. They need their daddy, is what they needs.'

'Pamela, I'm sorry,' she said, her own voice rising. 'I really am. But what damn good is their daddy gonna do them if he's in jail for killing their mommy? Then who's gonna feed your kids?'

'Bullshit!' she screamed again.

Alright. Maybe that was a little harsh. 'I can arrange transporta—' she began, but it was too late. All that remained of Pamela Johnson was the dead hum of a dial tone.

Julia hung up and rubbed her tired eyes. Then she spun her chair around and looked out her rain-streaked window, past the twin five-ton air handlers outside on the roof, over at the Dade County Jail and courthouse across the street. The streets in front of the Graham Building were completely deserted; puddles the size of mini-lakes the only thing left behind in the parking lots after the heavens had suddenly and violently opened up a couple of hours earlier. Once again, except for a few other diehards and social recluses, she'd be one of the last to leave the building tonight.

After nodding his head in sympathy for her plight, Mario had whipped out his thick directory of local police departments and deposited it on her desk, along with Pamela Johnson's last-known phone number, before catching the 4:10 bus back home to Hialeah. Thelma and the rest of the third-floor support staff followed shortly thereafter in the mad, high-heeled stampede for the elevators that was done and over with by 5:04 p.m. After prepping the morning's calendar, Julia had worked the phone lines the rest of the rainy evening, calling witnesses and beeping officers, hoping that after she picked a jury tomorrow, she'd actually have someone show up to put on the stand. At eight o'clock, she'd finally gotten a hold of Pamela Johnson. Five minutes later she was left talking to herself. She dry-mouthed another couple of Tylenol for the headache that had never really gone away and reached for the folder with her case law on excited utterances. Bedtime reading that was sure to be anything but exciting.

The Dade County Jail stared back at her through the miserable drizzle under roaming fluorescent searchlights, like some creepy downtown nightclub, looming large and gray and menacing and less than a couple of hundred feet from her window. Even now, strange undesirables squatted under its concrete overhang, smoking cigarettes and drinking on the sly from paper bags, some chumming for change with empty Big Gulp cups while they maybe waited for a friend or a relative to make bond. Behind the twenty-foot razor wire and heavy steel-barred windows were some of the most violent men in the state of Florida; women were held a few blocks away at the Women's Detention Center, or out west at TGK, the Turner Guilford Knight Center. Murderers, robbers, pedophiles, rapists – penned up, just yards away from where she now sat, waiting for a trial or their next hearing or to finally find out what state prison the Department of Corrections would be shipping them off to for the next couple of decades or so.

Never before had her job affected her the way it had today. Never before had a case or a criminal or a victim rushed back to consciousness the horrible, painful memories that her brain had long since purposely displaced. Memories that nightmares were made of. Memories that triggered debilitating panic attacks in the middle of bright, sunny days.

She put her head in both hands and closed her eyes. Life was funny. Happy childhood memories always seemed selectively random and spotty, like snapshots in a scrapbook. Why you remembered some and not others was anyone's guess. Eating watermelon atop the monkey bars at the Chestnut Street school playground, spitting black pits into the sand below. Her mom cutting her hair while she sat at a white Formica kitchen countertop, flecked with tiny gold dots. Good memories from childhood were never a continuous stream – the faces in them were always somehow obscured or a little bit foggy. But the bad memories, those were always so painfully vivid. They played instead like a movie in your mind, each second recollected in real time, every detail still crystal clear, even decades later. And the seemingly most innocuous moments and exchanges that preceded or succeeded something awful – moments that would otherwise never have formed a memory on their own – now they, too, became part of the *film noir*.

'*What time will you be home in the morning?*'

She put the fuzzy purple overnight bag on the kitchen counter. '*What time do you want me to come home?*'

'*Do you have homework due on Monday?*'

'*Just the report in Social Studies. But that's easy.*'

'*Then ten o'clock,*' *she said, rolling up the* Ladies Home Journal *she held in her hands. She had just painted her nails a delicate, sheer pink. Julia thought it was too light, too boring.*

'*But it's Sunday morning, Mom!*'

'*And you have an assignment due. Tell Carly no* Saturday Night Live. *You need to get some sleep. I'm sure Mrs Hogan doesn't want you two up after she's gone to bed, anyway.*'

'*Momma, jeez . . . ten o'clock?*'

'*You heard me, Monster. Besides, I'm gonna miss your face tonight.*'

A conversation she would never have remembered. One that should have just slipped away into the spotty, generic 'good' pile. Julia bit her lip to stop the tears that would surely rush out if she would only let them.

Perhaps the one and only good thing that could be said of Letray Powers was that he had kept her mind busy the past couple of hours, far away from places it shouldn't go, people it shouldn't remember. Far away from the dark, dark memories that had suddenly and without warning been brought back to life in the Marquette House of Horrors this afternoon. It was hard to believe that less than a dozen hours ago she'd been so excited to be a part of this case, so proud to have been asked, couldn't wait for the game to start up, and now . . . She looked down and saw that her hands were shaking.

She exhaled a measured breath as she began to pack up her briefcase. It was time to stop thinking, go home and let out poor Moose – her half-beagle and half-everything-else sweet-faced mutt who'd probably already had an accident – nuke a Lean Cuisine and pour herself a well-deserved glass of red wine. It was going to be a long night. She was sure of that now.

She pulled the crumpled *Herald* from her purse, and stared at the headline that was soon to be yesterday's news. She hadn't heard from Rick since they'd returned to the office, and she was more than a little anxious to find out what was happening with the detectives down at the hospital. Maybe Marquette had confessed. Maybe he was already in custody. Maybe this case would go the way of a quick plea, like ninety percent of all arrests. Maybe that would be a good thing . . . She toyed with the idea of calling him, but decided against it. This was his case – if he'd wanted to call her, he would have. He could be having second thoughts about her assisting. She pulled her hands through her hair and blew out another slow breath. God knows he wouldn't be the only one.

The phone on her desk rang, startling her – something that was happening a lot today. Most of the outside world correctly figured that their government had long since packed up and gone home by four thirty. After six, the phone ceased to ring at all. It was probably a hungry, company-seeking Dayanara demanding to know where the hell her funnies were. Julia tried smoothing the wrinkles out of the Lifestyle Section with her three-hole punch. 'State Attorney's,' she answered.

'Julia? Hey, you still there?' It was Rick, sounding surprised she'd picked up.

'Hey there. I'm leaving in a minute. I'm just prepping for my trial tomorrow.'

'The one with no witnesses?'

'No victim. I'm hoping for a change of heart, but it's not looking good. She hung up on me tonight.' Julia stood up and walked to the window, craning her neck to try and get a look at the SAO parking lot that hugged the building to see if she could spot his car. 'Where are you?' she asked.

'Heading home. I just got off the phone with John Latarrino.'

She stopped craning. 'Oh. How'd it go?'

'It didn't. The boys didn't even make it through the front door of Ryder. Mel Levenson greeted them in the parking lot.'

'Oh boy,' Julia said. Mel Levenson was a big-name defense attorney who usually handled big-name celebrities for a big-name price. A former Circuit Court judge and one-time Miami prosecutor himself, Mel successfully used his reputation and his thirty years in the system to intimidate the greener and even the not-so-green ASAs into favorable pleas. Because going up against him in trial was like stepping into the ring with Mike Tyson – he might not be all that he once was, but no one really wanted to go a round or two and get their ass kicked in a courtroom full of colleagues to find out. Pleading a case out still meant a conviction, and that was enough for most.

'That's right. Oh boy,' he repeated.

'So I guess Dr Marquette's doing okay. Well enough to

pick up the phone and call a high-priced lawyer,' she said as she began to pack up her briefcase again.

'His father in Chicago was the one who contacted Levenson. He's some hotshot doctor himself up there. I don't even know if Junior is actually up and talking yet. Mel wouldn't tell Lat. I have a call in to his office, but I'm not expecting a ring back tonight.'

'So what's next?' she asked.

'It sucks Lat didn't get a statement.' There was a brief static-filled pause. 'We wait for the DNA to come back. Let's see what the boys turn up in Orlando. I want to make sure we dot our i's and cross our t's on this one. We have a good case, one that's certainly going to generate a lot of press when we make an arrest. I don't want to look like an ass at the end of the day by jumping the gun.'

'He's not going anywhere anyway,' she offered.

'Nope. But that will change soon enough. And before he's capable of rolling out of town in a wheelchair, I want to have an arrest warrant ready.' He paused for a second. When he spoke again, his voice had lost some of its bite. 'So, did you enjoy your first homicide scene? Nothing like what you thought it would be, huh?'

'Really brutal,' she replied softly, wondering if Lat had maybe shared with Rick the details of her embarrassing sudden attack of stomach flu in the bathroom. *No, it wasn't anything like I thought,* she wanted to say. *Of all people, maybe I should have been better prepared . . .*

On her desk sat a copy of the 911 tape Latarrino had given her. She traced it with her finger. 'I'm having a hard time with the motive part.'

'Leave that to Latarrino and Brill. They'll dig up the reason. There's always one.'

She heard something slam in the background and then muffled silence before he returned. 'Sorry about that. I just pulled into my building,' he explained. 'So you're gonna head home now, too?'

'Yeah,' she said. 'I have to let my dog out. If he's still talking to me.'

'Uh-oh. I don't know about this.' Before she could even begin to wonder what he meant, he added with a laugh, 'I've got a cat. Look, I'm getting another call. Let me talk to you in the a.m. We'll get coffee.'

'Oh, yeah, goodnight,' she said and clicked off the phone before he could even say goodbye. She hated new relationships. She hated the way she felt right now, insecure and unsure, like the doe-eyed schoolgirl who'd fallen for the high-school star quarterback. Or in this case, his coach. He didn't owe her a phone call or even a goodnight before he left the office – there were no expectations to meet yet. She just hated thinking about someone who wasn't thinking about her.

She put her briefcase on the floor, popped the 911 tape into her boom box again, hit play and sat back in her chair. Recorded dead air filled the room for a few seconds before the tape began. A long beep signaled the start of the call.

'Police and fire. What's your emergency?'

'Help us . . . please.'

She closed her eyes. It was being in that house, smelling those smells, seeing the bloodstains on the walls, on the carpets, splattered everywhere. She knew there were places – nooks and crannies – that a cleaning crew would never get to in a death house, where the blood would seep and settle and become part of the walls and the baseboards and the very foundation. And when the sun went down and the lights were out, you could hear the screams, trapped forever in those walls. No matter how much you scrubbed, no matter how much you cleaned, she knew you'd never get that blood or those screams out. It would always be a house of slaughter.

'I'm going to help you, honey. I need you to stay on the line and tell me exactly what's happened.'

'I think he's coming back.'

'Who's coming . . . ?'

. . . she could feel the cold, heavy air, pressing hard against her chest. Already, she was breathing in death, feeling it fill her lungs and stab at her sides as she raced across the frozen, brown lawn, over icy patches of slow-melting snow, running faster and faster toward it. Even though she didn't want to see what was inside, what was behind all the flashing blue and red lights that lit up the two-story colonial, she still kept running, as fast as she could go. She knew she had to be fast, to be quick, to make it past all those policemen that were going to try and stop her from going in . . .

'Hello? Is there someone on the line? Is there anyone there? This is the emergency operator.'

'Oh, no, no, no . . .'

. . . please . . .

. . . no, no, no, no . . .

. . . he's back now, he's back . . .

The short, labored pants grew more and more shallow in between words, till they sounded like the final, gasping sprays left in a can of whipped cream. The chime of the grandfather clock grandly struck off the hours in the living room.

. . . is there anyone listening?

. . . can anyone . . .

. . . come?

. . . oh, no . . .

. . . please . . .

'No, Daddy!'

The hum of a dead line and then, finally, silence as the tape clicked off.

Julia opened her eyes with a start and stared once again at the Dade County Jail, glowing ghostly gray in the powerful beams of the searchlights.

It was time to go home.

15

'Julia?'

'Aunt Nora?' Julia asked, looking at the cell in her hand and almost missing the entrance ramp onto 836, the Dolphin Expressway. She hadn't even heard the phone ring.

'I sure hope so, honey,' her aunt chuckled. 'You called me. Unless you meant to call someone else.'

'No, no. I was calling you,' she replied, embarrassed. 'The phone didn't ring, that's all. How'd you know it was me?'

'I had Jimmy go down to Best Buy today. He bought me one of those caller ID phones,' she announced triumphantly. 'No more annoying telemarketers ruining my dinnertime.'

'Alright, then. Well, a hearty welcome to the twenty-first century, Aunt Nora,' Julia said, wondering how it was Uncle Jimmy had managed to talk her aunt into giving up the Mickey Mouse talking phone with the ninety-foot-long pigtail cord that had sat on her kitchen counter for the past twenty years. The next technological push would be to get her to use the cellphone Julia had bought her two Christmases ago. Or at least to answer it.

Aunt Nora laughed. 'So to what do I owe the pleasure of this phone call?' Julia heard the mixer start up in the background.

'Just wanted to say hi, that's all. See how Uncle Jimmy's back was feeling.'

'He's fine, don't worry about him. He's driving me crazy, though. Over my shoulder all damn day, looking for something to do. Driving the neighbors crazy, too, with all his stories down at the pool, when they're trying to get some peace and quiet with their sunshine. You should be worrying about *me*, is who you should be worrying about. Why don't you come on over? I can tell you haven't eaten yet, little one. I'll make you a little something.'

She couldn't help but smile. Her aunt amazed her sometimes. Instincts like a cat. 'Oh yeah? How do you know I haven't eaten?

'I can hear it in your voice.'

'Only you can hear hunger pangs. I'm just heading home, Aunt Nora. I'm still like, I don't know, maybe thirty minutes away and it's already eight thirty.'

'Heading home from where?'

'Work.'

'Jesus, Mary and Joseph, I was hoping you were out doing something fun. I was hoping, actually, you had a date. What you doing at work this late? Aren't all your criminals locked up safe and sound for the night?' Nora despised what Julia did for a living and didn't try very hard to hide it. When she'd sprung the idea of law school on Nora and Jimmy, it was *Julia Valenciano, Esq., Real Estate Lawyer* or *Valenciano & Associates, Practice Limited to Tax Law* they'd envisioned etched across the plate-glass doors.

'I have a trial in the morning.' She sighed at the thought. 'And my victim doesn't want to cooperate. It's just a mess.' There was no need to get into why else her day had gone bad. Or what else was on her mind. She'd really called just to hear her aunt's familiar, throaty voice. The content of what they said didn't matter so much.

'And . . . ?' demanded Aunt Nora, shutting off the mixer.

'And what?'

'And what else is bothering you?'

There went those instincts again. There was the briefest of silences before she answered, 'Nothing. Honest.'

'You're a bad liar, little one. And I know you're hungry. Now listen and listen carefully. I've got your little dog and I'm holding him hostage till you come over and have a bite of decent food. I know you've been using that microwave too much. Jimmy said there was butter sauce all over the inside of it. Those rays, they'll give you cancer, Julia, I'm telling you. They'll make that pretty hair of yours all fall out and your skin scaly, like a lizard. That's why the cancer rates are so high, you know. Everyone's in such a hurry nowadays, that they're microwaving themselves to death.'

Julia ignored all the clutter in the conversation. 'What? Why is Moose over your house?'

'Jimmy went by your apartment this afternoon on the way back from the track and figured he'd take Moose out for a walk. You know Jimmy and that dog.'

'And a walk turned into a sleepover?' Moose sometimes camped out at Nora and Jimmy's while Julia was at work. Uncle Jimmy was retired, and besides bugging her aunt all day long or getting lost for a few hours at the track, he liked to come by and take Moose to the dog park or for a walk on the Hollywood Beach boardwalk. Her apartment was about twenty minutes southwest of her aunt and uncle's condo on Fort Lauderdale beach, and about twenty minutes northwest of Gulfstream Racetrack – right smack-dab in the middle of all the excitement. Aunt Nora swore it was all the attention Moose got from lonely dog-sitters and girls in bikinis that kept Jimmy walking all over Broward county, when he never even liked to take the garbage down the hallway to the incinerator chute at home. On occasion, Jimmy would steal Moose and take him back home with him. Not that Moose minded being stolen – the food was much better uptown, and so was the view of the Atlantic from Uncle Jimmy's La-Z-Boy.

'What? What? You don't feed him,' whined her aunt. 'Poor baby.'

'He's not allowed to have human food, Aunt Nora. No more lasagne.'

'I didn't give him no lasagne.'

'Good.'

'I made ravioli. Come have some before your piggy little dog eats it all and turns himself into a Great Dane. He got into my pepperoni, you know.'

Julia grimaced. 'Oh no, Aunt Nora. Please don't give Moose pepperoni! It makes his hiney itch.'

'It's too late for that. He begged and Jimmy listened, the coward. Now I can't make chicken pepperoni tonight unless I go to Publix.'

Aunt Nora was a true night owl. Always had been. Her mom had told her that, even as a little kid, Nora would be up reading comic books under the covers with a flashlight, erupting into giggle fits that would wake up their dad and get them both in 'water hotter than the divil's piss'. As a teenager in Sheepshead Bay, Brooklyn, Nora had taught her mom how to sneak down the fire escape in high heels without it creaking so that they could go out dancing. Now it wasn't comic books or nightclubs pulling her aunt out of bed in the middle of the night anymore – it was her kitchen, which was probably why she looked a little like the food she liked to cook most: gnocchi. Soft and round and short – a 220-pound, five-foot-two little dumpling, topped off with a generous splash of teased red hair on her head, like a spoonful of marinara. Her most creative concoctions were made sometime between the wee hours of midnight and 3 a.m. – trays of eggplant rollatini and home-made manicotti, osso bucco that would melt off the bone. When most people were counting Zs, Aunt Nora was busy measuring cups of ricotta for cheesecake and leavening loaves of bread to twist into sausage and broccoli stromboli. Her aunt was the most ethnic Italian Julia had ever known outside of a *Sopranos* episode, and she was German Irish – although you'd never get her to admit it anymore. It was Uncle Jimmy who had the Neapolitan roots and the family tree you didn't want to shake too hard.

'You know, it is late,' Julia tried. 'Maybe you should keep Moose tonight, then, and I'll pick him up tomorrow after work.'

'Not on your life. The pepperoni's already giving him gas. For such a little dog, he can sure fill a room. That's why I'm in here and he's in there with Jimmy. The two of them deserve each other.'

'That's too much information, Aunt Nora.'

Nora laughed and turned on the mixer again. 'Come get your piggy, little one. He misses you. And while you're at it, let me feed you some ravioli. I have some pork tenderloin left over from dinner and some semolina. I'll make you a sandwich. Then you can tell me all about whatever it is that's got you so damned upset.'

'Know what I think?' said Perry. 'I think there must be something wrong with us. To do what we did.'

Dick was annoyed. Annoyed as hell. Why the hell couldn't Perry shut up? Christ Jesus, what damn good did it do, always dragging the goddamn thing up?

'There's got to be something wrong with somebody who'd do a thing like that,' Perry said.

'Deal me out, baby,' Dick said. 'I'm a normal.'

Truman Capote, *In Cold Blood*

16

John Latarrino rubbed his eyes with a yawn and struggled to focus on the road in front of him. In the dark car, the patter of driving rain and the constant, rhythmic swish-swashing of the windshield wipers were almost hypnotic, and right now he knew he was an easy subject. He slugged down a gulp of cold 7-Eleven coffee, turned up the static on the country music station, and set the AC to just below freezing to try and keep himself from dozing. Next to him, Detective Steve Brill hadn't even moved. His snoring face was still smashed up against the window, where it had been since they'd pulled out of Miami.

It probably hadn't been his best idea – driving to Orlando tonight – considering that, save for a quick nap yesterday, he'd been up for almost two days straight. But if fourteen years as a cop had taught Lat anything, it was never trust anyone else to do your job – not if you want it done right. Because it would always be *your* sacrificial ass getting reamed and *your* name on the proverbial serving platter when something inevitably got screwed up. So rather than let the Orlando PD handle his search warrant at the Marriott – like other detectives might have done – or assign another MDPD stiff to drive up in the morning and supervise a search on a case he knew nothing about, Lat knew enough to get his butt in the car tonight, drive up and do it himself. Orlando was the starting point of a night filled with terror and violence. And after Mel Levenson had greeted both him and Brill at Jackson, and told them, with a sad, but slick smile, that while his client would love to cooperate, he wouldn't be — Lat had decided there was no time like the present.

Although he didn't necessarily need or want the company on the three-hour ride, he'd invited Steve Brill along for a couple of reasons. To begin with, the first forty-eight hours of a homicide investigation were grueling enough, and a long drive could be a hazard. Another body meant another set of hands on the wheel. Second, and more importantly, this was still a Gables case. Officially, MDPD had been brought in to assist. Since it was unseemly for anyone to be killed in posh Coral Gables, thoughts were that the County would be more equipped to handle a quadruple murder, seeing as it actually had a Homicide Squad, a crime lab and experience with dead bodies. Enter stage right, the Miami-Dade Police Department and Detective John Latarrino to assist. He knew, though, that the reality of the situation was that the County would actually be taking over the investigation, and the responsibility to find answers would ultimately now rest with him. Lat knew it and Brill had accepted it, but out of respect, no one actually said it. Instead, everyone had just quietly slipped into their new roles.

But the truth was, Lat knew from past experiences with other PDs like Homestead and Sunny Isles, who also didn't have Homicide Squads, that this silent change of command would definitely not help forge the best of bonds between either the two departments or the two cops. It couldn't. Even if a department was completely inept at investigating homicides, no one really *wanted* somebody else coming in, peeing on their territory and taking charge of their mess. And that no one included Elias Vasquez, the Chief of Coral Gables himself, who'd been the one to call the County in on Sunday morning. Which created a delicate and potentially explosive problem. Because for the next few weeks – and quite possibly a lot longer – whether they liked it or not, John Latarrino and Steve Brill would have to function like partners. Manpower at Metro was not unlimited. In fact, besides an analyst, Crime Scene and the use of the MDPD lab, Lat wasn't getting any other bodies sent over to help him conduct interviews or run leads. That meant he still needed Brill and he needed the Gables and he needed the two departments to work together. The one thing he didn't need was to take a power trip to Orlando all by himself. Sharing the ride, he'd figured, would be the best way to befriend his new partner.

But, of course, he had no idea if the guy felt befriended seeing as he'd slept the entire way up. Although he'd never worked with Brill before yesterday, he'd heard all about the detective's reputation from those who had. 'Hot-headed', 'difficult' and 'obnoxious' were just some of the descriptions. 'A cheating, motherfucking asshole' was another, but that came from a female detective at Metro who'd actually dated him, so Lat didn't count that. God knows what his own ex-wife or ex-girlfriends would say about him behind closed doors. But snoring and abrasive adjectives aside, no one was denying that Brill was competent. Three of his last fifteen years had been spent heading up Persons, and he had a personnel file at the Gables filled with commendations. Before that, he'd put in another ten as a sergeant with the Florida Highway Patrol. Accomplishments not readily achieved by the lazy, Lat thought, then skeptically looked over at the stocky lump with the receding hairline that was still sawing wood on the passenger seat next to him.

Two marked Orlando PD units and a Crime Scene van sat waiting for them under the overhang of the sprawling hotel and conference center, which was still busy with cars and tourists and Disney shuttle buses, even at eleven thirty at night. 'Time to get up now, Sleeping Beauty,' Lat said, pulling in behind a cruiser. Then he got out of the car, slamming the door shut behind him. That should wake the guy up, he thought with a yawn as he joined up with the Orlando uniforms.

Albert Plante was the night manager on duty. A tall, stringy man with pasty, white skin and big, bulging eyes, Albert looked like an animated character in a Tim Burton movie. He twitched when Lat handed him the warrant, as if it were electric, and his lip curled in distaste. Then he quickly ushered Lat, Brill, the three uniforms and the Crime Scene tech through the towering marble atrium and lobby to the bay of glass elevators, all the while reminding them in a hushed tone that nothing like this had ever happened at this hotel before. When he actually asked with a strained half-smile on the ride up if they could turn off their police radios when in guest areas, Brill, who'd caught up to them, had yawned and told Albert to go fuck himself. That got a chuckle out of the Orlando guys.

Right off the elevators on the twelfth floor was room 1223. A *Pardon Our Appearance! Closed for Renovation!* card hung from the door handle. Lat felt his stomach knot up. It was always that way at a crime scene or when serving a warrant. When you're the first guy through the door, you never know what you might find. Not that he was worried about his safety tonight, but this was the room where Marquette had stayed right before he'd decided, for some as-yet-unknown reason, to drive 300 miles in the middle of the night and kill his whole family. The missing piece of the puzzle might just be on the other side of the door, like in a bad horror movie – written in bright red lipstick across the mirror.

'You call this secure?' Lat asked, looking incredulously

around the hallway while Albert slid the keycard in the lock with hands that shook slightly.

'Crime-scene tape and police officers can make guests very uncomfortable,' Albert offered in a defensive voice without looking up. 'Especially in this hotel. Don't worry, Detective. Only management can gain access to this room. The code was changed as soon as the police contacted us this morning. Housekeeping hadn't even cleaned, as there was a Do Not Disturb sign on the door.'

'Oh. The code was changed. I feel better now,' Brill said sarcastically. Then he tapped Albert on the shoulder. 'You do know this is a quadruple homicide investigation, right, Chief? Homicide, as in murder, and quadruple, as in four people are dead?'

Clearly Albert did not like Brill. He swallowed hard. 'No,' he hissed back, 'I didn't know that, Detective.'

Clearly Brill did not care. And that was the one thing Lat was actually beginning to like about him. The detective pulled no punches. 'Yup. Three little kids. And this is where their daddy stayed right before he killed 'em. Holed up right here, in the heart of everything Mickey. Right here in your hotel. Wonder how that's gonna look as a headline tomorrow?'

Albert Plante grew pale. He looked like he might drop when the door finally did open, probably fearing, Lat supposed, a dead body swinging from clean sheets in the closet and a confession taped to the mirror.

But unfortunately there was no profession of guilt – bloody or otherwise – to be found. As Lat walked around the unremarkable room, disappointment replaced anxiety. There'd been no maid service, but the bed had not been slept in anyway. Two business suits and a couple of pairs of slacks were still hanging in the closet; a shaving kit and assorted toiletries set out neatly next to the bathroom sink. Literature and brochures from orthopedic equipment companies, drug companies and Med-Net Technologies – some website design firm – were laid out on the desk next to a notepad and a laptop and a pot of in-room coffee, obviously distributed at the trade-show part of the medical conference. But that was it. No drugs. No empty beer or alcohol bottles. No suicide note. No evidence on the surface of a girlfriend or a boyfriend or a hooker. Lat didn't quite know what he'd expected to find in the room, but especially since Marquette had lawyered-up, he'd hoped it would be something more than this.

The next couple of hours were spent interviewing the hotel staff that had worked the weekend night shift, but unfortunately no one at the front desk could even identify a photograph of David Marquette, much less remember what time he might have left the hotel Saturday night. Same with housekeeping, concierge and security. The AMA conference that he'd attended and was supposed to speak at on Sunday had officially ended this morning, and most of its 500 attendees had checked out and gone back home, which seemed, unfortunately, to be everywhere across the continental US. That meant that everyone would need to be tracked down and interviewed, at least by phone. That was in addition to running other leads, subpoenaing and reviewing phone, business and medical records, and getting all the lab work back. Then there was the circle of family and friends – as well as all of David Marquette's business associates – that still had to be identified and interviewed.

Usually the hardest part of a murder investigation for a detective was figuring out who the murderer was. You arrived on scene, looked at a dead body, looked at the clues left behind and started from there. Normally, finding out *why* the victim might have been killed led you to the suspects. *Was he robbed? Was she raped? Was he in a gang? Was she having marital troubles?* But here, things were backwards. Here, they had their suspect – on scene and with what would probably turn out to be the damn murder weapon in the guy's own gut – but no why. Considering that the government was not legally required to prove motive, it would seem the easier case. But, as that prosecutor, Julia Valenciano, had pointed out, Lat knew that just because it wasn't legally required, didn't mean that a jury wasn't going to *want* to see why the dots all connected back to the smiling father in the Disney photo before they agreed to put a needle in his arm.

'Well, that was a bust,' Brill said, as they headed out of the hotel some three hours later, an evidence bag full of parking-lot security tapes in one hand and Marquette's laptop in the other.

'What'd you think?' Latarrino asked.

'I think we got a problem, bro.'

Lat sighed. 'Piecing his last hours here is gonna be a bitch.'

'Maybe he was just heading home in the middle of the night because he missed his wife, and then something went bad,' Brill said with a shrug.

'Please,' Lat said, shaking his head with a wry laugh. 'No one actually misses his wife. No one who's had one, anyway. But maybe he thought his wife wasn't missing him too much. If that semen stain is from someone else, could be Jennifer was getting a little action on the side. Maybe he came down to catch her in the act.'

'That would complicate things. That would also at least give you motive, something that you're running a little short on, in my opinion, boss-man.'

Lat nodded. 'And maybe premeditation.'

'All we'd have to do is find the Bill Clinton who left behind his little something special.'

'Let's wait till the labs come back,' Lat cautioned.

They stepped out into the parking lot. The rain had stopped and the night air was cool, the sky milky black. The birds had started to chirp; the sun would soon be up. It probably wasn't the best idea to drive back to Miami now, but the day was already filled with things to do and sleep wasn't making the list. 'Hey, don't call me boss-man,' Lat said quietly.

'Well it's the truth, ain't it?' Brill replied.

Lat stopped walking. 'I ain't your boss.'

Brill stopped too. 'And this really ain't my case no more, now is it?' he asked back with a smile that didn't look too friendly.

'That's not my decision.'

'Nope,' Brill said walking again. 'But that is *the* decision. And that makes you the boss.' He chewed on the toothpick he'd picked up in the restaurant and neither said anything. 'So, did you check up on me?' Brill asked finally, turning and walking backwards.

'Yup,' Lat said without missing a beat.

'And . . . ?'

Lat stopped again. 'You want a quote?'

'Lay it on me, brother.'

'Hot-headed, difficult, obnoxious and, I quote, "A cheating, motherfucking asshole." End quote.'

'That last one was Patti Corderi,' Brill said. 'You shouldn't count her. She's a whack-job.'

'I didn't.' They started walking again and had almost reached the car. Surprisingly, the conversation felt less tense than Lat thought it would. Brill had all the personality disabilities everyone had said he would. And yet, in spite of himself, he still kind of liked the guy. Unlike Sonny and Tubbs or Starsky and Hutch, Lat didn't have a regular 'partner' in Homicide. No one did. Sometimes you worked with somebody on a case, but more often than not you didn't. And while you could always run things by guys in the squad, it was actually cool to have someone involved on the same case at the get-go. Someone who wasn't trying to climb the same ladder with the same people you were. 'No sleeping this time, Rip,' Lat warned as he passed the driver's side and headed for the passenger door.

'I liked it better when you called me your Sleeping Beauty,' Brill replied.

'I never said *my* Sleeping Beauty.'

'That's how I took it. Now I'm sad.'

'It's your turn to drive,' Lat replied with another yawn, digging the keys to the Impala out of his pocket. For a person who normally paced the floors at night with insomnia he was dog-tired.

'Is this new?' Brill asked, running his hand over the hood.

'Yeah. 2006. I just got it. It took me three years to get on the top of the new-car list. I had a piece-of-shit nine-year-old Taurus before this.' He tossed Brill the keys over the car. 'Don't fuck it up. Besides liking my life, I don't think other drivers are covered.'

'Wow,' Brill said, catching them in one hand. 'Since the accident, I can't take home anymore. So I always get the crap drug cars seized by IMPACT. You know, the Fred Flintstone piece-of-shits with the holes in the floorboards? They never look like the dealer cars in *Miami Vice*, man. I've yet to see a fucking Lamborghini.'

'What accident?'

'You didn't know?'

Lat sighed and walked back around to the driver's side,

his hand out. 'You're a fuck. Give me my keys and get in the car.'

'I would have driven, Lat. I'm a team player,' Brill laughed, tossing the keys back and heading back around the car, his hands in the air.

'You fall asleep and I will personally beat your ass,' Lat growled, climbing in the car. 'I'll play fucking John Denver tunes the whole way home if I have to.'

'Now I know you're fucking with me. Ain't nobody got John Denver tapes in their car, except maybe the man's own momma,' Brill said with a yawn, taking off his jacket and rolling it into a ball. 'I guess I can live with hot-headed and difficult. And coming from that nutcase, asshole is quite a compliment.' He pressed the jacket up against the window.

'I'm glad you feel that way,' Lat said, reaching for the radio dial.

Brill closed his eyes and smiled. 'It's still better than what I heard about you . . .'

17

Julia watched Judge Farley climb down off the bench and hurry out of the courtroom, his swollen robe trailing behind him in a big black puff, like an enormous dark cloud. The door to the judge's back hallway slammed shut behind him – probably on purpose – leaving the courtroom in stunned silence. She stared at the empty bench in disbelief from her seat at the State's table, ignoring the fiery whispers of court personnel that suddenly erupted all around her.

Letray Powers whooped when Scott Andrews, the PD, explained to him that he was now free to go. Since nobody had shown up in court on his behalf, he hugged and high-fived Scott instead. Then, after a few more minutes of celebratory hollering, he walked up to the State's table and stood there for a long moment. 'Whoo, no, this can't be good now,' said one of the corrections officers from some-where in the room, with the excitement of a kid about to watch a schoolyard fight go down, but no one moved to stop it.

Julia could feel Letray's icy stare as he waited for her to look up at him. 'Tough break, bitch,' he said when she finally did. His smile revealed a mouth full of shiny, gold teeth, but it wasn't at all friendly. She was acutely aware that he was no longer wearing handcuffs or leg shackles.

'I'm sure I'll get another shot,' she replied coldly, her eyes meeting Letray's and not so much as blinking. 'I don't expect you'll last too long on the outside, Mr Powers.'

'Come on, Letray, don't talk to her. Let's go. You don't

need any more trouble,' Scott cautioned, as he firmly tugged on the elbow of the oversized sports jacket that the Public Defender's Office had lent his client for trial, leading him back over to the defense table. A few minutes later, a couple of corrections officers finally walked a whistling Letray through the empty jury room.

'I'll be seeing ya,' Julia heard him call out to her with a laugh. 'Tell Shorty, you know, I'll be seeing her, soon, too.' The door closed with a thud behind him.

She couldn't believe it. Just could not believe it. It had taken her a full day to pick a six-person jury, another to do openings and present her witnesses. But it had taken Judge Leonard Farley just five short minutes to JOA her.

A JOA was a Judgment of Acquittal. Normally only a jury could acquit a defendant, but in the event a reasonable jury with common sense could not be found, the Florida legislature had built a safety valve into the law, and that was the almost-never-used JOA. If, after the State had presented its case, the trial judge felt in his learned opinion that no reasonable jury could find the defendant guilty, he could save *his* jury the time and trouble and acquit the defendant himself. In this instance, Julia knew it wasn't so much Farley's learned opinion as it was his vindictive personality that had sent Letray Powers back home to Pamela Johnson whistling 'Dixie'. And the worst part about a JOA was there was no right to appeal, and hence, nothing either she or the State could do except hold open the door and wave Letray goodbye as he skipped merrily off into the pretty Miami sunset.

She continued to sit there for a few minutes in stunned silence. On his way out of the courtroom, Scott Andrews came up to shake her hand and offer the standard post-verdict condolences of 'Good job' and 'Nice working with you'. When he added, 'You know, I wouldn't have JOA'd you,' in a quiet voice, she bit her lip. It didn't make her feel any better.

In a jealous attempt to stop other men from looking at her, Letray Powers had taken a razor blade to his girlfriend's face and tried to rearrange it. The same man who had a record as long as her arm for violent offenses, including three prior domestics, and no one but Julia seemed to care. She'd proven her case even without her victim and she knew it, Farley knew it, Scott Andrews knew it – hell, even Letray Powers knew it. But it didn't matter anymore. And that's what left her feeling so incredibly empty and incredibly bitter right about now.

Julia quietly packed her two boxes of case law, statute books and rulebooks onto the pull cart and headed for the door herself. That's when she first noticed John Latarrino standing in the rear of the courtroom.

'Boy, don't you look happy,' he said as she made her way down the aisle.

'Hello yourself. What are you doing here?' she asked, looking around the empty courtroom to see who else he might be waiting for.

'I just came from the ME's,' he replied. 'I stopped up at Bellido's office and his secretary tells me he's out of town.' He reached for her pull cart. 'Can I help you with that?'

'Sure, if you want,' she said, handing over the reins. 'He's up in Atlanta teaching at a National Prosecuting Attorneys' conference. I think he's coming back tomorrow.' They walked out into the hallway, which was as deserted as the courtroom. It was almost five and no one was around.

The thick peanut butter feeling was back. This drop-by was obviously intentional and it was obviously about the Marquette case. Distancing herself from Monday's crime scene and diving into a difficult trial for the past couple of days had helped clear her head of ghosts somewhat, but she still found herself taken a little off guard. She hadn't expected to see Lat here, now. The house had spooked her Monday, no doubt – rushing back vivid, painful memories she thought she'd long ago shuttered away – but she could deal with those memories. She knew she could. She knew she had to. Julia wanted this case. She needed to succeed here, to make a name for herself as a prosecutor. To defeat your fears, didn't you have to face them first? Wasn't that a classic, tried and true, psychological cliché? Isn't that why abused children grew up to be guidance counselors and leukemia survivors to be doctors? Isn't that what some shrink would probably say about why she was here, doing what she did in court, day in and day out, slaying dragons that just kept coming back to life in different, more terrifying forms? Time over the past couple of days had given her distance, and distance had given her back the perspective she told herself she needed to continue. And if she was going to go forward on this case, if she was going to try and leave the past behind her, now more than ever, it was important that she look confident and prepared and in control. Because she definitely didn't want Detective John Latarrino thinking of her weak-kneed and retching over a toilet bowl whenever he saw her in court or her name came up in conversation.

'That's what Marisol said,' he replied as they walked toward the elevator bay. 'So I stopped up to your office and your secretary said you were in trial.'

'Was. It's over now.'

'I can see that.' He hit the button down.

'Were you here—' she started to ask.

'When Farley JOA'd you? Yup. I caught the tail end. You had a nice argument, but he wasn't listening. No offense,' he said, stepping into the elevator and holding the door open for her, 'but I don't think he likes you much.'

'You think?'

'Don't take it personal. I don't think he likes women.'

'I figured that out.'

'Your victim didn't show up for trial?'

'Nope. So I was trying it without her. And that's wherein the problem lies.' She looked around the elevator car and didn't offer any more information, so he didn't ask any more questions.

'Well,' he said after a moment, 'I need to run some things by you, then. We've got a couple of decisions to make and you're the "it" girl.'

Uh-oh. New-found perspective and self-proclaimed confidence aside, decisions were something she wasn't sure she wanted her name on making in this case just yet. She also wasn't too sure Rick would want her making them. She frowned. 'Have you talked to Rick today?'

'Nope. Beeped him, but he doesn't seem to want to call me back. You're still second seat, right?'

She nodded.

'Then you're the "it" girl as far as I'm concerned.'

'Alright. What's up?'

'We got some of the lab work back from the house. The footprints in the upstairs hall – one set was made by a size-eleven loafer that belonged to the Gables uniform who responded. The other set, well, we don't know. They're unidentifiable.'

'What does that mean?'

'The prints are too distorted for a comp. Not just smeared, but distorted. There's no tread base. Best guess, based upon size and what appears to be weight distribution, is a size twelve, which would match Marquette. Greg

Cowsert is our print and tread specialist. He's the best and he's thinking that our bad guy might have worn something over his foot, like a surgical bootie or something, although he found no fibers in the print, which would be consistent with a bootie. That would account for the distortion and smearing.'

'But there were no bloody booties found at the scene, right? Okay. I'm guessing this is not good news,' she said walking out of the elevator.

'No, I got good news. A nurse anesthetist at Sinai who works with Marquette's practice for the last couple of years ID'd his voice on the enhanced nine-eleven tape. It's not a forensic comparison, but it'll do for PC. Sure as she's breathing, she says it's him.'

PC stood for probable cause, which was the legal threshold necessary to cross over and arrest a defendant. Was it more probable than not that a crime was committed and that the defendant was the one who had committed it? 'Okay, that's good,' she said.

'Now, back to the not so good. So far, we've got sixteen different sets of fingerprints around the house that have yet to be identified,' he continued. 'Three of those are by and around the window sills. Now it could be the Terminix guy or a shitty cleaning lady who doesn't dust right for all we know, and in the long run, it probably won't matter a damn, but a defense attorney's gonna pick up on that and play the fingerprint game, so I just wanted to give you a heads-up.'

'DNA's not back yet on that semen stain, right?'

'Won't be for at least a week. The oral swab we took yesterday from Marquette for DNA won't be back till then either.'

'Do you think the semen's going to be an issue?'

'You're asking me? If it's not hubby's, hell yeah, it'll be an issue, although it shouldn't affect PC for his arrest.'

'I think Rick wanted to work up a warrant by the end of this week, before Marquette gets released from the hospital,' she said, starting toward the doors that led out to the back of the courthouse.

Latarrino stopped walking. 'We don't have that long, Counselor,' he said.

'What?' she asked, turning back to look at him.

'That's why I'm here. He's being released today,' Lat replied. 'In about three hours, give or take. His father's having him transported to Chicago's Northwestern Memorial tonight.'

18

'You're kidding me,' Julia said, staring at him in disbelief. The clock in the courthouse hall hung right above the detective's head. The numbers seemed to pop out at her, like a cartoon sketch in a Dr Seuss book. BOING! 4:58!

'Found out when I was at the ME's. A nurse over at Ryder called my Lieutenant and gave him the heads-up. Once Marquette's out of our jurisdiction it's gonna be that much harder to get him back. And we'll have lengthy extradition issues to contend with, not to mention a damn high flight risk. In addition to being the Chief of Neurology over at Northwestern, we've heard Dad's also pretty heavy-handed with a checkbook.'

'So he's got pull.'

'And money. We need to pick him up.'

'Alright,' she said. 'Hold on. I can't give you the go-ahead until I try to reach Rick.' The day just couldn't get any shittier, but there you go. 'Let's head back to the office and let me try his cell. If I can't get him, we'll go from there.' She speed-dialed while quickly walking across the street, praying like a nun for him to pick up.

A lot of legal clocks started ticking once a person was arrested. First and foremost was the right to a speedy trial, which, absent a defense continuance or a waiver by the defendant, ran out permanently after just 180 days. And there were no second bites at the apple if you screwed up and made the wrong call the first time, but subsequently found that murder weapon or that missing witness on the

181st day. Double jeopardy prevented that. In criminal law, the stakes were high for a prosecutor to make the right call at the right time all the time. Although Julia had made the decision to arrest someone before, she'd never done it in a homicide.

'What's up, Julia?'

There was a God. 'Hi,' she said into the phone, slowing down to catch her breath. 'I'm just heading back from court.'

'We're on a break. I was going back in myself in a second,' Rick said.

'I've got Detective Latarrino with me. There's a problem. I'm going to let the detective tell you.' She hit the speaker button.

'Thanks for calling me back,' Lat said.

'My beeper's off when I'm lecturing. So's my cell. We just broke not five minutes ago and you were next on the list, Lat.' He sounded irritated.

'Alright, I'll buy that. Look, I'll let your second seat fill you in on the gritty details, but the shoe prints are a bust. We also have sixteen unidentified fingerprints, three on and around the windows. DNA is still pending and won't be back till next week.'

'Great. Got any good news for me, Lat?' Rick said with what sounded like a sigh.

'Marquette's set for release tonight,' Latarrino said.

'No fucking way.'

'That's not the bad news,' Lat said.

'It's not?'

'Nope. He's hopping a private medical transport plane for Chicago in three hours.'

The silence lasted a long time. Only the crackle of cellphone static told them Rick was still on the line. She and Lat had reached the Graham Building, but she didn't want to lose the signal, so they stood outside. On the floor over in the corner by the concrete benches and planters she spotted a bunch of crushed cigarette butts scattered about. This was where the smokers met and chatted every day on their breaks, or on their way back from court as they stopped to finish the last puffs before heading inside. Julia herself hadn't touched a cigarette since college, but she couldn't help thinking how good one would taste right about now.

'The hell he is,' Rick finally said. 'I guess the state of Florida will be picking up the tab for those medical bills after all. Screw the warrant; we've got enough. Go pick him up, Lat.'

19

Lat waited until the wheelchair was actually pushed out the front doors of Jackson Memorial Hospital's Ryder Trauma Center before he walked up to the man seated in it. 'David Alain Marquette?' he asked, already knowing the answer.

'Jesus Christ! Not here!' shouted the older gentleman in dress slacks and a sweater who walked carefully alongside the chair. He had the slight cadence of an accent that had been worn away over many years, which Lat couldn't quite place. Lat figured it was Marquette's father, who had been successfully ducking the police since his arrival in Miami a couple of days ago. A handsome woman – probably Marquette's mother – flanked the right. She was dressed impeccably in an expensive suit with well-coiffed silver-white hair that was pulled back tight into a chignon. She looked elegant and reserved, but scared. The man now moved protectively in front of the wheelchair.

A private ambulance sat waiting underneath the awning. The two EMTs that had moved to assist Marquette hesitated, looking around dumbly for someone to tell them what to do. Steve Brill held up his badge. Although he had no jurisdiction outside of Coral Gables, no one besides Lat knew that. 'Mr Marquette and his family won't be needing your services anymore, boys,' he said. At that precise moment, three MDPD cruisers pulled up, their lights flashing. 'See, we've made other arrangements for him.'

'Are you Alain Marquette?' Lat asked the older man.

'Go to hell!'

'Step away from the wheelchair,' Brill cautioned.

'I'm Detective John Latarrino, Miami-Dade Police,' Lat said.

'He is sick!' said the man, his tone desperate.

'Step back, sir,' Brill said again, and the man finally did. Family members were always the ones you watched during an arrest. Emotions ran high and you never really knew what someone was capable of.

The figure in the wheelchair was pale. His light-gray eyes darted everywhere. An oxygen tube ran from his nose to a tank on the side. A portable IV connected more tubes to his veins.

Lat was unmoved. Images of the slaughter that he'd seen at the house flashed in his head. The crumpled, broken body of little Emma, hiding behind her Hello Kitty chair in her pink princess room. For as long as he lived, he'd never forget that scared, swollen face, her blue eyes wide open, the soft streams of sunlight from a new morning bathing the bloody carnage in a golden caramel hue. Lat nodded to a uniform. The nurse backed away as the officer took her spot, turning the wheelchair around and back toward the hospital. On the other side of Jackson, and a building away from the Ryder Trauma Center, was Ward D, the part of the hospital reserved for in-custody defendants who required hospitalization. Marquette would be booked in there, just a few short pushes away. Ward D was handled like a jail, with bolted doors and high security. But no matter how bad it might be, at the end of the day it was still a hospital, not a jail cell. For Lat, that was just not bad enough.

'Get Mr Levenson on the phone. Now!' shouted the man.

'Alain, calm down!' said the woman.

'Just do it!'

'His lawyer ain't gonna help him tonight, folks,' piped in Brill.

A blue Channel Seven news van pulled up fast behind one of the cruisers. The door slid open and a breathless Teddy Brennan jumped out, microphone in hand, Willie in tow. 'Dr Marquette!' he shouted while running toward them. 'Did you kill your whole family? Why did you do it? How do you feel right now? Or are you the victim here?'

'Jesus Christ!' Lat shouted, shaking his head and waving in the direction of the uniformed officers. 'Get them the hell out of here!'

Only a few limited ears at MDPD, the State Attorney's Office and Coral Gables PD knew about Marquette's arrest and Lat certainly hadn't authorized anyone to contact the news, even going so far as to keep it off the radio so no one would pick it up off the scanners. It didn't take a quantum leap to figure out the boat had a leak. As if on cue, another news van pulled up and a reporter scurried out, this one from local NBC Channel Six.

'Is it true there's a full confession?' yelled Brennan, ignoring the uniforms and pushing closer, hoping it was his question that got an answer, not the competition with the next microphone over.

'Was Jennifer Marquette raped before she was murdered?' shouted the newcomer.

'Is this a Miami-Dade case now?'

'Are you seeking the death penalty?'

'Where the hell is your warrant? Where's your warrant?' the old man shouted angrily at Lat. He, too, moved toward the wheelchair.

Another news van pulled up. Another reporter came a-running.

'Step back, sir,' commanded Brill, his hand on his taser. 'I said step the fuck back! You, too, Geraldo!' he yelled at Brennan.

'He's sick! He's sick!' pleaded the woman. Her handsome face had turned ashen white, matching her hair.

'Freedom of the press, Detective! We have a right to be here!' shouted Brennan, thrusting his microphone at the woman, and pressing close enough to Brill that Lat knew it was simply a matter of time before something really bad happened.

Time to wrap this up. 'David Marquette, you're under arrest for the murder of Jennifer, Emma, Daniel and Sophie Marquette,' Lat began. 'You have the right to remain silent, and anything you say can and will be used against you in a court of law. You also have the right to an attorney, but you obviously know that one already. Alright,' he said to Brill and the uniform, nodding back toward the electric double doors. 'Let's go. Get him out of here.'

That was when the woman fainted face-first onto the pavement with a thud, Alain Marquette started to scream and sob for the cameras, and all hell broke loose in front of Jackson Memorial.

20

The angry shouts from 5−3 could be heard all the way down the courthouse's fifth-floor hallway. Mel Levenson was a tall, lumbering man with two chins and an imposing voice even in a library. Now Mel was in a courtroom, he was mad and he wasn't holding back, either on the volume or the accusations.

'This was nothing but an ambush, Your Honor!' Mel complained on decibel ten to an already irritable Judge Irving Katz and a courtroom full of cameras. 'Rather than call my office and arrange for my client's surrender − which could have and should have been done,' he said, shaking an angry, swollen finger in the direction of Rick Bellido, John Latarrino and a sullen-looking Steve Brill, 'the Miami-Dade and Coral Gables Police Departments − with the blessing, I'm sure, of the prosecutor − set up a trap outside Jackson to nail my client as he helplessly rolls by in his wheelchair, an oxygen tank and critical-care nurse at his side. Not to mention the man's elderly parents. And without any concern for the devastating emotional trauma this man has already been through, losing his whole family, or the life-threatening injuries he's just had surgery for,' Mel continued, picking up a copy of Friday's *Herald* and holding it up for the judge. **DOCTOR DAD ARRESTED FOR MURDER WHILE ATTEMPTING TO FLEE** blared the headline across the front page. 'These detectives call the press to get their own fifteen minutes of fame in − all the while prejudicing everyone in the tri-county area against Dr

Marquette with their damn lies. Then they arrest him and ship him off to jail, when he belongs in a hospital.' Mel wiped his long jowls with his big balloon hands and moved back from the podium, almost stepping on a cameraman and Stan Grossbach, his co-counsel.

Lat felt the rush of anger flush his face and he looked over at Rick Bellido, waiting for him to say something about that fame comment, but he never did. Meanwhile, to his right, he could actually hear the knuckles in Steve Brill's hand crack as he clenched and unclenched his fists behind his back. He was apparently waiting for the same thing.

Due to the sheer volume of people who tended to do even more stupid things over the weekend than they normally did during the week, bond hearings on Monday mornings in Judge Irving Katz's courtroom were always busy, but never like this. Except for the judge, bailiff, an ASA and a PD, usually the claustrophobically small courtroom was empty. Today it was standing room only. Conducted via closed-circuit TV at DCJ, even the defendants didn't show up for court. At least not physically. Nothing more than a thirty-second pro-forma hearing that allowed the judge to review the arrest form, determine if probable cause existed and set a bond, a First Appearance was usually done and over with before the defendant had even figured out where in the room the damn camera was.

The judge shook his head. 'Great speech, Mr Levenson, and it's duly noted for the record, but your client is charged with murder. Four of them to be exact. This is just the First Appearance and you know murder's non-bondable at this stage.' He nodded at the TV screen before him, where a pale-faced David Marquette, dressed in an orange Department of Corrections jumpsuit, stood motionless at the metal podium, a wheelchair at his side. 'All I get to decide now is if there was probable cause to arrest him, and,' the judge continued, waving his copy of the pink arrest form from the bench, 'based on the facts cited in here, I have no choice. So there's not a lot I can do about your complaints except listen to them, and, frankly, I'm not Dear Abby. Besides which, if I'm reading this A-form correctly, Dr Marquette was wheeled off to Ward D, Mr Levenson. He got his medical care. It's not like the detectives threw him in a cement cell with the rats.'

'We all know Ward D is not like the rest of Jackson, Judge. Look at him,' Levenson said, pointing to the screen. 'Just look at him!'

The doctor had not moved. He hadn't even acknowledged that the judge was talking about him. In fact, Lat wasn't sure if the man had even blinked the five minutes or so he'd been standing up there, clutching the sides of the podium with bone-white knuckles, eyes vacant and expressionless. Behind him, a long line of bored-looking, tattoo-riddled defendants in various states of undress snaked its way through the middle of the crowded, peeling pea-green room to the back doors, where two correction officers stood watch against a wall. Another two kept the line moving at the podium and the noise down. Because a First Appearance was supposed to be held within twenty-four hours of arrest, more than a few defendants were still dressed as they were when the cuffs were slapped on the night before – bare-chested and in their boxers. Some even worse. The restless line began to talk again and the courtroom filled with the echo of incoherent chatter and noise.

'Keep them quiet over there!' yelled Katz to the correction officer at the podium, placing one hand over his ear. 'I can't hear. If they don't want to be quiet, then take whoever's yapping out and bring 'em back tomorrow.'

The guard nodded at the camera. Then he turned and yelled, 'Shut up!' to the crowd behind him.

'I could've done that,' mumbled Katz in disgust.

'He should be in a hospital bed right now,' Levenson continued. 'He never should have been released back to the general population this morning. He's still a very sick man.'

'HMOs do it all the time,' Katz said flatly. 'He had the weekend off as it was.'

'Mr Levenson's client was apparently feeling well enough last week to try and flee the jurisdiction before he was wheeled over to Ward D, Your Honor,' Rick interjected.

'He was being transported to another hospital,' protested Levenson, glaring across the courtroom.

'In Chicago,' added Rick.

'I made those arrangements,' said the man who rose like a tall shadow from the front row of seats. 'That is my hospital and my son needs acute medical care. He was not trying to flee.'

'Your hospital?' asked the judge.

'This is Dr Alain Marquette, Your Honor,' said Levenson. 'He is the Chief of Neurology at Chicago's Northwestern Memorial Hospital.'

'Ah, three sides to every story,' said Katz. 'Dr Marquette, you have good counsel here, and as I'm sure that good counsel has told you, there's nothing more that can be done for your son at this point in the proceedings. Mr Levenson will have another opportunity to seek bond at what's known as an Arthur Hearing or before the trial judge when one's appointed, but there's nothing I can do for him today.'

'This was unprofessional. It should have been handled differently,' Levenson grumbled.

'If I had a nickel for each time I wished for something I didn't get, I'd be a rich man, Mr Levenson. Instead, I'm just really old and really disappointed.' Katz looked into the jail camera. 'No bond,' he yelled, as if David Marquette were deaf. 'Now unless there's some other high-profile case that someone forgot to tell me was on my calendar this morning,' he said, pausing for a moment to throw an icy stare in the direction of his bailiff, 'you all can take this outside in the hallway so I can clear my courtroom. I imagine they're all with you, Mr Bellido,' the judge finished, frowning over his glasses at the reporters who had already started to gather their cameras and microphones and hightail it for the door. Then he turned his attention and his frown back to the correction officer on the TV screen. 'Bring the next one up, Sergeant!' he barked. 'And keep the rest of them quiet over there!'

Lat moved quickly, catching the elder Marquette as he opened the door to the courtroom's vestibule. 'Dr Marquette? I'd like to speak with you for a moment—'

'You're kidding me, right?' barked Mel Levenson, barreling up behind them, like a freight train without lights.

Alain Marquette turned to Lat, his dark-blue eyes angry and unforgiving. A long, uncomfortable moment passed. 'I have nothing to say to you people. Nothing,' he finally said.

Contrary to what police dramas portrayed on primetime, short of a subpoena or some really good leverage, there was really no way to make someone talk to the police who didn't want to talk to the police. And since John Latarrino had neither at the moment, he could only watch as Dr Marquette, flanked by his son's attorneys, walked out of the courtroom.

Less than thirty seconds later, a dapper Rick Bellido strode up in his expensive navy suit, frowning. 'Let's go,' he said with a nod, straightening his tie and reaching for the door.

'What about Brill?'

Bellido shot him a look. 'He said he'll catch up with you downstairs.'

That was smart, Lat thought, as he followed Rick out of the courtroom. Brill had been warned by his department in no uncertain terms to keep his mug far away from any and all cameras after last week's televised out-of-jurisdiction, expletive-filled, taser-waving takedown at Jackson.

A crowd of noisy reporters from all the local stations

buzzed around the Levenson camp, which had made an impromptu, teary-eyed press-stop by the escalators. Another crowd waited anxiously outside the doors for Team State. Lat had been in media cases before, but this looked Hollywood crazy. Flashbulbs began to explode as soon as they pushed the doors open, and a parade of reporters and cameras and boom mikes trailed behind them as they headed for the elevators, shouting out questions that they'd either just heard the answer to in court, or weren't going to get an answer to anyway. At least not from him.

'Does this mean Dr Marquette will have to stay in jail? When would his Arthur Hearing be? When could he be released?'

'What about the death penalty? Are you going to seek the death penalty for all four murders?'

'How did he kill the children? What was the actual cause of death? Why won't your office provide details?'

'Were the kids sexually assaulted? Was the mother involved? Was there evidence of a cult?'

'Is it true Emma Marquette was still alive when officers arrived at the house? Could she have been saved if they'd just gone in sooner?'

'Detective Latarrino, does your department take some blame for the injuries suffered by Nina Marquette when her son was arrested last Thursday?'

Some of the questions were just completely bizarre, as were some of the reporters asking them. Back in the front row once again, Lat spotted Teddy Brennan, from Channel Seven, and it set his teeth on edge. Rick stopped by the elevators and selectively answered a few of the easier ones, the perfect look of prosecutorial confidence and controlled outrage on his face, while Lat, of course, said nothing. He'd watched Rick Bellido work the cameras before on his other media-magnet Major Crimes cases, and also when the guy popped up on TV as a guest legal analyst, and he had to admit that the cameras sure did love the man. But if Lat was damn sure of anything it was that Ricardo Bellido, Super Prosecutor, loved those cameras right back. Every last one of them.

Just as the elevator doors opened on an empty car, Rick held up his hands, like the Pope at an attendance, and the crowd obediently quieted. 'That's all I have for now, folks. We hope – I hope – that you'll respect that. Right now, our thoughts and prayers are with the family of the victims, and, of course, our concern is to ensure the safety of the community, which was the purpose of this morning's bond hearing. The investigation's ongoing, and we'll keep the public informed. That is a priority. That's *my* priority.' Then he repeated the same thing in Spanish for the cute *Telemundo* reporter, just before the elevator doors closed.

Lat could practically hear the collective sigh of approval as thousands of *abuelas* across Miami swooned in their living-room easy chairs. 'That's *my* priority.' Like this guy was running the damn show by himself? As he watched the doors close on all those cameras, Lat began to seethe. With the exception of the serial killer Cupid a few years back, he'd never seen such media interest before at a bond hearing – which made today's unexpected circus all the more curious. David Marquette hadn't even been shipped over from Ward D and placed on calendar until the last second this morning. And since all bond hearings were videotaped, there was really no reason for the press to physically appear. All a reporter had to do was call ahead and order the bad guy of the day to go, zip by the courthouse and grab the tape twenty minutes before airtime. And that's what they usually did. Usually. Unless they thought they'd be getting a scoop.

'The cameras certainly eat you up, Bellido,' Lat said with a shake of his head when they were alone.

'Thursday was a clusterfuck, Lat,' Rick replied coolly, without looking over at him. 'Today was damage control.'

Marquette's arrest and the dramatics that followed had played out on an otherwise slow news night on all the local channels. Alain Marquette might have nothing to say to the police, but he sure had plenty to say to Teddy Brennan. His angry two-minute interview – the one where he clung to the sweater that had gotten soaked with blood from his wife's televised kiss with the pavement – had blasted both police departments. Rather than see it as the harmless emotional tirade Lat thought it was, the Director of the MDPD viewed it as a PR nightmare.

'What about controlling Mel Levenson?' Lat asked. 'What about making the detectives who are working this thing 24/7 a priority? You know damn well it wasn't us that called in the press. That's what turned Thursday to shit.'

'You need to know how to work them, John. Don't let them work you.'

The elevator stopped on four. 'I heard Jerry Tigler is passing the reins soon, heading to greener pastures. Charley Rifkin, too. I heard there's gonna be room at the top soon,' Lat said and then paused. 'Did you know the media was gonna be here today, Bellido?'

Rick finally looked over at him. 'I was just doing my job today, Lat,' he replied, the temperature of his voice dropping from cool to arctic freeze. 'And they just showed up doing theirs, I suppose. The two shouldn't affect each other, and they didn't. As for that rumor you heard, that's news to me.' He exited the elevator, holding the door as people pushed past him to get on. 'Your pre-file's next week. Call me the second you get that DNA back and keep pressing Holt for the pattern testing on that knife by the end of today. If you can't do it, I'll get on the horn with him and handle it myself. Like I said, I don't like waiting till the last minute. What you need to be worrying about now is the grand jury.' With that, he let go of the doors and walked off down the crowded hall.

Then the elevator filled and the doors closed, and the opportunity passed for John Latarrino to give Rick Bellido's camera-friendly face the finger.

'Are we done now, Ms Seminara?' Judge Farley asked with an impatient sigh, slapping his hand hard on the bench and spinning his throne in the direction of the nearest exit.

'I think so, Judge,' Karyn replied, as she quickly thumbed through the thick calendar, the division's brand-new bewildered C attorney at her side. The courtroom was all but empty; only court personnel remained.

'Good. Then we're in recess.' The judge capped his pen and stood up, turning his attention to the court reporter. 'Off the record, now,' he said sternly, and obediently the soft clicking of the stenography machine stopped. 'Word to the wise, Ms Gleeson,' he continued sharply, shaking his finger in the frightened direction of the new C, his brow buried so deep in wrinkles that it looked like his scalp was slipping off his head. 'Stop objecting so much. It's irritating me and it's certainly not getting you anywhere. Let's not get off on the wrong foot, now.' With that, he shot a dark look across the courtroom at Julia, who stood on the State side of the gallery against the wall, watching the minutes tick slowly by on the clock over the judge's head. Then he quickly flew off the bench, disappearing like the Wicked Witch of the West in a black puff down the judge's back hallway before Jefferson the bailiff could even yell, 'All rise!'

'Court is now in recess,' Jefferson managed weakly when the door slammed shut.

Finally. Julia grabbed her stack of files off the State's table and hurried past Karyn and Janet, up the gallery. She pushed open the doors and walked smack into Rick.

'Just the person I was coming to see,' he said with a frown. 'You missed all the fireworks. What happened to you this morning?'

'Damn. I'm sorry, I was just coming up,' Julia started.

'I happened,' said her DC, as she stepped out into the hallway, a glum and shell-shocked Janet Gleeson trailing behind with a pull cart full of file boxes. 'Good morning, Rick,' Karyn said rather brightly, but with a tired, woe-is-me smile. 'Look, don't get mad at Julia here, but mornings with Farley are just completely crazy. Even when it's not their trial week, I need all my attorneys in court. If something comes up on calendar, I can't be hunting them down all over the courthouse. I know Julia's been helping you out on this doctor case of yours, but I'm afraid I just can't spare the bodies around here. Especially on a Monday morning.'

'She's second-seating me on a first-degree murder case, Karyn, not helping me photocopy,' Rick snapped back. 'And a first-degree murder takes precedence over babysitting your crazy Monday-morning calendar, anytime and all the time. Call me in the future if there's gonna be a conflict, but let's get this straight, right here, right now – this bullshit's not going to happen again. Ever. Or it won't be Leonard Farley you'll be worried about babysitting.'

Karyn's face tightened up so hard and so fast, Julia thought it might crack if she ever did smile again. She also thought it might be a good long while before her division spent another Friday night sipping two-for-one mojitos together. 'Right,' Karyn replied coolly after a long moment, 'I understand.' She looked over at Julia, and, with some difficulty, added, 'I'll see you back at the office, then. You know, I'm still waiting on those dispos you owe me.'

'This case, Marquette, is your priority, Julia,' Rick said, turning to her after Janet and Karyn had finally disappeared down the hall, defeated. 'Word to the wise – a lot of people will be wishing it were theirs. Don't take their disappointment too personally.' He nodded toward the escalator. 'Come on, let's get some coffee,' he said, glancing at his watch. 'I think I'm having withdrawal. I haven't had a cup since eight.'

'So how'd it go?' she asked as they walked.

'A lot of media, which I expected. No bond, of course. Levenson was yapping about how unfair life is. Marquette's dad showed up, without his wife this time, thankfully. Latarrino and Brill were there, but apparently they're still ticked off at everyone but themselves over last week's fuck-up at Jackson.'

Julia said nothing. She'd watched the news Thursday night, too, and it wasn't pretty. She felt bad; circumstance had forced an early arrest. And she knew the media could distort absolutely anything.

'As for our defendant, be sure to tune into the news at noon for a peek. Corrections wheeled him over from Jackson early this morning, but he still looks like death warmed over. Good,' he scoffed, stepping onto the escalator. 'Hope he feels like shit, too. It's a damn pity that he's gonna be just fine. Anyway, Yars is taking Marquette to the Grand Jury on the second.'

Martin Yars was one of the State Attorney's Chief Felony Assistants. Besides handling administrative staffing matters, he was solely responsible for all of the office's Grand Jury presentations. In Florida, only first-degree capital murders and juveniles being sent over to adult court were indicted by the Grand Jury. Formal charges had to be filed within twenty-one days after an arrest or the court could ROR the defendant – release him on his own recognizance. That meant no bail, no bond, no house arrest, no ankle bracelet – nothing but a heartfelt promise to come back to court.

Julia counted off the days in her head. 'His arraignment's—'

'November third. The Grand Jury only meets on Wednesdays. That gives us a little time to prepare. I've got this protracted motion to suppress before Judge Gilbert this week, and I'm starting a murder trial next week, so I'm going to have you handling most of the pre-files. It's good for you to get familiar with all the witnesses anyway, and the experts, too. Jump right in. Who knows who you might end up directing at trial . . .' he added with a sly smile.

As a B second-seating her first Major Crimes murder trial, Julia figured that would probably be the Coral Gables PD records custodian, if she were lucky. Just sitting at the State's table was invaluable experience; directing or crossing a witness was a bone. And doing all the exhausting prep work to get there was the price of admission.

'Does this mean you're definitely going to seek the death penalty?' she asked. She suddenly, uncomfortably, recalled one of Charley Rifkin's overbearing, dire predictions from last week.

If Dr David Marquette becomes the next Scott Peterson du jour . . . the press will be camping out in both your backyards until Corrections finally sticks the needle in.

A conservative Republican some days, Julia's staunch opinion on the death penalty had always been an eye for an eye, but, then again, her opinion, until now, hadn't really mattered much. And now it would. Now if this case went that far, now she'd actually be a participant in the process that took a human life. And she wasn't as sure of her opinion as she once used to be.

He paused for a moment, studying her. 'It leaves the

option open. Of course, the official decision will be made after we sit down and examine what aggravators we have.'

To convict someone of first-degree premeditated murder in Florida you had to prove a conscious intent to kill; to put him to death you had to have more statutory aggravating factors than mitigating ones. Julia already knew the answer to her own question – thirty-seven stab wounds and a bashed-in skull pretty much spelled out the words 'heinous, atrocious and cruel' on a verdict form. So did hunting down your crying six-year-old with a kitchen knife in the middle of the night.

The escalator opened up onto the courthouse's busy, noisy lobby as it descended from the second floor. She looked down at the two long, restless lines of people that waited to pass through the metal detectors. Bored, indifferent correction officers shouted warnings that all bags would be searched and all weapons confiscated. Mixed in with the crowd below were the cops, who were waved in through a different wait-free door, and the lawyers, who stood out from everyone else with their dark suits and overloaded briefcases. In front of the courthouse directory, the dazed and confused gathered to find out where it was they needed to be in the nine-storied maze of courtrooms and administrative offices, while the more experienced casually strutted over to the right elevator or escalator, dressed in their courthouse best of wife-beater tees and baggy, underwear-showing jeans, laughing and joking with their friends, as if a day in court was just another fun day in the park.

'Will the prints be a problem for the Grand Jury?' she asked.

He shook his head. 'The Grand Jury won't even hear about them. And they shouldn't. It's not evidence that tends to exonerate the defendant; we have no obligation to address it. Right now, smeared footprints and unidentified finger-prints are just nuisance facts that a defense attorney will try to make more out of than he should at trial. Levenson can try it then as part of a last-ditch defense that the one-armed man did it, 'cause he's not bringing it up to the Grand Jury.'

Rick was right. For all its pomp and circumstance, Julia knew an indictment really wasn't all that hard to get. Especially since the facts in a first-degree murder were always brutal, and the juveniles bound-over for adult court beyond redemption. Cloaked in secrecy and masked by formality, the reality was that the Grand Jury only got to hear one side when determining whether to indict someone – the State's side. And it was all State. There was no judge overseeing the proceedings, no defense attorney screaming objections. The legal standard of proof was still only probable cause, and hearsay was admissible, so, of course, the facts tended to be a bit more slanted in favor of the prosecution. A criminal law professor of hers at Georgetown had once bragged that as a Cook County ADA in Chicago, he could have indicted a ham sandwich if he'd wanted to. That state-ment was probably not too far from the truth.

They'd reached Au Bon Pain, the courthouse sandwich shop that had replaced the old Pickle Barrel, which was slowly filling with people as the courtrooms broke for lunch. Rick ordered two coffees and walked Julia over to a quiet table in the back corner. She felt the eyes of several pros-ecutors and defense attorneys glance over, watching them as they passed. She felt a little self-conscious, strangely aware that her nails needed a manicure and her heels were a bit chewed. Two things she hadn't thought to think about until this very second.

'I've already arranged for Marisol, my secretary, to set the pre-files of the responding officers and Crime Scene techs with you. Just get with her on times,' he said, sliding into a booth seat. Then he paused and smiled at something or some thought. 'Have you met Marisol yet?'

She shook her head. 'I haven't met many Major Crimes secretaries. They don't get out much, I suppose.'

'Well you can't miss Mari,' he chuckled. 'Trust me. Oh, and as a warning, she can be a bit testy. Not with me, but I inherited her from C.J. Townsend when she left the office. C.J. swore she was the devil incarnate.'

'Wasn't C.J. Townsend the woman who tried the Cupid murders a few years back?'

He nodded. 'That was her. Were you in the office then?'

'No, law school. But it was all over the DC papers. I even caught a bit of the trial on Court TV. When did she leave?'

'Damn, do I feel old,' he said, shaking his head with a smile. 'You do know who the Rolling Stones are, right?'

'Very funny.'

'Just checking. C.J. left the office about a year or so back. Got married, took some kind of sabbatical. She had a rough time with Bantling, after everything that happened. She was always a pretty tough lady, but that bastard seemed to break her in the end.'

'He won a new trial, didn't he?'

'Yeah. Now she's supposed to come back home and try him all over again. It keeps getting put off, though. Judge Chaskel died in a nasty motorcycle accident on the 195 flyover and his docket was reassigned, which backed every-thing up. Then Bantling changed lawyers a couple of times. There were more appeals. I think Judge Stalder is supposed to hear it this spring. Anyway, to say Mari and C.J. didn't get along would be . . .' His voice trailed off. 'Well, just don't take Marisol's shit, if she tries to give you any. I've already told her you'll be calling. And I told her to be nice. I hope you don't feel dumped on, but that is why I have a second seat. Latarrino and Brill's pre-files are set for next week, after they get back from Philly. We'll try and do those together if my trial doesn't go.'

'Philly?'

'Jennifer was from Cherry Hill, New Jersey, a suburb outside of Philadelphia. The ME is finally releasing the bodies. They're being flown back tomorrow. Lat and Brill will interview the family up there.'

'Alright. I'd better get with Marisol, then,' she said, finishing the last of her coffee. 'Wish me luck.' She reached for her files.

'How was your weekend?' he finally asked.

'Great,' she said with a smile. She hoped she didn't sound too enthusiastic. That would be a telltale sign she was lying. 'Busy running around. You know before you realize it, it's Monday and you're nursing a hangover.'

'Ouch. Sorry to hear that. I was going to call you Saturday, but I got caught up.'

'No problem. I told you, I was crazy all weekend. And this, you know, *this*,' she said, looking right at him but not actually saying the word most men didn't want to hear anyway, 'it is what it is. I'm not expecting anything, is what I'm saying, so you don't have to explain anything.'

It had been more than a week since that Friday-night wine-soaked lapse in judgment, and Julia was still no closer to figuring out what they were or where they were headed, either as a couple or even as trial partners. Any other man, and she would definitely have written him off by now. She didn't believe in one-night stands, she didn't want a friend-with-benefits. Or a trial partner-with-benefits, for that matter. She hated mind games and she hated herself even more for playing them just now with that stupid, juvenile hangover comment. But Rick Bellido was not most men, and this case . . . well, it had changed everything. There was no way she could just write him off as a bad experience and never see him again. So her 'crazy weekend' had her and Moose hitting the vet and then the Bark Park. Then there were the trips to Publix, the gym and the dry-cleaner's, wrapped up by an exciting trek to the Galleria Mall Saturday night for an anniversary present for Aunt Nora and Uncle Jimmy. By Sunday she'd polished off the rest of the Halloween candy she'd bought three weeks too early, and spent the final remaining two hours of the day pedaling all over Hollywood trying to burn it off. Although she'd punched Rick's cell number into her phone a dozen times, she'd never actually hit send. It was pretty obvious to her by now, that hot and heavy one night didn't guarantee a steady Saturday-night date. Maybe the rules changed when you hit forty. Maybe it was a casual screw and then it's everybody back to work in the morning.

'I've got to find a home for my dad,' he said, looking into his coffee. 'That was my weekend.'

'Oh,' she said hesitantly.

'Alzheimer's. That's life, I guess.' He shrugged.

The guilt slammed her like a silent tsunami. 'I'm sorry. I didn't know,' she stammered. 'Did you find one?'

'Not yet. It's a long process, one not made easier by my mother, who insists on taking care of him herself. Even if that means strapping her body to the front door to prevent him from going for long, unaccompanied midnight strolls. But never mind that. Listen,' he said, lowering his voice. A finger found the back of her hand across the table and stroked it softly. 'I'd like to do dinner again.' He paused. 'That was nice. Maybe I shouldn't say this, but, damn, I've missed you.'

She felt her face grow hot. She wished she could say something witty and mature. Maybe, 'You have my number. Use it.' A line straight out of a Bette Davis movie. A line that wouldn't show him that she cared and that she'd missed him, too. But, of course, she didn't. She just nodded and smiled like a dolt. A smile that she knew gave away everything she'd hoped to hide. 'Any word on who the trial judge is gonna be yet?' she asked, standing up with her files.

He laughed and shook his head. He had the best smile, bright white, perfect teeth against deep Mediterranean skin. A toned-down Erik Estrada grin. 'Oh boy. I think you may need to sit back down, sweetheart.'

Julia felt her stomach drop and her palms instinctively began to tingle. From the look on his face, she knew exactly who it was. 'Please tell me you're not gonna tell me what I think it is you're gonna tell me,' she said, sliding back into her seat. 'Tell me it's Henghold. Or Gibbons. Or anyone else you wouldn't want to get.'

He just kept shaking his head. 'No can do.'

She sighed and slumped back in her chair, defeated. 'It's Farley, isn't it?'

He simply smiled.

23

'Look at me!' demanded Emma with a high-pitched squeal as she spun around the kitchen in her sparkly blue and white Cinderella gown, the one Jennifer had bought on a family trip to Disney World just a few months before. She'd kept the receipt, tucked into an envelope scribbled with the words *Miscellaneous Credit Card Receipts* and neatly filed away in the top drawer of her desk, where detectives had found it. Emma had worn the costume over her pajamas on the night she was murdered. The detectives theorized that she'd probably snuck it on after her mom had put her to bed. 'Mommy! Look! Look at me!' she continued to shout.

'Oh my, don't you look pretty,' Jennifer purred off-camera. The shot jumped across the cluttered kitchen to the pretty, slight blonde behind the island, a chocolate layer cake before her on a plate, a spatula full of frosting in hand. 'Don't get it dirty, Em. We still have the parade at school and Halloween to get through. Oh, please, David,' she said with an annoyed shake of her head when she spotted the camera. 'Point that thing at Emma.'

Obligingly, the camera jumped back across the room.

'I can make it spin!' Emma shouted as she twirled about, singing some pop song Julia had heard before but couldn't place who sang it. Maybe Hilary Duff or Christina Aguilera. The little girl's long, light-blonde hair was done in a French braid, and it whipped about behind her. Julia could tell she was trying to get it to wrap around her neck and touch her other shoulder. She'd done the very same thing when she was a kid and her hair was down past her waist.

The baby cried a cranky newborn cry in her scoop on the counter. 'Hush, now, Sophie. I'm getting it ready. Give Mommy a minute,' said Jennifer, fatigue straining her voice.

A barefoot little boy suddenly streaked across the kitchen in a cherry-stained Superman T-shirt and a droopy-looking Pull-Up. 'I'm hungggrryyyy.'

'You just ate supper, young man. Maybe you should have some more carrots, you're so hungry.'

Danny shook his head violently. He stood on his tiptoes at the island, straining to see what his mom was doing. 'Can I lick the bowl?'

'Danny! I'm dancing! Go away,' declared Emma with a pout, her hands on her hips.

'I want cake,' said Danny, rubbing his nose and pulling on his mother's pant leg. His tousled, brown hair stuck to his sweaty forehead.

'It's coming, it's coming everybody. The witching hour is here. Oh boy, oh boy, oh boy, is it here,' Jennifer mumbled, mainly to herself. 'Okay. We're going to sing now. Dave, are you ready? David?'

The camera focused back on Jennifer, and the picture bobbed up and down as the cameraman presumably nodded. The crowd in the kitchen sang *Happy Birthday, Mommy* as Jennifer carried the chocolate frosted cake with the single lit candle over to the kitchen table, navigating her way through a bobbing pool of colorful balloons on the floor. She blew out the candle and everyone clapped. Danny screamed, 'Yipee! I want some! I want a big piece!' The baby cried again. Jennifer picked up Sophie and began to feed her a bottle as she tried to eat a slice of cake with her free hand.

'Watch me,' Emma demanded into the camera, twirling

and spinning once again, ignoring the slice of cake Jennifer had cut for her. 'Look at me, Daddy! Look at me! Daddy!'

The camera watched Emma dance for maybe thirty seconds more before it suddenly just cut out. Black and white fuzz filled Julia's television, like two armies of fighting ants.

Coral Gables PD had seized nineteen home videos from the Marquette residence. Julia had had Investigations make a copy for her of each one, and over the course of the past few days had watched them all from her living-room couch. Watched as the beautiful Marquette babies came home from the hospital, one by one, bundled safely in their proud mother's arms. Watched as Danny and Emma learned to sit and crawl and walk and swim. Watched Emma learn to read and write and ride a bike. Watched birthday parties and Christmas morning free-for-alls under a tremendous, tinsel-laden, fake fir. Watched as the dead breathed and giggled and smiled once more. The tapes were her only link to a family she'd never get to meet. A family she felt a desperate, almost compulsive need to know. A family that reminded her too much of her own . . .

Like Danny, her big brother, Andrew, had loved cars as a little kid, too. Especially fire trucks. He'd carried a metal Matchbox fire engine around in his pocket wherever he went. In a department store one time, he'd gotten in trouble for something. Playing with a mannequin? Running off? Hiding? Momma had sent him to stand in a corner by the fitting rooms. And there he was, forever embedded deep in her memory, all of seven or eight, red truck in hand, not a tear or so much as a defiant pout on his freckle-smattered, milky-smooth face, a mop of soft black curls spilling past his forehead over his dark eyes. When Momma had finally turned her attention back to the sales girl, he'd waved mischievously over at Julia, turned around to peek his head into the ladies' fitting room behind him, and with a hand over his mouth to stifle the giggle, he'd sent the truck careening underneath the row of stalls.

Julia closed her eyes tight, hoping to shut off the memories. It had been a long time since she'd allowed herself to think of Andy. Even though he was five years older than her, when they got along, they'd been the best of friends. Her brother could make her do the goofiest things with just the flash of his lopsided grin and a double dare: walk on the train tracks; ring Mrs Crick's doorbell on Halloween when everyone knew she was a witch and her creepy house with the caved-in roof was haunted; eat the red squishy berries off the unknown bush by the garage. It was Andy she'd go running to when a thunderstorm would wake her in the middle of the night, and he would let her come into his bed and under the covers, counting off the seconds for her between the thunder and the lightning until he could assure her the storm had moved far away. She could still smell his breath, sweet with mouthwash and the chocolate he'd snuck after he'd brushed his teeth, as he whispered words in the dark to distract her.

'*I hit a home run today at practice, Ju-Ju. Coach said I was good, but I should work harder on my pitching, 'cause that's what I do best. Says I'm the only one on the team he's seen that can throw a damn curve ball. No one can hit it. And no one can touch my split finger, neither. He thinks I could even play JV next year. Imagine that — me pitching JV my first year in junior high. That would be so cool . . .*'

Planning for a future that would never be.

The rain pattered softly against her living-room windows, as it had all night, blurring the streetlights outside into twinkling streaks of soft yellow. Moose, maybe sensing things were not right, jumped up and joined her on the couch, curling himself into a little brown and white ball by her side and immediately falling into a deep sleep. She watched his warm chest rise and fall under her fingers. They'd found each other six years ago, when he was just a pup and she was a first-year law student. He was wandering around in snow that was deeper than his body one night and she was on her way to a boring torts class. He'd had a deep cut on one paw and his short fur was a bit mangy, but he had the most soulful brown eyes. Lost and completely alone in a big, intimidating city, he was a survivor, just like her. At first he was skittish, but she wouldn't leave and he didn't run off, and eventually, with a lot of coaxing, he'd let her pet him. When she reached to scoop him up, he'd actually kind of jumped into her arms, snuggling into her scarf. The rest was history – she'd missed her class, brought him home to a chicken dinner and a warm bath and there he'd stayed, never straying further than a stone's throw away from her ankles ever again if he could help it. She'd given him his name from the Archie comic-book character. Moose was so completely trusting, so vulnerable, she thought, looking at him now, especially when he was sleeping. Like a child. A shudder ran through her as the tape finally clicked off and the screen went to blue.

She slid Moose gently off her lap and went over to the DVD/VCR player. She hit the eject button and the last video ever shot of the Marquette family slowly popped out. With the back of her hand, she wiped away the tears that streamed down her face, and slipped the video into the sleeve marked *Mommy's Birthday 4/10/05*. Then she put it back in the cardboard evidence box, along with the others.

Jennifer and her babies had less than one week left to live.

24

Three days after David Marquette's First Appearance, and twelve days after they were murdered, Jennifer and the children were flown up to Cherry Hill, New Jersey and finally buried.

Lat and Brill pulled their rental car past the large crowd that had spilled outside onto the steps of St Mary's, just as the three tiny, white caskets made their way up rain-slicked steps to follow the full-sized coffin of their mother into the church. Once inside, they listened as grief-stricken family and friends struggled to console one another and a father remembered the little girl he'd given away, on the steps of the very same altar, to the very same man now accused of killing her. Standing awkwardly next to Brill in the back of the church, dressed in his best black suit, Lat could not even begin to imagine what the man could be thinking. He didn't have any kids himself, but he knew that if it were him, they'd have to take his gun away.

Hours later, in the slip-covered living room of Renny and Michael Prowse, the two detectives sat in a couple of tired Queen Anne side chairs, a stack of flower-covered photo albums and two hot cups of coffee in front of them. An antique cuckoo clock loudly ticked the stagnant seconds away. On top of a worn Baldwin piano, a makeshift shrine to Jennifer and the Prowses' only grandchildren had been created – complete with pictures and burning candles and watched over by the outstretched arms of a crucified ceramic Jesus. Like in the Gables house, family pictures were everywhere here. Yearly school pictures, displayed in black plastic certificate frames, age-progressed the Prowses' three daughters up the colonial staircase, from nursery school through high school and college graduations.

If asked to give a short history right now on the Prowse family, Lat felt pretty confident he could nail it, just from having sat in the room for five minutes. And not just from looking at the pictures. Hummel figurines crowded glass shelves in a corner curio and the shelves of a wall unit were filled with still-tagged Beanie Babies. On the wood mantel, tiny crystal figures had their own red velvet-lined display case. Obviously the Prowses were a family of collectors. A family that never liked to give anything away. A family that would be especially hard hit by the deaths of their daughter and their grandchildren.

The entire neighborhood must have come and dropped off food; platters and steaming casserole dishes overflowed from the kitchen, and were now stacked on the dining-room table in the next room. The smell of lasagne, garlic, coffee and sausage filled the house and there was apparently more on the way. The doorbell rang constantly.

'It's been like this for a week now,' Renny Prowse said absently, setting down a platter full of butter cookies and slices of apple cake on the coffee table. She was a well-kept woman in her late fifties, dressed in a neat black suit, her blonde hair pulled back into a clip. But Lat noticed the band of long, gray roots that framed her face, the dark circles that sunk her eyes. She had put on some make-up, but with no real purpose and her round face was puffy and blotched red from days of endless crying. 'People are so kind. I just can't get over how kind they are. Some of them we don't even know, do we, Mike?'

'No, no,' said Jennifer's father, Mike Prowse, who sat on

the plastic-covered couch across from them. 'We don't even know them.'

Jennifer's older sister, Joanne, sat next to her dad, her hand on his, while her younger sister, Janna, stood quietly by the door that led to the kitchen. Both women were blonde and blue-eyed, like their sister and mother. Joanne was only in maybe her mid-thirties, but dressed in a matronly tent dress, with no make-up and horn-rimmed glasses, she was already forging full speed ahead for middle age. Janna, on the other hand, must have been the Prowses' late-in-life surprise. Lat guessed late teens, early twenties, with a fit figure and a coquettish, wholesome, pretty face.

'Please. Eat something, Detectives. There's so much,' Renny said, finally taking a seat on the other side of her husband. She licked her dry lips and clasped her hands together, obviously bracing herself for the conversation ahead.

Lat hated this part of his job. Hated it. He could look at mangled, mutilated bodies – even nasty decomps – and brutal crime scenes well enough, but it was meeting the family of the victim that always got to him. That, by the end of the interview, always seemed to have gnawed a piece of him away. After enough years and enough interviews, he figured his soul would eventually be picked over and eaten to nothing. That would be the day he retired – probably to a good bottle of Jack and an isolated log cabin somewhere in the mountains of Montana.

As a street cop in Miami, John Latarrino had long ago learned how to distance himself from his job and the people he arrested. All cops did. The bad guys were no longer people, but mopes, skells, perps, subjects, defendants. His ex-wife, Trish, who had minored in psychology for way too long, had once told him that labeling individuals with derogatory slang terms was a mental coping mechanism cops used to separate good from evil, their job from their everyday lives. *Us against them* helped a cop get through the shift, and restore power to what was oftentimes viewed as a powerless situation, she had theorized. When he was assigned to Homicide a few years back, Lat had taken that over-analysis one step further, and had learned how to distance himself from death, so that no matter how bad the scene, the bodies in it were not really people, either, but DBs, or victims, or stiffs. His job as detective was to simply solve the mystery of how they got that way. That's when Trish had finally stopped analyzing him and just called him cold and unfeeling. The papers were filed six months later.

Right about now he would give anything to be at a scene. Or in a Chiefs' Meeting. Or at his damn dentist's having root canal. Anywhere but here, doing anything but this. Maybe it was because the family suddenly made it all real. Maybe because, like now, he couldn't pretend when he looked into Renny Prowse's confused, red-rimmed eyes, or leafed through the stacks of photo albums she'd dragged out. Maybe it was because he couldn't lie to himself anymore that it was just a job he was doing.

'We know this is a difficult time for you, Mr and Mrs Prowse, Janna, Joanne. But we are just trying to get some background on Jennifer and your son-in-law. What might have caused this,' Lat began softly.

Renny was already shaking her head. 'We don't know, Detective. Oh God, David is – he seemed like such a good man. Such a good father. But . . .' She buried her nose in a tissue.

'But?' asked Brill between bites of his cookie. Crumbs fluttered to the floor. Lat shot him a look.

'She's been gone from us for so long, now, Detective. Down there in Miami. I couldn't get my hands on her like I could my other two girls. I couldn't help her when she needed me. I couldn't be there when . . .' her voice trailed off again, but she never finished the thought. 'I still remember the day she pulled out of my driveway, her car packed with all the teddy bears she'd gotten over the years. That's when I knew she shouldn't be leaving home. She wasn't ready to grow up yet, you see . . .'

'Jen met David in the emergency room at Temple seven years ago,' said Joanne, taking over as her mother buried her face back in a tissue. 'She fell rollerblading in the park and David was doing his residency in emergency medicine. They dated for a few months and then decided to get married. Everyone liked David. He was a doctor. He was handsome. He was . . .' she paused, searching for a word. 'He was great. Jen was crazy about him.'

'Crazy,' murmured her father.

'They got married at St Mary's right before his residency was over. My parents invited the whole town and everyone showed,' Joanne continued.

'Just like today,' Renny said, almost proudly.

'Two weeks later they left for Miami. Last year they bought that house in Coral Gables. It was very expensive.'

'How often did you see them?'

'Two or three times a year. Jennifer would always try and come up for Christmas,' Joanne said. 'It was difficult for any of us to get down too often. We have to work, you know.' Lat thought she might have overemphasized the 'we'.

'When was the last time they were here?' asked Brill, reaching for another cookie.

'Memorial Day. Mom and Dad had a barbecue.'

'Were they getting along?' asked Lat.

'Oh yes,' said Joanne, nodding quickly. 'They always got along.'

Lat already knew that David Marquette had completed his residency in October of 1998. Emma's birthday was 31 March 1999. It wasn't hard to do the math. 'Jennifer was pregnant when they got married.'

Renny looked away, embarrassed, and Michael closed his eyes. 'Yes, she was,' Joanne said quickly. 'But that didn't matter. They were going to get married anyway. Emma was just a little earlier than they had planned.'

Obviously it was a sore subject. Lat thought of the ceramic Jesus. 'What about David. What can you tell us about his family?' he asked.

'Nothing,' said Mike bitterly. 'They didn't come to the wedding. His father was some hotshot doctor in Chicago. He couldn't come because there was an emergency. So no one came. No one at all.'

'You didn't think that was odd?' asked Brill.

'My father didn't talk to his own father for some years, Detective. It's not so odd,' said Joanne in a voice that was both calm and patronizing. 'Families fight. The point is, we all liked David. None of us can believe this has happened. None of us saw it coming, if that's what you are getting at.'

'Did he have a temper? Did you ever see or hear them fight? Did Jennifer ever tell you about any fights?' asked Lat.

'That's just it, Detective. I was very close with my sister. They were the perfect couple. They never fought.'

'Or she never told you,' cautioned Brill.

'Or she never told me,' conceded Joanne with some difficulty. She shot Brill a cold look.

'When was the last time you spoke with Jennifer, Mrs Prowse?' asked Lat.

'Two days before she was . . .' Renny's voice trailed off again and she bit her lip. 'We talked about two times a week. David was out of town and she was taking Emma and Danny shoe shopping. No one ever heard from her again.'

Joanne shook her head. 'I talked to her a few days before that. She never mentioned any problems.'

Her dad shrugged. 'I'm not sure. It was the week before she died. She wanted to know how my foot was feeling.'

'He twisted it jogging,' said Joanne.

'And you?' asked Brill to Janna.

Janna looked startled. 'I don't know,' she said, crossing her arms across her chest. 'A couple of weeks before, maybe.'

'Janna's still in college, Detective Brill,' said Joanne sharply. 'Syracuse. She's had to come home for this. She's a very busy girl.'

Lat sighed. This was not very productive. 'Is there anything, then, that any of you can think of that might be important for us to know? Anything at all,' he prodded.

'There was one thing,' began Jennifer's father, his voice trembling slightly.

'There was nothing,' said Renny loudly, shaking her head, reaching for his hand. 'Stop doing this to yourself, Mike. Please.' She started to cry again.

'Anything at all,' offered Lat.

'Damnit! I'm going to speak! I'm finally going to speak!' Michael Prowse said, his voice rising. He waited for a moment. 'There was something about David,' he began. His eyes welled up and he looked away, to an unseen memory in the room.

The past week and a half had probably aged Mike Prowse ten years. Lat knew the next six months would add another ten. The physical transformation of a murder victim's family from arrest to when a trial was finally had was unbelievably sad.

'There always was something not right,' continued Mike. 'Something that I can't explain to you. It was like, when David looked at you, he never *stopped* looking. He never turned away, or got lost in something else. When he talked to you, he always listened very carefully. It was like he was studying you. And he always knew the right thing to say. The *perfect* thing.'

'And?' Lat prodded.

Mike looked at Lat finally. Silent tears ran down his cheeks, but he didn't bother to wipe them away. 'That was it. David Marquette was . . . he was . . .' He stumbled to find the right words. 'It was almost as if he were *too* perfect. And he fooled us all.'

25

Renny began crying again, her shoulders heaving up and down as she struggled for air. 'Don't, Mike. No more. I don't want to hear it!'

Lat shifted uncomfortably in his chair. 'Do you want to take a moment, Mr and Mrs Prowse? We're almost done here.'

Mike nodded and stood up. He looked around the room absently, as though trying to remember where he was. 'Come on, hon. Let's take a break. This is too much,' he said, leading her out of the room.

'Dad, I'll take her,' said Joanne, getting up off the couch. The doorbell rang and she looked at the detectives blankly. 'I'd better get that. Give us all a minute or two, won't you?' Then she followed her parents out of the room.

Janna still stood by the kitchen door. An awkward silence settled in the room, broken only by the loud ticks of the grandfather clock.

'Hey, Janna, honey,' Brill said with a wink when everyone was gone, 'do you think you could get me another couple of those cookies your mom set out? I didn't have any lunch.'

'Sure,' she said and shrugged, heading into the kitchen.

Lat looked at Steve Brill like he had three heads. 'Another cookie? What the fuck is that?'

'She was porking the brother-in-law,' he announced with a big smile and a shake of his head.

'What?'

'The younger sis. College girl. Something's going on, boss-man. She knew something, saw something, heard something, did something. I'm not sure what, although my money's on the doc teaching her a private anatomy class.'

Lat looked back toward the door Janna had just slipped out of. 'You think?'

'Female body language, brother. If there's anything I know, it's that – a pissed-off broad, or one that's hiding something. It sure as hell gave her away. Standing the polar opposite away from Waltons. Arms crossed. Nibbling the corner of her cute, pouty mouth. Scared rabbit look. And the older sister is the new matriarch now that Momma is breaking down. Ain't nobody gonna disparage the Prowse name. And that includes us. So your interview with the rest of the family, I'm afraid, is done, boss-man. They saw what they wanted to see, when they wanted to see it. Even their hindsight ain't twenty-twenty.'

Lat nodded slowly. He looked Brill up and down as if he were seeing a new person but somehow couldn't trust his own vision. Brill just kept beaming like a Cheshire cat. 'So you sent her for more cookies to tell me this?'

'No. I'm still hungry. I'd actually like to get my hands on some of that real food,' he said, pointing to the dining-room table and rubbing his stomach. 'I just think it might be rude to ask for some. But you're good at this interrogation shit, Sherlock. You talk to her. You have a way with people, I can tell.'

Janna walked through the kitchen door at that moment with another platter full of cookies. 'Do you want more coffee, too, Detective Brill?'

'No. We want you to sit down, Janna,' Lat said softly, but sternly. He hoped Brill's sixth sense was right or he was really gonna feel like an asshole by the end of the day. 'We think you might have some information that you may want to share with us before everyone else returns.'

Janna sat down slowly on the couch. 'I . . . don't know anything,' she said softly, looking around. Her blue eyes were large and scared.

'Were you sleeping with your brother-in-law or was your sister?' asked Brill, reaching for another cookie.

'Excuse me?' Janna asked. Her eyes narrowed and she looked surprised, but what she didn't look was pissed off that Brill had asked the question in the first place.

The man had absolutely no tact. Lat shook his head. 'That would be something we would need to know, Janna; if there was something going on between you and David. Something that would help us make sense out of all this. We're having a hard time with everyone telling us how wonderful the man was. And if there was something happening between you, it would be better if we heard it from you first, than learning about it from someone else later.'

'He wasn't so wonderful,' Janna said in a soft voice after a moment. 'But I never slept with him. Neither did Joanne. God, never. Joanne is really religious. She'd burn in hell for sleeping with anyone before she got married, much less her sister's husband.'

'So why wasn't he so wonderful?' asked Lat.

Janna grew quiet. She twisted her hands in her lap and looked around the room again, before lowering her voice to just above a whisper. 'He made a pass at me. In May. At the barbecue.'

'Did Jennifer know?'

'Yes. She saw him talking to me. I was home for the summer. She came over just in time to hear him ask me to go out with him to a local bar after Jen went to bed.'

'That was a pass?' asked Lat.

Both Brill and Janna shot him a look.

'So what did she do?'

'She ran into her room and cried. She was pregnant with Sophie. Everyone else thought it was the hormones that were making her upset. I never said anything to anyone. David went back to Miami the next day without her.' She grew quiet again. 'Apparently it wasn't the first time either. With me, yes. But Jen knew about the others.'

'There were other women?'

She nodded and sighed. 'Yeah. But I don't know names or dates. They might even have been hookers for all Jen knew. But there were a couple of late nights and perfume-soaked shirts. I think she blamed Memorial Day on me, though. We stopped really talking after that.'

Finally. The perfect husband was not so perfect after all.

'Was she gonna leave him?' asked Brill. 'Were we talking divorce here?'

She almost laughed and shook her head. 'Don't take this the wrong way, Detectives, but my sister, even though she was pretty, was always insecure. So when she met David, he became like an obsession for her. He was the guy she got but couldn't ever believe she really did. My parents, my sister, they never saw that. Only I did.'

'So the first pregnancy?'

Janna shrugged. 'She never 'fessed to planning an un-planned pregnancy. And she never would.' She rose from the couch and looked nervously back at the foyer, lowering her voice again. 'I've said enough. But you asked me if she was going to leave him? Let me just say this, Detectives. Jennifer was desperate-crazy about David. He could do anything to anyone and she would never leave. Never. He couldn't get rid of her, even if he tried.'

26

'That is one fucked-up family,' said Brill as they climbed in the rental car and headed to the airport. 'I'm sure as hell happy my parents just beat my ass.' He lit up a cigarette and rubbed his head.

Lat looked at him and raised an eyebrow. 'Yeah. Just imagine how you might have turned out.' He started up the car. 'You know, they are in mourning.'

'They're in denial, bro. Big-time.'

'Of course they're in denial. Right now they're sifting through every memory they ever made with their daughter and grandkids and that man they called their son-in-law to see if any of them were real. They'll relive every word of every conversation for the last seven years for the missing clue that would have tipped them off that he was a fucking cold-hearted psychopath. And then for the next seven, they'll get to blame themselves and each other for not seeing the telltale signs of catastrophe that, by the end of this case, the prosecutors will have painted as obvious to everyone. So, yeah, right now they're still in denial. 'Cause if they deny it, then it didn't happen, got it? And then they're not the ones at fault for letting it.'

Brill stared at Lat in amazement. Then he exhaled a thick plume of gray smoke. 'Oh shit. That's deep.'

'That's the five stages of grief and an ex-wife who's a psychologist.' He fanned his hand in front of him. The Marlboro sure smelled good. 'Blow that shit out the window, man. I'm off the death sticks six months now.'

'Christ, you have had it rough. An ex-wife who's a mind-fucker. I take back most of the things I was thinking about you, Nitchy.'

'That's Nietzsche, you idiot.'

'"If you gaze for long into an abyss, the abyss gazes also into you." Watch who you call an idiot.'

Now it was Lat's turn to stare.

'Why is she an ex?' Brill asked.

'Could you live with me?'

Brill didn't even blink. 'Good point.'

Lat blew out a long breath. 'It just wasn't in the cards. How about you? Exes? Wives? Kids?'

'An ex-wife and an ex-kid.'

'That sucks.'

'Only the ex-kid part. Lisa, the ex-wife, poisoned her, so she hates me, too. But she still loves my money. Sure does love that. She's past eighteen now. Not supposed to be my problem anymore, but I still pay the tuition bill at college and she still ignores me. I'm hoping when she moves out of Transylvania that she'll see her blood-sucking mother is a fucking nut job. Maybe then she'll give her old man a call.' He threw his cigarette out the window. 'Got any worldly advice for me, Nietzsche?'

'Forget Nietzsche. You need Freud, man,' Lat laughed. 'What's her name?'

'Nicole – Nicky. I haven't actually seen her in five years. But, damn, she was a cutie. That college girl reminded me of what she must look like now.' He sighed. 'Hey, this is a fuckin' cheery-ass convo we're having, boss-man. Say, have you written up your will yet?'

'Well, at least we've got a motive now.'

'Yeah. Trying to bang your pregnant wife's younger sister would get the claws out on most women. And most lawyers.

173

Maybe the denying relatives are wrong. Maybe she was gonna divorce his ass and he wasn't having no part of splitting everything he'd earned.'

Lat nodded. 'Especially if he was roped into a marriage to begin with.'

'Then there's the insurance. What was the death benefit on that MetLife policy you found?'

'Two million.'

'There's another two million reasons to make it hurt.'

'The house was worth some ching, though. And he's still got a one point two mortgage to pay off. It's not such a crazy amount, given the guy's a surgeon.'

'I got a friend from grade school, became a surgeon up in Connecticut. I saw him at a reunion a couple of years back. Said there ain't no money in it anymore. Not what people think there is. Wasted a hundred G's on med school.'

'Maybe your friend's just a shitty surgeon.' Lat paused for a moment. 'Even if he was scraping for change and decided to collect early on his wife's insurance policy, I still can't figure out the kids.'

Lat couldn't understand a father actually killing his own children, even though he'd seen it before far too many times. A wife – maybe you'd be angry enough to pull the trigger. But a three-year-old in Pull-Ups was just crazy. An infant who could never be a witness anyway? A screaming little girl?

Brill shrugged. 'Maybe he wanted to wipe the slate clean. Maybe he wasn't the Poppa type. Some aren't. Look at that freak in California who killed his nine kids last year with a bullet to the back of their heads. Or the dad who hated his wife so much he drove his two kids cross-country from New Hampshire, killed 'em and buried 'em in some state along the way, but then offed himself so she would never find their bodies. The list goes on. But I don't need to tell you about all the fucking psychos in this world. Just pick up the morning paper.' He paused for a second, flicking his cigarette out the window. 'I hate doctors,' he said in a low voice. 'I never go to 'em and I don't trust 'em. God complexes, every damn one. My dad went to see one – first time in twenty fucking years he goes for a check-up. Walks in the door laughing and smiling – healthy as a goddamned horse, I'm telling ya. Then this idiot in a white coat straps him to a treadmill and makes him run like the devil's chasing him. Two hours later he's lying in a hospital bed. Two days after that he's dead. Can you believe that shit?'

Lat's cellphone rang then. He looked at Brill and flipped it open. 'Latarrino.'

Brill lit another cigarette and turned to look out the window. He'd never been to Philly before. And now he knew why. With the naked, twisted trees, gray skies and bleak rain, it looked depressing. Plus, right now Latarrino was driving past what looked like a few hundred graffiti-stained chemical plants, all belching white smoke up into the rain, where it hung in the humidity like a giant poisonous cloud over the city. Brill, like a lot of other transplanted New Yorkers, had lived in Florida long enough to be suffering withdrawal. He needed to see some green grass and blue skies and white-haired golfers in plaid pants and he needed to see them soon.

Two minutes later, Lat snapped the cell closed. 'Just when you thought it was safe to go back in the water,' he said with a sigh. 'That was the lab.'

Brill looked at Lat's face. 'The knife don't match.'

'No. It matches, bro. But something else doesn't.'

'No fucking way,' Brill said, sitting up straight.

Lat shook his head and slapped the steering wheel hard. 'The semen found on Jennifer's nightshirt doesn't belong to her husband.'

27

Nora and Jimmy's condo in the aging Galt Towers was tightly sandwiched between two other high-rises at the far south end of an overdeveloped, mile-long stretch of Fort Lauderdale beach known as the Galt Mile. Julia pulled her Honda into a bright yellow spot that conspicuously warned GUESTS ONLY!! turned off the engine and sat there for a moment listening to the crashing sound of the ocean, hidden behind the building's elongated shadows, less than a hundred feet away. The sun was beginning to set, and to the west, the sky over the Intracoastal was a warm tangerine color, infused with fiery streaks of copper red and deep orange, and the faintest whisper of purple clouds. The air smelled and tasted of coconut oil and sea salt, like pina coladas and margaritas. It was Julia's favorite time of day, the beach her favorite place to spend it. And to top it off, it was finally a Friday. She could feel the stress of the past week begin to melt away with the sun as it slipped under the horizon. She savored the moment a little while longer, then grabbed the Macy's bag off the front seat, along with the bottle of Uncle Jimmy's favorite Chianti, and headed across the parking lot.

During the crazy South Florida real-estate market of the past five years, big-name developers like Donald Trump had snatched up a lot of the older condos and co-ops and spring-break hotels that lined the beaches of Fort Lauderdale. They'd either renovated the old with fabulous façades and ultra-chic lobbies, or torn them down to construct opulent spa/resorts and multi-million-dollar oceanfront condos. The much-needed facelift was helping reshape the city into a younger, edgier, metropolis-by-the-sea. The Venice of America was the new catchy nickname the Mayor hoped would catch on.

But not here on the Mile. Donald Trump and downtown might be looking for the young, up-and-coming professional, but the Mile still had its sights set on the older, down-and-almost-out-of-here retiree – fifty-five and older with No Pets, No Renters and definitely No Kids.

On her salary, Julia was lucky to afford a one-bedroom apartment that was just west of 195, so a place on the beach was definitely not happening anytime in the foreseeable future without a little divine intervention from the Florida lottery. Her aunt and uncle, though, were two of the Mile's pioneering snowbirds. They'd bought their unit twenty years ago as a vacation home for next to nothing. After Julia had left New York to go to law school and Uncle Jimmy had slipped a disc at work – prematurely and painfully ending a thirty-year career with the Department of Sanitation – they'd decided to make the move down to South Florida permanent.

Julia was only seven or eight when Nora and Jimmy got their condo, but she could still remember a time when the hallways didn't always smell like boiled meat, before the crimson flowers on the lobby wallpaper had faded to a dull pink. Her parents had combined their first visit to Aunt Nora's new vacation pad with her family's only trip to Disney, which was probably why she still remembered it so vividly. The endless drive down from Long Island in the family station wagon that – thanks to her brother, Andrew, spilling an entire container of Nestlé Quik in the back seat the week before – smelled like rotten milk in the afternoon sun. The stops on 195 so her dad could collect cuttings from all sorts of strange plants he had no business disturbing. Fighting with Andy over who would get to rest their head on the console. Playing Jaws and Marco Polo and Jellyfish with Andy in the motel pools. Clutching Andy's hand as the two of them waited nervously in line to ride Space Mountain. But the clearest memory of the trip was the smiling, tan face of her mother, dressed in blue jeans and an orange T-shirt, running down the aisle of McCrory's five-and-dime, clutching bunches of plastic flowers in her hand. 'They're perfect, Nor!' she shouted as she ran. 'Just perfect!'

McCrory's had long since closed, and her mom was dead now, but whenever Julia tried to picture her mother, that was exactly how she saw her. Young and happy – maybe just a couple of years older than Julia was now – her long, wavy, dark hair flopping behind her, the lemony smell of Jean Nate body splash on her skin and bubblegum on her breath. The moment was framed forever in her mind like a brilliant, perfectly detailed picture, with one strange exception – she could never remember the color of the damn flowers Momma held in her hand. Strange because they were still sitting in Nora's bathroom, and Julia looked at them every time she was over.

She shook the memories out of her head and walked through the warm, musty lobby to the elevator, nodding at the white-haired security guard who sat watching *The People's Court* on a portable TV set and couldn't care less if she was dressed in black and wearing a ski mask. A couple of tables of bridge were still going strong in the resident rec room, along with a few bitter squabbles. For a late Friday afternoon the place was jumping.

She heard the blaring televisions as soon as she got off the elevator on ten, shouting at her from behind every door.

Oprah. Ellen. Judge Judy. Judge Alex. Judge Milian. Today the fluorescent-lit, teal-carpeted corridor smelled like cabbage, chicken soup and boiling eggs. Finally, outside 1052 she caught a fragrant whiff of sausage and peppers and garlic cooking in olive oil. Before she could actually knock, the door opened. Moose ran out to greet her with a happy howl and a crazy-dog circle dance.

'Uncle Jimmy!' she said with a big smile as she stooped down to pet Moose before even the deaf neighbors heard him. 'Happy anniversary! How'd you know I was here?'

'Hey there, Munch,' Jimmy said. 'Freddy called up.'

Munch was short for Munchkin, which was really funny since in heels, Julia took her uncle by at least an inch. She stopped petting Moose and shook her head. 'Who's Freddy?'

'Fred. Freddy. The guard downstairs. He called up. Told us you were on your way.'

'Oh.' Good thing she'd left that ski mask back in the car. 'Where's Aunt Nora?' she asked, giving Uncle Jimmy a kiss and walking into a mauve and gray living room that still looked like it did that day in 1985 when her dad had packed them all back into the smelly, overgrown wagon and headed for home. Moose merrily followed. In the corner, he had his own little mauve dog bed and a basket full of dog toys.

As if on cue, Aunt Nora came out of the kitchen, swaddled in aprons and holding a spoon. 'Well, there you are,' she said, giving Julia what she called 'a Sicilian hug' – a squeeze with all her body and generous bosom, followed by a hard kiss on the cheek that was sure to leave a bruise. 'We were getting worried about you.' Julia navigated her way around Nora's breasts and hugged her back hard.

Aunt Nora was her mom, Irene's, older and only sister. Her only sibling, in fact. It was Aunt Nora and Uncle Jimmy who she'd gone to live with fifteen years ago after her parents had died. After her world had been turned completely and horrifically and instantly upside down. She'd been only thirteen at the time – old enough, unfortunately, to understand what was happening to her and around her, and definitely old enough to know that she was being sent to live with her aunt and uncle in Staten Island. There were no relatives left on her dad's side. His only brother had died as a teenager – suicide, her mom had told her – and both his parents had died within a year of each other before Julia had turned five. She didn't even remember them. All of the pictures were gone, now, too.

They'd tried for years, but Nora and Jimmy could never have kids of their own. After tragedy struck, Julia had become their daughter, and they'd raised her through the rest of adolescence into adulthood just that way – adored and sheltered and completely overprotected. The fragile porcelain doll they knew could easily shatter into a zillion pieces at any moment. But Nora had rules. Crazy rules. From the day Julia had walked through the door of Nora and Jimmy's two-family house in Great Kills – a single, fuzzy purple overnight bag stuffed with clothes in one hand and a shoebox full of what was to become her most cherished possessions in the other – certain subjects were never spoken of again, as were certain people. Familiar pictures simply disappeared from Nora's clean, white walls; treasured keepsakes were quietly put away, never to be seen again. Aunt Nora dealt with the pain of losing her only sister by ordering it from her house. Exiled mementos and the faces of the banished were replaced with new knick-knacks and smiling photos of Julia, which Aunt Nora hung everywhere.

Unlike her aunt, Julia, over the years, had only mastered hiding her pain. Hugs and kisses smothered in tomato sauce and cannoli cream were Aunt Nora's well-intentioned cure-all for an emotional anguish that both of them knew never really went away. For Julia, time had only dulled the constant ache that was always in her heart. And on occasion, like a crippling case of arthritis on a cold day, that ache would flare up without warning into the most excruciating, debilitating physical pain, as if someone had torn a hole in her heart and then ripped the stitches out once again.

She could hardly blame Nora for wanting to scrub the horror of the past completely clean from her house. And given how Julia had turned out – a relatively successful lawyer who didn't do drugs or even smoke, and who wasn't downing Prozac with her Rice Krispies each morning – even she had to admit that her aunt's nurturing recipe for success had seemingly worked its magic. Perhaps most importantly, all these years later, she was still in one piece when others would surely have crumbled.

'Come in, come in,' Aunt Nora finally said, taking her hand and leading her into the kitchen. 'And don't you beg now,' she scolded Moose with a wave of her spoon as she tossed him a sniggle of something.

'He's getting fat,' Julia said, shaking her head.

'Nonsense. He just needs a haircut.'

'You shouldn't have cooked. I wanted to take you out,' Julia tried. A ridiculous proposition. Aunt Nora thought no one in the world cooked as good as her. And she was right. Hence, there was no reason to go out.

'Where do you think you can get sausage 'n' peppa that's not dried out like shoe leather? Save your money, sweetie.'

Julia conceded with a shrug and a smile. 'Happy anniversary,' she said, handing the package from Macy's to her. 'I also brought Chianti. Maybe you won't let me take you out, but I'm leaving that present here. I thought it would go with the kitchen. Don't you dare return it.'

'Tell me you got it on sale.'

'I got it on sale,' Julia lied.

'Okay, then I'll keep it,' Nora chirped.

Uncle Jimmy appeared behind her with a full glass of wine. 'So how's that big case Nora said you're working now?' he asked, handing her the wine. 'I don't see you on TV.'

'He's been looking,' piped in her aunt while cutting cucumbers for a salad big enough to feed the entire floor. 'I told everyone at the pool my Julia's gonna be famous.'

'I shouldn't even have said anything,' Julia replied with a smile, shaking her head and reaching for a slice of cucumber. While she'd mentioned to Nora the other night over pork loin sandwiches and ravioli that she'd gotten assigned to a really big case, she hadn't mentioned exactly what that case was. And she hadn't mentioned it for a reason. She tried to keep the tone light. 'But it's pretty exciting. It's my first murder, Uncle Jimmy. A prosecutor in Major Crimes asked me to try it with him. Can you believe that? So I had to go out to the scene, and I've been handling all the pre-files of the witnesses, getting the case ready for the Grand Jury.'

'What'd this guy do? What kind of murder are we talking?' asked Jimmy.

Julia took a long sip of wine. 'It may even be a death-penalty case.'

'Oh my,' said Nora with a frown.

'But what'd he do?' Jimmy asked again.

She hesitated a second and took another sip. 'It's the doctor case, Uncle Jimmy. You know, the man who killed his family.'

Aunt Nora stopped cutting.

'Are you gonna be on TV?' Jimmy asked, looking carefully over at Nora.

'Maybe, but I'm not the lead attorney. I'm what they call second seat.'

'Second string,' Uncle Jimmy said absently, nodding at the thirteen-inch TV that was mounted under a cabinet in the kitchen. Jimmy Rose had started talking about Sunday's upcoming Dolphins game.

'Is that the man who was just in the paper?' Aunt Nora asked quietly. 'The one with the wife from New Jersey?'

Besides the excessive local TV coverage of the arrest, both the *Herald* and *Sun Sentinel* had run pictures of the funerals in their local sections this past week. 'Yes,' said Julia quietly. 'That's the one.' She looked down into her wine and swirled it around, avoiding Nora's stare.

Before she found out they were going to be held in Philadelphia, Julia had wanted to go to the funerals. She'd wanted to say a proper goodbye to the family whose deaths she was now charged with avenging. It was not normal practice for a prosecutor to get personally involved with a case, but, for her, Jennifer, Danny, Emma and Sophie were no longer just names on the back of an A-form. They couldn't be. She felt an intimate, growing connection to each one of them, a connection that had frightened her as she walked through the halls of a slaughterhouse with John Latarrino, still decorated with last week's artwork and tomorrow's to-do lists, closing her chest and clutching at her throat – overwhelming emotions that she'd struggled to keep in close check ever since she was thirteen years old. It had triggered horrible, vivid memories that had then become bloody, familiar nightmares – nightmares that seemed to grow worse each night, worse than they'd been in years. When the terrors woke her before dawn, her body drenched in an icy sweat – that was when she would lay in the dark with her eyes wide open, seriously considering once again just backing off the case, of distancing herself far away from anything and anyone that could take her back to the night that she'd struggled for years, like Nora, to completely forget. Running away until a dumb ache was all that remained of her pain once again. But the closer it seemed she got – the more frightened she became – the more she was inexplicably drawn in. And as daylight broke through her blinds each morning, thoughts of backing away and trying to simply forget it all again faded along with the night sky.

'Mary, Mother of God,' said Nora, putting down the knife altogether and walking over to the sink. She put her hands across it and took a deep breath.

Julia nibbled on a lip and turned back to her uncle. 'Well, I'll be trying it with the Major Crimes prosecutor, Uncle Jimmy. His name's Rick Bellido. Maybe you could meet him sometime. I could have him over for Aunt Nora's sauce.'

'I don't like you around these people, Julia. These—' Her aunt's bitter voice trailed off. 'You shouldn't be around criminals. It's not good for you.'

'Criminals are not good for anyone, Aunt Nora. I'm not becoming one. I'm trying one.'

'Sounds like something serious,' said Uncle Jimmy, eyes still glued to the TV. After twenty-nine years of marriage, he knew enough to stay out of Nora's way. She'd get the job done herself. 'Is this a boyfriend?'

'I don't know, Uncle Jimmy. Maybe. I hope so. I'm working on it.'

'A boyfriend?' Nora asked, raising an eyebrow and her voice. Jimmy walked back into the living room.

'I said maybe.' Julia held her hands up defensively. 'We've gone out. That's all.' Rick had actually made good on his musings about missing her – and in a big way. While she wasn't yet clearing her calendar on Saturdays, she was officially booked for dinner tomorrow night at Prime 112, a hot spot on Miami Beach.

'I want to meet him,' Nora said quietly.

'We'll get to that,' she replied, finishing her wine with a gulp. 'Now let's eat, okay? This stuff smells amazing.' She picked up the salad bowl to move into the dining room and head off the rest of the conversation.

Aunt Nora grabbed her arm and held it fast. For such a little woman, she had quite the powerful grip. 'Listen to me, little one. Jimmy and I never wanted you doing these cases. Never. I'll admit that. I don't know why you can't be a lawyer in an office, with some nice people. Maybe make some money, find a good man. I worry about you. My God, do I worry. Every day. But you're a big girl and I suppose you can pick what you want to do for a living.' Her voice lowered to just above a whisper. 'But I don't want you on *this* case. I've read about it. It's too close, Julia. Too close. Please, I'm begging you to stay away. It can only bring . . .' she stumbled to find the right word. The word that could possibly describe a lifetime of tears and loneliness, nightmares and stolen memories. 'It can only bring *despair*.'

Julia bit her lip again and blinked back hot tears. She nodded and quickly turned her face away so that her aunt would not see her. Would not read her. Then she took the salad and walked into the dining room.

Aunt Nora had no idea how right she was.

28

When the red digits on the bedroom clock changed from 3:59 to 4:00, Julia finally gave up the fight and climbed out of bed. Lying there with her eyes closed was useless; sleep would not come again tonight. She padded into the dark living room, twisting her long hair up into a bun as she looked out the window. Her skin was clammy from the night sweats, and she wrapped her robe tightly around herself. Downstairs, her building's sprinklers had just turned on, lightly misting the lawn and the maze of deserted walkways that weaved in and around the sprawling apartment complex. The sky was black; the streets empty. She put a kettle of water on for tea in the kitchen and flopped down on the couch to wait for it to whistle. Everything in the apartment was dark and still. Back in bed, Moose was sound asleep, lost somewhere under the warm covers.

Julia hated waiting for morning to come, waiting for the world to finally wake up with her. It was the loneliest time of night. The first couple of years after she'd gone to live with her aunt and uncle were the worst. If she was lucky, she'd get three or four hours of sleep a night. Most early hours, though, were spent staring out her bedroom window at the empty street outside, like a bird in a cage, watching neighbors either stumble home drunk or leave for work that started long before the sun came up. Watching, night after night, as winter turned to spring, spring to summer, summer to fall, fall back into winter – as the world kept on turning and life speedily marched forward without once ever missing a beat. And every night she would wish she was any one of those neighbors, with a different life, full of different worries. Some nights, when the loneliness and pain proved too overwhelming, she'd sneak out and defiantly wander the unfamiliar streets of Staten Island or hop the ferry into Manhattan, hoping some would-be robber or rapist or killer would find her and do her the favor of ending what she herself could not. But nothing bad ever happened.

She stared at the black television screen, absently rubbing her socks to keep her feet warm. Her nightmares lingered with her now in the darkness, raising goosebumps on her cold skin. She squeezed her eyes shut, struggling to hold back the tears and the memories that continued to force their way out anyway, like a blistered, rupturing infection.

'Julia? Julia? Sweetie? You have to get up.'

She heard the words, but they were so far away. Too far away to be real. Julia buried her head in the pillow and reached out her hand to touch the person who had called her name, but she couldn't quite reach. The distance had grown between them by what felt like miles. She squinted, trying to see the face that was only a blur. It was when she felt the cold hands on her shoulders, gently shaking them, that she realized the voice was no dream.

'You have to get up now, Julia.'

She struggled to open her eyes, which felt like they had lead plates on them. It seemed like she'd just fallen asleep, maybe only a few minutes ago. The room was as cold as an icebox and she remembered the news said it might snow. Outside the window, a bright moon lit the stripped, bare branches of an elm, which was still sprinkled with a thin, crusty layer of last week's snowfall. What time was it? Tomorrow was Sunday, right? She didn't have to be home till ten. She blinked again and sat up, rubbing her eyes. She looked over at her best friend, Carly, who was already awake and sitting up in the other twin bed across the room, chewing on a strand of her brown hair. Carly stared at her, then looked away. She looked strange. Scared, maybe.

Mrs Hogan, Carly's mom, was the one shaking her shoulders. Standing over Julia in her nightgown and robe, she wore the same weird look on her face as her daughter. She clutched her pink velour robe by the bosom.

'What's the matter?' Julia asked. 'Is everything okay?'

Mrs Hogan hesitated for a moment and looked around the room while searching for the right words. 'There are detectives here, honey. Downstairs. Two of them. They want to speak with you.' She spoke quietly, her voice just above a hushed whisper, as though she feared waking up the rest of the house.

'Detectives?' Julia asked, reaching for the jeans and sweatshirt that Mrs Hogan held out in front of her. She shook her head, letting the word roll around her brain like a pinball. Waiting for it to hit a memory or something and light it up. Her heart started to race and a lump formed in her throat. She automatically felt guilty, even though she knew she hadn't done anything. She turned to her best friend again. Carly still had that awful look on her face, so Julia was the one who looked away this time. Her eyes trolled the bedroom while she pulled on her jeans. Carly had the coolest room. It was painted a freaky purple that was almost blue. Her mom had let her pick out the color and paint it herself. U2 posters hung on every wall and neon yellow and pink butterfly mobiles dangled from the ceiling. And her mom let her have a phone in her room, too. Julia had sometimes been just a little envious of Carly – of her cool room and her cool clothes and her cool mom – but never more so than at this very moment. Right now she just wanted to be Carly – the one who wasn't in trouble – and she really wanted everyone to stop looking at her in that strange, scared, pathetic way.

She pulled her sweatshirt on over her pajama top and slid her feet into her sneakers. 'What do they want?' she finally asked, tying her sneakers. 'I didn't do anything, Mrs H. I swear.'

Mrs Hogan suddenly began to cry. 'It's not you, Julia. It's nothing you've——' She stopped herself and reached over and hugged Julia tight. Then she wiped her cheeks with her hands and folded up the sleeping bag on the bed, tying it closed. She took a deep breath and handed the bag to her. 'Something has happened, honey. You have to go now. You have to go home.'

Julia opened her eyes with a sudden start and looked help-lessly around the dark, still living room, her heart beating fast.

In the kitchen, the kettle had begun to shriek.

29

Marisol Alfonso – the secretary with the unholy reputation – sat at her cubby in the Major Crimes secretarial pool, chatting away on the telephone, twisting the pigtail cord around white and pink striped fingernails that were so long they curved inward, like a hawk's talons. Rick was right – it wasn't too hard to pick his secretary out of a crowd. Especially this crowd. She was the only one in the lair dressed head-to-toe in varying shades of pink. Glossy fuchsia lips framed an oversized toothy grin; a rose-covered headband held back a jet-black wild mane of thick, coarse curls. She wore sparkling carnation-pink corduroys that someone must have poured her into, resulting in a love handle around her middle the size of a small life preserver. Her ultra-tight bubblegum-pink T-shirt, from which her considerable breasts were attempting to escape, was embroidered in glittering rhinestones.

Even though John Latarrino and Steve Brill's pre-files had been set for ten and it was already ten fifteen, Julia carefully made her way around the maze of cubicles and through the gaggle of suspicious secretaries over to Marisol's colorful little corner of the world with a smile glued to her face. Her impatiently tapping toes hidden from view, she waited for Marisol to finally notice her and get off the phone, acutely and awkwardly aware while she waited that, in a room full of women, the only sound she was hearing besides a phone ringing and the hum of an incoming fax, was the nasally, abrasive laughter of Rick's oblivious secretary.

It didn't take a soul-searching session with Dr Phil to figure out why Marisol Alfonso had a problem getting along with others. A thirty-second phone call had been enough for Julia. In their one and only conversation last week, Marisol had managed to make it perfectly clear – through a conveniently thick, and definitely annoyed-to-have-even-been-asked Cuban accent – that her days were far too busy to be doing work for some attorney who, A) wasn't in her division, B) wasn't even Major Crimes and who, C) already had her own damn secretary. And, true to her short, mispronounced words, she hadn't. Hadn't sent subpoenas, hadn't set pre-files, hadn't lifted one painted claw to do much of anything. And with thirteen-plus years on the government payroll, it was pretty obvious in those thirty seconds to an equally annoyed-to-have-been-practically-hung-up-on Julia that nobody was going to make her. Present company especially included.

Under normal circumstances, Julia Valenciano would never let so much as an ant walk all over her, but these were no ordinary times. Superman could fly naked over Madison Square Garden before she'd run to Rick to complain that his secretary was an obnoxious, lazy lump. Three years in the office was long enough to appreciate the politics of how things *really* worked around these-here parts: the pay might be dismal and the résumé credentials short, but secretaries wielded the power that counted in the office. They could easily make you, or worse – break you – in front of judges and colleagues and Division Chiefs. And lovers. That was something she definitely did not need.

'What can I do for choo, honey?' Marisol finally asked with a sigh, covering the receiver in her clawed hand. The toothy smile was gone.

'Good morning,' Julia began brightly. 'I'm so sorry to

interrupt. Marisol, right? We spoke on the phone. I'm Julia Valenciano with Judge Farley's division. I'm here for the pre-files with Rick Bellido. Is he in?'

Little yellow Post-it notes cluttered the fabric walls of Marisol's cubby like cheap wallpaper, as did thumb-tacked pictures of bare-chested, oily men. Ricky Martin sat poolside next to Antonio Banderas and a few other cut-outs from *People en Español* that Julia didn't recognize, mixed in with a few familiar courthouse faces that she did, but wished she hadn't – including an undercover City of Miami narcotics officer she'd once respected. And once dated. She swallowed her grimace.

It took a moment for the light to switch. 'Oh yeah, yeah,' Marisol said suspiciously. 'You here on the new case, right? Go 'head down. The detectives are 'ready here for a long while now.'

'I know, I'm running so late ... thanks,' Julia replied, walking quickly down the hall. Then she turned and, still smiling, called out, 'I love your T-shirt. It's so funky. And that color is great on you.'

Marisol looked down at herself as though even she couldn't believe what Julia had just said. 'Thanks,' she replied, a smile once again taking root as her face defrosted. 'Did it work on those subpoenas choo needed?' Before Julia could answer, she sighed and waved her free hand excitedly across her cluttered desk, speckled with orange Dorito crumbs. 'I wish I could have helped choo, honey, but they have me so busy here. It's crazy, you don't know. I mean, look at this!'

The statement simply invited a snappy retort, but it wouldn't come from Julia. 'Tell me about it. I figured you were busy. No big deal. I had my Victim Witness Coordinator and secretary help me and, so far, everyone's shown for their pre-files and everything's worked out.'

'Okay, well, maybe next time I won't be so busy. Maybe I can help choo then, choo know.'

The ice was melting. Julia could see spring just up ahead. 'Great! That would be great!'

'I like your hair,' Marisol said, making a curling motion with her claw.

'Thanks! The humidity kills it, though,' Julia said, sighing herself. 'Frizz was always my nickname. I better get down there. It was nice finally meeting you! We'll talk soon!' She waved cheerily behind her before rounding the corner and finally disappearing down Rick's hall. The exchange was like swallowing Mylanta without a chaser. It might be good for you in the end, but it sure as hell tasted awful on the way down.

Damn, damn, damn. She hadn't meant to be late again. She tapped lightly on the door and someone called out, 'Come in.' She slowly opened the door. John Latarrino and Steve Brill sat in front of Rick's desk, a box of files at their feet. Rick was on the phone, his back to them. The tension in the room hit her like a stiff breeze and she hoped it didn't have anything to do with her.

'Hey there,' she said hesitantly. 'Did I miss a lot?'

'Nah,' said Lat, rising. 'We're waiting on your boy to get off the phone, anyway,' he said, coming around from behind the chair and motioning for her to take his seat. 'Sit, please, Julia. I like to stand.' He kicked the boxes at Brill's feet. 'Look. We brought you a big present.'

'I thought your name was Julie,' said Brill, scratching his head, as if trying to remember something.

Lat slapped the back of Brill's head. 'Smooth. And so chivalrous. Lazy bastard. He gets more obnoxious the longer you know him, Julia, but he does kind of grow on you after a while. Like mold.'

'What? I've got a corn,' Brill said, lifting his foot and waving it in Lat's direction. 'I can't stand.'

'How was Philadelphia?' Julia asked. 'How's the family doing?'

'We were just telling Bellido. Apparently our defendant had a wandering eye,'

'For his wife's baby sister,' Brill finished with a laugh.

'And there's more. The semen on Jennifer's shirt isn't our guy's,' said Lat, leaning up against one of Rick's bookcases.

'Huh?' she asked, stunned. 'Whose is it?'

'That's the question of the day,' Lat said, tapping his pen absently against the spine of *Practical Investigation of Sex Crimes: A Strategic and Operational Approach.* 'We ran the swab again, just to be sure. We've been trying to find the lawn boy our desperate housewife might have taken up with, but so far no one's come forward to claim ownership. While Jennifer didn't have too many friends here, the girlfriends that she did keep play dates with all say there was no one else. At least not that they knew of. They thought everything seemed just dandy in the bedroom department at home. She was talking about having a fourth. Of course, none of them had actually met the husband of the year.'

Julia hadn't seen John Latarrino since the day he'd shown up in Farley's courtroom with the news that David Marquette was hitching a ride out of town. His dark-blond hair was a little bit longer and a little bit blonder than she remembered it, and the rough, three-day stubble gone from his face. He wore Nikes with jeans, and a silk black mock-turtleneck sweater that definitely wasn't tight, but didn't need to be. It was obvious he had a nice body. Out of habit, she glanced down and wondered why there was no ring on his finger. 'Was it a rape, then?' she asked. 'Were we wrong about him?'

'There was no other evidence of rape trauma. They did the kit. The semen could have been days, weeks, even months old for all we know,' Lat said.

'Months?' she asked skeptically.

'Think Monica Lewinsky, Jules,' said Brill.

She made a face, at both the thought and the nickname.

'The point is, there's still no evidence to support a burglary gone bad, if that's what you're thinking,' Lat continued, remembering Julia's persistent questions at the Marquette house. 'We have some more interviews to go back and finish up, but everything still points to Marquette, including the two-million-dollar insurance policy we found, the alarm, the lack of forced entry, his own kid screaming Daddy's name at the nine-eleven operator, and the knife in his gut with his prints all over it. At least the patterns matched on that. That's our weapon.'

'And that's enough for an indictment,' Rick added, spinning his chair around. 'Unfortunately it might mean our victim comes to the table with a few issues, which may or may not be relevant at trial. Even if she did have an affair, it doesn't make her a bad person,' he chuckled. 'Hey there, Julia,' he said acknowledging her from across the room with an intimate smile. A smile that she hoped didn't let everyone else know that he thought she was good in bed last night.

She felt her cheeks betray her thoughts and she quickly looked down at the box on the floor. 'I got stuck in court,' she began.

'I figured,' replied Rick. 'That judge of yours. Do the boys here know who's got our case?'

'Who?' asked Lat skeptically, looking at both of them.

'Len Farley,' Julia replied, with more than a hint of resignation.

'No shit,' said Brill with a laugh. 'Well doesn't this just

get better and better? First we get you, Bellido, and now we have that old fart. I wonder who's going to win the wrestling match for the cameras?'

Lat was liking Brill more and more.

'Funny,' said Rick. 'Alright, Julia, you missed me swearing at them. So let's finish this up and get this thing ready for the Grand Jury. We still have some work to do.'

'Any idea what the defense is gonna be?' asked Lat as he reached in the box for his accordion file.

'Even if he could knock around a manslaughter or self-defense with the wife, he can't run from the kids. My bet's on the one-armed man who reset the house alarm right before he ran past the cops pulling in the driveway.'

'And when Mel Levenson finds out about that semen stain, it's gonna play right into his defense. A one-armed man with no staying power,' cracked Brill with another chuckle.

'Maybe he's posturing for a plea. You know, Mel's been around a long while. He's not shy about trying out a new defense when one of his scumbag clients boxes him into a corner. Any attorney worth his weight will tell you it's better to come out the door with both fists swinging – you're a hundred times more likely to hit something than the guy that doesn't do shit to defend himself. It only takes one juror to fuck up a verdict', finished Rick cautiously. 'So just what defense Levenson's going to try and mount remains the question of the day. The trick is to try and see the punch before he throws it.'

30

On Wednesday, 2nd November, at three thirty in the afternoon, the Grand Jury returned an indictment charging Dr David Alain Marquette with four counts of first-degree murder. The thirteen men and eight women who comprised the jury had deliberated a little under twenty minutes. Although the concurrence of only twelve was needed to indict, Martin Yars reported to Rick that he had it on good authority the vote was unanimous. By law, the substance of Grand Jury deliberations – including the actual vote – was supposed to be kept secret.

Marquette's arraignment was the following morning at nine before Judge Farley and the courthouse was definitely jumping. On three, Judge Flowers was trying a thirteen-year-old aspiring serial killer for slitting the throat of his best buddy in their middle-school bathroom. On five, Judge Macias was sentencing a nineteen-year-old to life in prison for the shotgun murder of a drug dealer and his hard-nosed mother. At eleven o'clock in 6–10, Judge Houchens would be hearing a motion to suppress the statements of a father accused of molesting his five-year-old twin daughters and giving them gonorrhea while on a church camping trip. Arson in 2–6 before Judge Johnson. Home invasion in 2–10, cocaine trafficking, 5–7. Pick a courtroom – any courtroom – and you'd be sure to be horrified. But as Julia hurried across the street, dodging raindrops and puddles the size of small lakes along the way, she knew it was *State vs. Marquette* that was drawing the crowd. There was a pile-up of local news trucks in front of the courthouse, their monstrous satellite antennas towering forty, fifty feet into the downpour.

It was funny, she thought, as she ran past them in her now-ruined new suede heels, you never knew what would make a headline. Like a sleeper-of-the-year at the box office, or a best-selling novel from an unknown writer, you just could never predict what would strike the public's nerve and what wouldn't. Some cases made a lot of noise in the beginning, but faded to barely a mention in the local section as the case made its way through the process and interest inexplicably petered out. Others never hit the paper at all. The aberrant exceptions – the Lyle and Erik Menendezes, Scott Petersons, O. J. Simpsons, Michael Jacksons, Bill Bantlings – those were the defendants who grasped and held the ultra-elusive *national* attention. Those were the big-name cases that made and ruined careers and fixated an entire country of workaholics in front of their TVs in the middle of busy afternoons just to watch a verdict be delivered.

Fortunately, that kind of intense media scrutiny wasn't the case here. At least, not yet. But while David Marquette might not be making the headline desk over at *Good Morning America* or CNN, there was no denying he'd attracted and kept the fickle attention of the local desensitized press here in Miami. And that was intimidating enough for Julia. She spotted the jumble of cameras and the familiar faces she usually watched report the eleven o'clock news as soon as she stepped off the escalator, all gathered in front of the grand mahogany doors of 4–10. Corrections had set up shop with another search table, metal detector and an extra set of plastic stanchions. A decent crowd of curious onlookers lingered to watch what was not going on, thickening the already-congested morning hallway.

She took a deep breath as butterflies began to flutter furiously about in the pit of her stomach. She'd never been a newsmonger, or had a lifelong desire to 'be on TV', but seeing the cameras and knowing that they were here on *her* case made her more than just a little anxious. It was a few minutes to nine, and Rick was either inside already, or, as was more likely the case, still across the street sipping coffee in his office and flipping through the paper. He hated sitting around any courtroom waiting for court to start, so Julia knew she was probably the first to be making an appearance for Team State. She worried about doing or saying the wrong thing in front of all the cameras and familiar-faced reporters who were sure to ask for her thoughts and comments.

She needn't have worried. She walked right past everyone and into the courtroom without anybody even asking her for the time of day. Inside, a jabbering, excited crowd of correction officers, attorneys, cops, defendants and witnesses filled the courtroom. Most were there for cases other than *State vs. Marquette*, but Julia suspected the tripod-mounted cameras in both corners of the room had definitely added to both the crowd and the excitement. Farley had no problem with the limelight and being in it every night on the evening news. In fact, he was probably backstage right now, chomping at the bit to come out and ruin someone's day in front of a TV audience.

She looked over at the jury box as she made her way up the aisle and into the gallery, but the in-custody defendants had not yet been brought over and the box was empty. She settled into a seat against the wall on the State's side. Karyn was chatting with an ECU prosecutor by the podium, and Julia flashed her a smile, but all she got back was a cool, indifferent nod. It was hard not to take it personally; things had definitely been strained between them since the First

Appearance. Thankfully, the strange, potentially contagious aloofness that Rick had warned her to watch out for had not spread to anyone else in the office yet. Of course, it was only the arraignment, and her involvement on the case certainly hadn't been announced to the world.

She glanced over at the still-empty jury box. Although she'd seen his face in photos and on the First Appearance tape, in just a few moments she would finally get to see Dr David Marquette in person. She'd never been as curious, as excited, as angry, or as scared to meet one of her defendants before. A million strange emotions charged the adrenaline that pulsed through her veins.

Julia had seen killers before – chained and shackled and only steps away in a jury box or behind a defense table. In Miami courtrooms, they were not that uncommon a sight. But even though she'd met more than her fair share of bad people on this earth, she still needed to look whenever a murderer was brought into the room or stepped up to the podium as the prosecutor called out priors. Look and see the person who'd taken someone else's lifeblood with the pull of a trigger or the quick jab of a knife. Look and see if there was anyone there, if there was anything left that was human in his eyes. She always expected those defendants – the murderers – to look remarkably different somehow, to sound different, to bear a sign or a disfiguring stain or a mark – something, anything that one could immediately recognize as that of a killer. Of one who was *capable* of committing murder. But more often than not, it was frightening how completely normal a killer could look . . .

Outside in the hallway, the press must've pounced on prey. Everyone turned to look as the doors swung open and Dr Alain Marquette and his wife both hurried in, closely tailed by Mel Levenson and Stan Grossbach. Insistent reporters, held back at the door by Corrections, continued to shout out questions that were not being answered. Dr Marquette kept his arm protectively around his wife's shoulders as he ushered her to the front row of seats. But even with her head hung low, it was hard to hide the yellowing bruises under her puffy, red-rimmed eyes and the white bandage across her nose – long-lasting souvenirs, presumably, from her fall outside Ryder. Julia watched them for a long moment. Nina Marquette was a large, statuesque woman, elegantly styled, with strong features and squared shoulders. Julia suspected she dominated a room on most occasions. But not today. Today she looked frightened and overwhelmed, small for her size. She looked like a woman who had been crying for days, maybe even weeks, on end.

How did it feel to be the parents of a killer? How did it feel to have created a human being so reviled, so loathed – a person who would grow up to murder his own children in cold blood? She wondered if the Marquettes felt any sense of responsibility for the sins of their son. Were there warning signs that they chose to ignore over the years? Was there anything that they could have done that might have made a difference? She supposed it must be doubly hard for them – they'd violently lost their daughter-in-law and grandchildren. They had them to mourn, too, although she knew that friends and family closest to Jennifer had discouraged their presence at the funerals. Now they stood to lose their son – not to a prison cell where they could maybe visit once a week, but to a needle that would stop his heart and kill him, too. And they would not be allowed to mourn him when he passed, either. They were just supposed to watch quietly with the rest of the witnesses when the warden pulled the black curtain back and the crowd outside the prison gates began to cheer.

The door to the jury room suddenly opened, pulling her out of her troubling thoughts. A human chain of defendants shuffled into the courtroom, chains rattling and mouths running as Corrections barked instructions. Fresh from the farm across the street, most looked mean and tough and larger than life somehow – no matter the physical stature – with their tattoos and piercings and gangsta attitudes. All except one. Towing the back of the line, and separated from the others by a few chain lengths, was a slight man in physical comparison, wearing a red jumpsuit, looking down, his face hidden from view. An electric murmur ran through the spectators as they asked each other, 'Is that him? Is that the doctor?'

Without any warning, the door to the judge's hall opened and Jefferson, the bailiff, stepped out. Before he could even open his mouth, the courtroom rose to its feet as a sour-faced Judge Farley rushed from behind him to the bench.

'All rise! No beepers, no cellphones! No children, no talking! Court is now in session,' Jefferson hesitantly shouted. 'The Honorable Judge Leonard Farley presiding. Be seated and be quiet!' Jefferson was relatively new to his job. He looked back at the judge for a nod of approval, but Farley was giving out none of that today.

The courtroom quickly settled into quiet as the judge stirred his coffee and surveyed his kingdom, seemingly oblivious to the cameras and the crowd presence. Even the defendants in the box shut up, as the judge's reputation for not taking shit stretched across the street and upstate, as well. Julia saw John Latarrino and Steve Brill slip in the back of the courtroom and move to a spot up against the wall, next to Dayanara, who'd popped in for support and to get a look at 'the sonofabitch' herself. Lat smiled and gave a short wave. She smiled back. Allies, finally.

'Alright,' Farley began after a moment, studying the long line of attorneys that already snaked behind the podiums. 'It looks like we've got a full house today. Let's get this party started. Who's first, Ivonne?'

Julia prayed that Rick would walk fast as Ivonne called calendar and the parade of defense attorneys slowly worked their way up to the podium. Farley hated passing cases for attorneys who weren't present, and she definitely didn't want to be the first one to face his wrath this morning. Just as the room began to get really hot and Stan Grossbach moved into the number-three position, the muffled shouts of the press started up in the halls once again. The courtroom door opened, the crowd hushed momentarily, and Rick strode in, well-dressed and ready to save the day.

'Mr Bellido,' Farley said, raising a lip – the closest Julia had ever seen to a smile. 'Let me guess. You're here on—'

'The State versus David Marquette. Page nine. Good morning, Your Honor,' Rick answered back smoothly as he made his way up the aisle. 'Ricardo Bellido for the State,' he said to the court reporter with just a hint of a Spanish accent that Julia had not heard before. Somehow he'd gotten to the head of the line and no one had complained.

'I heard this was coming my way,' said the judge, waving off the defense attorney at the podium, whose mouth was still open and in mid-sentence. Mel lumbered his way up and bumped the fly-catcher back into line.

'Good morning, Judge,' Mel said gruffly. He flashed a familiar smile at the judge as Stan headed over to the jury box. 'Mel Levenson and Stan Grossbach for the defendant, Dr David Marquette. I've already filed my appearance.'

'Good to see you, Mel. I heard your office was handling

this,' Farley said. 'Looks like we've got quite a crowd.' In between careers as a prosecutor and then a defense attorney, Mel Levenson used to be a Circuit Court judge. In fact, he'd had the courtroom down the hall from Farley. That was a number of years ago, but the Good Ol' Boys Club offered lifetime memberships. The judge leaned back in his seat and raised his lip once again. 'I'll tell you, gentlemen, this is going to be some match-up. Tyson versus Holyfield. Alright, let's get this party started.'

'Page nine, State vs. David Alain Marquette, felony case number F05-43254,' said Ivonne. 'Today is the twenty-first day, Your Honor.'

'Is the defendant present?' asked the judge, looking at the box.

'He is,' said Mel. 'As are his parents, Your Honor.'

Farley didn't bother acknowledging them.

Julia craned her neck, but Marquette's face was still obscured. Someone began sniffling loudly. It was Marquette's mother.

'Please stop that,' said the judge, annoyed.

'As I think you know, the Grand Jury has indicted the defendant on four counts of first-degree murder. The indictment should be in the court file,' said Rick, looking around the courtroom. His eyes caught Julia's and he discreetly motioned with a nod of his head for her to come up beside him.

'I have a copy of the indictment. We wave formal reading, enter a plea of not guilty and demand discovery,' responded Mel.

'Fifteen days,' said the judge, taking a slug of his coffee. 'Ivonne, what's my calendar looking like?'

Julia took a breath and walked across the gallery to the podium as Ivonne began to toss out dates. She felt Karyn and the other prosecutors watching her, some probably wondering what she was doing up there. Others, as Rick had warned, perhaps jealous that she was.

Across the room, David Marquette finally looked up.

Julia sucked in a breath. She wasn't sure exactly what she'd expected to see, but it definitely wasn't what she saw. The young, handsome doctor with the soft face and easygoing, trusting smile that she'd seen in the hallway pictures was gone. His light skin was sallow and pale under the courtroom's harsh lights; shadows made his well-defined cheekbones appear drawn and sunken, and either Corrections had purposely sized his jumpsuit wrong – which they were known to do on occasion with child molesters and other particularly repugnant inmates – or David Marquette had lost a lot of weight since he'd moved in. His tousled blond hair was now stringy and long, his face a matted carpet of blond/gray stubble. He clenched the jury-box railing so hard that Julia could see the raised vein lines in his chained hand. His strange, light-gray eyes stared out at nothing, vacant and lifeless, like that of a mannequin in a department-store window – watching everything but seeing nothing.

Stan stood next to the box, whispering in his ear, most likely explaining the proceedings and the charges in the indictment. But whatever Stan was saying – whatever it was his client was hearing – the words were having no effect. When Farley began to recite some of the more grisly facts from the indictment after Mel requested a bond, the man didn't even blink. A strange wave of goosebumps erupted across Julia's skin, leaving her cold and clammy, and she finally had to look away. The whole strange scene reminded her of some nineteenth-century traveling circus that'd come to town and had finally unveiled the show's main attraction – the hideous Human Monster, a freak chained and shackled to his stage. The terrified, fascinated audience gaped in fear and disgust at the very sight of him.

'Look,' Judge Farley said with a shake of his head, holding his hand up to silence Mel, 'I'm not giving him a bond. If you want an Arthur Hearing, take your arguments to Judge Solly. That's what she does and that's all she does. If she wants to give you a bond, I guess I won't have a problem with it. Although,' he finished, looking over at Rick with a smirk and a smug look in his eyes, 'I'm pretty confident Mr Bellido will.' The judge finally noticed Julia at his side. Maybe she was being paranoid, but she swore his bushy brow furrowed slightly.

'Correct, Judge,' Rick replied coolly. He reached across the aisle divide and, with a snap, handed a piece of paper to Mel. 'Especially since the State intends to seek the death penalty in this matter. I've already filed my written notice with the court.'

'I've got it right here,' said Farley.

'Naturally, we will be strenuously objecting to any release,' said Rick.

Another electric murmur buzzed the crowd. One of the defendants in the box started to cackle and another let out what sounded like a 'Whoo-Whee!' The judge shot them all a testy look. 'I think your client might need to find someone to take care of both his patients and his houseplants for a while longer, Mr Levenson,' he said when the courtroom had settled down. 'Alright, let's set a trial date. Give me something quick, Ivonne. I don't want to die before I get a chance to try this thing.'

'February ninth for report. February thirteenth for trial,' replied Ivonne.

'Whose week is that?' asked Farley.

'That's a B week.'

'Fine. February ninth for report—'

Julia looked at Rick. She was still a bit shocked over seeing Marquette and then there was the death-penalty announcement, which had just come as official news to her. 'Julia Valenciano for the State,' she interrupted, moving into the podium and clearing her throat. 'Judge, excuse me, but that's my week. I'd like to request you set Marquette down in an alternate week.'

Farley frowned. 'Ms Valenciano, this decision doesn't concern you. Step back.'

Obviously the judge had not yet heard the news. How ironic was it, she thought as she nibbled on the wall of her cheek, that of the twenty criminal Circuit Court judges in Miami that were assigned to handle the county's forty thousand felony arrests each year, it was the Honorable Judge Leonard Farley who the computers had randomly spit out to hear this one. In a case that could catapult her career into another stratosphere, she'd beaten Las Vegas odds to get the one judge hell-bent on destroying it.

'Ms Valenciano will be second-chairing this with me, Your Honor,' Rick coolly cut in. 'I think we'll need a date that can accommodate her trial schedule as well.'

The judge said nothing for a long moment while the courtroom sat in silence. Julia felt like she was naked in a room full of leering voyeurs. 'Okay, Ivonne. Give me another date,' he finally said. 'One in an A week, please.'

'February sixteenth for report. February twenty-first for trial. That's the Tuesday after President's Day.'

'The sixteenth it is, people. I'll see you all then,' said Farley. 'Motions in thirty. And no delays.' He peered menacingly over his glasses. 'As I'm sure Ms Valenciano here can tell all of you, I've got a very busy docket.'

32

'Wow. You're famous now. Can I touch you?' Dayanara asked with a laugh as she and Julia slipped into a booth in a Miami Subs a few blocks removed from the chaos that probably still lingered around the courthouse. 'Even though you're skinny, don't forget the camera adds ten pounds.'

'Very funny. Notice who Farley kept addressing in that courtroom, who it was the press wanted to interview. It wasn't me, Day. Fame doesn't become me.'

'Give it a little time.'

Julia made a face as Day rummaged through the abyss of her enormous purse. She dug out a box of Table Toppers – disposable kiddie placemats – stuck one to the table, and then neatly spread out her soda, burger and French fries, carefully covering all images of a smiling Dora the Explorer. 'I wish they'd make these without the damn characters,' she mumbled, sounding annoyed. 'Speaking of people not wanting you to have fame, I saw your DC shooting optical death daggers your way as you ambled up to the podium. Bitch. I never liked her. What's up with that?'

Julia smiled and sipped at her iced tea. 'Your guess is as good as mine. She's none too happy I'm trying this, that's for sure. She's blaming her anger on the fact that I'm about three months behind on my dispos.'

'Try more like six. I've seen your office floor. Or rather, I should say, I haven't seen your office floor.'

'Dispos are the least of my worries now.'

'True,' Day said as she wiped an alcohol pad over the disposable fork she'd just ripped out of a sealed plastic baggie. 'As a fellow self-professed workaholic, I have to say I'm beginning to worry about you, though. All you're doing, all the time, is this case, girlfriend. I'd almost forgotten what you looked like, it's been so long since we lunched. At least now I can turn on my TV at night and remind myself, should I forget again.' Through a bite of her burger that she held in hands wrapped up like a prizefighter in napkins, she asked, 'Doesn't that boyfriend of yours actually *do* anything besides stand up and take all the credit?'

The press had pounced once again after court and Rick had held another impromptu press conference, this one downstairs in the lobby. For maybe a moment or two this morning – when Julia had first stepped out beside him into a crowd of cameras that no longer dismissed her – the attention was exciting. She thought about Uncle Jimmy and Aunt Nora mixing Bloody Marys poolside, proudly pointing their celery sticks at Jimmy's portable Sony Watchman while their neighbors asked them to turn up the volume. But the initial excitement quickly faded, replaced by an uncomfortable, guilty sort of feeling that told her the limelight was just not for her. At least, not on this case. As the questions started up, she quickly fell away from the crowd that followed Rick around like he was the Pied Piper, ducking into a staircase off the judge's back hallway. Lat and Brill apparently had the same idea; she saw them drive off a few minutes later as she made her way back to the Graham Building.

'He's not my boyfriend,' Julia said. 'At least, I don't think he is, and that's the price of being second seat on a murder, I guess. I get all the pre-files and the legwork. It's fine. I learned a lot.'

'Nice speech. Tell me, is Lover gonna let you actually *do* anything at trial? Like speak?'

The thing about Day that Julia both admired and feared was that she always, *always* said what she thought – even if you didn't like it, and even if she knew you weren't gonna like it when she said it. You got what you saw with Dayanara. And like a lot of pit prosecutors – resentful, perhaps, of his revered reputation and much larger paycheck, and maybe put off by what they saw as arrogance and pomposity – Day didn't like Rick Bellido. Tall tales of skirt chasing – around the office, courthouse and PD water coolers – didn't help either. Then there was the rumor that he'd picked out the trial outfits of a senior Division Chief who he'd once tapped to try a Major Crimes murder with him – right down to the shade of her lipstick and the height of her heels. 'If you let him so much as suggest the color earrings for you, Julia, I'll hurt you. So help me,' Day finished, menacingly shaking a forked fry at her, 'you'll go naked into that courtroom when my scissors find you.'

'Down, Fido. That's not ever gonna happen. I can assure you that dressing me has not come up. Undressing me, maybe . . .' she laughed.

Day held up her hands. 'TMI. Too much information. Yeuch.'

'Listen, I don't know what he'll let me do at trial,' Julia continued, 'but as the speech is *supposed* to go, "I'm just grateful for the opportunity to be here." And stop calling him Lover; you're gonna slip. No one knows anything about that. Please. I was desperate to talk and you were sworn to secrecy.'

'Trust me, he'd be flattered to be known as your lover, honey. You make stunning arm candy. Men who nab young, beautiful girlfriends when they're in the middle of a mid-life like to show them off. And while I hate to burst your bubble, don't think that conclusion hasn't already been drawn in everybody else's mind after today.'

'Maybe,' Julia said, thoughtfully crunching on an onion ring. 'But I'm certainly not going to confirm it. I want my reputation made on this case and that's it. So make that young, beautiful and *smart* arm candy.'

'I hate to break it to you, honey, but I didn't include smart in the definition for a reason. Not because you aren't, but because intelligence is not required for the job and is generally discouraged.'

'Thanks,' Julia said, raising an eyebrow.

'You're welcome. And that onion's gonna give you bad breath. You never eat that stuff once you finally get yourself a man. Didn't your momma ever tell you that?' This time she pulled floss and a small bottle of Listerine out of her purse and pushed them across the table. 'Thank me when the kids are born.'

'You're too much.'

'Speaking of bearing children for someone, your detective's hot. Not the lawn patch. The rebel. And he's Italian. My favorite food. Yum.'

Julia frowned and crunched another onion ring. 'I'll be sure to mention that to him.'

'Please do. And don't forget to credit the author.' There was a slight pause before Day asked, 'How does it feel to be on a death case? Are you okay with it? Pretty heavy shit.'

'No. Yes. I'm not sure,' Julia replied softly as the conversation subtly changed direction. 'I didn't know that was coming today, Day, so I can't answer that question right now.' She kept expecting things to be either black or white in the courtroom, like they'd always been. For her feelings to be as sure and as unwavering as they'd once seemed to be . . .

Your client scores to twenty months state prison; take the plea or go to trial – that's your choice.

This is the law, right here in the statute, and this is what the law means, right here in the case. I didn't write it and I didn't interpret it, but you broke it and now here's the penalty – conveniently spelled out for you, right here in the sentencing guidelines.

Now the lines seemed to be dulling, the sharp colors that demarked the all-important boundaries of order were fading, and all she could see today was gray – a defense attorney's favorite color – and it was making her uneasy.

'As probably the only registered Democrat in this county,' Day said, 'I can tell you that I'm not a proponent of the death penalty. But your defendant, Julia, is a damn freak. Gives me the creeps just looking at him, the way he looked in court today. He's got nothing – no emotion whatsoever. And those eyes of his – they're like what you'd see on a horror-movie poster hanging outside the theater. Dead eyes. When the judge started talking about the things he did to those kids . . .' she said with a shudder as she finished off the last bite of burger. 'Well, you're not gonna have any problem finding twelve people to vote for the needle. So be prepared, is all I'm saying.'

Julia nibbled on her straw but said nothing. A Channel Ten news truck pulled into the crowded parking lot. She recognized one of the three faces that stepped out as a reporter from court and she turned her head away from the window. 'Time to go,' she said to Day.

'Better prepare yourself for that, too,' Dayanara said, slipping on her sunglasses and nodding in the direction of the trio as they came in and joined the long line at the counter. 'I have a feeling you just might make the big time after all with this one. Forget Lover – you may need to hire a stylist to dress you.'

'I'll take that under advisement,' Julia whispered, her head bowed, as the two of them ducked out the back door of the restaurant.

33

Charley Rifkin opened one of the gray double doors that led into the fourth-floor private office of the State Attorney and stuck his head in. 'I've got Rick Bellido with me,' he said.

Jerry Tigler sat behind an enormous cherry desk, his slight body swallowed up in an oversized leather executive chair that was turned facing the row of windows and the skyline of Miami. Sheets of rain whipped against the glass, then ran down in jagged streaks, making the windows appear shattered from a distance. 'Good, good,' he answered absently, although he didn't turn around. 'Bring him in, Charley.'

Rick straightened his tie and followed Rifkin into the State Attorney's office, as he had a thousand times or more in his long career as a prosecutor. But instinctively, he knew this time was different.

The Graham Building had been built only twelve years ago, but it would be at least another decade before the SAO would see one more penny from the state legislature for renovations. The room looked and felt tired: the mauve carpet was worn thin in a few spots; the gray walls scuffed and beaten from too many run-ins with office furniture.

'Take a seat, Rick,' said Rifkin, as he settled himself in one of the two leather chairs in front of the desk.

A few moments passed in polite silence. Finally, Tigler spun the chair around, leaned across the desk and shook Rick's hand. He was smiling, but definitely distracted. 'Rick, good to see you, son. How'd it go this morning?'

'Good. You know we have Farley?'

Tigler shrugged his small shoulders and settled back into his chair. 'I heard. And yet you still said it's going good. That's encouraging.'

'The case is pretty open and shut. I don't think even Len Farley can screw it up,' Rick replied with a laugh.

'We need to get that disaster off the bench somehow,' Tigler said, scratching at the back of his head. 'I'm working on Putnam to put him over in civil where at least he can't hurt anybody. Let the big boys over there try to oust him — hell, they got more clout and more money and a lot less patience than me. But, you know, there's not much Gene Putnam's gonna do. Lenny's blood.'

'Which means Len Farley isn't going anywhere Len Farley doesn't want to go,' Rifkin finished with a resigned nod. 'I was in court watching this morning, Jerry. Even with a cantankerous judge doing his best to muddy waters, your boy here did a great job. You think Mel's gonna try and plead him, Ricky?'

'I'm sure. What Mel's going to try is to get his client a life sentence. But I don't want a plea, Charley. The man killed his whole family. There's a price to pay, and I'm going to make sure he pays it.'

Rifkin let out a low whistle. 'A dog with a bone.'

'Send the message. Loud and clear to the masses. They'll listen.'

'You announced today?' the State Attorney asked.

'There was no sense in waiting, Jerry,' Rick explained. 'The Grand Jury took twenty minutes to come back with an indictment. Martin was offering them tissues on their way out of the courthouse. The facts on this are so outrageous, the murders of the children cold-blooded and premeditated. I've definitely got the aggravators. If anyone deserves the death penalty, it's gonna be this guy. I have no problems with it.'

Tigler paused for a moment. 'I got a call from the French embassy this morning.'

Rick shifted in his seat just slightly. 'The French embassy? What the hell?'

'David Marquette's a French citizen,' Tigler said quietly.

Charley Rifkin shook his head, like he'd just remembered something. 'Oh, shit.'

Rick felt his throat dry up. It was an unfamiliar feeling. 'What?'

'His parents – they're French citizens, and he has dual citizenship. Somebody called the embassy and raised a stink. Apparently there's international protocol to be followed by the police when a foreign national is arrested. The Vienna Convention on Consular Relations says that the consulate of the foreigner's country must be notified within twenty-four hours after the arrest and allowed access to the individual. That wasn't done here. Of course our doctor is actually a *dual* citizen, so the argument's going to be that he should be treated like every other American and the convention's not applicable in this instance.'

Rick shook his head. 'No one knew he was a French citizen, Jerry. He certainly didn't announce it.' He slapped his hands hard on his thighs. 'Damn it. Alright, what's the penalty?'

'That's a gray area,' Tigler returned slowly. 'A pissed-off country's a sure bet. The courts are apparently split. Some defendants have sought release as a remedy, dismissal of the charges – even executive clemency. Some courts have said that short of an apology and a heartfelt promise by the United States to try and do better with the next foreign criminal, there's not much else that has to be done, because the treaty does not confer any rights on the individual arrested, rather it's just a nation-to-nation protocol – a guideline, so to speak – on how foreign nationals should be treated if arrested abroad. But, I'm not gonna kid you boys; it's a testy situation right now. Real testy. The International Court of Justice in The Hague – the World Court for the United Nations – ordered the US last April to review and reconsider the convictions of some fifty-one Mexican citizens sitting on death row in American prisons in response to a complaint by Mexico that their consulate wasn't notified of the nationals' arrests as the treaty requires. So now that you announced today that we're seeking the death penalty on yet another foreign citizen, I'm sure it will be a *really* pissed-off country, especially since France, like the rest of the European Union, does not have, and does not support, capital punishment. I'm sitting here waiting for the phone to ring again and someone with a French accent to start screaming at me.'

Rick wanted to strangle John Latarrino right now, even though Lat probably had no way of knowing Marquette was a dual citizen. There was no computer system that popped out that kind of info on US citizens as a matter of course, at least not on a local level. But he abhorred looking unprepared – ever. And given his rocky past with the detective – who was still sore over a filing decision he'd made a couple of years back – it was a distinct possibility Lat might try and make him look like a fool. Or if not try, then sit back and just let it happen without intervening. But he resisted the urge to pass the blame. 'I'll look into it and speak to the consulate. If they're entitled to access, then I'll see to it that they get it, Jerry.'

'Good,' the State Attorney replied. Another sudden and furious downpour blew sheets of rain against the windows.

Outside, the skyline disappeared completely. 'Can you believe this damn weather?' he said, turning back to the window. 'I feel like I've been looking at rain for a month. We've had, what? Eight hurricanes in the past two years? Jesus, where the hell is the sun in the sunshine state?'

'I think even *my* tan's fading,' Rick said, looking down at his hand with a laugh.

'Now I know we're in trouble,' Tigler chuckled back.

'I'll tell you what's in trouble, boys. My golf swing,' Rifkin piped in.

'You'll get time enough to work on that drive, cowboy. How much longer do you have now?' asked Tigler.

'Let's see. One year, six months and twenty-two days,' replied Rifkin with a wistful sigh. He was already in DROP – the State's Deferred Retirement Option Program. The five-year countdown to monthly pension checks had already begun. 'But who the hell's counting, right? How about you, Jer? What are we doing here? You joining me on that course anytime soon, or are you staying in the game?'

Jerry Tigler sighed. His red, plump face had deflated, as if the last of the laughter had been squeezed out of the tube. Tired lines sliced across his forehead, pulling at his mouth and crinkling his blue eyes. He looked every minute of his sixty-seven years right then. And a few more for good measure. 'I'm done, Charley,' he said, shaking his head slowly. 'Thirty is enough.'

'No. It's a damn legacy,' insisted Rifkin.

'I don't know about that.'

'You're gonna be missed, Jerry,' Rick joined in.

'I don't know about that either. What I do know is that I'm not up to another campaign. The last one kicked my old, tired ass.' Tigler looked at Rick. 'Which brings us to you, young fellow. You've done exemplary work here in this office. You know that. You're one of my closest confidants. And while I've offered this opportunity to my good friend and golf partner, over here, he doesn't seem to want to put the target on his back at this stage in life.'

Rifkin waved a dismissive hand in front of him. 'My biggest challenge in a year and a half is gonna be to break a seventy-seven. I don't need to be managing any more headaches. My wife already gives me enough of those,' he chuckled. 'Thanks again, Jerry, but I'm still gonna pass.'

'I don't want to see this office go to the wrong party, Rick,' Tigler began, smoothing his hair back, subtly checking it to make sure his hairpiece was still in the right place. 'I want to pass the reins while I still have enough clout with the Governor to pass them. And I want to give the person I pass them to enough time to prove himself to the citizens of this county, the folks in this building, and the all-important moneymen in Tallahassee, before he's forced to actually put his name on a ballot and take a chance at the polls in 2008. What you want is to get in there, prove yourself and scare off any challengers early on.' He wagged a cautionary finger at Rick. 'There's a lot of people that count on stability in this office, Rick. They need it. And they need a name and a face of a leader they can identify with – align sides with – so they don't go out trying to place bets on the wrong pony because they're unsure of the future.'

Rick nodded. He felt the excitement bubbling inside him, like when a jury was about to come in with a verdict; he could always tell by the looks on their faces when they'd come back as charged. Always. Now he was looking at Jerry Tigler's tired face in this tired room and he knew the next words out of his mouth.

'With twenty years in this office, Rick, you're well-respected by the staff, the attorneys, the defense bar and the bench. I don't need to go into your management skills – you've paid your dues as Division Chief in the pits and as Assistant DC in Major Crimes. We all know that. You're a hell of a leader; Charley is always singing your praises. I think you know the system, the politics and, most importantly, the people. I also think your surprising choice of a trial partner on this Marquette case was wise, too. She's green, but that might make the lawyers in division not feel so isolated now. Morale's been a big problem the past few years around here, with those in division feeling like they're underpaid and overworked while the specialized unit attorneys – especially the elite in Major Crimes – rest on their laurels and kick back with a caseload of ten. I think your trying this with her can make Major Crimes attorneys look more accessible. In the end I think that will make *you* look more accessible to the pits, and that's ultimately what will be important in your run in 2008.'

'Thank you, Jerry. I appreciate your confidence,' said Rick, drawing a slow breath.

'So you know where I'm going with this. Are you game for the chance?' Tigler finally asked.

'As I think I've made it clear before, I am more than ready for this opportunity. I welcome the challenges that running this office can bring.'

'Good, good,' Tigler said, nodding his head slowly, as though finally accepting what he'd just said himself. 'Then I'd like to start the transition; get you familiar with the ins and outs – the headaches, as Charley, here, likes to say – of daily life in my chair. I'm planning on making my departure official next September. I'd like to get your name in Jeb's ear now, so there's no hiccup when I make my announce-ment. I'm having lunch with him next week when he's in town. I want to drop it then. What's the time frame on Marquette?'

'February.'

'It won't go then, will it?'

'Probably not, but Farley can be funny. If Mel doesn't look for a continuance, he could push it,' Rick said with a shrug. 'Most likely the summer.'

'Winning that case would be a good note to start on, Rick. Free publicity can make you a household name quicker than any paid political advertisement. The quicker, the better.' He stood up and walked out from behind his desk.

'Congratulations, Ricky,' Rifkin said with a big smile, rising and shaking his hand. 'You're the man.'

'Yes,' Tigler said, taking his hand and shaking it as well. 'Congratulations are definitely in order.'

34

Somewhere in the distance – somewhere in this cold, putrid, green maze that he was trapped in – he heard the gritty click of the guard's heels start up again. Slow and easy, they made their way down empty, fluorescent-lit cement hallways, silencing all in their path. *Click, click, click.* Coming this way. Coming *his* way, he knew.

He cocked his head and listened intently until his brain began to hurt. There were two sets of footsteps now, walking almost – *almost* – in sync. The heavy click, click, clicking slowed to a shuffle, and then stopped. An electric jolt of adrenaline seized his chest and froze his body. Somewhere along the parade route, the heels must have paused to observe one of the crazed zoo animals they'd caged.

Although he couldn't see them, he could definitely picture his captors, peering through thick iron bars into squalid cells that were always brightly lit – 24/7 – shaking their clumsy utility belts for attention. With mace cans at the ready, and black steel asps dangling from their sides like menacing third arms, their suspicious eyes searched for a reason to call in an extraction team. Sadists, every one of them. He could hear their radios, chirping and squawking, blurting out strange codes. If they found something, he knew the screaming would begin, but he never knew why, and he didn't want to know.

In the thick fog that swirled inside his head, it took minutes – maybe hours for all he knew – for the footsteps to make their rounds. For him, time had no reality anymore:

no significance, no consequence, no definition. And that frightened him, perhaps most of all, as he sat on the cold cement floor waiting for them to come for him. He closed his eyes and drifted off.

The drugs they fed him were drowning him alive, making his head feel as if it were trapped in the spin of a crushing wave. Lucidity would be there one moment, and then suddenly a wave would buckle him at the knees and drag him under into the murky blackness. Just above the surface, and a fingertip out of reach, was the world he'd slipped away from. He could see the watery shadows, the blurred faces. He could hear the distorted, muffled drone of their conversations as he tumbled over himself, but he couldn't reach them. He was forced to watch in horror as life went on as though he'd never even gone under, as though he were not being pulled further and further out to sea. The screams of despair only sounded in his own head.

He opened his eyes and realized with a frightening start that the *click click clicking* had gotten much closer. He felt the panic grab at his throat. *Where were they now?*

The man in the cage next door began to scream. The blood-curdling shrieks ripped at the inside of his brain like a sharp bread knife. It was impossible to think, hear, feel, breathe, in here.

The footsteps slowed to a shuffle and then stopped. The keys jingle-jangled, the radio squawked. He felt eyes crawl over his person, and he heard the muffled, heavy breathing of those who watched him.

'This him?' asked a voice filled with disgust.

'Yep. Yo, Marquette, get up. Let's go, Doc. Time to go again. Pisses me off,' he said to the other guard. 'We just got him ready for court this morning, and now they want him out again.'

'Where the fuck's his clothes?'

'Suicide watch,' said the one jingling his keys. 'No nooses on this floor. I guess you never worked on nine before.'

'How's he supposed to make a noose out of a jumpsuit? Where's he gonna hang himself from anyway?'

'You wouldn't believe what they do on this floor. Crazy fucks. I saw one guy stuff his own shit in his mouth once, then choke to death on it. That's why they're up here, man. That's why he don't have no clothes. We're saving him from himself. From choking on his panties,' he laughed.

Jingle coughed up a wad of phlegm and spit it on the floor in the cell. It landed next to his foot, oozing slowly toward him, white and frothy. He watched it out of the corner of his eye, as it melted and spread. He felt the anger rise up in him, like the crushing wall of a tidal wave. When it touched his toe, he *wanted* to stand up and scream. He *wanted* to take Jingle's fat neck in his hand and put his nose into his own spittle – like a dog – and rub it around until it finally broke off.

But he didn't.

'Me?' Jingle continued, wiping his mouth with the back of his sleeve. 'I say let him fucking kill himself. Guy offed his whole family, including a little freakin' baby. Save the taxpayers' money for once – let him do it himself. But I ain't in charge, man.'

'Thank God for that,' said the other guard with a short laugh. 'Well he ain't coming downstairs like that. Is he violent? Do we need additional restraints?'

'Ain't given no one trouble. Yet. He don't say nothing. He don't do nothing. He just sits there like that. You can fart in his face and he don't fucking move,' Jingle chuckled. 'Freak.'

'Well, let's get him dressed,' the other guard said with a sigh, and looked at his watch. 'He's got company, and I'm betting that his lawyers don't want to see him like this neither.'

'I have to warn you,' Mel said, as he signed the log and waited for the CO to give him back his ID. 'This is a jail, not a hospital, Alain. As you can tell from this morning in court, David's in a fragile state. It's been difficult communicating with him.'

'Why is he still in here, Mr Levenson?' Alain Marquette demanded, a frustrated, angry frown on his face. 'That is my question. Why is he still in here?'

'They will not bring him to visiting hours, Mr Levenson,' said Nina Marquette softly, running her hand gently over the lapel of her husband's jacket as she tried to soothe him. 'This upsets us, not being able to see our son when we should be permitted to see him. Weeks he has been here and we have not been able to even speak with David. I don't think that is right.' She turned to her husband, and said in a quieter tone, '*Alain, l'homme essaie de nous faire plaisir. Nous devons être patients ou alors nous ne reverrons jamais David. Les tribunaux américains rendent les choses très difficiles.*'

No one offered to translate.

David Marquette's mother nervously clenched and unclenched the tissue that she held in her small palm. The reception area of the Dade County Jail was filled with all sorts of sordid, dirty-looking people, and she wished she hadn't worn her good jewelry. Every eye was fixed on her, probably wondering what she was here for, how much money she had in her purse to bond someone out. She ran a finger over her nose, aware that it was still bandaged and bruised where she'd broken it weeks before. Perhaps they thought her a crime victim.

Thick bulletproof glass separated the waiting area from the cluster of green-uniformed correction officers on the other side. A bold-faced sign above the glass warned that all weapons would be confiscated, all violators arrested and prosecuted. Circled pictures of guns, knives and bombs with black lines drawn through them illustrated what a weapon was for those who could not read. Although the jail was also filled with correction officers, she felt no safer. They watched her, too. She remembered what her father had warned her once: *Never stare down an animal, Nina. They will get angry and bite.* So she looked down at the dirty floor and at the tips of her designer boots, focusing on the wet spots the rain had made on the suede accents.

'It's up to the discretion of Corrections to allow an inmate visitors,' Mel continued patiently. 'David hasn't been allowed. That's a problem, but one, unfortunately, that I have no control over. I've been able to get in to see him when I need to, and that's what matters.'

Mel Levenson had been in and around the criminal justice system for close to three decades now, and there was no doubt that, in Miami, he was the best at what he did. Mel could afford to be selective with his clients because his clients could afford to be selective. But privilege, he'd found, came with its own set of problems – most clients had no experience with the criminal justice system, which virtually guaranteed Mel some shocked and outraged relatives to deal with at the end of the day. Outraged at a system that strip-searched Uncle Joey after he was arrested for securities fraud. *What did they think would be up his ass? Stock certificates? He's not a real criminal.* Outraged to find out that horrible jail conditions and toothless cellmates named Bubba really did exist. The system that had been falling apart in front of them on the front page of the paper their entire lives suddenly had to be fixed yesterday. Over the years, Mel had learned to listen to the rantings, but never to feed them – after all, it was the relatives who usually footed his bill. But today was a little different. Given what his client was charged with, it was difficult to feign outrage because the man couldn't get a bond or visit with Mom and Pop on a Sunday afternoon.

Just as the silence began to feel a little heavy, the steel outer door buzzed open. Mel quickly ushered the Marquettes out of the reception area, past the plastic booth of COs and through a set of metal detectors. Painted arrows on cinderblock walls directed them down a series of hallways to yet another solid steel door. Mel waved his ID badge at the camera above the door and it, too, buzzed open. They walked down another green hall in silence. In front of a third door, with a small square-foot wire-mesh window, stood a bored-looking CO. He ate a yawn, mumbled a few words into his shoulder pack, then nodded at Mel.

'Are we ready?' Mel asked him.

'He's in now,' the guard said, unlocking the door with a key. 'The buzzer is on the wall under the table. Call if you have a problem. We opened the mikes so you don't have to wait for him to hit the button to hear him if he wants to talk.'

The room was small, maybe 8 x 10, divided in half lengthwise by a metal table and a clear inch-thick plexiglas partition. The walls were the same color as the rest of the jail – a pasty mint green. The floor was cement gray. Long fluorescent tube lights were caged to the ceiling.

Behind the plexiglas, in a metal chair that was chained to the floor, sat Dr David Marquette, his scraggly, overgrown face pale against the bright red of his jumpsuit. Behind him was another solid steel door, which he must have been brought through. As he had at his arraignment, he stared out at nothing.

Alain walked up to the table, palms open against the plexiglas, but his son did not flinch. 'David? David?' He suddenly slapped the partition hard with both hands.

'It's only been a few days on the meds, Alain. The agitation is gone, which is good, but the negative symptoms—' Mel stopped himself. 'Lawther is the jail doctor. He says it could be weeks before the medication sets in. Before we know what is the drugs or what is—'

'What are they giving him?'

'Thorazine. A thousand milligrams.'

'Jesus Christ!'

'They are still diagnosing him, Alain. Remember, this is a jail, not a private hospital.'

'Thorazine?' Alain angrily hit the glass once more. 'No wonder he's like this! They're killing him! They're making him nothing but a zombie!'

'Thorazine? Is that different than what Darrell—' Nina cautiously began to ask.

'Yes, Nina! Yes, it's different!' shouted Alain bitterly, cutting her off. He knew what she was going to say before she said it.

Nina bit her lip and turned away from her husband, looking down at her lap, the tears silently falling once again. She dabbed a crumpled tissue at her eyes, trying to remain as dignified as she could in this awful place. 'I cannot do this, Alain. Don't ask me. Not again,' she whispered. 'There is only so much one person can take.'

He watched them all watching him, studying him. He felt his eyes roll in his head. Roll, roll, roll around the room as the wave smashed him from behind and washed over him once again. Their voices became muffled and thick, as if they were all underwater with him.

'Enough,' Alain said finally, throwing his hand up. 'This place is horrible. It's barbaric. We need to get him out of here!'

'It's not that easy, Alain,' said Mel, shaking his head. 'He's charged with four counts of murder. This is very serious.'

'Yes, that I know. That man, Mr Bellido, wants to kill my son.' He blinked back tears as he stared at the vacant figure behind the partition. 'Look at him,' he whispered softly. Alain leaned across the table and, with his hands on the glass once again, suddenly shouted. 'David? Do you know what you've done? Do you know where you are? Do you know why you're here?'

There was no response.

'We're going to get you out of here. We will.'

'Don't promise him that, Alain,' Mel replied quietly, reaching over to touch the senior Marquette's arm. 'We've got to be realistic. This is Florida, not France, and there is no bond in Florida for murder. We have a long road ahead of us.'

Alain abruptly pushed back from the table and stood. 'Then shorten it. This is no place for him,' he said. 'Make it happen, Mr Levenson. Find a way – *any* way – but make it happen. That's my son in there. I'm paying you enough. Make them all understand.'

Although seated just a few short feet away, his mother had yet to actually look at him. Now, as his father screamed at the man they called his attorney, she finally managed to pull her stare from her lap. On her black, tailored skirt was a pile of twisted and shredded white tissue pieces. She still clutched a few ragged strips in her fist, dabbing them gingerly at red-rimmed eyes. He could see now that her always-elegant face was swollen and disfigured from crying. Even through all the make-up, greenish-yellow bruises shaded the delicate bags under her eyes.

Everything about his mother was always so refined, so picture-perfect – even now, she made the bandage that was strapped across the bridge of her nose look like a fashion statement. Not a hair out of place, not a drop of mascara running with all the tears. But beneath the cultured, polished, expensive exterior, he knew that she was squirming inside – worrying about all the vile germs she might be touching or inhaling in this very room, just by sitting here with the son she could not bear to even look at. Maybe it was the curiosity, maybe the guilt – maybe it was because to *not* look would be too obvious to his father and his lawyer, but she finally did, her deep-blue, always-questioning eyes falling on him. She squinted just a little, her head tilted slightly to the left, watching him as a tourist at the zoo might study the monkeys. He felt those eyes silently roll over his person like a lint brush, picking up all in their path, missing nothing. Finally, they found his own and stayed there for a long moment, locked in his vacant stare.

'Let's go, Alain. Please, let's go,' she pleaded, rising from her seat, her face bleach white. The tissue shreds fluttered to the floor. She turned and walked back to the door where she'd come in, her arms wrapped around herself, as if she was incredibly cold.

'Nina,' Alain began.

'Now. I don't feel well, Alain.'

A few minutes passed before the guard came and let the three of them out of the room, but his mother never turned around again. It was clear to him that she could no longer bear to look at this man who was her son.

Or at what he had become.

36

'Avon Lady,' Julia said with a shy smile when the door opened.

'I'll take it, whatever you're selling. In fact, I'll take two,' Rick said, leaning against the doorframe that led into his apartment, looking her up and down with a smile of his own. 'Come in. *Please*, come in.' He kissed her softly on the cheek as she stepped out of the hall and into what looked like a photo spread for *Architectural Digest*.

An open living room, decorated in cool shades of blue, sea-foam green and arctic white, led into a modern kitchen with shiny stainless-steel appliances, gleaming glass cabinets and polished black granite countertops – all, remarkably, streak- and fingerprint-free. Sleek, modular furniture was purposefully arranged on dark bamboo floors; contemporary – and what looked like probably expensive – art hung on the walls.

'This place is really nice,' she said softly, as she walked up to a set of open sliding glass doors that led to a covered patio and an amazing view of a twinkling Miami Beach. Even through the stocky maze of buildings, she could make out the rolling white surf of the black Atlantic just a couple of blocks to the east. She thought of her own cluttered apartment – the one with the stunning parking-lot views – that she still hadn't finished completely unpacking from her move south three years ago. Pre-framed posters from Michael's Arts and Crafts decorated her walls; Glade scented oil candles accessorized the coffee table and mismatched furniture. She hadn't made a bed since she'd moved in, and had no idea which box the real plates were even packed in. Considering it was her bed that she and Rick had always ended up in, she couldn't help but wonder, with some embarrassment, what he thought of her when the lights were turned back on. 'What a view,' she managed. 'Are you sure you're employed by the same government agency I am?'

He laughed. 'Remember, it's just me here. No kids, no wife. No alimony, no child support. I got into this building years ago, before real-estate prices went through the roof. Before art deco was a really hot new word and South Beach was a cool place to be. A bit before your time,' he added, smiling. She heard the pop as he worked the cork out of a wine bottle in the kitchen.

'There was a time when South Beach wasn't cool?' she mused.

'Yup. You might not know it, but I'm one of the few native Miamians that grew up in this city. My parents were from Cuba – fled during the revolution. Back in the day, it was old Jewish men who used to line Ocean Drive and Collins Avenue in their wheelchairs and oxygen tanks, instead of rappers in their tricked-up Benzes headed off to the VMAs. Rent *Scarface* one of these days, sweetheart. *That* was Miami Beach in the seventies and eighties – complete with domino games and ugly Guayabera shirts and cocaine cowboys just dropping bales of soft white snow from the sky. A city that had left its heyday a couple of decades back at the Fontainebleau with Frank Sinatra and the Rat Pack. Aaah,' he said with a sigh, 'a time when you could actually get a parking spot on Ocean Drive.'

'Hey, I like Guayabera shirts.' She couldn't help herself. 'Were hot dogs really a nickel back in the day?'

'You're a wise-ass.'

Julia smiled. 'You really are old.'

'Don't tell anyone,' he said, as he headed across the room to her, two glasses of white wine in hand. 'And you really are young.'

'Don't tell anyone,' she returned.

He handed her a glass, then kissed her – this time on the lips. His mouth lingered over hers. His breath smelled sweet and oaky, like Chardonnay. 'Are you kidding me?' he whispered. 'I tell everyone. I'm very proud.'

She thought of Day's words from lunch and felt herself blush. 'Not everyone, I hope.'

He took a long sip of wine. 'You mean the folks down at the rumor mill? No. I think we're on the same page there, Julia. I want our business to stay our business; neither one of us needs to be handling personal PR during this case. Besides,' he added, flipping her long hair playfully off a shoulder, and running his fingers down her arm, 'secrets can be a lot of fun.'

She sipped her wine as he headed over to slip CDs in the stereo. She still hadn't been able to fight off the queer, uneasy feeling from the morning's arraignment. It had nagged at her all day in the office, until she finally decided to leave early and go for a quick run on the boardwalk in Hollywood to clear her head. A quick run had turned into ten miles, and her head was still no clearer. When she got back, there was a message from Rick, asking if she wanted to come over.

'I was gonna order Chinese, if that's okay with you,' he said from across the room.

'That's fine. I like Chinese. I'm not really very hungry, though.' Outside, the rain began to fall again, lightly between the buildings. The drops looked like tiny, platinum daggers in the yellow blur of the streetlights.

'Where'd you disappear to this morning?' he asked, looking over at her. 'I turned to introduce you and you were gone.'

She hesitated for a moment. 'I'm sorry, but I just don't think the cameras are for me. I don't want to say the wrong thing. So if it's okay with you, I think I'll just bow out when you hold a conference.'

He shrugged. 'That's fine with me, but I do think you're gonna need to get over your camera phobia. And soon, too. I fielded a phone call from the French consulate this afternoon. Followed a couple of hours later by one from CNN.'

'The French consulate? Why?'

'Because our defendant is apparently a citizen of France, and the French historically don't like it when we try to execute one of their own, even if he does also carry an American passport. They get very proprietary.'

Julia almost choked. 'A French citizen?'

He reached over and took her wine glass from her. 'More?'

'What are you talking about?'

'A dual citizen, actually. Big difference. Or no difference, in my opinion.' He headed back into the kitchen. 'I'll take that as a yes.'

She was stunned. 'What does the consulate want?'

'Access to Marquette and a promise not to seek the death penalty,' he called out. 'The first I apparently have to give them under the Vienna Convention. The second, I won't, which I'm sure will get all the bleeding hearts at the ACLU hemorrhaging. It sets a dangerous precedent if we let our office be bullied by other countries that don't like or agree with our laws,' he continued when she hadn't said anything. 'Besides, I don't care where you're from, if you commit a crime here, then you should be subject to the penalties of

US and Floridian law. I'm sure this will rise to some form of an international incident; it has before with other countries that don't have the death penalty.' He poured another two glasses of wine and headed back across the living room.

Julia said nothing. Smooth jazz floated from the speakers. She could feel the alcohol begin to work its magic and she closed her eyes. 'I didn't expect you to file the death-penalty notice today,' she said suddenly, surprising even herself that she'd said it.

'You didn't expect me to file the notice, or you didn't expect me to seek the death penalty?' he asked quietly.

She was silent for a long moment. 'Both, I guess. I thought it happened later on.'

'Are you okay with it?' He raised his eyebrows and those dark magnetic eyes asked the real question on his mind. *You're not a bleeding heart, now are you?*

She nodded and looked away. 'Yeah, yeah, I'm fine with it. I was just surprised, that's all.'

'This is fuckin' bullshit!' shouted Uncle Jimmy into the phone. He slapped his hand hard against the refrigerator, sending Nora's magnetic fruit clips and to-do reminders to the floor.

'Jimmy, Jimmy, please. Julia's in the other room,' Aunt Nora pleaded in a hushed voice. 'Keep your voice down.'

'Excuse my language,' Jimmy said, heeding Nora and lowering his voice just enough that Julia had to get out of bed and open the door a little more to hear. 'I'm just upset here.' She could see him through the crack in the door, red-faced and pacing in the kitchen, Aunt Nora sitting at the kitchen table, wringing a dishtowel in her hands. She could hear her own breath catching in the doorframe.

'What do they want from us, Jimmy?' Nora demanded, crying, her voice a scratchy whisper. 'I'm not letting her go through anymore! I already told them that.'

'I know it's not your decision, but . . . yes, yes, I know that, too,' Jimmy said into the phone. *'Listen to me . . . no, you listen to me – this bastard needs to fry for what he's done. Did you see the pictures? Did you see them? Did you see what he did to them? You ask me, sir, what we want to see happen? You ask me what we want to see done? We want him dead! That's justice.'*

She shook the cold memory out of her head. 'What do you think went wrong with him?' she asked softly, thinking now of the pictures that lined the pale-yellow upstairs hallway. Nothing was ever what it seemed. 'I mean, he led the perfect life . . .'

'Never pretend to know someone's life, Julia. You'll only know what they want you to know, when it is they want you to know it. Remember that in this job, and nothing, and no one, will ever surprise you again.'

He came up behind her and ran his hand through her hair, moving it off her shoulder and exposing her beautiful, sculpted neck. He lightly traced the bowl of the cold wine glass over the soft curve of her throat. A delicious chill ran down her spine and she closed her eyes, losing herself in the moment. A few drops of wine splashed her skin, and he sensuously kissed them off with warm, wet lips as they ran down her neck and disappeared into her silk shirt. Her breath came in rapid starts, her chest heaving under his touch. She heard herself moan softly as his tongue slowly worked its way up to her ear, devouring an earring in its kiss. Pressing his body close to hers, he wrapped his free hand around her arm and across the front of her chest, finding the buttons on her blouse and undoing them slowly, one by one, with his deft fingers. She felt him growing, pulsing hard against her back. 'Now let's not talk anymore,' he whispered, unbuttoning the last button. 'And especially not about him.'

She nodded, arching her neck back into his lips, offering her throat to him. 'You're in a good mood tonight,' she whispered back.

With the fluted stem of the wine glass, he parted her shirt, revealing her ample, supple breasts. A fading tan line disappeared into a black lace bra. 'Mmmm . . .' he murmured at the sight. Slowly, he moved the cold, wet crystal over the delicate lace, making her nipples hard and erect. Running the glass slowly along the curve of her cleavage, with the stem he pushed the cup off of one breast, exposing it. Then the other. She knew she should turn away from the open sliding doors that she stood in front of, but she could not move. They were on the fifth floor, but with the living-room lights on, anyone could see in. She sucked in her breath as he poured the rest of the cold wine down her arched throat, letting it run over both breasts and down her pants.

He kissed her neck once again, his warm tongue lapping up the wine. 'Despite the best efforts of the French, I had a great day, that's why. A fantastic day,' he murmured in her ear. 'And now I think it's getting even better.'

He turned her around to face him, slipping the shirt off her shoulders. She stood before him in the living-room light, trembling, her breasts exposed, the front of her slacks soaked with wine. He put down his glass and carefully unhooked the catch on her pants, pulling them over her hips with a tug of both hands till they fell in a heap on the floor with her panties. He exhaled a deep breath as he looked at her. 'You are something special,' he said softly.

Then, without another word, he picked her up and carried her into his bedroom.

37

'Hool-ee-ah!' The voice called across the lobby of the Graham Building. 'Hool-ee-ah!'

Because it sounded nothing like her actual name, Julia kept walking with the crowd from the elevator across the lobby, dragging three humongous file boxes on a metal dolly behind her. As usual, she was running late, and today was her plea day, which the judge began right after morning calendar. She'd gotten three new cases this week alone, and five others in the two weeks before that, so just to keep her already unmanageable docket status quo since her last plea day, Julia knew she'd have to either try, plea, or in some other way get rid of, at least eight cases. With the state guidelines as strict as they were, and half her defendants qualifying either as habitual offenders or for minimum-mandatory sentences, she knew it wasn't likely she'd be able to plea much out, unless the PD was in a good mood and willing to work with her on a bunch of crap drug cases. If not, she'd probably be in trial all next week, and because she'd surprised Farley yesterday by announcing she was counsel on Marquette – thereby making him look unprepared in front of the cameras – there was a strong chance the judge would look to even the score by sending her to back-up court the week after that.

'Hool-ee-ah!'

The voice was almost at the level of an insistent scream now, and as people turned to look, so, finally, did Julia. That was when she spotted an obviously annoyed Marisol Alfonso across the crowded lobby. Dressed in a light-pink corduroy mini-skirt and matching jacket, she practically blended in with the dull Pepto-Bismol-colored lobby walls behind her.

'Hool-ee-ah! Over here, honey!' With one hand on her pink hip, the other impatiently waved Julia over. Marisol herself did not move an inch.

There was really only one reason why Julia, already stressed and already late, actually turned around and began to walk quickly back across the lobby with a smile on her face – and even she knew it was pathetic. 'Hi there, Marisol,' she said sweetly as she rushed up. 'I'm running really late,' she began, trying hard not to sound impatient.

'What? You no hear me calling you?' Marisol said with a frown, her fleshy face growing dark.

'No, I guess not. I'm in a real rush and I was thinking,' Julia replied. *Perhaps if you'd actually said my name right I might have heard you*, was what she wanted to say, but, of course, didn't.

'Tha's alright,' Marisol said, dismissing the excuse with a wave of her hand. As quickly as it had come, the frown was gone, replaced by a big, toothy grin.

Julia could picture Marisol nailing a boyfriend in the head with a frying pan one minute, and then having hot sex with him on the kitchen floor the next. Her on/off switch flicked fast. Way too fast. 'What's up?' she asked.

'Look,' Marisol said, dangling a yellow mailing envelope in front of her, 'I have something for you. It just came in and I was going to bring it upstairs to Rick, but I thought maybe you want to see it first. Ees, ah, on your case with him. The one from yesterday. The doc-door.' She leaned in a little closer and grabbed Julia by the wrist, with her long pink claws and jingling bracelets. The dark look was back. 'My friend in the mailroom says it come in this morning by messenger. He says ees *really* important,' she said with a wink of her ultra-long lashes, dragging out the syllables in the word 'really' for as long as possible. 'I thought you should take it upstairs yourself.'

Julia didn't know if Marisol was just trying to spare herself a trip back up to the second floor, or if she was really trying to help her out. Either way, she figured this must be progress. 'Sure. Thanks,' she said with a nod of her head and a smile. 'I'll give it to Rick. I'm heading over to court—'

Marisol shook her head and the dark look disappeared again, replaced by another pink smile. 'Don't wait, honey. My friend says you need to look at this *now*,' she said with a toss of her black mane before walking off. She held her hand up to silence any further discussion. 'You can thank me later,' she called back over her shoulder and then teetered off into the lobby crowd on a pair of three-inch pink platforms.

Julia looked down at the envelope and saw that it was already sliced open. She slipped her hand in and brought out a five-page notice, neatly paper-clipped together in the corner and styled *The State of Florida vs. David Alain Marquette*. It was already stamped by the SAO mailroom with today's date, and the time of 9:43 a.m.

Less than thirty seconds later, she was running like hell for the elevator.

38

With Marisol busy getting coffee in the lunchroom, there was no one to call down to Rick's office anyway, and no point in calling to announce herself. Besides, although they weren't up to steady date-nights yet, they should at least be at the point in their relationship where her presence in his office didn't always have to be announced by his secretary – Major Crimes Assistant Division Chief or not. She walked down the hall as fast as she could, past the secretarial pool and a sour-faced, surprised Grandma at the copy machine.

'Come in,' Rick called out gruffly when she knocked at the door, but he actually looked pleasantly surprised when she opened it. 'Hey there,' he said, breaking into an intimate smile and settling back into his chair with a mug of coffee.

'Hey yourself. Good morning.'

'What a coincidence. I was just thinking about last night. Mmmm . . .' he said, with a shake of his head. 'Sit down. Are you just getting back from court?'

She shook her head and took a seat in front of his desk. 'It's my plea day. I was on my way across the street when I ran into Marisol downstairs. She handed me something that got clocked into the mailroom less than a half-hour ago on Marquette. It was brought over by messenger from Mel Levenson's office.'

'Okay. What is it?' he asked slowly, trying hard to read her expression. The smile disappeared.

'It's a change of plea,' she said, handing him the envelope across his desk.

'A change of plea? What the hell do you mean?' he asked. Now his face grew dark and suspicious. 'Is Mel throwing in the towel already and pleading guilty? Saving the taxpayers the time and trouble of a trial? How kind.' But Julia could tell by the look on his face that he wasn't joking. And she also thought he'd just guessed what was coming.

'It's a 3.216 notice. He's pleading insanity.'

'You're kidding me.'

'I'm not.'

He slammed his coffee cup down on the desk. Coffee sprayed everywhere, but he ignored it. He stroked a long finger against his temple and said nothing for a minute while he stared down at the envelope she'd just handed him. 'Surprise, surprise,' he finally said, but more to himself, she thought, than to her. 'That damn freaked-out blank look in court. All the sickness crap from his dad. I should have seen this coming. The set-up.' He reached into his desk drawer and pulled out a stack of napkins. He shook his head while he mopped up the coffee splatter. 'I thought Levenson might try an insanity defense out once he realized he wasn't gonna get the one-armed man past that alarm and an army of cops on the front lawn. But, you know, maybe it's smarter for him to go in full force with an insanity claim from the beginning, even before discovery. Maybe this way he figures he'll have a better shot at me actually believing him, and maybe give his piece-of-shit client a plea. Get him into a warm bed in Chattahoochee and off death row. Like that's gonna happen,' he scoffed. He reached for his reading glasses. 'Have you ever had a defendant plead insanity before, Julia?' he asked, abruptly regaining his composure.

She shook her head.

'You know why that is? Because insanity defenses don't work.' He slid the notice out of the envelope. 'Not in Florida.

In twenty years, I've seen maybe fifteen, sixteen attempts. Let me tell you, all but two have failed miserably. The two that did work, the guys were nuttier than fruitcakes and they weren't charged with murder, so I actually pled them both NGI.'

NGI stood for Not Guilty by Reason of Insanity. At least she knew that much.

'What's the law on insanity in Florida?' Julia asked. 'The bar exam was a while ago.' All she could remember from her law-school days was that each state had a different legal test for sanity, and that some were stricter than others.

He shot her a quick look that she couldn't quite read. 'Florida follows M'Naghten, as about half the states in this country do. "Every person is presumed sane, and to be found not guilty by reason of insanity, a defendant must establish at the time of the act he suffered from such a defect of reason from disease of the mind such that he did not understand the nature of the act, or that it was wrong." End quote. What does that mean? Unless Mel Levenson can come in and demonstrate that his client had some mental disease, defect or infirmity that remarkably no one ever knew he had until now, and because of that condition he either, A) didn't *know* what the hell he was doing or, B) he knew what he was doing, but he didn't *know* it was wrong, then he's legally sane. The emphasis, Julia, is on cognition – on a defendant's ability to know what's going on and discern right from wrong. An inability to control one's actions or rage is of no consequence, as long as that person knew what he was doing. So being commanded to kill by God or Satan or Santa, and irresistible impulses of rage due to seeing your wife fornicate with the plumber in the marital bed don't fly in this state.'

'Well, Mel Levenson just might have that first part down,' she said quietly as Rick started to read.

'What first part?' he asked, looking back up at her, his glasses precariously perched on the tip of his nose.

She blew out a low breath. 'The mental disease, defect or infirmity part. Keep reading – it's all in there. Levenson is claiming David Marquette's schizophrenic.'

39

They sat in silence while Rick finished reading. When he was done, he spun his chair around to look out the window at the Miami skyline and the overpass of the Dolphin Expressway, which, even though the HOV signs all said it was past rush hour, still looked like a parking lot. A few more minutes passed in silence. Then, without a word, he spun back around, picked up the phone and dialed, staring at Julia somberly as he did. 'This is Bellido,' he said in a quiet, controlled voice, though obviously angry. 'I need you to call me the second you get this message. I'm in my office, or try my cell, 305-794-0114. We have a problem.' Then he hung up and turned back to the window.

She wasn't sure, but Julia could pretty much guess that the call was made to one John Latarrino. And she could also venture a guess that Lat had seen who was calling him and let it go directly to voicemail. Despite displaying a unified front at yesterday's arraignment, she knew things were tense between the two men, although she had yet to figure out why. This latest news was definitely not gonna make their bond any stronger. Latarrino was the lead, the one who had conducted the interviews, asked the questions, written the reports. Even though the investigation had only just begun, and no one had suspected the case would take this direction, she knew Rick hated being caught unawares. Chances were that Lat would take some heat for that misfortune, especially if, in Rick's eyes, that investigation *should* have raised everyone's suspicions a while back.

'What now?' she finally asked, breaking the silence.

Rick blew out a long, slow breath. 'We get both Lat and Brill in here. We get them to dig up everything and anything on Dr David Marquette – dating from the day he was born to what he ate for breakfast this morning in DCJ.' He spun back around to face her. 'There's no way something like this should come as such a big surprise, which means either we're all idiots or, much more likely, Marquette's faking it, because there is no past.'

'Levenson claims Marquette spent some time in a psychiatric hospital outside of Chicago when he was younger, but under an alias. That's probably why no one knew about it,' she offered. 'I mean, how could they? No one in Marquette's family is talking to us, and Jennifer's family obviously didn't know. Maybe Jennifer didn't even know. Remember what Lat said about her family holding back, seeing only what it was they wanted to see all these years?'

'Well we sure as hell know now. Now we get ourselves a court order and get those medical records from his three-week stint at Parker Hills, along with any other psych or medical records he might have here in Miami. I didn't know that he was being housed on nine over at DCJ. Where to cell an inmate is a CO decision. Nine's the crazy floor. They sometimes put high-security inmates there who're on suicide watch. Maybe Marquette picked up a couple of ideas while he's been up there. We interview every guard who works on that floor to see what Marquette's like when his lawyer's not around and the cameras aren't looking and the jail doc's not taking notes. We research all we can about the disease, in the event he actually does have it: what it is; what causes it; what the treatment options are; what the effects of the illness are. I know some of the answers from cases I've had over the years, but I'm betting you don't, and I need current information. Because what I do know is this: just because you're schizo, or manic, or have whatever flavor-of-the-day mental illness there might be out there, that doesn't give you a license to kill without responsibility. Especially not here in Florida. And not with me.' He paused. 'Have you handled a competency hearing before?'

She so badly wanted to tell him yes, but she couldn't. She shook her head.

He sighed and motioned to her *West's Criminal Laws and Rules* softcover book that sat on top of her file boxes. She could tell in just that one split second that he was having second thoughts about her – the case was getting far too complicated for a rookie.

'Rule 3.210,3.211,' he said. 'I suggest you not just learn it, you memorize it. First up, besides being insane, Levenson is claiming Marquette's incompetent to proceed to trial – which has nothing to do with his client's sanity on the night of the murders, and everything to do with his ability to remain in the here and now during court proceedings. Insanity's only a legal term – there's no actual medical diagnosis of 'insanity'. But before we get to have a trial to decide if he was legally insane, Farley first has to determine if he's *competent*. Does he understand the nature of the charges against him and the penalties he's facing? Does he understand what a lawyer is for, why he needs one? Will he sit in a chair at trial and assist his attorney or will he scream for the mothership in his pajamas?'

He paused for a long moment, lost somewhere in his thoughts. 'We can't forget that this is a man who, just weeks ago, was performing surgery and lecturing on the beauty of hip replacements to colleagues at the AMA. We need to make sure both the judge and the psychiatrists know that. And ultimately, of course, a jury. Marquette's educated and he's bright, which makes him much more dangerous than your average criminal. *And* he's facing four murder counts and a death sentence, which makes him much more desperate. It behooves him to try his best at winning a spot on the next bus going to the state mental hospital up in Chattahoochee.'

'I don't mean to be difficult,' Julia interrupted softly, with a shake of her head, 'and I know this is new for me, but what if he really is sick? I won't pretend to know anything about schizophrenia, but you're planning three steps ahead, as if he's got to be faking. Isn't there a real possibility that he could be ill and we just didn't know enough to look for it before today?'

She couldn't forget those vacant albino-like eyes. Dead eyes. *Staring at her. Staring through her.* Her uneasy feeling from yesterday was still with her, and it was growing – spreading through her bones with a chill, settling in them like a cold for the winter. The deeper she was drawn in on Marquette, the closer she inevitably seemed to come back to her own past, no matter how much she resisted.

This case . . . It's too close, Julia. Too close . . . It can only bring . . . despair.

She pushed Aunt Nora's prophecy out of her head. 'Maybe we should let the doctors who examine him decide.'

'Almost every day,' Rick began, with a shake of his head, because she obviously wasn't getting it, 'somewhere in this courthouse, someone tries to win a spot on that bus, Julia. Why? It's simple. Because if they can get to Chattahoochee, then they can get out one day. It's the golden ticket. And any time they might have to spend fooling the docs locked away in a mental hospital is not like life over at Florida State Prison. It's a hell of a lot sweeter. For someone like David Marquette, who's ultimately looking at either death row or life behind bars without the possibility of parole, Chattahoo-chee is the *only* door out. And, of course, if he's ultimately found NGI, that's it, you know. Once the doctors say he's no longer a danger to himself or others, he walks away, free as a bird and there's absolutely nothing either the State or a judge can do about it. No matter if he killed one person or a hundred – he *walks.*

'Listen, I've seen everything from feces-throwing to devil-worshipping in a courtroom, but only two real nuts in twenty years. *Two.* Forgive me if I'm a bit skeptical when someone suddenly tells me they're crazy. Someone who, as far as I know and you know at this moment, was fine until two days before he decided to Ginsu his entire family. We simply can't afford to hedge the bet that the man's a little off and let him take an extended vacation in Chattahoochee to collect his thoughts while we work out our case. If he's found incompetent, it'll be another six months before he comes up on calendar for report and another eval. That's time spent in the loony bin perfecting the craft with the real loons, and time doesn't help a prosecutor, Julia. Remember that. Witnesses forget, die, retire, relocate. Evidence gets lost and destroyed. Juries feel bad for defendants who have spent a long time locked away in a mental hospital. They tend to think there's really something wrong with them. They tend to think they're not responsible for their actions after all. They tend to acquit them. So Marquette's com-petency is the first and most important hurdle we need to jump right now. After we get past that, then we can tackle his sanity.'

Two fresh Christmas trees, decorated only with simple white lights, stood on each side of the altar. Wreaths of fragrant evergreen hung below arched stained-glass windows; garlands adorned the communion railing and hung in giant swoops with big red bows under the fourteen Stations of the Cross, above the wooden pews. Just last Sunday morning, a veritable sea of red poinsettias had filled the sanctuary floor at Mass, but today they were gone. In their place were dozens and dozens of pastel flower baskets and sprays and ornate funeral wreaths. The church smelled like Christmas and spring and incense, an overpowering scent that was strangely fresh and crisp and noxious and made her nauseous each time she inhaled, so she tried not to – breathing in through her mouth and her fistful of tissues and only when necessary.

Her mom had loved flowers, though she'd always joke she had a black thumb that could even kill silk. On her way home from work on Fridays, she'd buy herself a simple bouquet of white peonies from Country Arts & Flowers, a local florist up by the Turnpike and the only store in town her family kept a house account with. 'The poor man's rose, but it still smells sweet,' Momma would say. She'd put them in her grandma's vase and leave them in the kitchen next to the sink so she could look at them doing stuff she hated doing, which was the dishes. And when the flowers died, she'd put the petals in a dish, dry them out and then sprinkle them in bath water or make little sachets for everyone's drawers, ignoring the constant complaints of Julia's dad that his underwear smelled like flowers. Julia clenched the tissues in her hand until she thought her fingers might never open again. Until she felt the warmth of her own blood as it seeped through her fingers, where her nails had dug into the soft flesh. She wondered suddenly how many of the sprays and wreaths on the altar were arranged by Country Arts and if the shop owners knew they had made them for their most loyal customer? Or would a few more Fridays have to pass before they missed her smile?

'Sometimes we don't know why the Lord does what He does,' young Father Ralph was gently saying in a feather-soft voice. 'We don't understand the plan He has for us. We can't understand it. But it is a Divine Plan. We know that Irene is in His plan. Joseph is in that plan, too. And Andrew is in His plan. And we must, we must learn *to trust in the plan the Lord has made for us. We must learn to forgive, for that is what He expects—'*

Aunt Nora abruptly stood up in the front pew. Without a word, she grasped Julia by the wrist, and with Uncle Jimmy following, led her out of the pew and back down the aisle, past too many familiar and unfamiliar faces. Neighbors, friends, Mr Leach the dry-cleaner, classmates, teachers, the cashier from P&E Bagels, total strangers. The story had made the front page of Newsday, *so they came from all over. Father Ralph stopped talking. The massive church held its breath as the three of them made their way down the marble aisle and out the back door.*

'Julia? Are you listening?' Rick was looking at her funny.

'Yeah,' she said, nodding absently. 'I'm sorry. I was just thinking. What's our next step?' she asked, trying her best to focus on a book on the bookshelf. She noticed that her legs were shaking and she leaned forward, pressing her weight on her knees to get them to stop. *Understanding Gunshot Wounds and Trajectory Patterns. Sex Crimes and the Psychopathic Personality.*

'You look a little pale.'

Five, four, three, two, one . . . breathe.

Six, five, four, three, two, one . . .

'No, no, I'm fine. Too much caffeine.'

Seven, six, five, four, three, two, one . . . breathe.

'I need to get this set down for a hearing before Farley asap,' he continued, eyeing her carefully for another moment. Then he pulled open a drawer on his file cabinet and took out an accordion file. 'The judge is gonna order a psych eval. He'll appoint at least two, possibly three, shrinks off the list to evaluate Marquette's competency to stand trial, and then the experts will have twenty days to report back. I don't want to drag out that time. Remember, that's our enemy. Especially with the holidays upon us. So we'll need to get on those medical records right away, along with all the police reports, labs, witness statements and anything else we can think of that may help inform the shrinks.'

'The list' referred to a court registry of licensed independent forensic psychologists and psychiatrists in Miami that performed psych evals in criminal cases.

'Does it matter who we get?' she asked.

'Hell, yeah. Farley'll ask us for our choice and we're gonna jump up and say Christian Barakat. He's the best for the State. If we get a stab at the second, I want Pat Hindlin or Tom McDermot. Levenson, of course, is gonna want Al Koletis. Every defense attorney wants Koletis. He's useless; everyone's incompetent and we're all nuts. I could save him the paper.'

Her cellphone suddenly buzzed at her side. It was a 545 exchange, from across the street. *Farley*. Oh shit. She had completely forgot about her plea day. She looked at her watch and her stomach suddenly dropped out, as if she'd rounded a blind curve on a bumpy roller coaster and saw the plunge just up ahead. It was already ten thirty. They were probably all waiting for her over in court.

'Speaking of the devil, I've got to get across the street,' she said, rising with her phone in hand. She took a deep breath. Her legs were still shaky, her head light, and she thought of that day in the bathroom with Lat. She knew passing out in front of Rick would somehow be worse. 'I'm late. In fact, I'm more than late. I'm probably in contempt.'

'I'll walk you. Maybe I can keep you out of the box and we can get this noticed for next week,' he said, reaching for his jacket. The phone on his desk rang just then. He hit the button and left it on speaker. 'State Attorney's. Bellido.'

It was Lat. 'I just got your message. What's up?'

'You need to get in here asap. And bring Brill.'

'What's happened now?' Lat said after a second, obviously annoyed. 'You're not holding another press conference, are you, Bellido? I'll definitely need to take a shower, then.'

'I don't think I'll be the one holding the press conference this afternoon, Lat,' Rick snapped. 'But Mel Levenson and David Marquette's pissed-off daddy just might. They dropped a bomb on us a half-hour ago, so forget searching for the owner of that semen and those footprints and get your ass in here. Marquette's just pled insanity.'

40

HUNDREDS PROTEST OUTSIDE US EMBASSY IN PARIS

CHIRAC DECLARES SEEKING OF DEATH PENALTY AGAINST MENTALLY ILL SUSPECT IN FLORIDA SLAYINGS 'BARBARIC'

It wasn't the front page, but it was the *New York Times*. And the *Washington Post*. And the *Chicago Tribune*. And the *Los Angeles Times*. Even a brief mention by Ann Curry as she did the morning news on *The Today Show*. Seemingly overnight, Dr David Marquette and the Coral Gables Family Massacre, as it was known in Miami, quantum leaped from relative obscurity as a Local Section tragedy to international incident and a world news headline, and the phones at the State Attorney's Office had not stopped ringing since. Charley Rifkin's foreboding prediction, uttered just a few weeks back, of an impending media circus, was apparently coming true, although it wasn't just the shock of Marquette's crime, his farm-boy, handsome face and esteemed profession, or even the haunting smiles of his children that were launching his name into the dark stratosphere of infamy. Unlike the serial killer Cupid, who drew crowds and cameras to Miami from all over the world because of the lurid details and random brutality of his crimes, and his ability to terrorize a major metropolitan city by eluding a task force of homicide detectives for eighteen months, David Marquette's case had developed into a political hot potato. An *international* political hot potato, ripe with all the wrong issues: Capital Punishment. Seeking Capital Punishment of a Foreign Citizen. Seeking Capital Punishment of a Mentally Ill Foreign Citizen. Add in the shockingly wholesome face and the MD suffix and the lurid details, and the hot potato had all the sensational ingredients necessary to become a firestorm. The *perfect* storm, Julia remembered, was Rifkin's prediction. While it was too early to say if all the attention would wane or pick up speed, judging from the high-caliber news trucks parked outside the Graham Building's glass doors for the past few days, and the bitter debate over capital punishment now being waged on American embassy steps and in the international press, it was pretty clear that David Marquette's fifteen minutes of fame weren't up just yet. The circus had definitely come to town. The only question being asked by everyone on the other side of those glass doors was how long would it stick around?

She lit a cigarette from the pack of Parliaments she'd picked up at a gas station on the way home. She'd smoked in college, and it had taken her almost a year of trying and failing to finally quit. When she did, she vowed never to touch another butt again. But never was a long time and right now she needed something to calm her unraveling nerves. A cigarette was like an old, familiar friend, it was legal, and getting cancer in twenty years was too remote of a worry right now.

She rubbed her eyes and pushed herself back from her kitchen table, away from the pile of medical and legal treatises, psychology books, layman's reference books and the blur of thick, boring case law on insanity that she'd gathered and read a few times over already. Her notes read like a jumble of thoughts from a twisted, psychological thriller.

—Severe, debilitating mental illness ... profound disruption in cognition and emotion

—Symptoms frequently include <u>psychotic manifestations</u> and bizarre delusions that other people regard as totally implausible ... <u>assaultive, destructive and violent behavior</u> in some schizophrenics

—Prominent <u>auditory hallucinations</u> — voices keeping up a running commentary on a person's behavior, or two or more voices conversing with each other

—<u>Catatonia</u> — state of minimal movement and responsiveness (think mental paralysis)

—<u>Paranoia</u> — an unwarranted feeling others are trying to harm you

—No lab test, CAT scan, brain imaging test (MRI) or clinical presentation of an individual that can yield a definitive diagnosis of schizophrenia

—<u>Strikes young</u> — Average onset: males — between the ages of 17 and 25; females — onset appears delayed by 3–4 years, developing usually between the ages of 21 and 29

—No cure. Anti-psychotic meds include Risperidone, Haldol, Mellaril, Clozaril

Schizophrenia. While she'd definitely heard of it before David Marquette, she'd never known more than what the media chose to print about it in news stories or the scary symptoms that Hollywood selectively twisted into a movie plot. What she did know before last Friday was that schizophrenia was *the* mental illness that defined the word 'crazy', no matter what circle you traveled in. It was the 'condition' that caused people to talk to themselves — or scream at themselves – as they walked down the street, as if there were someone else walking right there alongside them. It was the 'illness' that statistically seemed to plague the homeless, the 'affliction' that made people see little green men, or God, or clandestine government agents.

The jumble of facts and statistics spun inside her head, like unsorted clothes in a dryer. Over the past few days she'd taken a self-taught crash-course in mental illness that was both eye-opening and frightening. An estimated one percent of the world's population – at least 2.2 million Americans – had schizophrenia. But even though its numbers were pervasive and widespread, that didn't make it a socially acceptable disease by any stretch. Schizophrenia still carried with it the most damning stigma of any disease a person could have, outside of leprosy or maybe the plague. It struck young, healthy people with little or no warning – robbing them of, in a word, reality. And the disease didn't discriminate – crossing lines of color and culture, targeting the smart and the stupid, the rich and the poor alike. It did make people see things that were not there, and hear voices that did not speak, but it also changed the very way thoughts were processed and organized in the brain. A misfire somewhere in the circuitry made thoughts and ideas sound just fine in the schizophrenic's head, but once spoken, made no sense to anyone hearing them.

Perhaps the cruelest effect, though, was how the disease stole the ability of its victims to recognize that something had gone very, very wrong inside their brains – a clinical symptom referred to as a 'decreased awareness of illness'. To not know you were sick, while the rest of the world crossed the street just to avoid you, was incredibly sad, Julia thought. No other medical condition could possibly be more isolating or more frightening.

She finished her final gulp of wine and poured herself another glass. Although she wished it would help her sleep, she knew that alcohol, unfortunately, made her insomnia worse. What it was effective at, though, was helping calm the anxious jitters and the disturbed, growing unease while she was awake. But wine was the only vice she permitted herself to have, and only at night. No hard alcohol. She knew that would definitely signal a problem. It had before. She walked into her living room and stared out the window at the night. The moon was full, hanging low in the sky – a funky, ethereal, orange-yellow color, dimpled with craters.

'Andy, why does the moon shrink every night?'

'That's a stupid question.' He sighed an annoyed sigh as only an annoying big brother could. 'It doesn't shrink, Ju-Ju. It's hiding.'

Even though he'd practically just called her stupid, she still wanted the answer. So she swallowed her pout and her pride. 'Okay, why does it want to hide?'

'So it can come back out and make everyone look again. Think about it,' he said, looking up at a full, yellow moon dancing in between the whispery clouds, right outside his bedroom window. It was so perfect, you almost expected a witch to fly past. 'If it stayed fat and round all the time, no one would care. People wouldn't even notice it. Like the sun. No one pays attention to the sun until it disappears and rains for a few days. Then everyone wants it back.'

'Ohhh . . .' It all made perfect sense now. Andy was so smart. He was going places, Momma always said. Julia hoped he'd take her with him when he did.

She blinked back tears.

This case . . . It's too close . . . It can only bring . . . despair.

Is this it? Is this despair, Aunt Nora? Or is this empty,

hollow, dread-filled feeling just the beginning? A prelude to anguish . . .

She looked down at the cordless phone she held in her hand, as she had all day, as she had all night, as she had all week. Only this time she actually hit the speed-dial number.

'Hello?' said a sleepy voice on the second ring.

'Uncle Jimmy?' Julia asked, hesitating, stamping out her cigarette as if she'd been caught. She looked over at the clock on the VCR/DVD player and just then realized it was already half past eleven. She'd waited so long that she'd waited too long.

'Julia? Honey? Waz a matta?' Jimmy asked, wide awake now. She hung her head, mad at herself for not looking at the time before she dialed. While Nora would be up till three baking a calzone, Uncle Jimmy was often out cold by ten.

'I'm sorry, Uncle Jimmy. I just wanted to talk to Aunt Nora. I, ah, didn't realize it was so late,' Julia said in a hushed voice herself.

'What time is it?'

'It's after eleven, so maybe I'll call her tomorrow—'

'Is that Julia?' asked her aunt in the background. 'What's a matter?'

'Hold on, Munch. She's right here.' Julia heard Jimmy say, 'I don't know. She wants you,' to her aunt as he passed the phone. 'She sounds okay, I think. She didn't say nothin' was wrong.'

'What's a matter?' Nora demanded when she got on the phone.

'Nothing, Aunt Nora. I just wanted to ask you something, that's all.'

'At eleven thirty at night? Are you feeling okay? You want me to come over there, honey? I can just get dressed—'

'I didn't mean to wake you.'

'You didn't. I was in the dining room cutting out a couple of coupons – my Valpak came in the mail today. Jimmy got the phone first.' She laughed, relieved. 'At this hour, I thought maybe somebody died.'

'I, ah, I just got done working on this case I've got.'

'Oh.' The laughter stopped. 'The murder? I read the paper this morning. They're saying that man is insane.'

'Yes, and I . . .' Julia hesitated and closed her eyes. 'I wanted to ask you some questions about Andrew.'

There was complete silence on the other end of the phone.

'Aunt Nora? Are you there?'

'Why do you want to ask me about him?' Nora asked quietly.

This was so hard. Much harder than she'd imagined. 'I've been thinking a lot about, um, not just that night, but about the year before it happened. And how things were so different.'

'What's wrong, Momma?' Julia pressed, trying to look past her mother and down the stairs where the den was. 'Who's he yelling at? Why's he so mad tonight? I'm scared.'

'I said go to bed, Julia Anne!' commanded her mother, the fear betraying her strong voice and making it crack. 'Now!' Then she disappeared back into the small room where all the screams were coming from, closing the door behind her.

'There's no one left that would've known him – you know, no other family or friends – and I thought maybe my mom had talked to you about him,' Julia continued. She pulled the hair back off her head, hoping to rein her thoughts in and pull them together. 'About what was going on with him after he left for college. And I thought maybe—'

'I have to tell you that no good can come of this, Julia,' her aunt said in a firm, dismissive voice. 'None. Leave the past in the past. For all of us. Please.'

'What happened to Andy?' Julia finally came out and asked. 'I think I need to know. I think I should know. I have a right, Aunt Nora—'

'I don't want to discuss this. I told you this case was too close. Remember what I said to you, Julia. Remember my words. You're not sleeping again, you're asking crazy questions, you're tired and you're stressed.' She paused. 'You're drinking. Yes, I can hear that, too.'

Julia purposely set the wine glass down on the window sill and stepped over to the couch. She sat and closed her eyes.

'You're opening a box that you don't need opened, is what I'm saying,' Nora continued. 'One that Jimmy and I have worked very hard to keep closed for your own sake. Walk away, Julia. Walk away now, and just let it be before any more people get hurt.'

'Aunt Nora, I can't just walk away. I love you, but I have to know what happened—'

But Aunt Nora cut her off once again, her voice chipper and forced. 'I don't think this Sunday's gonna work. We'll be in Jupiter at a bridge tournament, but we'll have to start talking about Christmas I suppose, right? I know Jimmy's watching Moose next week while you do your trials. You're welcome to come for dinner if you can find the time – we'd love to have you. On Christmas, I don't know, maybe you can bring your boyfriend, the one you've been hiding. That would be fine. But I don't want to talk about this anymore. I have to go to bed now. I love you, but I have to go,' she finished, with what sounded like a whimper. Julia could hear

Jimmy asking her what was wrong before Nora hung up the phone and the line went dead.

She stared hard at the receiver in her hand. No matter how much she tried to keep them back, no matter how much she tried to concentrate on other things, the memories continued to rush forward. Ghosts kept knocking on her door, anywhere, anytime. All the time, now.

Banging, banging, banging just trying to get back in.

41

'You have her?' squawked a raspy male voice over the handheld.

'Yeah, she's in the car.'

'ETA?'

'We're en route. We'll be there in two.' The detective whose badge said Potter turned his head just a little and smiled a weak smile at the young girl who sat by herself in the back seat. Then he cast a silent look over at the driver before turning his attention back to the road. No one said anything.

Julia saw the mass of flashing blue and red lights as soon as the car made its painfully slow turn onto Maple from Hempstead Avenue. Her mouth went dry and she nibbled on her lip, clutching the still-warm sleeping bag in her hand. She probably should have realized long before this moment that something was horribly wrong, but she hadn't. Or she hadn't wanted to. But now she suddenly got it and she just as suddenly knew that she didn't want to see it yet. She turned to look out the side window and blinked hard, trying to force the leftover sleep from her eyes. Just ten minutes ago she'd been at her best friend's house, in the middle of a really good dream that she couldn't remember anymore. Now she was in the back of a cold police car that smelled like smoke and stale cologne and pee. She wondered what Carly was thinking right now. She tasted blood from where she had chewed her lip. What a difference ten minutes could make.

Most of the homes on the block had turned off their Christmas lights when they went to bed, but there were still a few colored lights that twinkled through the night in the tall pines and plump evergreens. The car slipped into slow motion as it passed familiar houses and familiar lawns, where familiar faces gathered in their pajamas and wool coats to see what all the commotion was about. They turned and pointed and squinted at the police car, straining to see its passenger in the back seat, and Julia buried her face in her sleeping bag. The car stopped in front of her house.

Potter turned around again. Red and blue lights spun across his face. No one said anything for a few long moments. 'Something's happened, honey,' the detective finally managed in a low voice.

She nodded furiously, wanting him to stop talking. She couldn't look at him. Blood from her lip seemed to fill her mouth and she was afraid to speak.

He paused and then sighed. Not an aggravated or impatient sigh, but one that was resigned and weary. 'You wanna wait here for a minute, hon?' he asked, but it was more like a statement. She said nothing and he opened his door, nodding at his partner. She watched as the two of them walked across the frozen brown lawn, dotted with gray patches of old snow, and then disappeared into her house.

Ten years earlier, her dad had hung his first and last strand of outdoor lights on the sagging two-story colonial, and more than a few of the oversized and now-obsolete painted bulbs had blown. A glowing plastic Santa Claus waved at the middle-class neighbors and their fancy reindeers and glittering sleighs, the red on his coat and hat faded over the years to a dull pink. She had put out the decorations herself this season, because no one else in the family had wanted to and she couldn't imagine a Christmas without tinsel and lights and gaudy lawn figures, but all she could find in the garage was the aging Santa and a weathered wreath.

Julia squeezed the warm sleeping bag tight against her chest and watched as faceless silhouettes moved through the upstairs rooms of her house. She could feel her heart pound furiously — faster and faster, harder and harder — like a freight train out of control, barreling down open tracks. Any minute now it was going to jump the line.

Icy cold slowly began to seep back into the dark car, stealthily wrapping its invisible, wispy fingers around her body like the coils of *a snake. She counted the ticks as the engine slowly cooled back to silence, and she wondered why she hadn't asked either Detective Potter or his partner what had happened or where her family was or why there were two ambulances just sitting there in her driveway . . .*

Something has happened to me – I do not know what. All that was my former self has crumbled and fallen together and a creature has emerged of whom I know nothing. She is a stranger to me – and has an egotism that makes the egotism that I had look like skimmed milk; and she thinks thoughts that are – heresies. Her name is insanity. She is the daughter of madness – and according to my doctor, they each had their genesis in my own brain.

Lara Jefferson, *These Are My Sisters*

42

'Man, do you look like shit!'

Julia looked up from the pile of paperwork on her desk to see Steve Brill standing in her doorway, paper bag in hand, wearing a Chicago Cubs baseball cap and a half-smile, half-grimace on his face.

'Are you sick or something?' he asked, plopping into a chair. 'You want me to get you a coffee or something? Maybe a doctor?' he added with a chuckle. He looked around the cramped room, where boxes of files sat stacked on top of each other, pushed up against the walls in the corner. Her dispos had been piling up and there was no end in sight. 'This place looks like my apartment,' he said with another laugh. 'You and I might just hit it off, after all, Jules. Looks like we do have something in common – we're slobs. Although I think you're a pack slob. That's a lot worse.'

'You've got so much damn tact,' said another voice from out in the hall. Two seconds later, Lat walked in with just what she needed – another box. 'Someone needs to train him, Julia.'

'Others more brave than you have tried and failed, boss-man. First one gets it right, I think I'll marry again.' Brill looked up at Lat and blinked coquettishly.

'In your dreams,' said Lat, dropping the box on Brill's feet. 'Ignore him, Julia. I've learned to,' he said, flopping into a seat himself. Then he looked at her and his brow crinkled with concern. 'You do look a little tired, though. You okay?'

'Thanks, guys,' she replied, reaching for her glasses, suddenly self-conscious. She thought she'd gotten rid of the dark circles under her eyes this morning with liquid concealer. 'Gee, what a welcome. I'm fine, just not sleeping well. Farley is punishing me. I've been in trial for like two weeks straight and it's getting to me.' She smiled a soft half-smile. 'No big deal.'

Actually, she was exhausted. It'd been more than a few days since she'd been able to get a decent night's rest. Just turn her brain off and go to sleep. And when she finally did manage to nod off, the nightmares would begin. She still had no answers to the questions she'd asked her aunt the other night. As a prosecutor, she knew she had the power and resources to find them out herself, but there was a part of her that didn't want to run the necessary computer checks, or pick up the phone and call strangers in the Nassau County Police Department up in New York to find out the facts. There was a part of her that feared actually hearing the truth. She just needed Aunt Nora to tell her what she wanted to hear and she'd be able to move on.

'That co-counsel of yours keeping you up late at night?' asked Brill. 'No offense, but he can be quite the asshole,' he finished, holding his hands up in the air defensively, before Julia could even think of how she should take the question.

She felt her face redden and she looked down, pretending to pull out a drawer and search for a pen. She definitely didn't want Brill or Lat to know about her relationship with Rick. Especially not Lat. 'I'm just not a good sleeper. Never have been. Are you guys here to see him?'

'We've both decided that we'd much rather see you from now on. You're easier on the eyes and you have a much better personality,' Lat said, grabbing the wax bag from Brill's hand and slapping down the brim of his cap. 'We just got off the plane from Chicago,' he said, handing her the bag. 'We brought you back some pistachio cannolis from D'Amato's to nosh while you're reading through the thick stack of reports we've come to personally deliver. There's an extra copy for the defense in there, too.'

'You know guys like girls with meat on their bones,' Brill said matter-of-factly. 'That skinny shit might sell clothes, but it don't work for the boys. Eat a cannoli.'

She smiled. 'Pistachio cannolis, huh? Thanks. Boy, my aunt would love you two.'

'Valenciano I figured had to be Italian,' Lat said. 'A little taste of home.'

'Like my new hat?' asked Brill.

'No,' she replied. 'I'm a Mets fan.'

'Ouch,' said Brill, smacking himself upside the head. 'A New Yorker. I should have known . . .'

She smiled again. For all of his obnoxious qualities, she was coming to figure out that Steve Brill was harmless. He reminded her of an eleven-year-old boy entering adolescence – snapping the bra straps on the girl seated in front of him just to be annoying. 'Rick might be in his office. I can call him,' she said to Lat, reaching for the phone.

'Seriously, we don't need to see him. Everything's in the reports. And you're co-counsel, so our duty here is done,' said Lat firmly. 'If I need to speak with your boss, it can be on the phone and without a camera stuck in my face.'

She shrugged and looked at him apologetically. 'He can be a bit intense.'

'That's an understatement. But, whatever. At least we have you.' He smiled. The moment lasted longer than she expected and she looked down again at her desk. She could feel the Irish curse flaming her cheeks. 'So, when's the competency hearing?' he asked. 'Do you have a date yet?'

'The Wednesday before Christmas. The judge appointed Barakat and Koletis.'

Brill rolled his eyes. 'Jesus . . . I can tell you the outcome of *that* match-up.'

'Rick will handle the hearing if it's a toss-up and the doctors don't agree. If they do see eye-to-eye, I suppose he'll stipulate to the reports,' she said.

'Well,' Lat said, 'we've pretty much interviewed and re-interviewed everyone in Miami we could find who ever dealt with David Marquette as either a patient, employee or colleague.'

'And?'

'The media always brings out the best in people. Some are remembering things a little differently than they did a few weeks ago. You know, everyone wants to be the first on the bandwagon to say they saw the signs.'

'Not such the great guy Jennifer's family insists he was?' Julia asked.

'You always try to impress the in-laws, Jules,' said Brill.

'Marquette was a loner,' Lat said. 'Jennifer's family, as we've already figured out, twelve hundred miles away and blinded by his checkbook and credentials, didn't know him. They saw what they wanted to see. End of story. And they'll make great witnesses for the defense. But the favorite son-in-law could be actually very difficult to work with, so goes the jaded opinions of the nurses, office managers, receptionists and underpaid, overworked, bitter hospital staff that had to work with him.'

'Unless you were good-looking and female. Then he was sweet and smart and dedicated,' noted Brill. 'Misunderstood.'

'Affairs?' Julia asked.

'One-nighters, we think, but nobody waiting in the wings and no one willing to go on record,' said Lat.

'How was he difficult?' she asked.

'God-complex difficult,' replied Brill.

'He blew off appointments on occasion, missed two surgeries in the last couple of weeks that had to be rescheduled. "His time is important to him and no one else" sort of complaints, but there's no doubt he was a good surgeon on the rise, to the point of being cocky in the operating room.'

'And there was that nurse,' Brill added.

'Yeah,' said Lat, nodding. 'He got into a screaming match with a nurse over something she said in the operating room a couple of weeks before the murders.'

'Which was?' she asked.

'She says nothing. But the doc flipped out on her, called her all sorts of nasty names in surgery and kicked her out of the OR.'

Julia nodded at the box that Lat had dumped on the floor. 'What've you got there? That can't all be reports.'

'Nope. Better. Medical records,' Brill replied.

'We went back to Marquette's old stomping grounds in Kenilworth, which is a suburb on Chicago's North Shore,' Lat said. 'Outside of a two-year stint in Paris when he was five and his dad headed up some international program at Pierre and Marie Curie University, that's where he was raised.'

'Nice 'hood,' said Brill with a low whistle.

'Interviewed a few former teachers, found a few old classmates, most of whom either didn't remember him, or didn't care to.'

'Even as a kid, the guy was definitely a misfit,' Brill said. 'A Charley in the Box. Stuck to himself, had no real friends. Bright, but could be lazy and definitely arrogant. Sailed through private elementary and middle school – hit a huge snag as a junior in high school. Grades tanked until Daddy built a wing or something, and then it was smooth sailing again until young Davy went off to college at DePaul – thanks again, I'm sure, to Pops.'

'Drugs?' asked Julia.

'That's what we think,' said Lat with a nod. 'Personality change coupled with a sudden drop in grades.'

'But, of course, when we go near the Marquette family compound to get their take on things, the curtains draw and everyone starts to boo us,' added Brill. 'You want to talk to somebody? You better have a subpoena in your hand.'

'He left DePaul after his three-week vacation at Parker Hills. Or DePaul booted him – his GPA was below a two. He started at Loyola the following September,' Lat said. 'The few former acquaintances who we did find that were credible remember Marquette as either extremely charming or extremely manipulative. Self-assured or completely full of himself. There's no middle ground.'

'I guess you have to be charming to be manipulative, don't you?' she asked.

'My ex-wife sure wasn't,' piped in Brill with a snort. Even Julia laughed.

'We pulled, record-wise, what we could from DePaul and Loyola, but again, nothing remarkable. No one remembers him. Grades were okay at Loyola, occasionally great. Looks like when our defendant likes something, he excels, but other than that, he doesn't try too hard. He went to med school at Northwestern down the hall from his father, made the final walk to "Pomp and Circumstance", but by a hair. In my opinion, Daddy definitely pulled strings to get him wherever he was going,' Lat said with a shrug.

'You know what they call the guy who graduates last in his class from med school?' Brill asked.

'What?'

'Doctor.'

'Good point,' Lat said.

'And I think that's gonna be our biggest hurdle. We need to get a jury past the fact that he's a successful surgeon,' Julia added.

Lat leaned forward in his seat, and tapped his finger on her desk. 'We did find something very interesting, though. An old arrest when young Davy was sixteen. Saw it referenced in the DePaul admission papers. A misdemeanor. Animal cruelty.'

She raised her eyebrows in surprise. 'Did you get the case file?'

'Nope. It's been sealed and expunged, that's why we didn't find it before on NCIC.' NCIC stood for the National Crime Information Center, which maintained criminal histories from every state in the country. 'It's gone, and only the original charge is left in the county computer, it was so long ago. Your guess is as good as mine as to what happened, but you know what I'm thinking.'

She nodded. Cruelty to animals, particularly in childhood and adolescence, evidenced an alarming emotional detachment from living things – a classic warning sign of a budding antisocial personality. Many famous killers experimented with animals long before they tried anything on humans. Jeffrey Dahmer impaled dogs; Richard Allen Davis set cats on fire; Richard Speck threw birds into fans. The list went on. 'But there's no way of making that jump without knowing all the facts.'

He tapped a finger against his temple. 'Just store it upstairs. Second year at DePaul, Marquette checked into Parker Hills, like his attorney says. That was nineteen ninety. We faxed ahead with the subpoena, so they had the records ready for us.' He pointed at the box. 'Some late-night reading for you. Maybe it will help you sleep,' he added with a soft smile.

Her eyes followed his finger to the floor. 'Is that when he was diagnosed schizophrenic?' Marquette would have been nineteen or twenty at the time – right smack-dab in the average onset for males. And once a schizophrenic, always a schizophrenic. The disease didn't just run its course and go away, like a cold. You didn't become 'schizophrenia-free', like a cancer patient in remission. Although another surprising fact Julia had discovered was that schizophrenics were not *always* psychotic, either – seeing things and hearing voices for the rest of their life. Which would explain why Marquette might have led a relatively normal life for the past decade or so – at least at a glance. The disease itself was unpredictable in whom it affected and how it affected them. Like rheumatoid arthritis, MS and Parkinson's – some people came down with the 'bad' progressive type of the disease, where symptoms never got better, only worse, while others received the better prognosis. In some, medicine worked wonders. In others, it didn't work at all.

Lat shook his head. 'Nope. Not directly, anyway. The only thing the doctor wrote on the notes was "Rule out schizophrenia", but there is no reference to an actual *diagnosis* of schizophrenia, or that it was ruled out. He was admitted involuntarily by his dad apparently, according to the records, suffering hallucinations and for, and I'm quoting here, "violent, combative, erratic behavior". End quote. But the records upon admission only refer to a probable *cocaine psychosis* as a true diagnosis. By the time he was discharged, his "psychosis" had been downplayed to a simple anxiety disorder. Probably, I'm guessing, at the request of his dad. Marquette's a big name in Kenilworth and Chicago.'

'Cocaine psychosis?' Julia said, taken aback. 'So this was a drug rehab?'

'That's what it looks like to my untrained eye. But I'm not a three-hundred-dollar-an-hour defense attorney grasping at straws. I'm sure that in a courtroom anxiety disorder will become a misdiagnosed psychotic break. Make the illness fit the crime.'

'Is the doc who diagnosed him still there?'

'Hell, no. Left a year later. Died of a heart attack five years ago.'

'And the violent behavior?'

'He assaulted his mother with an iron.'

'That was plugged in at the time,' Brill added.

'Ouch,' she said, shaking her head at the picture. 'Was he arrested? Were the cops called?'

'Nope and nope,' Lat replied. 'Looking at the admission remarks, Dad apparently dragged Junior's ass into the family Range Rover and drove him to this exclusive Betty Ford-like rest-stop. Under a different name, of course. It was all very hush-hush, which is why we couldn't have found it, even if we'd known where to look.'

'This is a family that likes to keep secrets, Jules,' Brill added with a strange smile. 'Big ones. And, for you, we've saved the biggest for last.'

Her eyes darted between the two of them. 'Why am I getting a bad feeling?'

'You can either hear it now or read about it tomorrow,' Lat replied. 'Levenson's scheduled a press conference in an hour or so.'

'A good defense attorney's rule of thumb – when your client's just not making the headlines anymore, spoon-feed some fun facts to the press to keep interest up,' Brill scoffed.

'Now I don't know just how this is gonna play out, and

I don't even know how much it's gonna matter in the end, but it is pretty damn interesting – especially if psychotic behavior runs in the family and swims in the gene pool,' Lat began.

She stared at him, waiting.

'David Marquette has a brother,' Lat finished. 'An *identical twin brother*, quietly stashed away in a psych hospital. His name is Darrell Armand Marquette, and he most definitely *is* a nut job.'

43

'Officially diagnosed schizophrenic in ninety-two when he was twenty-one,' Lat said. 'Had a breakdown two months after a new girlfriend dumped him and Grandma up and died. He was supposed to be up at MIT studying nuclear physics, but instead Wackenhut Security found him re-arranging the lawn furniture of a high-school buddy at three in the morning, preparing for the second coming of Christ with sixteen rolls of heavy-duty tinfoil and a few hundred yards of electrical tape. The family kept him hidden away at the homestead for a couple of years, like Norman Bates's mother, but in ninety-eight, he was moved to South Oaks, a locked psychiatric hospital in the 'burbs. He's there under the name Darrell Lamoreaux.'

Her head was spinning. An identical twin? 'How'd you find him?'

'That was tough. As Stevie Wonder here just said, this is a family that likes to keep its secrets, Julia. We only found out this guy even existed after a couple of old teachers we interviewed asked us *which* Marquette boy we were referring to. That's when we discovered that even though David Marquette had an identical twin, not everything about the two of them was the same. Evidently Darrell was the one who stood out. *He* was the genius, one teacher told us. Our boy, Dave, struggled in comparison. It was Darrell who was valedictorian, Darrell who'd jumped a year ahead in school, Darrell who won track meets, Darrell who dated the prom queen, Darrell who was accepted to MIT on a scholarship.

Everyone we spoke to after that who remembered both boys, all wondered what had become of *Darrell*. And so did we. Nothing came up on Autotrack, NCIC or with the locals. We got his social from school recs and checked with the Bureau of Vital Statistics and knew he wasn't dead. It's like he just up and disappeared. Of course, no one at the house would talk. So we found ourselves a former house-keeper who didn't mind chatting if we helped her out on a bench warrant for some unpaid moving violations. She gave us the name of the hospital. We used Mom's maiden name to figure out the alias.'

'Did you interview him?'

'Not much there to interview, Counselor,' Lat said with a shake of his head. 'He's got what the docs call hebephrenic schizophrenia, also known as the disorganized type.'

'Who knew there were different types? I thought it was one size fits all nuts,' Brill said with a throaty laugh.

Lat ignored him. 'You can't follow what this guy Darrell's saying when he does talk, which is rare. Nurses told us he just sits for hours and hours on end. He's in his own little world. Looking at the daily activity log, only Dad's been paying visits the last six months, which is how far back the records go. No Mom, no bro. In fact, no one who works there can recall visits ever from a brother. And since they are identical twins, you'd think someone would remember seeing *that*. The doc at South Oaks must have called Alain Marquette as soon as we hit the parking lot, 'cause the phone was ringing by the time our plane touched down at MIA. Levenson wanted to know exactly what we were doing over at Looney Land, who told us about it and what we'd found out. It sounded like he might not know too much himself.'

'What did you say?'

'I told him Nextel has a problem with dropping calls.

Then I hung up. It'll be interesting to hear what he decides to spill to the cameras this afternoon. What he's been *told* he can spill.'

'Ya know, I knew the parents were holding out,' Brill said gruffly, twisting the end of his mustache with his fingers. 'Why not talk to the police? We're your friends.'

'Unless you got something or someone to hide,' answered Lat.

'They wouldn't be the first parents to want to distance themselves from their children,' she said quietly. 'Especially these kids.'

Lat shook his head. 'And now? The reversal of engines? The high-priced attorney? Calling out the embassy? Holding press conferences?'

'Heading you off at the pass on the last one. If the story's inevitably coming out, better to put their spin on it than ours. As far as backing this son,' she shrugged, 'maybe they feel guilty for abandoning the other.'

'Maybe. Wait a sec, you weren't a psych major were you?' asked Lat.

'No. Why?'

'Just asking. So what do you think this twin thing means? Anything?'

'Maybe Dave's been taking notes all these years on how a nut's *really* supposed to act,' said Brill. Then he shrugged. 'Or maybe that house was hell, drove 'em both crazy.'

'There's no known cause of schizophrenia, but it's thought that there is a genetic link,' she said slowly, remembering some of the things she'd been reading. 'The DNA of identical twins is the same. So if one twin has the disease, there is a markedly increased risk of the other twin developing it. I think it's like almost a thirty percent chance or something like that. So yeah, this arguably might be very relevant. At least to the court-appointed psychiatrists. Is there any other family history of mental illness?'

'*That's* gonna be a problem,' said Brill with a sigh. 'And not just because Dad and Mom and the rest of the hired help don't want to cooperate.'

'Huh?' she asked.

'We told you this case was full of surprises,' Lat said. 'And they just keep on coming. There are no other blood relatives, Julia. Darrell and David are both adopted.'

44

The same body, two completely different men. The same story, two completely different tales. Julia didn't need to tune in to Mel Levenson's late-afternoon press conference to hear just how his closing argument was shaping up. She could spin the yarn herself for both sides.

She washed down the last bite of her cannoli with a gulp of warm Diet Coke as she skimmed through the thick stacks of disturbing police reports, interviews and medical records that now covered her desk. In serial crimes, police often used profilers to develop psychological composites of possible suspects to help them hunt down rapists and killers. Like a slow-developing photograph, the background of David Marquette's life was now gradually beginning to emerge, the fine details were being filled in, completing the picture of the strange man in the foreground, hidden in shadow. On paper, those details read like a profiler's psych composite. *White male, age 25 to 45, average to above-average intelligence, probably educated and in a high-risk profession. Has a problem relating to people – women in particular – with a controlling, domineering mother, a probable history of animal cruelty and substance abuse, and few, if any, friends.*

She spun her chair around and looked past the air handlers at the Dade County Jail across the street. Somewhere behind the iron bars and steel-mesh windows sat her defendant, locked away from the general population and buried deep within the screaming corridors of the ninth floor. The Crazy Floor.

The same story, two completely different tales.

A boy who didn't fit in from day one: strange, odd, a loner, an underachiever, a misfit. A Charley in the Box with an identical twin who was anything but identical. In fact, he was perfect. Perfect grades, perfect personality. Wins track meets and scholarships and walks little old ladies across the street. Dates the cheerleaders and prom queens and makes Mom and Dad very proud. The Misfit Boy fits even less. He begins to act out. Hurts animals just to watch them suffer. Tries drugs. Flunks a couple of classes. If he can't be his brother, then he *won't* be his brother. As the Perfect Brother grows older and more perfect and his long list of accomplishments hits double digits, The Misfit's behavior gets worse. Drug use intensifies. The violence reserved for animals escalates now to humans; he focuses on the object of his rage and tries to kill his mother. He gets kicked out of school. Again and again, Dad has to help him out of jam after jam. Dad has to clean up the verbal messes The Misfit leaves behind on arrest reports and admission papers so that no one gets 'the wrong impression' about the family with the good name and deep pockets. It's Dad who pulls strings again to get The Misfit into another good school, buy him another chance. He is nothing like his brother. He is nothing but a scary, bitter disappointment. But then Perfect Brother gets sick. Comes down with the Mother of Bad Diseases. The most shameful: schizophrenia. Perfect Brother suddenly falls hard and fast from grace and becomes the son who Mom and Dad now want to hide away somewhere. Dad pushes The Misfit into his new role as Number One Son. Gets him through school, gets him a degree, gets him a prestigious job. The Misfit's given a license to practice medicine and officially stamped a success. Only he's really not. He's really a time bomb, ticking away in this new, uncomfortable, socially enviable role, with a clingy wife and three kids he didn't plan on having, until he finally, inevitably, just explodes.

But the same facts could just as easily tell a different story; the same brush could paint a much more tragic picture – that of a boy who was always a little odd, who struggled to fit in but never could for a reason. Because, like his twin, deep inside his brain an insidious disease was taking hold and growing silent roots, destroying and disrupting communication pathways as it spread out, stealthily seeding images and voices in his decaying mind like deadly landmines – so incredibly real, his own brain was sure to be fooled. Layer by paper-thin layer, the disease slowly breaks the boy down from the inside out, leaving only his body intact as his frightened adoptive parents willfully misread all the warning signs, hoping against hope that their son's more and more obvious distress is anything but a mental illness. Anything but the horrible disease he is inevitably to be diagnosed with. And even then, the diagnosis is unacceptable. It's changed, for the sake of the family name. When the boy's identical twin suffers the same fate a couple of years later, he is locked away in a room, then shuffled into a psychiatric facility, never to be seen again. But his brother's affliction is far worse, far more disabling, and so the boy must have recovered from whatever it was that had ailed him in college. A bad case of nerves, it was. Stress. He's fine now, the denying family rationalizes once again with a hushed whisper. Only he wasn't fine. The boy with the unmentionable disease was sick. He was denied the help he needed all these years because of stigma and embarrassment, and now four people are dead.

'The world is either cheerfully rosy or depressingly gray; it all depends on how you're seeing it,' Julia's mom used to say. 'You choose the glasses you want to wear everyday. You choose how you want to see it.'

The same body, two completely different men.

Dr Jekyll or Mr Hyde.

Who was David Alain Marquette?

45

'Tell me this guy's not a real nut, Chris,' Rick said with a smile and a shake of his head as he and Julia followed the cute, young secretary with the tight Christmas sweater into an office that was a lot nicer than what one would expect the office of a psychiatrist on the State's list to look like. Faux-painted hunter-green walls, leather club chairs, an antique burnished oak desk and an address on ritzy Brickell Avenue – business was clearly booming in Christian Barakat's private practice. Forensic psychiatry was obviously the side-job. ''Cause if he is, *I'm* gonna need a standing appointment in that overbooked Day-Timer of yours. Julia Valenciano, this is Dr Christian Barakat, the man who's going to save my perfect case from going to shit.'

A tall, dark and handsome man, who looked nothing like what Julia thought a psychiatrist should look like, stood up and stepped out from behind the desk. Dark hair, sculpted chin, incredible blue eyes – no wonder the desperate house-wives were lining up outside to spill their secrets. 'Hey there, Ricky,' he said, shaking Rick's hand, his perfect grin endcapped with saucer-sized dimples. 'Nice to meet you, Julia.'

'Yes. Nice to meet you, too,' she answered.

'Please, sit. You want some coffee?'

'Nah. We just came from lunch. Julia's second-seating me on this Marquette mess. I figured we'd stop in for some good news and a bite of that report you owe me,' Rick said. 'So what's the final verdict on this guy?'

'Ariana was about to messenger it over. She just finished typing it up,' Dr Barakat said, taking a seat back behind his desk. His eyes narrowed and he smiled a thoughtful, teasing smile. 'Feeling anxious, are you, Ricky?'

'Cut the psychiatrist act, pal. Nothing like breaking my balls and waiting till the last goddamn minute. Christmas is breathing down my neck, every judge wants to get a head start on the holidays and wrap up their calendar for the rest of the year this week, and I've got this thing going on Wednesday. Not to mention that I haven't even started my Christmas shopping.'

Julia was willing to venture a guess right then that Rick and Christian Barakat's relationship was more than just professional – the two of them were obviously good friends. She felt a little out of place in the conversation, and wondered why Rick hadn't shared that with her before walking in here today.

'Only eight shopping days left. And with the length of your list, you're right. You *are* running out of time,' Dr Barakat replied with an inside-joke sort of laugh.

Good guess. Rick ignored the comment with just a smile, while Julia tried to, looking down at something on the carpet. Obviously the good friend didn't know about her either.

'The press on this has not been favorable.'

'I know. I've been reading about you on line at the supermarket.'

'*Et tu, Brute?* The French consulate's now threatening to file a complaint with the World Court in The Hague if we don't drop the death penalty. They want Marquette examined and treated by their own psychiatrists.'

Dr Barakat shook his head.

'Exactly. I don't need any more performers in the circus. They had their ten minutes with him to make sure he was being fed and read his rights. I'm not letting them build on this bullshit insanity defense by throwing in a few more store-bought, jaded opinions simply because they don't want to see one of their displaced countrymen take the walk. As you well know, I've got a lot riding on this case. A lot. I need ammo to throw at my detractors, show them that I'm not such a bad guy after all.'

'For trying to execute an insane Frenchman?' the doctor asked.

'Exactly. So tell me he's not.'

'French?'

'Insane.'

Dr Barakat sighed. 'I can't do that. *Yet*. At least, not officially. But what I can tell you is that he's competent to stand trial, despite his very best efforts to convince me otherwise.'

Rick slapped his hand on the desk. 'I knew it. Is he schizo?'

A strange look crossed the doctor's face, as if he were remembering something and wasn't sure if he should reveal it. 'I can't be official on a diagnosis until I do the full psych eval,' he said slowly, 'but I don't think it's schizophrenia that ails him.'

'Al Koletis found him incompetent. He filed his report this morning,' Rick grumbled, running a hand through his hair. 'Which is one of the reasons I'm so uptight, even though I can't say I wasn't expecting it. In my twenty at the State, I can't remember Koletis ever finding anyone competent. That's why Len Farley let Mel pick him, 'cause he loves all the drama. It makes the old coot's decision in front of the cameras all the more important.'

Dr Barakat slowly shook his head. 'Don't go celebrating just yet. I'm telling you, this is a tough call. You're gonna have a hard time with this guy, Rick.'

A chill suddenly ran down Julia's spine. The strange, un-comfortable unease was back once again, creeping through her bones. She remembered the figure in the red jumpsuit from the arraignment. The Human Monster on display, with his dead eyes and shackled hands. The smiling man from the hall photographs who, strangely enough, never appeared in any Marquette family videos.

Never pretend to know someone's life, Julia. You'll only know what they want you to know, when it is they want you to know it.

'What do you mean?' asked Rick.

'Psychiatry is not an exact science, you know,' Dr Barakat explained. 'There's no scan, no physical test, to detect mental illness. Only after taking a history, and listening to the symptoms a patient *claims* to be experiencing in his head, can you try and figure out his mental malady. The biggest challenge to a *forensic* psychiatrist is, of course, malingering – how to tell when someone is faking it to get a pass on a lifetime in jail or a final walk down the long hall to the execution chamber.

'Now, your average person thinks being "crazy" means seeing little green men and shouting obscenities at the devil all day long. So that's exactly what they'll do when they're trying to convince the world they're insane – whenever they're in a courthouse or come within ten feet of a doctor. But that's not an accurate portrayal of schizophrenia. While the disease afflicts people differently, many don't experience visual hallucinations at all. And it's not usually the devil yapping in their ear. You see, *delusions* are the hallmark symptom of the disease – fixed false beliefs held by the schizophrenic that defy logic and persist in spite of rational arguments or evidence to the contrary. From there, the audio, and *sometimes* visual, hallucinations will spawn and then feed the delusion.

'Take Margaret Mary Ray, for instance, the schizophrenic known as David Letterman's stalker. Ray *believed* she was Letterman's wife, despite being arrested multiple times and being told by everyone, including Letterman himself, for years that that was just not the case. *But the delusion was her reality.* Now that's a difficult enough concept for someone in the mental-health field to understand and treat, and an almost impossible manifestation of the disease for someone to try and successfully imitate – twenty-four hours a day, seven days a week – if he or she's not actually in the throes of a delusion. For example, when Ray stole Letterman's Porsche from his driveway in Connecticut and, with her three-year-old kid in it, headed off to see him in New York, she really believed it was in *her* car with *his* child. Her actions followed, or furthered, the delusion. And that's just the sort of behavior – or lack thereof – that'll give a malingerer away most of the time. They'll steal the car and get caught at a chop shop. Or they'll present with questionable symptoms – like seeing the proverbial little green men. Or being symptomatic only at specific times – like when they're in court – and fine during others, maybe when they're around other patients and feel no one is watching. Or perhaps they'll continue to claim they're having hallucinations or hearing voices long after the medication would have helped to subdue their symptoms, because they're unaware of when and how a psychotropic drug actually works. These are all classic signs to watch for to detect malingering. Most of the time, though, you just know ten minutes after meeting the person by the feeling in your gut whether or not he's faking it.'

Dr Barakat hesitated for a moment and his face grew dark. 'But then there is a different breed of malingerer. A different breed of human being, actually. This one is much more rare. Extremely smart, cunning, manipulative. Dangerous. He will convince those that want to be convinced of his illness, including professionals, and he will adapt to the tests they put upon him because he is a survivor. He feels no remorse for what he's done, because he feels no empathy for others, no matter who they are. He has no conscience – that internal Jiminy Cricket voice in all of us that keeps us on the straight and narrow, and turns us, so to speak, from evil.' Dr Barakat paused for a long moment, reflecting on his thoughts. 'And I think that just might be your defendant.'

46

No one said anything for a moment. The air felt almost electric. 'Is that just your gut talking?' Rick finally asked.

'I spent two hours with him at the jail,' Dr Barakat replied slowly. 'He did present with some of what we call the negative symptoms of schizophrenia: poor hygiene, blank expression, what's known as blunted affect or flat emotions, zombie-like behavior.' He paused again. 'Most malingerers don't know enough about the disease to do that, as I said before. But again, this guy's not your everyday malingerer. He's got a degree in medicine. Now it's difficult when someone's on a drug such as Thorazine to distinguish what may be these "negative" symptoms, and what might just be the effects of the medication,' he said with a shrug. 'But, frankly, I don't think it's either.

'Let me just say,' he continued, when no one said anything, tapping his pen on his notepad. 'Personally, if I was going to try and fake being legally insane to beat a court case, I'd probably go the same route with the same symptoms. Why? The less said, the less for anyone – including a team of court-appointed psychiatrists – to interpret. It's the *smart* choice. It's perhaps not as egotistical as trying to verbally outwit the shrinks and nurses and cops, but yet it's much more controlled. Much more cunning, actually.

'So maybe I'm a bit skeptical, but in my time with Dr Marquette I was looking for certain bizarre behavior characteristics that are peculiar to catatonic schizophrenia – the type of schizophrenia he's demonstrating symptoms of. One of these characteristics is echopraxia, which is basically mimicking, or mirroring, the movements or speech patterns of another. Or inflexible muscle movement, where you'll move a catatonic's arm and it will stay in that exact position, sometimes for hours, even if it's suspended. These are characteristics even most medical professionals, such as Dr Marquette, would not be familiar with unless they'd worked specifically and extensively with catatonics before.' He paused and then added, 'But *I* have. And I didn't observe any of those behaviors. When I raised his arm above his head, it fell to his side, carefully missing both his face and the table on its way back down.

'So, while we don't know exactly where a catatonic goes when they are in that state of extreme withdrawal, I feel pretty confident telling you that David Marquette is not in that place. He's right there in the room with you. Carefully watching you watch him with blank eyes. Waiting for your reaction to plan his. *That's* my gut talking.'

'Did he speak?' asked Julia.

'Yes. Although, for the most part, he was mainly monosyllabic answering my questions. As I said before, I thought he was carefully reading my reaction, and I think he read that his act was clearly missing something.'

'Did he talk about the murders?'

'Only in a limited capacity as it related to his competency. But he was oriented to time and place. He knows what he's been arrested for and what penalties he faces. He knows his entire family is dead. Bottom line, in my opinion, with a medication adjustment, he's definitely competent.'

'This twin brother of his,' Rick said carefully. 'Darrell. Where does he fit in? Or does he?'

'That's the interesting twist to all this,' Dr Barakat said, frowning. 'You see, no one knows exactly what causes schizophrenia, but we do know this much: genetics definitely play a role in who gets it. So, yes, it will be a factor in his defense. For decades, everyone thought schizophrenia was caused by bad parenting. More particularly, bad mothering. Obsessive, overanxious, domineering, bad mothers created stressed-out, psychotic kids who couldn't cope with reality. But bad mothering has been displaced by science. We know now that schizophrenia is an organic brain disease, in that the brain's *structure* is physically changed. As for suspected causes for the changes, they still range from viruses and food allergies to neurochemical deficiencies, infectious agents or physical trauma in utero, or a dysfunctional endocrine system.'

Rick made a skeptical face, but said nothing.

'Blame the cause on whatever you want,' Dr Barakat continued, 'but the genetic link can't be ignored. With each family member afflicted with the disease, the risk factor for fellow family members does go up. To put it in perspective, the worldwide general population, with no family history of schizophrenia, has about a one percent potluck chance of developing the disease. Now, take a parent afflicted with schizophrenia. His or her child is *thirteen* times more likely to develop it. If both parents have it, the risk jumps to *thirty-six* percent. And with identical twins, the risk leaps close to *thirty* percent, even with twins separated at birth and raised in different households. And the risk is cumulative. So if Mom, Sis and Grandma have schizophrenia, Junior is at least twenty-six times more likely to develop the disease than, say, you or me. Since this guy's adopted, the argument, I'm sure, will be that his tree was loaded with bad fruit. We've seen whole families, unfortunately, afflicted with the disease. Margaret Mary Ray, who I was telling you about before, was a classic example of this. Two of her three siblings had schizophrenia, as did her father. All three kids committed suicide, including Margaret Mary who knelt in front of a train in 1998. The identical Genain quadruplets from the thirties – all four girls developed schizophrenia before the age of twenty-four. Now whether genetics *cause* the disease, or merely *predispose* someone to it, no one knows. And no one has yet found a gene that causes schizophrenia. All that is clear is that it definitely runs in families.'

Ariana came back in with the report. She handed it to Rick with a coquettish smile. 'Happy holidays,' she said sweetly.

'Thank you. You, too,' Rick replied thoughtfully, matching her smile. He stood up and waved the report in his hand. 'Good job, my man. I'll call you after I've digested all this and you and I can go over your testimony for Wednesday. Dress nice and don't forget, nine thirty sharp. It's Len Farley and he's unforgiving. Especially with our poor Julia here.'

'Good luck with the shopping,' Barakat said in that same inside-joke voice, rising himself. 'Remember, stay the hell away from jewelry stores.'

Julia remained seated. She suddenly didn't care anymore about what Christian Barakat and Rick might really be saying. Instead, her brain was spinning with everything Dr Barakat had said moments before. What it meant, what it could mean. 'I have to ask you something, Dr Barakat,' she said slowly, still not yet rising. 'If David Marquette is not schizophrenic, if he's faking it like you're suggesting – what is he, then? You said before, he's cunning, he's smart, he's manipulative – but what does that really mean? Without an obvious motive, what kind of person could murder his entire family and then be devious enough – smart enough, as you said – to successfully fake the symptoms of catatonia and schizophrenia?'

Christian Barakat didn't hesitate at all. 'For once, that's an easy enough answer to give, even for a psychiatrist,' he answered coolly. 'It would make him a monster.'

47

'He's competent,' Julia said to Lat over the phone. She slugged down a long sip of cold coffee, and looked around her desk drawer for a couple of quarters to go get herself another one from the machine downstairs. She only found three.

'That's not what I heard on the news at noon,' Lat replied. 'Says who?'

'Tune in again. Says Christian Barakat. He just handed us his report this afternoon. He thinks this zombie act is just that – an act. Says it could be a medication issue, or more likely it's because David Marquette is, get this,' she said, hesitating just a bit, 'a psychopath. He needs to do some more tests to make that official, but the doctor scored high on this "Psychopathy Checklist" Barakat referred to.' She raked the bottom of her pocketbook with her fingers and finally found another quarter, covered in lint and purse dirt.

'A psychopath, huh? That makes sense. Who the hell else breaks out the kitchen cutlery on their family in the middle of the night?'

She closed her eyes. *A monster.*

'Well that should make for an interesting Wednesday morning,' Lat offered when she hadn't said anything.

'You'll be there, right?'

'Definitely. I wonder if Levenson will put his client on the stand.'

'I doubt it. He'd be crazy to.' *Crazy.* The word sounded strange on her tongue. It had such a different meaning now. She rolled the quarters around in her sweaty fist.

'Will you be handling the hearing?' he asked.

The idea was so funny that she actually laughed out loud. She had a better chance of winning Powerball before Rick would let her handle an expert witness at a competency hearing. 'I'll be sitting at the table,' she said in a conciliatory voice.

'Too bad.'

She wasn't sure if he meant that as a compliment to her or a slam against Rick, so she said nothing.

'Farley sure picked some week,' Lat said. 'Four days before Christmas.'

'He did that on purpose,' Julia said. 'He does everything on purpose, and ruining holidays and vacations would be one of the things I imagine he does best.'

Now it was Lat's turn to laugh. 'Did he ruin yours? Family out of town?'

She felt the sudden pain stab her heart. She should've prepped herself for that question, but she hadn't, and she felt as if someone had rushed her from behind, knocking her to the ground and stealing the breath from her lungs. She hated this time of year. Hated it. Starting at Thanksgiving and lasting past New Years, every day was a chore to get through, every night filled with bad memories that just seemed to get worse year after year. She hated seeing everyone happy and together – in every commercial, in every print ad, on every box of cereal and can of Coke. She hated the intrusive questions that people seemed to ask each other without thought. *Are you going back home for the holidays? Who are you spending Christmas with? Is Mom making the turkey this year? Does she let you help?* Nora and Jimmy and she always went through the motions of having a holiday dinner, complete with turkey and non-stop Christmas music, but Christmas at Aunt Nora's was like a bad wake with good food – there was nothing joyous about it and everyone couldn't wait till it was over. This year, Julia knew, would be especially difficult because she'd gone and brought up Andy.

The box was wrapped so pretty, she knew it couldn't have been Andy who'd wrapped it. It must have been wrapped at the store – a fancy store. The ribbon was thick and tied into a bow that you only saw in department-store Christmas displays, but never under your own tree. A sparkling plastic angel ornament hung from one of its many pretty loops. 'To Ju-Ju, Hope this makes it merry. Love, A.J.' read the tag. A.J. was the new nickname Andy had been trying to get everyone to call him. Momma said names that started with initials sounded too much like confidential informants.

She closed the door of the bathroom softly behind her, turned on the lights and took a deep breath. There were only a couple of hours left to wait till Christmas morning, but she just couldn't help herself. The idea of a present under the tree with her name on it bugged her like an itch – there could be no relief until she knew what was in it. She moved the ribbon out of the way, slid a bread knife under the tape and then unwrapped one end of the thick paper. She slid out the box, careful to keep the shape of the wrap intact so she could just slide it back in when she was done peeking. No one would be the wiser.

When she saw the box was from Cosby's Sporting Goods she stopped breathing. She wiped her palms on her robe, then took off the top and pulled back the folds of tissue paper. Shining under the lights of the broken overhead bathroom fixture was the white satin New York Ranger jacket that she'd asked for, first for her birthday and then again for Christmas. It was the only thing she wanted, but it was almost a hundred dollars and her mom had said they couldn't afford it. Now, here it was, hers.

She couldn't help herself again. She put the box on the sink and took the jacket out. She slipped off her robe and put the jacket on over her pajamas, running her hands over the smooth satin. It felt soooo amazing . . .

'How does it fit?' came the voice on the other side of the door.
She froze, her arms wrapped around herself.
'Come on, Ju-Ju,' Andy whispered. 'How does it fit?'

'Julia?' Lat asked.

'No,' she said slowly, pushing the ghosts back once again. 'I'm just going to my aunt and uncle's on Christmas Day. They're down here. And you?'

'I don't know yet. I might head over with a buddy to the Bahamas. He's got a fishing boat up in Fort Lauderdale and an ex-wife who gets the holiday with the kids this year.'

'Christmas on the high seas? That sounds kind of nice,' she said. She realized just then, like an unsettling epiphany, that Christmas was only a week away and she and Rick hadn't even discussed the holiday yet. She had no idea what he was doing.

'You're welcome anytime,' Lat replied.

'Thanks for the invitation. I might take you up on that one day.'

'Egg-nog's overrated. And fattening. I'll stick a candy cane in your pina colada.'

She was quiet for a moment, thinking about the other reason she'd decided to call Lat when she got back to the office.

'You still there?' he asked after a second.

'I have a favor I need to ask you, Lat,' she said quickly, twisting the phone cord around the fingers of one hand, crunching the quarters in the other. 'Can you run an NCIC for me?'

It was actually a crime to run a criminal history without a legitimate law-enforcement purpose. And since it was an NCIC she was asking for, it was technically a federal crime. Julia had never asked anyone to do something that was illegal for her before. She'd never done anything illegal herself. She felt guilty making Lat an accomplice, but she couldn't run one herself, and she didn't want anyone in her own office doing it.

'Sure. What's the name?' Lat asked without hesitating. If he sensed something was up, he said nothing.

Julia took a deep breath and closed her eyes. 'Cirto,' she said. 'C-I-R-T-O. Andrew Joseph. Date of birth, March fourteen, 1972.'

48

'What is it you want, Mary? What do you want? You want the moon? Just say the word and I'll throw a lasso around it and pull it down.'

She stared at the TV screen from her spot on the living-room couch at three in the morning, watching, of all things, *It's a Wonderful Life* on TBS. It had been her mother's all-time favorite movie. She used to let Julia stay up to watch it with her on Christmas Eve after midnight Mass, when the rest of the house had gone off to sleep. They'd make popcorn and snuggle on the couch under the cotton and fleece pink blanket stolen off Julia's bed. Momma knew every line. Every single word, in fact. Sometimes she would say them along with the actors, with the same inflection, too. She'd had Jimmy Stewart down pat.

'Hey! That's a pretty good idea. I'll give you the moon, Mary.'

They'd never had the chance to watch it that last Christmas. Christmas Eve that year was spent in her new room at Aunt Nora's in Great Kills, far away from her living room in West Hempstead, far away from Carly and her friends and her school. Sitting on her new bed, with her new pink comforter and her new ruffled curtains, she'd watched out the window as carloads of well-dressed, smiling people pulled up in front of her new neighbors' house, platters of food and bottles of wine in their hands, arms loaded with Christmas presents. She'd sat there for hours in the dark, her numb body trapped in place, watching the comings and goings of what was now to be her new life, reciting sad, cheesy lines from her mother's all-time favorite movie, which now played like a bad memory in her head. Only, unlike a TV movie that you didn't want to watch anymore, she couldn't turn it off. Instead, it just kept running, running, running, as she sat at that window, until the entire film had played out in her mind. She'd spent the last fifteen years hating herself for taking those two hours and twelve minutes for granted every year. If she could go back and have one more moment with her mother, just one more, that would be it.

'Strange, isn't it? Each man's life touches so many other lives,' Clarence the Angel said to a sad and shocked George Bailey. 'When he isn't around he leaves an awful hole, doesn't he?'

She mouthed the words along with Clarence and closed her eyes to stop the tears. She could still smell the damn fleece blanket – the one Aunt Nora had replaced – and the lilac-scented fabric softener her mom used to use. Since she'd moved into her own apartment, she'd tried every brand known to man in the stores, but she'd still never found it.

49

Julia sat by herself at the State's table Wednesday morning and just silently prayed he'd walk in. Farley tapped his pen impatiently against the bench, in tune with the second hand of the loud clock that hung in the back of the courtroom, above the doors. It read 9:42. Surprisingly, the jammed courtroom stayed eerily quiet.

'I think that's enough time, State,' the judge finally said with an impatient sigh.

'Your Honor, if we could just wait a little bit longer. I'm sure Mr Bellido will be here,' she said anxiously, looking back at the courtroom doors. At that moment, they opened, but it was John Latarrino who walked through them, not Rick. He shook his head.

'Ms Valenciano,' the judge began with that all-too-familiar, I'm-going-to-yell-at-you-now look. 'I don't have the time to —'

'Excuse me, Judge,' interrupted Lat, as he walked up the center aisle to the State's table. 'I apologize, but if I could have a word with the prosecutor?'

The judge sighed loudly, threw the pen on the bench and spun his chair around to face the wall, like a two-year-old having a temper-tantrum. 'Take as long as you need, Detective. It's not like we're waiting to start court or anything.'

'Tell me something good, Lat. Please,' Julia whispered quickly, hoping all the cameras that packed the courtroom wouldn't pick up her words or her desperation. She could feel them focusing in on her.

Lat looked her in the eye and shook his head again. 'No can do, sweetheart. I just got his message. He was on his way back from Orlando and he's had some kind of accident. Nothing bad. He wants you to reset it, is all. Get a continuance.'

'What?'

'Are you two done chitty-chatting?' Farley finally sniped. 'Or do you think we can maybe resume court today?'

'Um,' Julia began hesitantly, slowly turning back to face the judge. 'Detective Latarrino has just received word about Mr Bellido, Your Honor. There's been an accident. It's nothing serious, but he is going to be delayed for a while. He's requesting – the State is requesting – a continuance.'

The judge looked around the courtroom. 'No,' he said finally. An excited murmur ran through the crowd.

'No?' asked Julia. Her hands began to sweat.

'Not that I mean to sound uncaring, but he's not dead, is he, Detective? He's not in the hospital? And even if he was,' Farley explained, motioning to Julia for all the cameras to see, 'he has a second seat handling this very important case for him. A hand-picked second seat, I might add. And that means that *my* time should not be compromised because of some fender-bender or morning traffic on 195. I have the reports of doctors Barakat and Koletis in front of me, and from what I can tell, the experts are split on whether the defendant is competent. So I'm thinking that we're all here for a full hearing this morning. The defense is present, and ready to go, I presume. Everyone's valuable time is ticking away while Mr Bellido waits for a tow-truck. I'm sure, Ms Valenciano, you're ready to proceed, lest only the defense present evidence here today.'

So much for the Good Ol' Boys Network and all the sporting courtroom banter exchanged just a few weeks ago.

Julia looked at a knot in the wood table. This was bad. This was really bad. She might officially be second seat, but even she knew the title was really only a warm-body position. She remembered Rick's use of pronouns with Dr Barakat and Charley Rifkin. As Dayanara had cautioned and everyone higher up in the office already knew, the most he was probably going to let her do during this trial – besides all the grunt work – was pass him his file, and maybe do the direct examination of a few insignificant players. If she was really lucky, he'd let her do the opening statement. She knew her participation would be limited and she accepted that as part of climbing the ladder of experience. Now Judge Leonard Farley was going to demand she handle a competency hearing in a first-degree murder by herself with the news cameras all rolling and the international press closely watching.

Day was seated in the front row next to a couple of other ASAs who'd come to watch. She leaned over the railing and whispered calmly, 'I'll call Legal, Julia. Don't do anything till they get here!' Julia nodded and Day dashed out of the courtroom.

'Mr Levenson, are you ready to proceed?' asked Farley.

'Yes,' said Mel, rising. He was no fool. He smelled the chum that the judge had just tossed into the water. 'We're ready to proceed. And due to my client's delicate mental condition and need for immediate treatment, I'd say that time is definitely of the essence and that we conduct the hearing this morning without hesitation,' he said, making sure he hit all the right appellate buzz words. Mel motioned to his client, who sat flanked between him and Stan Grossbach, in the same red jumpsuit and in pretty much the same condition Julia had seen him in at the arraignment, except more overgrown. His hair had not been cut and his carpet of facial hair was now a full-fledged wiry beard. Julia knew that most defense attorneys would do anything to make their clients appear more sympathetic in court – dressing them up in expensive suits and covering them up in modest dresses when the case called for it, hiding tattoos, changing hair color, removing body piercings. In big-name cases, some had even gone so far as to hire stylists and body-language consultants to help mold their clients into the defendants they ultimately wanted a jury to see. Image was everything in the courtroom. The scraggly caveman look, she figured, just might be Mel Levenson's idea to make sure his client fit the role he was here to play today. Once again, Marquette stared blankly out in front of him at nothing and no one. The thousand-yard stare, Dr Koletis had called it in his report. If the eyes truly were the 'windows to the soul', Julia thought with a sudden shudder, recalling Dr Barakat's chilling words to her only days before, then David Marquette just might not have one.

. . . there is a different breed of malingerer. A different breed of human being, actually . . . He will convince those that want to be convinced of his illness, including professionals, and he will adapt to the tests they put upon him because he is a survivor.

'Wonderful,' said the judge. 'State? Are you ready to proceed? Or are you willing to stipulate to Dr Koletis' report that the defendant is incompetent?'

'No, Judge, the State is not willing to stipulate. Dr Barakat's report clearly states that the defendant is competent.'

'Then let's go. Call your first witness.'

'Your Honor, someone from the State's Legal Unit is on their way over—' she tried.

'Oh no, Ms Valenciano. You want to play with the big boys, then you're the one who's gonna play. Call your first witness.'

'Judge, I believe the defendant is presumed competent under Florida law. The burden is with the defense, then, to prove he's incompetent by a preponderance of the evidence,' Julia protested, hoping that if Levenson was forced to put on his case first, that would buy some time for Rick or someone from Legal to show up. Lat could go pick him up, wherever he was, and bring him back. And everything would be okay.

'Nice try, Counselor. But the Federal Courts have interpreted the United States Constitution as requiring the government to only bring *competent* individuals to trial. Particularly those they are trying to execute. So I believe the burden of proving the defendant actually knows what's going on in a courtroom falls on you, State.' He smiled a devious smile. 'Welcome to the big league, Ms Valenciano. As I was saying, call your first witness.'

50

She had no choice. There was no way she could just let David Marquette be found incompetent and sent off to Chattahoochee for the next few months, or even years, while the case here against him went to shit. She heard Rick's dire warning in her head: *Time doesn't help a prosecutor, Julia. Remember that.*

Ultimately, the determination of a defendant's competency was within the sole discretion of the trial judge. And that meant Julia had to do whatever she could to prove to Farley that Marquette was competent, and she had to do it now. God knows he was vindictive enough to send the guy for treatment he didn't need just to burn her for not trying. Prove to the world that she was not good enough to be here.

She exhaled a low breath. 'The State then calls Dr Christian Barakat to the stand,' she said, without even knowing if Dr Barakat was actually present. She heard the prosecutors behind her start to whisper among themselves, like siblings who know that their little sister is *sooo* gonna get it when their dad gets home.

Jefferson stepped out into the hall and, less than ten seconds later, Dr Barakat, in a tailored charcoal suit and powder-blue dress shirt, strode to the witness stand to be sworn in by a swooning, blushing Ivonne. He settled into his seat, acknowledging Julia with a nod, but it was clear he was more than a little puzzled to see her sitting at the State's table instead of Rick.

Julia had never put a psychiatrist on the stand before. Or any doctor, for that matter. As far as experts went, she'd only qualified a records custodian, a fingerprint tech, and a Breathalyzer maintenance tech. Before a witness was allowed to give expert testimony on a subject, counsel first had to establish to the court that he or she was, in fact, an expert on that subject. Important passages about qualifying medical experts from the Rules of Evidence flashed in her head, not staying long enough, unfortunately, for her to actually remember what they said. She opened her statute book and stared at the criteria for competence under rule 3.211. Words that suddenly made no sense stared back at her, and she felt the room begin to spin, the shrink-wrap tighten around her lungs.

'Look at me, Daddy! Look at me!' screamed little Emma suddenly as she danced across the courtroom in her blood-soaked Cinderella ball gown, her French braid matted black with dried blood. Her little face looked like it did in her autopsy pictures – swollen to almost double its size, her lips blue, the whites of her eyes red where the blood vessels had burst. A twisted ringlet of thick black thread spooled from the neckline of her gown where the ME had neglected to cut the autopsy thread. 'Look at me now, Daddy!' she demanded with a distorted pout as she spun around. 'Look at what you've done to me!'

Julia closed her eyes tight. She was it. She was the only person who could make justice happen today. Who could make sure little Emma's father was held responsible for what he'd done. She was the only one who could make sure David Marquette didn't slip through the cracks of an unsympathetic system that was more than willing to forget its victims and move on to the next tragedy. She had to look past the mess at the defense table and do her job.

'Look at me now, Daddy!' Emma screamed again.

Lat leaned over the rail and touched her shoulder. 'You

can do this, Julia,' he said softly. 'You're better than Bellido. Trust me.'

She nodded and took in a deep breath. *Here goes, Emma. Let's put this bastard away where he belongs.* Then she stood up, and for the next three hours, to the surprise of every single person in that courtroom, including herself, she proved John Latarrino right.

He ran a finger slowly over the deep red dents that cut across his wrists, where the steel handcuffs had dug into his flesh and pressed against the bone. A razor-sharp pain radiated up through his right arm into his shoulder, but he resisted the urge to acknowledge it. He imagined that the lines were on someone else's wrist, the pain was not in his body. He knew that the correction officers made the cuffs extra tight on purpose because of who he was. Because of what he'd done. He'd watched them smile and heard them chuckle when they snapped the cuffs on behind his back, clicking them until they reached almost the very last notch.

But he'd never complained. Not even once.

. . . he did present with some negative symptoms of schizophrenia, but, as I explained in my report, Your Honor, there were also no peculiar behavioral manifestations such as echopraxia . . .

He heard what they shouted at him in his cell and in the hallways as they shuffled him past the other inmates on the way to court. *Baby Killer. Daddy Death. Doctor Death. Psycho. Norman.* He knew they spit in his food and tried to trip him in the hallways. He knew if they could, some of the animals in here would shank him or fuck him, or both, if they could just get close enough. That was probably the only good thing about the floor he was on. The crazies each had their own cell.

. . . Some of those symptoms can possibly be attributed to the medication that Dr Marquette is taking; however, yes, to answer your question, Ms Valenciano, I'd have to say it's my opinion he's malingering . . .

He wondered what they would be like if he weren't in his chains. If it were just the two of them, alone in a room. No asps. No radio. No cuffs. No laughing buddies. He wondered how long it would be before Mr Correction Officer pissed himself when he looked into the eyes of madness. There was always safety in numbers. Take away the numbers . . .

. . . again, it is possible that Dr Marquette has what's known as a psychopathic personality disorder. In the Diagnostic and Statistical Manual of Mental Disorders *it's referred to as an antisocial personality disorder . . .*

Or any of the animals, really. Any of the caged zoo animals on the other floors. So big and tough with their gang colors and their tattoos. Again, take away their brothers, and they were nothing. And they underestimated him, which would be their downfall.

. . . probably the most dangerous of all mental disorders. In varying degrees, the psychopath is unable to actually feel emotion. He's like an empty shell. A machine. He doesn't know empathy, he doesn't feel love, he doesn't experience guilt. No one will change him, and nothing will affect him. He has learned, though, through watching society, what the appropriate emotional responses are, and he has learned to mimic *those responses. So he's* learned *to cry at funerals, even though he doesn't actually feel the emotion of sadness, no matter who it is in the casket, and he's* learned *to say 'I love you' after sex, even though he really cannot actually feel the emotion of love . . .*

He had caught a couple of the big bad ones looking at him in the box or in the halls, when the buddies weren't watching them. A quick glance over in his direction. He knew they wondered what the hell went on in his head. It was one thing, after all, to kill a man because he owed you money. Or maybe take out a girlfriend because she cheated on you. But even the big and the bad had a code of conduct, a set of rules to live by. And when someone operated outside those rules, it frightened even the worst of them. As it should.

. . . take Ted Bundy, for instance. Good-looking, by all accounts. Educated. A law student at a top-ranked law school. Some speculate the number of women who fell prey to Bundy may be close to one hundred. See, it's a common misconception people have, you know, that psychopaths somehow look different. That they sound different. That they're all drug dealers or bouncers or unemployed roofers. Everyone thinks they'll spot the Charles Mansons right off, when the truth is, we encounter psychopaths in everyday life and never know it, Ms Valenciano. It was Scott Peterson's charm and good looks that were perhaps his most disarming weapon. They can be bankers and CEOs and basketball coaches. Of course, not all psychopaths are murderers, and not all murderers are psychopaths. But the one textbook warning that does ring true is, especially, I believe, in this case, the smarter the psychopath, the more dangerous and destructive he will be . . .

It was strange to sit in a room surrounded by people talking about him in the third person. Attempting to define him with tricky medical terminology. The cameras were a bit distracting. It was so important to listen right now, but so hard to focus. The medicine still clouded his brain. The waves still washed out their words sometimes. He swallowed a yawn.

. . . Like a chameleon, he will take on the persona he _knows_ you want to see. He will say the words he _knows_ you want to hear. That's what makes him so difficult to identify. Almost impossible to catch . . .

He looked over at the prosecutor. Valenciano. Julia Valenciano, she'd said. She was so pretty. So young, he thought. Younger than him. An apprentice, obviously. An ingénue. *Was he her biggest case? Was this her biggest moment?*

He watched as she walked around the courtroom, with all those cameras trained on her. She was so sure of herself, but so . . . *not.* He caught her quick, awkward glances over at him, studying him with her suspicious but, yet, curious green eyes, as if he were a specimen in a science lab. She looked at him with contempt, but also with maybe ... compassion? Even through the fog of the drugs that made his tongue heavy and sometimes carried off his thoughts, he could tell she somehow doubted the confidence of her own questions. He had a thing with reading people. He always had. And he was never wrong. He could tell right then just by watching her that she was the one who would listen. Of all the people in the courtroom, he knew *she* wanted to understand.

'Why?' she demanded, narrowing those fiery green eyes and looking right at him. 'Why would he do this, Dr Barakat?'

Never ask a question you don't know the answer to. Even he knew that.

In not-so-clinical terms, Ms Valenciano, he's a monster.

He needed to show her the *real* him. It was time to tell her what he knew she wanted to hear.

52

Farley leaned back in his chair, a wrinkled talon wrapped around his chin. 'I've read the reports of both doctors. I've listened to their testimony here today from both Dr Barakat and Dr Koletis. I've had the opportunity to observe the defendant in court, not just today, but on several occasions. Let the record reflect that this hearing is approaching its third hour now.

'The defendant hasn't been a disruption in court. He's able to conduct himself in front of a jury. Both psychiatrists have testified that he knows he's been charged with murder and knows the penalty he's facing. The defendant himself is a doctor. He's not mentally deficient. He's highly educated, and until the week before his arrest, he was performing surgery down the block. While this court recognizes that intelligent people can be mentally ill, too, his intellect has to be considered as a factor when determining his competency. And even though it might be sad that his twin suffers from schizophrenia, that's all it is – a sad fact.

'I'm not going to get into whether the defendant is malingering. That's something for a jury to decide. The standard for competency is whether a defendant has the present ability to consult with counsel, *and* whether he has a rational, as well as factual, understanding of the proceedings. Now let me say this – no one and nobody is going to escape justice in my courtroom by faking a mental illness. Just by refusing to answer questions, even when it's your own attorney or psychiatrist asking them, doesn't mean you're going to evade the long arm of the law. The defendant has a lot at stake in going forward to trial, and a strong motivation to fabricate or exaggerate the symptoms of mental illness. The law allows me to make sure Dr Marquette is properly medicated when he is in my courtroom so that he can proceed to trial. And so, based on the testimony presented here today—'

Hushed, heated whispers erupted at the defense table. Mel and Stan leaned across the defense table toward each other, their backs to the court, obscuring their client from view. It sounded, at first, as if the two of them were having an angry exchange.

'Is there a problem, Mr Levenson?' grumbled the judge. 'We're not disturbing you and Mr Grossbach now, are we?'

'Don't,' Mel whispered one final time. Then he reluctantly pulled back from the conversation to face the judge. He shook his big head, making his jowls wobble. 'No, Your Honor.'

'No, no, no,' said a small voice. It was one Julia didn't recognize, because she'd never heard it before. The courtroom fell completely silent as David Marquette stood in his red jumpsuit. His waist irons jangled.

'David,' said Stan forcefully. 'Sit down.'

'No, no, no . . .' the voice continued. Marquette shook his head violently from side to side.

The judge waved off Stan. 'Dr Marquette, do you have something you'd like to say to this court? Something you think I should know? Although I should warn you that anything you do say can, and most likely will, be used against you.'

In the hushed courtroom, his voice was nothing more than a broken whisper. He looked at Julia, who was sitting at the State's table watching the scene unfold. His dead light-gray eyes stared right at her, right through her once again. 'I *saved* them,' he said softly, as though answering her last question to Dr Barakat.

And with those words, the world as she knew it came suddenly and irreversibly crashing down around her as the protective firewalls in her mind slowly toppled, one by one by one, like dominoes, until, finally, only the frightening truth was left standing before her.

Like frenzied bats freed from a dark and musty attic, the horrifying memories swarmed her. The ghosts had finally found their way back in.

53

The car door opened and Detective Potter leaned in the back seat. His round face looked puffier in the yellow overhead dome light than it had at Carly's; his small eyes even squintier. 'Julie,' he began with a sigh and Julia smelled the cigarette smoke on his breath.

She swallowed the blood that filled her mouth and breathed in the blast of cold air. Don't say it. Whatever you're going to say, please don't say it. Let me have more time before you say something bad. More time before everything changes . . .

'Sorry to keep you waiting, honey,' he started with a gentle, sad smile, 'but we needed to make sure that—'

She stopped listening.

Her eyes suddenly caught on the two police officers in bulky dark-blue nylon coats that had stepped out her front door. They sandwiched a man dressed only in a T-shirt and jeans. She suddenly pushed past Detective Potter and out of the car, at first walking, then running full speed across the lawn. She heard the shouts behind her calling her to stop, but they didn't make any sense.

'Andrew?' she shouted while running, the cold wind stinging her cheeks. 'Andy? Andy!'

He turned to face her then, and she saw the bright red splatters on his white undershirt, the smears on his face, the dark stains that soaked his jeans.

At first she thought he was hurt, then her eyes fell on the handcuffs on his wrists and she knew. Both of his hands were wrapped in white kitchen towels, like a boxer's, but blood had begun to seep through in spots. Her legs suddenly collapsed, refusing to hold her up any longer and she fell to her knees next to the Santa.

'Oh my God, what did you do? Andy! What did you do?' she screamed at him. 'What did you do?'

The handsome young man who still had the face of a boy smiled. Tears spilled from his eyes. They met the smears of blood, running down his cheeks in watery red streaks. 'I saved them, Ju-Ju. I saved them. I had to. It had to be done.' He thrust his hands up to the sky, creating a reactionary panic among the blue coats, who rushed to regain control of his arms. The kitchen towels fell away and ribbons of bright red blood streamed from his mangled hands. 'Alleluia!'

She stayed on her knees, screaming, her fists clutching at the frozen ground, the cold, melting snow seeping into her jeans. Detective Potter and the other officers who had rushed to catch her on the lawn stopped and backed up slightly, awkwardly looking at each other, watching her as she rocked back and forth.

The blue coats escorted the young man to the back of a waiting cruiser, forcefully ducking his head and placing him inside with a hard shove. He smiled softly at her once more out the window. Then he hung his head as the car drove off down the block.

She never saw her big brother again.

54

The courtroom stayed strangely quiet for a few seconds, like the eerie lull right before the scream of a child who's just skinned his knee – mouths hung open and contorted, but no sound escaped. Then the excited chatter started up, fast and furious, rising to an almost deafening crescendo before Farley silenced the crowd once again. 'I'm ready to rule,' he barked into the microphone on his bench – the one that had always been there but had never before needed to be used. He looked around for something to slam on the bench and shot an angry look over at his bailiff.

'Be seated and be quiet!' Jefferson nervously proclaimed, as if reading from bailiff cue cards. 'No cellphones, no talking!'

The courtroom quickly settled back down to whispers, as the reporters ignored Jefferson's warning and finished sending off the last of their text messages to their editors. When there was complete silence Farley began to speak again. 'I find the defendant competent to stand trial. Now we need to know if he was sane. I'm extending the trial date by two weeks for you all to find out. Mr Levenson, clear your calendar.'

'Yes, Your Honor,' Mel replied, rising.

'State, I'm accommodating you in so far as to make sure this matter is set down in a C week. You will have no other trials set down that week.'

There was no response.

'Ms Valenciano? Hello?'

How could it all be so clear now? So clear, like physically stepping back in time and into a memory. A memory she had shuttered away for so long. She could suddenly smell the cold air, heavy with the snow that was expected by morning, the burning leaves, the pine trees and evergreens, the cigarette smoke, the hint of Tsar cologne — strangely enough, her father's favorite — in the back seat of the police car. She could hear the squawking of the police radios, the crackle of the operator's voice, erupting over a dozen handhelds at the same time, the frantic, excited, hushed whispers of her neighbors who stood on the sidewalk behind her, held back by garish yellow crime-scene tape. She could taste the blood, thick and warm and coppery in her mouth. And Andrew . . .

'Julia? Julia?'

She felt a hand on her shoulder again. It was Lat. 'The judge,' he said with a whisper, nodding over at Farley. The courtroom sat in strange, excited silence, as if everyone in the room had collectively held their breath as they watched her. She looked around, dumbfounded. Lost.

'Not a problem, Your Honor,' the Chief of Legal said, rising from the front row and stepping purposely into the gallery and up to the podium. 'Penny Levine on behalf of the State. We appreciate your working to accommodate Ms Valenciano's trial schedule. Mr Bellido has asked that I assure the court that the State will be ready for trial on whatever date Your Honor sets.'

The judge frowned at Julia, but decided to move on. 'Trial is resct for Monday, March sixth, then. Report date is Thursday the second. That's two extra weeks to get your case together, everyone. Short of one of the attorneys in this case actually dying next time around, we're going on the sixth. I'm not letting this drag on for a year or so while we go back and forth squabbling with the experts. I'm appointing both Drs Barakat and Koletis again under 3.216. If you're planning on using anyone else, let the other side know within thirty days. No surprise witnesses and no last-minute additions or substitutions, so get your acts together and plan every move carefully. I will not tolerate delays. I hope you all heard me on that,' he finished with one final, annoyed glance over at the State's table.

Then the judge sailed past Jefferson and off the bench as the courtroom erupted in chaos once again.

55

It no longer really mattered whose semen was on Jennifer Marquette's pajama top, whose distorted footprints had walked the halls the night she and her children died, whose fingers might have slid open the windows of the lavish house on Sorolla Avenue, did it? David Marquette was a confessed murderer now.

A mob of well-wishers from the State's side spilled into the gallery. The very same prosecutors who had gossiped just hours before about her uncertain career move all wanted to shake her hand now, including the Chief of Legal herself. It was, perhaps, a moment every trial lawyer dreamed of, but one only a rare few would ever experience – winning *the* case or *the* argument in a crowded courtroom jammed with colleagues and cameras from around the world. A moment others would surely bask in and cherish, as they watched their careers soar to a new stratosphere on *NBC Nightly News*. But not Julia. For her, the moment felt frightening, pressing, claustrophobic, sickening, exploitative. The old courtroom looked the same as when she'd walked in just hours before, but everything and everyone in it was completely different now, like the final scenes in *It's a Wonderful Life* when George stumbles upon his brother Harry's tombstone in the town cemetery and finally grasps the terrifying truth that Clarence the Angel has been trying to tell him: George Bailey was never born. The town, the homes, the buildings – even the faces – might physically look the same as George remembered them, but they weren't. One fact had forever changed everything and everyone. One fact had changed history.

'Clarence! Clarence! Help me, Clarence,' she heard her mother whisper along with Jimmy Stewart. 'Get me back. Get me back. I don't care what happens to me. Get me back to my wife and kids. Help me, Clarence, please. Please! I want to live again! I want to live again. I want to live again. Please, God, let me live again.'

Of course, in the movies, George Bailey gets his wish. He gets to go back to the life he knew, with all its 'warts and pickles' as Momma might have said. But Julia knew that no movie magic would happen here today. No matter how much she prayed, she could not undo the truth that, despite repeated warnings, she herself had gone searching for. There would be no Hollywood ending for her.

It's too close, Julia. Too close. Please, I'm begging you to stay away. It can only bring . . . despair.

She quickly moved to gather her files, watching as Corrections fit David Marquette – this shell of a man in his oversized jumpsuit – back into his frightening get-up of iron shackles and steel handcuffs.

He's a monster. A psychopath. Like a chameleon, he will take on the persona he knows you want to see. He will say the words he knows you want to hear. That's what makes him so difficult to catch.

She looked away, not trusting her eyes anymore, and finished packing up her briefcase. The noisy, restless crowd of reporters and onlookers seemed to have surreptitiously moved closer to the gallery while she had her back turned. She heard her name being called, mentioned, discussed in a dozen different conversations, but all she wanted was to get the hell out of the courtroom. Right now. Before she fell apart in front of everyone.

A warm hand gently tapped her back. 'I knew you were better than him,' said a familiar voice in her ear, as she threw

Ehrhardt's *Evidence* into her briefcase. She turned to see Lat standing beside her. 'Although, you do know there's no guarantee Bellido's gonna let you take any of the credit,' he added with a soft grin.

She tried to smile back. She tried to make everything look normal, but she wondered if that was even possible anymore. The mask she wore surely had cracks. Behind Lat, Corrections worked to clear the courtroom and move the reporters out into the crowded hallway, where she knew they would wait for her to come out. *Hold on. Hang in there. Just a minute more and then you can run. Run to . . . where? Anywhere but here.* 'Any word on how he is?' she managed.

'Except for the blown ego, I'm sure he'll be just fine. Don't worry about him.'

She blew out a measured breath. 'What a day. Thanks for before. I, I really . . .'

'You were great. Quite the shark. I was surprised. You always look so nice. And him . . .' he said, his voice trailing off as he looked over at Marquette. He shook his head, but didn't finish his thought. 'You know, Julia, nothing surprises me anymore. And that's not a good thing. Try not to take it home with you.' He placed a thin manila folder on top of her statute book. 'For you. Your NCIC. I also ran an Autotrack, which is in there, too.'

'Thanks,' she said quietly, looking down at the folder. She tried to swallow the hard lump that had formed in her throat. 'I've got to go,' she finally managed.

'Alright, then. Well, let me know if you need anything else,' he said as he turned to walk away.

She saw Steve Brill standing in the back of the courtroom, talking with Charley Rifkin and Penny Levine and her DC. All four of them were looking over at her. Brill was laughing, but the others weren't. Why was it, that in a crowd full of people cheering your name, you could always hear the one or two small voices that weren't? Why were they always the loudest? She looked away, back down at the State's table, before they could see what she was thinking, and grabbed her briefcase, swinging it across her shoulder as she headed for the judge's back hallway and a quick escape down the back staircase.

'Oh yeah, Julia,' Lat called out behind her. 'I almost forgot.' She stopped at the door Jefferson was, for some reason, still standing guard at and turned to look back at him. 'Merry Christmas!' he said with an easy smile when she did. 'Have a good one.'

56

The air was so cold and dry, it felt as though she swallowed a dozen knives every time she breathed, and an intense pain ripped through her chest. She knew that everyone was watching her while she cried on the lawn, her world spinning like the red and blue police lights that lit the night sky — around and around and around and out of control. Blue coats and detectives, paramedics and neighbors had all begun to gather on the sidewalk, and she felt their eyes upon her, watching her as she writhed in pain on the frozen ground. Awkwardly fidgeting with the change in their pockets, or adjusting the scarves around their mouths, they watched and waited for someone to do something to stop the scene in front of them, even though a part of them secretly hoped to see it play out to its natural conclusion. There was something fascinating, titillating, about watching bad things happen to other people live. Those who surrounded her now were able to participate — view the most excruciating emotional pain someone could experience — but not have to actually feel it for themselves. They were macabre voyeurs, and they crawled over her lawn and sidewalk and driveway, edging closer, ever closer, to get a better look.

'*Poor kid,*' *one said.*

'*That sucks.*'

'*Are they dead, Officer?*'

'*Poor thing.*'

'*Oh my God! Oh my God! Oh my God!*'

'*Is the news here? Will this be on the news?*'

'*Are they both dead, Officer?*'

'*What the hell happened in there?*'

'*Poor Julia.*'

She wanted to crawl into a ball right there on the lawn, bury herself into a black hole and cry. Just cry and cry and cry until the earth swallowed her and she simply disappeared. Strange, fragmented thoughts flew through her head.

What did he do to them? Why was there so much blood? They can't be dead. My parents can't be dead. Please Lord, no. Where will I go if they're dead? I have a Spanish test on Monday. Why didn't I stay home tonight? What would have happened if I did stay home? Why was there so much blood? Where is Andrew going? Will he be back? Do I have to get him out of jail? Who should I call? Who will take care of me? They can't be dead. I have a track meet on Friday. Why the hell was there so much blood?

Then an instantly sobering, chilling thought . . .

Maybe they're still alive.

She pulled herself up quick, before the voyeurs could even gasp, and she ran as fast as her feet could take her. Faster than she'd ever run before. She heard Detective Potter again yell for her to stop, but she just kept going. Across the brown, snow-patched lawn and past the blue coats smoking cigarettes on the broken walk and the EMTs chatting it up in the driveway.

Up the front steps and back into the decaying old house she'd once called home.

She slammed on the brakes with a deafening screech, and the Honda fish-tailed, skidding to a stop on 195, missing the Lexus in front of her by only an inch or two. She blew out a breath and waved apologetically at the guy who was now angrily shaking both his head and his fist at her in his rear-view. Drivers and passengers alike stared at her out their car windows in the stop-and-go early-afternoon rush-hour Miami traffic. With trembling hands, she reached over and picked up her briefcase, purse and pack of cigarettes from the passenger floorboard where they'd landed after flying off the front seat.

For Julia — Personal and Confidential

She sat up with a start.

The folder from Lat lay on the floorboard. She hadn't opened it yet. Peeking out a corner was a black and white booking photo. She knew the face in an instant, the soft dollop of curls, the wide brown eyes.

She leaned her head against the steering wheel and closed her eyes. The memories kept coming at her now, popping into her head like a screensaver the second she stopped concentrating on something else. Each time they were a bit clearer, though. A little brighter. More in focus. She lit a cigarette with trembling fingers.

The picture was almost complete.

57

She deliberately put the folder down on the kitchen table, along with her briefcase and purse. She took an attention-craved Moose for a walk and fed him. Instead of going for a long run on the boardwalk, she popped two Tylenol, lit a cigarette, poured herself a large glass of wine and sat down in the living room to wade through her thoughts.

Like smoking, alcohol was another indulgence that had taken her a couple of tries to quit once. A rough patch with a rough boyfriend in college had made her drink a little more than she should have, a little more often than she should. The counselor at Rutgers had called it 'problem-drinking' – drinking as a means to forget or cope with a problem, something she was advised to never do again. Of course her counselor could never have imagined the scope or magnitude of problems she was dealing with at this very moment. If he had, she was sure he'd buy the bottle for her himself. And it was still only wine, she told herself. And it was almost nightfall.

I saved them, Ju-Ju . . . I had to. It had to be done.

She put her head in her hands and rubbed her eyes. Andrew. Her big brother. She saw him there on the front lawn – as if he were beside her this very second – standing barefoot in the snow, with their house all ablaze in Christmas lights behind him. His handcuffed, butchered hands dangling in front of him like he was holding fistfuls of chop meat, dripping bright red blood on piles of melting white snow like in some crazy horror movie. Smiling sadly, as if he knew it would be the last time they would ever see each other . . .

'In the matter of the petition for adoption of J.C., a minor, by Nora Clair Valenciano and her husband, James Anthony Valenciano. The parties are all present for a final hearing,' said the clerk.

'Have the minor brought forward,' called the judge with a wave of his hand as he read over his docket with a frown and sipped a can of Diet Dr Pepper.

A dozen people bustled about the small courtroom. The building was so old that a permanent smoky, yellow haze clung to windows that hadn't been washed in years, and fat dust particles danced in the stagnant air. Boxes were literally stacked to the ceiling in one corner, and papers cluttered every inch of the clerk's metal desk.

'Mary Ellen Kelly appearing as guardian ad litem on behalf of the minor child,' said the chubby woman with gray hair that went down to her butt. Julia had met her once when she came to Aunt Nora's. 'We have no objection to the petition.'

'What is the relationship between the minor,' the judge said hesitating, then looked down at the file to read her name, 'Julia Anne Cirto,' he said slowly, 'and the petitioners?' Only he said it as Cur-toe, instead of Sir-toe. He looked at Julia for the first time. 'She's how old?'

'Julia will be fifteen at the end of the month,' answered Mr Singh, Aunt Nora's attorney. 'She's the petitioners' niece, Judge. She's the daughter of Mrs Valenciano's deceased sister, Irene Cirto.'

'Where is the father?'

'Dead as well.'

'There's no other family?'

Ms Kelly shook her head. 'No, Your Honor,' she said into the microphone then cleared her throat. 'There's no one else. Everyone's gone. Her aunt and uncle are all this girl has left in the world now.'

Was it possible to hate someone in an instant? Someone who you loved with all your being just seconds before? Could you turn it all off in a heartbeat? In the blink of an eye? Could one horrific memory change the meaning of so many good ones? Should it? That night, as she sat in the cold, gray interview room of the police precinct, her sleeping bag wrapped around her shoulders, she remembered it was Andy she still wanted. It was her big brother she needed to hold her hand and hug her and tell her it would be alright, that this was all a crazy mistake. An accident. Because it had to be.

This bastard needs to fry for what he's done. Did you see the pictures? . . . Did you see what he did to them? . . . You ask me what we want to see done? We want him dead! That's justice.

'No, no, no . . .' she whispered out loud to an empty room, trying to shake the images out of her head. She pulled the picture that had fallen out of Lat's file from her pocket and unfolded it.

CIRTO, ANDREW JOSEPH; NASSAU COUNTY SHERIFF'S DEPARTMENT, DIVISION OF CORRECTIONS #11970; 12–21–90

Even in black and white, she could still see the faint dark streaks on his smooth cheeks, the sweat that matted charcoal-colored curls to his forehead, the pure fear in his almond-shaped eyes. The only pictures of Andrew that had survived these past fifteen years were the select few that remained in her mind. This was not one of them.

It was too much. Her brain threatened to shut down like an ATM that's been fed the wrong password too many times. Everything was going white, nothing was making sense anymore. But it couldn't, now could it? How could any of this ever make sense? Maybe that's why her mind had chosen to forget. Selective memory retention – the brain takes on only what it can handle and nothing more. Julia looked back now at the dark kitchen, where the final secrets lay, stashed away in complicated computer printouts and court files. The answers she had been seeking were right there, only steps away, and yet she couldn't move.

So she checked her mail, changed her clothes, listened to her messages – everything and anything tedious she could think of to stall for time. Finally, there was nothing left to hide behind. She walked into the kitchen and flipped on the light.

For Julia – Personal and Confidential

She sat down at the table, her empty wine glass in hand, her heart pounding, watching the folder as if it were a sleeping alligator, ready to snap her arm off at the first sudden movement. Once she opened it, once her worst suspicions were confirmed, she knew there would be no turning back. That was what frightened her the most.

Leave the past in the past. For all of us. Please.

Maybe it was a minute. Maybe it was five. Maybe it was longer that she sat at that table, hearing the tick-tick-tock of the kitchen clock above her. Slowly, she flipped open the manila folder.

The time had come for her to face what destroyed her family fifteen years ago tonight.

58

Julia — FYI. Andrew Joseph Cirto is currently being held at Kirby, Ward's Island, NYC. Verified 12/20 by telephone with M. Zlocki in records.

The yellow sticky note in Lat's handwriting was stuck to the top sheet of the NCIC. She sucked in a sharp breath and sat back hard in her chair, as if someone had shoved her into it.

He's alive. Jesus Christ, he's alive . . .

Lat had highlighted the criminal history for her. It was out of New York. The date of arrest was December 22, 1990. The charge was two counts of first-degree murder. Her eyes searched the printout as they had millions of times before in court, skipping past entries that detailed every court hearing — from arraignment to case status — to find the final case disposition. Lat had highlighted that, too, for her, on page four.

08/12/1991
Judge: R. Deverna
Disp: Adjudicated not responsible mental disease/defect

She stared at the words on the paper — relieved to know he was still alive, and yet sick to her stomach at the same time. She hung her head between her legs but it wasn't enough. A minute later, she ran to the bathroom and threw up the wine, along with whatever remained of breakfast.

Sitting on the bathroom floor, up against the cold tiled wall, the tears rushed out like a broken water main. Her whole body shook and she tried to catch her breath. Counting to ten or thirty or a million was no longer going to ward off the bad memories – memories she'd long ago packed away and buried for dead. Some were happy, some were sad. Some were bittersweet.

'You know, you don't have to call me Mom or anything like that,' Aunt Nora said quietly as they stepped inside the courthouse elevator that stunk of coffee and body odor. Uncle Jimmy had gone ahead to get the car out of the parking garage. 'This,' she said, shaking the rolled-up stack of legal papers in her hand, 'this is just, you know, to protect you and other nonsense.' The small elevator lurched with a loud creak and then started down. 'It's what your mother would have wanted,' she added when Julia still hadn't said anything.

Her aunt must have aged a dozen years since just the morning car ride to the courthouse. Today was the final chapter in a bad book that they both knew there would never, could never, really be a happy ending to. Tears rolled down her cheeks, but she didn't wipe them away. She just stoically looked at the elevator doors in front of her, tapping the rolled-up legal papers against her leg.

'The legal name of the minor child shall be changed to Julia Anne Valenciano. Best of luck to all of you,' the judge had said before moving on to the next case on his docket. With a swift level of the gavel and an official stamp from the clerk's office, the past had been officially erased.

'Where is Andrew?' Julia asked suddenly.

Nora looked at her, her wet eyes instantly filled with hate, and Julia wished she'd never asked the question. The forbidden question, even years later. 'He's in hell,' Aunt Nora said flatly just as the doors opened onto the lobby. 'Where he belongs.'

He was supposed to be dead. Dead and gone from her life and her memories. But he never really was, was he? Maybe it was just easier all these years to assume Andy was dead than to deal with the responsibility of knowing he wasn't. Maybe not looking was the same as not seeing. But now she knew the truth. And there was no more running, no more hiding from it. So why was it suddenly so crippling to imagine her brother as mentally ill?

It's this night. It always gets to you. It's the worst night of the year, Julia.

Moose nudged her hand with his wet nose, trying to get her to pet him. He whined and circled when she didn't, finally settling his head down on her lap. After a second she picked him up and hugged him close, burying her face in his fur as he licked her hand, trying, in his own way, to bring her back.

After her parents' funeral, they'd never spoken of her brother again in Nora's house. Ever. Mention of even Andrew's name was strictly forbidden. Uncle Jimmy stopped getting the paper for maybe six months, maybe even longer, and the news was never permitted to be on – so how could she have known what had happened to him, right? For fifteen years she'd rationalized her own ignorance. Her own indifference. *She was only thirteen, after all. A kid, right?* There was no one else – no other family, no friends – she could've confided in or gotten information from, or a ride down to the courthouse or jail or prison, or wherever he might have been held. The day after the murders, she'd moved away physically from her home, while everyone she knew moved away from her emotionally. And they didn't just gradually move on – they ran. Carly included. So Jimmy and Nora and Great Kills became her world. In her heart she knew Nora only did what she thought was best, but she also knew that her aunt would never, could never, get past her own anger at losing her only sister and best friend. There was no such thing as therapy or counseling – Jimmy would never allow that. It was not what 'good families' did. They solved their own problems. As the years passed, Julia learned to deal with the pain and isolation in the only way she knew how – by simply pushing it all out of her mind, like Nora had taught her. But now the responsibility was all hers, and she knew it. She couldn't blame her aunt or uncle any longer, or excuse herself because she was thirteen and naïve and without a mode of transportation or access to a newspaper. For better or for worse, Pandora had opened the box, and the answers were right there, spread out on the kitchen table.

She wasn't sure how long she sat on the floor for, holding Moose close and crying. Finally, she pulled herself up, splashed cold water on her face, brushed her teeth, and headed back into the kitchen. She poured herself a glass of water and followed it with a warm shot of Stoli from the bottle she kept in the kitchen cupboard. With the NCIC in front of her, she turned on her laptop and with shaking fingers typed words in Google's search box.

Kirby Ward's Island New York

In 0.40 seconds, she had 673,000 hits. The very first one was headed 'Kirby Forensic Psychiatric Center'. She clicked on the site. She could hear her heart beating in her head, feel it pulse in her temples.

> ... maximum-security hospital ... provides secure treatment ... forensic patients and courts of New York City and Long Island ...

Julia leaned back in the chair and closed her eyes. She knew exactly what Kirby was. It was the state hospital in New York for the criminally insane.

And her big brother was still a patient there.

59

Julia stood outside apartment 1052, her hand poised over the bell for a few seconds while she tried to gather her thoughts. Before she could actually hit it, the door opened.

'What's this?' Nora demanded with a big smile that quickly melted into a concerned frown. 'A Friday afternoon? You didn't get fired, did you?'

Julia smiled back softly. 'No, I didn't get fired. I wanted to talk to you and Uncle Jimmy.'

Her aunt raised an eyebrow. 'You just wanted to talk to us? Hmmm . . . that doesn't sound good.' She reached out and took Julia's hand and brought her inside, giving her a big kiss on the cheek. 'Come in, come in. Jimmy's at the track, though.' She looked behind Julia into the hall. 'Where's the pooch?'

'I left Moose at home.'

'Oh,' her aunt shrugged and then started for the kitchen. 'I bought him some new chewies, is all. So, what time you want to come over on Sunday? I'm gonna make a turkey this year, and of course lasagne. Do you want me to make a panettone?'

'If you want.'

'Is this about that man you're dating? You're not engaged, are you? He better know to see Jimmy first,' Nora called out behind her as Julia followed her into the kitchen.

'I don't think you need to be worrying about that just yet.'

Nora turned to face her. 'Pregnant?'

'Aunt Nora . . .'

'Just checking,' she replied with a smile. 'You know, that wouldn't be the worst thing. Not that I'm pushing, but you're not getting any younger and I want some grand-children.' She flipped on the kitchen light. 'Come. Have something to eat before we talk about a subject serious enough to take you away from your criminals.'

For two days, all Julia could think about was how to have this conversation. She'd rehearsed her thoughts again and again in her head, reducing them to carefully constructed sentences, like she would an opening statement, but some-where between the elevator ride up and the walk down the hall to the door, she'd forgotten them all. She wished Uncle Jimmy were here to keep things calm, like he always did, but she just couldn't wait any longer. 'I've been doing research on my murder case,' she began.

'I saw you on the news. Why didn't you call to tell me you'd be on? Deb Casalli had to tell me.' She turned her face away, pretending to wipe invisible crumbs off the coun-ter, but Julia heard the warning in her voice. The subtle signal to stop right there.

Leave the past in the past. For all of us.

Julia's eyes fell on the happy picture of her aunt and her mom hamming it up in front of the Hamilton House, a catering hall in Bayridge, Brooklyn, the day of her mom's high-school graduation, both dressed in white patent leather boots and psychedelic mini-dresses. It was two years before her mom had met her father. 'I've been thinking about what happened with,' she said, taking a deep breath, '. . . my family.'

Aunt Nora stopped wiping and watched her carefully for a long moment, then headed over to the refrigerator. 'I could make you a sandwich. I made Jimmy meatballs last night. I have some semolina. How about a sandwich?'

'I found him.'

Nora hesitated, her head still in the fridge. But she said nothing.

'Andrew. He's in a mental hospital, Aunt Nora. In New York City. It's a hospital for the criminally insane. He's been there for fourteen years now.'

'He might as well be dead,' Nora said quietly, closing the refrigerator door.

'Aunt Nora . . .'

'You have no business looking for him. He's a murderer.'

'I got a copy of the court file yesterday from New York. He has schizophrenia, Aunt Nora. He's sick.'

'Call it what you want to,' Nora snapped, her blue eyes suddenly igniting with anger. 'Go ahead, give it a label! To me, he's the devil. What he did to your mother, to your father. He's a monster, a—' A choked sob cut the rest of her words off, and Nora turned away to face the cabinets. Her aunt was such an incredibly strong person; it was hard to be the one doing this to her after all she and Uncle Jimmy had done, after all they'd sacrificed. But then Nora slapped her hands hard against the counter and the anger was back. 'You have no place looking for him now,' she hissed, her back still to Julia. 'None. You owe it to your mother to stop this craziness right now and move on with your life. Let him rot with his. I hope they never let him out. They should've executed him. They should've given him the god-damned death penalty. That's who it's there for. Animals like him.'

'He's my brother. My brother . . .'

'And she was your mother!' Nora shouted, spinning around. 'And she was *my sister!* My baby sister! You and Jimmy and your *forgiveness* . . .' Her cranberry-red lips folded in on each other, as she fought hard to hold back the words. 'It's so easy to forgive when you're the one who wasn't

345

home that night, Julia! Don't you kid yourself, little one. If you'd been there, warm in your pretty pink bed, he would've dragged you out, too. He would've carved you up, gutted you like a pumpkin. He would've taken that knife and butchered you, too, while you begged him on your knees for your life!'

The blond-haired, blue-eyed reporter tried hard to hold back her smirk of excitement. Battered yellow crime-scene tape still blocked access to the front door of the blue and white colonial behind her, the faded plastic Santa stood alone on the brown lawn. The white patches of snow had all melted away. '. . . the Long Island woman, and her husband, Joseph Cirto, were found brutally slain inside their home early last Sunday morning,' she said with the charged inflection of a seasoned professional. 'Nassau County police today released Mrs Cirto's desperate nine-one-one call, which recorded the final moments of her life. Their son, eighteen-year-old Andrew Cirto, has been arrested and charged in the killings, which shocked this small town of West Hempstead, only days before Christmas.'

The audiotape crackled to life then, as the transcription ran under a montage of still family photos of Momma, Daddy and a smiling Andrew at his high-school graduation. Then came the footage of the black body bags making their way to the waiting ambulance.

'Police and fire. What's your emergency?'

'Help us.'

'I'm going to help you, honey. I need you to stay on the line and tell me exactly what's happened.'

'I think he's coming back.'

'Who's coming? Are you hurt? What's your name?'

'I think he's coming back.'

'Who's that? Has someone been hurt? Do you need an ambulance?'

'. . . please . . . no, no, no, no . . . he's back now, he's back . . . oh God, don't . . . don't hurt him . . .'

'Ma'am, hold the line. Don't hang up, I'm dispatching units right now.'

'. . . is there anyone listening? . . . can anyone . . . come? . . . oh, no . . . please . . .'

Julia felt like she was going to be sick. The room began to spin. She put her hands over her ears. More than once she'd wished she had been in that house that night. She'd wished she had died. It would be so much easier.

'You – she gave birth to you, Julia. You were her everything. *Her everything!* The little girl Irene always dreamed of. Do you remember her at all? Anything you wanted, anything at all, Reenie would see you had. She loved you more than anyone could love a baby!'

'She was a great momma, Aunt Nora. I do remember . . . I never forget . . . I never forgot,' Julia cried as the words stumbled out. 'How could you say that?'

Nora turned away.

'And I miss her.' She grabbed her aunt's shoulder, trying to get her to listen. 'So much that it hurts. It *physically* hurts. Oh God, so much. Sometimes it feels like – it just feels like my chest – and my head – like they're going to explode.'

Nora shrugged off her touch. 'And for you to betray her now . . .'

'I'm not betraying her.' Julia ran her hands through her hair, trying to pull her thoughts back together. They were starting to get jumbled with her emotions and things were not making sense like they should – like they did when she'd rehearsed them. The conversation was laced with static, like a bad cellphone connection. 'I lost everyone that night, not just Momma. I lost Daddy, too. And I lost Andy. My whole family!'

Her aunt looked as if Julia had sucker-punched her in the

gut. 'Jesus, Mary and Joseph, Julia! He was the one who *took* your family from you! Don't you see that? Can't you get it?'

'He was sick, Aunt Nora. I remember him being sick when he came home early from college.' Maybe she could make Nora understand. 'Momma said he was tired and stressed, that it was all the pressure from a new school, but he was a different person than when he left.'

'Why's Andy eating in his room again?' Julia asked softly as she watched her mom at the kitchen counter, making up a dinner plate of chicken and mashed potatoes – her brother's favorite.

'Andrew's had a difficult couple of weeks. So we have to baby him a little,' her mom answered softly while she cut the chicken into bite-size pieces. She looked so tired. So incredibly tired. Like the mother of a newborn.

'Is he ever going back to college?'

'I'm sure.'

'When?'

Her mom sighed. 'I don't know, Julia. Soon. Someday. I don't know.'

Julia thought for a moment. Andy'd only been gone a few weeks to UNC Charlotte before he'd suddenly shown up back home. Maybe he'd lost his scholarship! 'Did he get kicked off the baseball team? Is that why he's back?' she asked.

Her dad suddenly slammed his hand hard on the kitchen table, and all noise abruptly stopped. 'You need to eat your own supper and stop worrying about where everybody else eats theirs,' he said flatly.

'And now I know what it was,' Julia said softly. 'This case I'm working has made me see the signs – they were all there, even before he went to North Carolina. He wasn't right; he was distant and cold and *not there* sometimes. We used to be so close – he was never just a brother. We were friends,

Aunt Nora – but then he just, he just *went somewhere*. He was in his room all the time. And he wouldn't let me in. He wouldn't let me come in . . .'

Nora stayed quiet. She stared at Julia as if she were a stranger, speaking an odd foreign language.

'Maybe . . . maybe it wasn't his fault. Maybe he had no choice. Because it's a sickness,' she stammered, trying to explain it to herself as well as her aunt. 'In his brain, eating it away like acid, and maybe it wasn't his fault . . .'

Nora finally spoke, her voice cold and detached. 'You're right, little one. It wasn't all Andrew's fault. As much as I hate your brother for what he's done, you go ahead and place the blame where it really belongs. On *who* it really belongs. But he's not here anymore, either, so I don't see much point in that.'

Julia felt her chest suck in, as if someone had taken all the oxygen from the air and she was waiting for it to be put back in before she inhaled the poison she knew would kill her. 'What are you talking about?' she finally managed. But down deep the bells had begun to ring, the alarms had sounded. She knew the answer, but she willed her aunt not to speak the words. *Please, please, please, I don't want to know this . . .*

Nora looked at her for a long moment. The anger that had fired her eyes bright blue was gone now, and she looked unbelievably sad and tired. 'Your father, Julia,' she said quietly. 'Don't you see now, little one? It was your father who brought this crazy *sickness*, like you call it, into your house, who gave this to his own son. Your father had it, too.'

60

It all started to make sense. The pieces of her childhood that had never seemed to fit before now began to slide deliberately into place, like hidden walls in an old house that led to a labyrinth of caves and secrets; each wall opened another and then another, forcing her to plunge further and further into the darkness of the unknown. Once she stepped inside the maze, she knew it would be impossible to turn back. The best she could hope for would be to find her way out once again, or else end up hopelessly lost, forever trapped in the new reality she'd created for herself.

For the first thirteen years of her life, her mother had obviously done her very best to create the illusion of a normal family life. For the last fifteen, Nora and Jimmy had tried hard to keep up the charade. To protect her, they'd simply pretended that the past had never happened. And Julia had let them. Partly because she had no choice. Partly because it was much less painful – a new house, a new name, a new identity and no questions to be answered. She'd taken the name Valenciano so she wouldn't be teased or ostracized at her new school, on the remote chance some parent figured out the familial connection from the newspapers and told their kid, 'That new girl in class has a psycho brother who killed their parents! Stay away from her!' The second they'd returned home from the funerals, her aunt had taken down all pictures of her brother and thrown them away. Then she went into her room and cried. When she finally came out, days later, the 'subject' was never spoken of again. She was the niece from upstate whose parents had been killed in a terrible car crash. Andrew had never even existed.

Julia sat down at the kitchen table, her head in her lap. The pieces kept snapping and clicking into place. 'When?' she asked.

'I've said enough. You were raised right, is all. Reenie was a saint. She did the work of both parents.'

'When, Aunt Nora? When?'

Nora turned away again, her lips pursed tight.

Up until the night of the murders, her family had seemed as average as the Musemeci family and their twelve kids down the block. But normal is always a relative term – it depends on who's doing the judging and who your competition is. Through the crime victims she'd dealt with, she'd learned some hard truths, one of which was when you're in a dysfunctional family, it's hard to see it the way others do, because to you, it's just life. And it's the only life you've ever known. A battered woman thinks all men beat, a sexually abused child accepts a father slipping into her bed at night. It's only when you get out, and examine your life from the outside looking back in, do you see it for what it really is – sick and different.

It was as though someone had suddenly placed a silk screen over all of her memories, allowing her to see behind the scenes, while the actors changed places and clothes and the sets moved. She remembered the time she was sent with Andy to live at her Nana's tree farm up in Hunter Mountain. She couldn't have been more than six, Andy must have been ten. She didn't know exactly how long they were gone, but they had to sign up for school there. Momma told them Daddy had broken his arm climbing a painting ladder in the living room and needed to recuperate, but when they finally got home, nothing in the house had been painted, and her father didn't have a cast. And his arm sure looked fine from a distance. But, then again, they were never allowed too close to him after that, because . . . *why?* She couldn't remember. Even for months after they'd been back, she couldn't remember seeing Daddy much outside of his room. When she did, he was always in pajamas. Soft, blue-striped pants and a white undershirt. Everyday.

Was that the break? Was it the first one? Did he get better? Why could she not see it all before? Why was it all so clear now?

Her mother began to work a lot after that – waitressing, or at the Pearl Paint store as a sales clerk – but Julia couldn't remember a time after the farm when they were left alone again with their father. There was always Mrs Musemeci's, or friends' houses, or, on occasion, they would go to the restaurant with their mom and sit outside on the steps that led to the parking lot reading comics or playing handball until she got off. Funny how she never thought that odd until this very moment.

Julia tried hard to remember her dad, the handsome man with a quirky temper who took her sometimes to fly kites at the Chestnut Street playground. Who got crazy mad when a single pencil went missing from the holder on his desk, but belly-laughed when Peanut the dog ran away. Then there was the time he bought her an ice cream off the Mister Softee truck when she didn't even know he was outside. Or when he let her steer his new car as she sat in his lap and rode around the block more times than she could count. The memories were there, but they were different. Her mother was like a continuous stream of good memories, assembled into a person. Her father was a person who she had a few good memories of.

'Why didn't anyone tell me?' she said softly, the tears still falling, even though she would have sworn there were no more left to shed. 'Why didn't I know about Andy?'

'Because she didn't want you to know,' Nora replied quietly, pulling another paper towel off the roll and handing it to her. '*We* didn't want you to know. There was no sense. You were only a kid. It was for your own good, Julia. You've got to know that.'

'But why?' Julia pleaded, looking up. But then she just as quickly answered the question herself. The last piece had slid into its place, the final wall had opened into the darkness. She looked back down at her lap. 'Because everyone thought I might get it, too,' she said softly.

61

The genetic link can't be ignored. With each family member afflicted with the disease, the risk factor for fellow family members does go up.

She heard Dr Barakat's words play over and over and over again in her head, with the same inflection and reflective pause as when he had said them in his office last week. She saw herself in that room, admiring his faux-painting and rich leather chairs, never once thinking he was talking about her.

And the risk is cumulative. So if Mom, Sis and Grandma have schizophrenia, Junior is at least twenty-six times more likely to develop the disease than, say, you or me.

Than, say, you or me.

We're different, was what he meant. *We* don't have mental illnesses like the defendants do. *We* wouldn't get that dirty disease.

And in the courtroom just two days ago, casually discussing the cause-and-effect relationship of schizophrenia with the experts, she'd been right there on center stage, with all eyes on her, asking the dramatic, breathless questions and secretly relieved to be part of the club. The Majority Club. A part of the Than, Say, You Or Me crowd. At that moment she was an intellectual, able to discuss and examine the clinical causes and frightening symptoms from an objective perspective in a courtroom full of other intellectual professionals. Now that was all gone. She was a percentage now – a statistic waiting to be realized. And just the word alone suddenly sounded repulsive and dirty and terrifying. Schizophrenia. *Schizo.*

She wiped the tears with the back of her hand, but it was useless. It was like an unending stream that she had not been able to shut off for two days. Maybe something was broken, she thought. Maybe the crying would never end.

Rain poured off her windshield in heavy sheets, whipped around by the gusty wind. Even with headlights, it was impossible to see more than a few feet in front of the car, and traffic on 95 had slowed to a stop-and-go crawl. She probably should've called the airport before she'd left her apartment to see if her flight had been delayed or cancelled, but she hadn't. After finding a seat on the last JetBlue flight of the day, she'd quickly thrown some clothes into a duffel bag and hurried to drop Moose at the kennel before they closed. She had to keep packing, moving, going, hurrying – or else risk stopping to think. And right now, she knew that was just too dangerous. Because she didn't really know what she was going to do when she got off that plane in New York. And with too much thinking, she might not go. There were still stacks and stacks of memories inside her head that she couldn't bring herself to drag out and examine just yet. The ones that she knew now might never have even existed the way she once thought they did.

It was like the shock of suddenly finding out Santa wasn't real, without ever having once questioned his existence. One small fact had changed everything. It had even changed history. Only it wasn't just Santa she'd found out didn't exist today. Or the Easter Bunny. It was her whole life. She turned the music up on the radio, hoping someone could sing loud enough or strong enough to stop the thoughts that kept running through her head while she waited for the traffic to inch forward in the driving rain. She wondered if the voices did come for her, would she know they weren't real? Would she know the difference between a DJ on the radio and a phantom?

She felt so alone. So incredibly alone with shameful secrets no one could ever know. No one wanted to be friends with the girl whose parents were murdered. The girl whose brother was a murderer. Old friends had stopped calling right after the funerals. Even Carly. New friends wanted no part of someone who was so different. So she'd made sure she wasn't. She buried her past in secrets and lies that she kept from everyone. Friends, boyfriends, teachers, professors, bosses. *Her parents had died in a terrible car crash. She was raised by her aunt and uncle. She was an only child.* She'd told the same lie for so long that, on occasion, even she'd thought it sounded right. For just a little while, sometimes even she'd forget what it felt like to be so damn different.

Andrew's sweet, young face flashed before her, with his milky skin and dark curly hair. The deep dimples when he smiled. Bobby Brady, her mom thought he looked like. He had never looked evil to her, even that night when he pulled away in the police car, covered in the blood of their parents. A boy of barely eighteen. That's all he'd been. A boy. Ten years younger than she was now. She'd abandoned him all this time, while he sat alone, going through a cold, indifferent justice system that she knew he didn't understand and that didn't understand him.

She chewed her thumbnail till it started to bleed, staring straight into the blurred red brake lights of the Mazda in front of her. Now there was one more horrible secret to bury from friends and co-workers and boyfriends. She blinked back tears again. Only this one she might not be able to keep all to herself.

'Schizo,' she said aloud in the empty car. Then she opened her window and spit the dirty, scary word out into the rain.

62

'Whoa, little lady. I know you don't want to be in here now,' said the deep voice of a blue coat whose whole large body blocked the front foyer. His broad arms grabbed her and held her tight.

She screamed something, anything. And she punched out at him, hoping to distract him with a claw to the face. Make him flinch so she could run past. It was her house, damn it!

Maybe they were still alive.

It was no use. Her small body was no match against Burly Man. 'I have to go in,' she pleaded. 'Please! Please! You don't understand! I have to go in!'

'No, you don't, honey. No, you don't,' he said in a voice that was too calm. Too soothing. As if to say, 'There is no emergency anymore, there's no need to be rushing.'

'They're my parents! I have to see them!'

'No, honey. You don't want to see them this way. Trust me. Where's Potter?' Burly yelled to one of the blue coats in the living room behind him. 'Have him get a psych out here, will you? Get me one of those EMTs!'

'That's my mother! My mother!' she screamed. 'Momma! Oh God, Momma!'

Through Burly Man's legs, she could see the puddle of bright red blood that stained the cream living-room rug behind him. It looked like it ran up the walls. Sticking out from behind the couch her eyes caught on the bright yellow rosebuds and pink ribbon that trimmed the sleeve of her mother's new nightgown. The one Julia had given her for her birthday last week. Long, slender fingers still held a bloody phone in their frozen grasp, the nails painted a dainty, soft pink. Her legs began to shake uncontrollably.

Potter ran in the front door. '*Julie, you need to come with me.*'

'*No! I want to see them! I have to see them!*'

'*Julie, it's very bad,*' said Potter.

She turned and screamed the words at him. '*My name is Julia, you asshole! J-u-l-i-a. And that's my parents in there! That's my mom! I want to see them! You can't not let me see them!*' She began to cry again and she felt her body weaken with exhaustion against Burly Man. There was little fight left. The blue coats and cheap suits in the living room had all stopped what they were doing to watch.

'*Get me Disick,*' Potter said into his handheld, running a palm through his sweaty hair. The detective was more than a few pounds overweight and that last run across the lawn had left him red-faced and wheezy. '*Have him meet us down at the precinct in thirty.*'

Julia had seen enough movies. She knew from Detective Potter's tone just who Disick was and she slumped down, defeated, on the floor. It must be a dream. This must all be a dream. Life can't change this fast.

'*Take her outside,*' said Burly Man to Potter. '*Let them finish up in here.*'

'*We need to find your family, Julia,*' said Potter softly, stooping down to her eye level. '*Do you have any other family, honey?*'

Any other family. Hers was all gone now. She stared blankly at the pinprick-sized spot of grease on the detective's tie.

He reached over and gently lifted her up by the arm. '*Come on, Julia. Let's go. There'll be someone down at the station you can talk to while we try to find your relatives. I have a couple of questions . . .*'

Potter's voice finally tapered off. She could tell from his moving mouth that he was still speaking, saying something, but she couldn't hear him. She couldn't hear anything anymore. Sound had suddenly been sucked up into a vacuum, replaced by an intense, deafening pressure inside her head and she thought she might pass out. She watched as the different characters slowly came back to life all around her, busying themselves once again in her living room and moving across her lawn and her driveway. Burly nodded grimly at her before turning his attention back to the officer behind him, giving him directions with animated hands.

And just like that, the world went on.

She let Potter lead her back through the small foyer with the fake brick linoleum that her mother had always wanted to replace, and out the front door into the cold night air. Yellow crime-scene tape held back the growing crowd of pajama-clad neighbors. When she reached the cement walkway that led down to the sidewalk she stopped, turning to look back for one long last second at the house she'd lived in for thirteen years. She knew she would never see it again. Every room, including hers, was ablaze with lights, crawling with silhouetted strangers. Through the living-room window, she could see the technicians and photographers and detectives do their handiwork right alongside the Christmas tree that she and her mother had decorated just last week.

Oddly enough, no one had thought to unplug it.

63

On a Saturday morning, the taxi ride from the hotel at LaGuardia Airport to Ward's Island only took about twenty minutes. It was strange. Here it was, she'd grown up in New York, volunteered during summers in college at both the Queens and Bronx Zoos, spent countless weekends down at the Seaport or in Greenwich Village clubs, gone to dozens of concerts in Washington Square and Central Park. She was probably one of the only New Yorkers who'd actually visited the Statue of Liberty and the Empire State Building, and she'd memorized the NYC subway system like a treasure map. But until three days ago, she'd never even heard of Ward's Island. How ironic that for years and years, she was just a short taxi ride away from her brother.

After the tollbooth at the Triboro, the cab turned off, following insignificant green and white signs for Randall's Island and Ward's Island – the same ones she'd always somehow managed to overlook. The road twisted around what was, by New York City standards, a veritable forest of tall oaks, sycamores and maples, as it wound down a hill and under the bridge itself. Even though it was winter and the trees were barren, the million-dollar-plus view was breathtaking. The skyline of Manhattan loomed less than a mile to the west, over the dark waters of the East River. But there were no homes here to appreciate it. No office buildings or restaurants or gas stations or, even among all this glorious outdoors, parks to play in. This piece of prime real estate was eerily undeveloped, overgrown and devoid of life.

The taxi pulled up to the gate of an old stone guardhouse. Another insignificant green and white metal highway sign next to the door read *Manhattan Psychiatric Center*.

Julia lowered her window. 'Kirby?'

'Name and picture ID,' said the guard, holding a pen and clipboard in front of him.

'Valenciano,' she said, holding out her State Attorney's badge, hoping it might work the same powerful magic in New York as it did in Miami. She was too tired to answer questions.

It did. The guard nodded and pointed, dropping the clipboard to his side. The fact that she'd come by taxi instead of in a marked police unit didn't seem to bother him at all. 'Take this straight ahead. Kirby's on the left after the turn.'

'What's the number on that?'

He looked at her blankly. 'It's the building with two forty-foot razor-wire fences around it, lady. Trust me, you ain't gonna miss it.'

She nodded and sat back in her seat as the taxi pulled away from the gatehouse. From research conducted on the Internet she already knew that Manhattan Psychiatric was made up of three buildings: Meyer, Dunlop and Kirby. All three had been constructed sometime in the fifties to house the city's overwhelming number of mentally ill residents – 28,000 at one point in time. But in the sixties – after the first generation of antipsychotics were discovered and institutionalization fell out of public favor – the number of committed residents fell from the tens of thousands to only a few hundred. Dunlop and Kirby closed their doors shortly thereafter, sometime in the seventies, leaving Meyer as the sprawling center's only facility to offer both in-patient and out-patient psych services. Eventually Dunlop housed administrative offices, but the Kirby building remained shuttered and abandoned until 1985 when it reopened as a maximum-security forensic psychiatric hospital – a present-day criminal insane asylum. Julia watched out the dirty window, already caked with winter, as the taxi made its way through the hills and past the first two buildings, presumably Meyer and Dunlop. Though it was near freezing out, a few green scrubs and white uniforms were seated outside at bolted-down metal picnic tables, sipping coffee or smoking cigarettes or simply staring off into the trees. Given what they had to do for a living and where they had to do it, it was easy to see why someone would take their break as far away from their day as possible, no matter what the weather.

The guard was right. As the taxi rounded the final turn, it was impossible to miss the double chain-link fence that wrapped around the perimeter of the twelve-story building. Thick rolls of steely barbed wire topped both fences. She paid the driver and watched him turn around and take off back through the parking lot. She fought back the sudden urge to run after him, scream for him to stop, pull out another twenty and demand he take her back to the airport. Back to Miami. Back to where everything was a mess, but at least it was safe and it was familiar.

But her feet didn't move. And she said nothing as the cab disappeared from sight behind the trees. She lit a cigarette with cold, shaking fingers, watching as the cab's trail of white exhaust fumes floated off into the sky and disappeared. She knew she couldn't just go back. Nothing in her past was real anymore. Nothing was truly safe or secure or even familiar – not even the happiest of memories. It was as if she were standing on a precipice, with one foot dangling over in mid-air. One more step in the wrong direction and she would surely free-fall out of control. But what was the right direction anymore? Inside the building behind her was not just the past she never knew she had, but the future she might not want to ever meet. Backwards or forwards, the ground was unsettled, no matter where she stepped.

She finally turned away from the road to face the dirty gray institution that loomed behind her. The black steel-mesh windows stared back at her like cold, vacant eyes; the rolls of prickly barbed wire formed a twisted smile of razor-sharp teeth. She wondered how many faces might be watching her at that moment from behind those windows and through the checkered steel of the fence. Watching her hesitate. Watching her deliberate. The faces of murderers and rapists. The faces of the criminally insane. Were any of them Andrew? Would he know her if he saw her? Had he been waiting all these years for her to come? Every Saturday and Sunday and holiday for the past fourteen years?

She sucked in the final puff of her cigarette and made her decision. She stepped forward off the ledge and into the darkness of an unknown future, not sure if anything would hold her up when she did. And as she made her way along the concrete walkway, past the razor wire and the abandoned picnic tables, through the double security doors and metal detectors, one last question burned in the back of her brain.

Did he still wait?

64

'Who you here to see?' asked the guard behind the bullet-proof window as he examined her driver's license and badge. Behind him, maybe a half-dozen other uniforms milled about in the small room, eating donuts and drinking coffee. Saturday morning cartoons played on a small portable TV. On the foldout table next to the metal detector, another officer went through her purse looking for weapons.

'Cirto. Andrew Cirto,' she said.

'Cirto, huh? That's a first. You a detective?' he asked with a thick New York accent, fingering her badge. Under where it read *State Attorney's Office*, a red enamel sun rose over a green palm tree and blue water. Even she'd thought it looked fake the first time she'd seen it.

'No. I'm a prosecutor. In Miami.'

'Oh. You seeing him for a case you got? You know, he's been locked up as long as I been here.'

She shook her head and cleared her throat. 'It's personal.' She looked around the empty screening/waiting room. On a table in the corner, a fake silver Christmas tree flashed on and off. She knew from friends in Corrections that visiting day in prison could get pretty busy. Obviously, from the looks of it, that was not the case here at Kirby. Not even on Christmas Eve.

'Well, they got to call up to the ward and bring him down to the visiting room. It may take a while. Have a seat.'

'Okay,' she nodded, turning away. Then she thought of

something and turned back. 'Do they tell him who's here to see him?'

'I think so.'

'Make sure they tell him it's Ju-Ju,' she said quietly, taking a seat on a ripped vinyl bench close to the door. She glanced down at the stack of worn *People* magazines on the chipped end table.

She closed her eyes and attempted to gather her thoughts. She tried to imagine the conversation she wanted to have with Andrew, but couldn't even get that far. Past 'hello', she wasn't sure what was going to happen.

Maybe a half-hour later the door to the waiting room opened. A slight, balding man in a dark suit and white doctor's coat came in. His dark eyes were buried in a deep frown. He didn't look happy. 'Ms Valenciano?'

'Yes,' she said, rising to meet him.

'I'm Dr Harry Mynks, the Director of Psychiatric Services here. I'm one of Andrew Cirto's doctors.'

She nodded. There was an awkward pause.

'The SHTA told me that someone was here to see Andrew,' he continued coldly. 'I'm sorry, but I don't recognize the name Valenciano.'

'I didn't know you were supposed to,' she said, shifting uncomfortably. 'What's that, an SHTA?'

'That's one of our Secure Hospital Treatment Assistants. An aid on the ward. He called me to say that Andrew has a visitor.' He paused, again waiting for her to say something. 'I've been the director here at Kirby for eight years, Ms Valenciano,' he continued when she didn't, pulling down on his bony chin, 'and, well, to be honest with you, that's never happened before. In fact, since I'm quite familiar with Andrew's records, I can tell you that in all his years at this facility, he's never had a single visitor. That's why I took an interest in meeting you. I wanted to speak with you before you actually met with him today.' He nodded at the uniform in the booth, who then buzzed the door. 'Can you accompany me to my office for a moment, so we can go over a few things?' Dr Mynks asked, holding the door open for her.

Julia swallowed hard and nodded, following him into a deserted hallway that looked a lot like the basement of the science lab in her high school, windowless and clinical. The metal in her worn heels clicked softly on the shiny cement floor and she shifted her weight to the balls of her feet. She'd meant to get them reheeled.

'These are just administrative offices,' he said, watching her as she looked about. 'The wards are on the upper floors. Visitors are not permitted up there. I have to ask,' he said when they'd arrived at his office door. He held it open and motioned her in. 'All the way from the Miami State Attorney's Office. Who are you?'

Julia looked around the sparsely furnished room, her eyes hoping to land on anything besides Dr Mynks's disarming stare. A degree from Johns Hopkins hung behind the desk. As did one from Cornell. She took a breath. 'I'm his sister,' she said after a moment, finally taking a seat. 'Andrew is my older brother.'

'Oh,' he replied, sitting himself behind the desk.

'I just want to see him again. I didn't know he was here. I just found out. I thought he was . . . well, I thought he was dead,' she said carefully. 'I just want to see him again, Dr Mynks.' She probably didn't have to tell him anything, but there you go – he was a psychiatrist and although it wasn't a couch, she was sitting in his office.

'Andrew murdered your—'

She nodded and cut him off with a deliberate wave of her

hand. 'Yes. I, ah – I know he was sick now. I didn't know that before.' She shifted in her seat.

'Oh,' he said again, but she could tell he didn't believe her. Then he paused. 'He's better, Ms Valenciano. Since I've been director here, he's been a model patient. Are you familiar with his history?'

'I know he has schizophrenia. I've read the court file.'

'And you didn't know that before? Were you living with him when he was first diagnosed?'

'I was very young at the time. What medication is he on?'

He shook his head. 'I can't discuss that with you. HIPA privacy rules.'

She waited a moment. 'I've read the plea transcript. I know he's paranoid, Dr Mynks. I know from those transcripts what he thought that night. What he was thinking . . .' She cleared her throat. 'About the CIA. About my father. I know what the voices told him to do to them.' She took a deep breath.

'The murders were very brutal.'

'I'd rather not discuss that.'

There was a long and difficult pause. 'I don't know how much you know about the disease itself, but schizophrenia doesn't go away, Ms Valenciano. So I don't know what you're expecting to find today. With paranoids, some hold on to the same delusion or auditory hallucination their whole lives, others may develop different delusions, or perhaps hear new or different voices. Medication can do wonders for some patients – completely quieting the voices they hear, or dulling those voices to whispers. In others, we unfortunately have limited success. There are some that will always exist in a foreign world that no one, and no medicine, can ever reach. I can tell you that your brother is one of the lucky ones. But since he hasn't seen you in so long, without divulging any privileged information, I have to suggest that you show him your hands before you sit down. Palms up. Let him inspect them carefully, so that he does not become agitated.'

She stared at him. A wave of goosebumps suddenly erupted down her back.

'He needs to look at your hands to make sure they have no implants,' he explained. 'To make sure that you are not a robot or a CIA spy. Medication successfully helps your brother learn to live with his illness. To him, though, his delusion and the people in it can still seem as real as you or me. Without medication, I'm sure he'd bet his life on it.' He hesitated for a deliberate second. 'And yours.'

I saved them, Ju-Ju. I saved them.

'I know there are privacy rules,' she said finally, and paused again. She looked down at her hands, rubbing them slowly together, thinking of what Dr Mynks had just said. 'But, well, how is he now?'

'You can see for yourself in just a moment. He's in the visiting room upstairs, waiting.'

'Does he know I'm here? Does he know it's me?'

'Yes. Yes, he does.'

She tried to read Dr Mynks's face, but he gave nothing away. She still didn't think he liked her.

'Thank you for speaking with me,' he said, rising. 'I was just curious to meet you. You know, fourteen years in here and no one. Not even a phone call. Now, with just weeks before his release, he gets his first visitor. It couldn't just be coincidence, I thought. I wanted to make sure you weren't with the press, trying to stir up some reaction in the community. From what I understand, his case did receive a fair deal of coverage in the news at the time.'

'Release?' she asked, startled.

'Yes,' Dr Mynks said, turning back to face her as he opened the door. He studied her with that same suspicious frown. 'Andrew just had his two-year review. The Forensic Committee met last month and reviewed the report of the ward psychiatrist, the staff psychologist and the OMH social worker, and this time recommended that he be released to a less-secure, civil psychiatric facility. He's being sent to Rockland Psychiatric within the next ninety days or so, as soon as there's a bed available for him. The hope, of course, is that from there, he can eventually be released back into society.'

65

The stairwell that led to the visiting room on the second floor smelled like fresh industrial paint, but the gray walls still looked as if they were about to shed, bubbling and flecking in many places. Everything, in fact, was painted the same bleak gray – the ceiling, the air ducts, the pipes. Caged fluorescent tube lights buzzed overhead, bathing the lifeless halls in a ghoulish, purple tint.

Julia walked up the center of the steps, her hands in her pockets, careful not to touch anything, her head down and her nose buried in her turtleneck. She thought of the very first time she'd walked into the Dade County Jail to take a statement from an inmate. A brand new C, the awful stench had hit her like a hard slap across the face. The air had smelled of not just urine and shit and old paint, but it also smelled *dirty*. Like the rancid men in the holding cells next to her and the catwalks overhead, who leered and cackled and coughed and breathed back into the same air that she then had to inhale. And right now – in this bleak, gray stairwell, in the waiting room downstairs, even in the administrative halls – all around her, it was not so much *dirty* that she smelled as *sick*. Like the stink of a hospital. The smell disinfectant never washed away. She held her breath for as long as she could, breathing in and out through her mouth only, wishing she were outside under the winter trees in the freezing weather with the aids and nurses, sucking in the icy air. Far away from this peeling, probably asbestos-filled building where she breathed in the panicked breaths of sick, crazy people.

A handwritten sign on the second-floor landing read 'Visitors', and an arrow pointed toward a door at the end of a short hall. Above that door, the face of a guard peered through a security window, watching her with a disinterested stare. He didn't even blink and the door below him suddenly buzzed open. Julia quickly moved to grasp the knob in her sweaty palm, pushing it in before it could lock again. She hesitated for just a second longer, then took a deep breath through her mouth and walked slowly into the room.

In here, administration had picked a soft, powder blue for the walls. A nice calm color, she thought. Round faux-wood Formica tables and mismatched plastic chairs were scattered about the large room, but there was no one seated at any of them. Another fake Christmas tree blinked in the corner. Cardboard dreidels hung on the wall beside it.

Bright sunlight streamed in from the wall of security metal-mesh windows that overlooked an empty exercise yard, casting diamond-shaped shadows across the tables and on the white floor. A few pumpkin-orange easy chairs that might have been left over from when the building had originally closed in 1975 sat empty, too, in front of a console TV. To Julia's left, two guards sat like DJs in an open booth that was mounted against the wall and above the room. A young, muscular black man in a white polo shirt, who she assumed was what they called a SHTA, stood in front of the booth, his arms folded across his chest, watching her intently. No one said anything when she walked in. In fact, the only noise in the room was from the boom-box radio on the ledge of the booth that played soft Christmas music. She looked behind her, wondering if they were going to bring him in after her, but there was no one. Then she scanned the room once again. It was on that second glance that she saw the heavyset man at a table in the far corner.

Dressed in a tan button-down shirt and brown pants, he practically blended in with the dull furniture and the barren landscape out the window behind him.

His face was cast down at the table, his fingers folded neatly in front of him. The first thing she noticed was the tousled mop of thinning black curls on his head. She knew right away that it was Andrew although, just last week, she probably couldn't have picked him out of a crowd at the supermarket. She forgot all about breathing through her mouth and sucked in a deep breath that probably sounded more like a gasp to the SHTA, who shot her a cold look.

Andrew didn't move, though. Didn't even lift his head. Julia walked slowly across the stretching room, her heels clicking softly on the polished floor, but she no longer cared if anyone heard them. The room suddenly seemed like a football field. Feet turned into yards. Yards could have been miles. 'Andrew?' she heard herself ask softly, standing awkwardly in front of him. 'Andrew, it's me. It's Julia.'

The man seated in the chair slowly looked up. His large brown eyes found hers. A long moment passed. It was Julia who finally looked away.

'Can I sit?' she asked softly, clearing her throat. 'Do you mind if I sit down?'

He watched as she pulled out a chair, but said nothing.

So she sat and she waited. Waited for any one of the million sentences rushing her brain to just come out. Waited for him to say something. Waited for the SHTA to say something from across the room. And she tried not to stare at her big brother, the person she'd idolized from the time she could walk. The person who'd taught her how to play guitar and climb a tree. Who'd held her hand every morning on the walk to the bus stop, even when their mother wasn't looking. The person who'd introduced her to Led Zeppelin and Steely Dan and Pink Floyd, when everyone else was singing along with Madonna.

Andrew was only five years older than her, but he could easily have been twenty. Once lean and fit, she guessed he was about forty or fifty pounds overweight now, his soft, dark curls peppered with gray. In high school, he'd been the varsity starting quarterback *and* captain of the baseball team, earning a full athletic scholarship to the University of North Carolina at Charlotte. Every girl had wanted to date him, every guy had wanted to be him. It had obviously been years now since he'd done more than a short walk through an exercise yard. Deprived of sunshine, his face was pale, his skin blotchy, probably from all the medicine he took. But it wasn't so much the dramatic change in his physical appearance that finally made her fidget for something in her purse. It was his eyes. Not just your ordinary brown, Andrew's dark-chocolate eyes had sparkled and fizzed when the light hit them. 'Root-beer brown' her mom had always called them. Now they were flat and dull. Devoid of light. Devoid of life.

She finally broke the silence, her voice barely above a whisper. 'It's been so long, Andrew. I came today because I wanted to see you. I didn't know you were . . .' She paused, looking awkwardly around the room, '. . . *here.*'

'I understand,' he answered back softly, nodding. His voice sounded exactly as she remembered it. They sat in silence for a few more tense moments. 'How are you?' he asked finally.

She smiled a little. 'Okay. I live in Miami now. I moved from Washington DC a few years ago. I work on my tan when I'm not actually working. As you can see, I'm in the office a lot,' she said with a short, desperate laugh, holding out her arm.

'Washington?'

'I went to school there.'

'What do you do?' he asked, his eyes on her hands.

'I'm a lawyer. I work for the government.' There was no need to get into details. 'How about you? What's it like in here? Are the people nice?'

He shrugged. 'It's okay. It's better than it was. It wasn't so good when I first got here. It was,' he paused for a moment, as though remembering something. 'It was hard. We watch TV and see movies. We have computers to use, and someone comes in and teaches some of us how to use the Internet. I like to read the paper. The *Times*, when they let me.' He smiled again. 'You see, I'm a Republican now.'

'Maybe you do belong in here,' she said, laughing.

He laughed, too. 'It's a good thing I can't vote, right?' Then his face grew dark and he scratched at the back of his head. 'I don't like the screamers, though.'

The goosebumps were back. She felt them race up her arm. 'The screamers? What are they?'

Andrew quickly shook his head back and forth. He blinked a few times and looked back down. 'Are you married?'

'No, no. I date people – I'm dating someone, but that's it right now.' Given where she was and what Andrew had been diagnosed with, part of her wanted to speak to him like he was an imbecile or a little kid: in short, loud and carefully enunciated Dick and Jane sentences. But he obviously didn't need that. She felt herself gently slipping into a conversation instead of just sentences. The awkwardness was still there, but it was getting better.

'Any kids?' he asked.

'I'd like to try marriage first. We'll see about kids after that.'

'You probably have your pick of boyfriends. You're a

pretty woman, Julia. Not just a little sister anymore. Your hair, it got so long. And you got so tall. You look so different from the pictures I have in my head. Good, I mean.'

'Thank you. The height's an illusion, though.' She stuck out her foot and pointed. 'Three-inch heels. You look good, too, Andy.'

He shook his head again. 'Nah. No more baseball for me. Only on TV. The medicine makes you gain a lot of weight. It used to make me real tired, and it does other things, too.' But he didn't say what those other things were.

'What are you taking?'

'I think it's Risperdal. I'm not so sure of the name. I've been on a few. I don't like when they change them, though.' He blinked a few more times and rolled his tongue about the inside of his cheeks. She heard his foot tapping and moving underneath the table.

'I think you look good,' she said. 'And I hear that you're gonna be released soon. You must be excited about that.'

'Can I see your hands, please?' he asked suddenly with a frown, blinking fast. 'I'm sorry, but I just need to – I really would like to see your hands. Can I see them?'

She swallowed hard. She had totally forgotten what Dr Mynks had said. She nodded and put her hands out on the table, palm side up. Andrew had grown very intense very quickly. She could hear both feet tapping away busily under the table as if he were running a marathon in place.

He moved his rough lumpy fingers over hers, and she felt an electric jolt run through her. The thumb on his left hand was twisted inward, flopping uselessly at the wrist; his other digits were strangely deformed. They were the hands of her brother, but yet the hands of a murderer – the very hands that had brutally taken their parents' lives. She could see the raised, jagged red scars and white lines that haphazardly sliced across the palms, dissecting his fingers into tiny pieces, like a ripped-up piece of paper that someone had tried to glue back together. She fought the urge to pull away while he probed her palms, carefully feeling every knuckle, every joint, every line. Her hands began to sweat and she wondered if he would think that meant she was hiding something. Then she went one step further and wondered what he might do if he did think that, which made them sweat even more. Suddenly he grasped both her wrists. He was strong, very strong. 'Where have you been?' he demanded, staring at her, his face dark.

She could feel her heart thumping loudly in her chest, so fast and so hard that it felt like it might actually push right through her shirt, like some love-demented cartoon character. The adrenaline instantly tensed every muscle in her body; icy fear froze her right where she sat. But, strangely enough, she didn't try to pull her hands back or scream for the SHTA or even stand up and run out. Rather, she looked into those sad, flat, root-beer eyes and just knew Andrew wasn't angry or even dangerous. He was scared. And he was pleading with her for an answer. An answer she'd owed him for fifteen years. It was at that moment that she just knew it was the scarred, broken hands of her brother that held her fast, and he was no murderer.

'I'm so sorry, Andy,' she whispered softly. 'I should never have left you.' She felt his grip relax and he looked down at the table again, defeated. She could have pulled away then, gotten up and walked out on shaky knees, promising to come back but not meaning it. But instead, she slid her palms back into his, taking his hands in hers. She squeezed them lightly. 'I'm here now, Andy. I'm here. And I won't go away again. I promise.'

The moment stayed there, held in suspension. It was just

the two of them in the world right then and time had simply stopped. He closed his eyes. 'I'm sorry, Ju-Ju. Sorry, sorry, sorry, sorry, sorry,' he rambled, over and over again, his words barely a whisper. 'I didn't mean for you to hate me. I know what I've done and I wish I didn't do it. I wish I could go back. I wish I wasn't born. I wish, I wish, I wish . . .' He squeezed her hands tightly and then started to weep. So did she.

They sat together like that, holding hands across the table for hours, talking and crying until the light faded from the winter sky behind them and the SHTA named Samuel came over to tell them that visiting hours were over.

66

The ranch-styled house with the stone façade sat in an
emerald-green clearing, encircled by acres of towering pines,
magnolias, live oaks and the occasional requisite palm tree.
On the front porch, an antique rocker creaked and tipped
in the breeze; white smoke puffed from the chimney into an
ink-black sky scattered with diamonds and conspicuously
missing a moon. An overnight frost warning had brought
all the flowering baskets that normally hung from the porch
trellis inside for the night. A long dirt driveway rambled
down through the trees from the main road, running alongside the house and finally ending in front of a small, four-stall
stable. Two beaten horse trails wound back into the woods
behind the house, past a rusted metal swing set and a Little
Tikes plastic playhouse.

Nestled in the black shadows of the pines less than fifty
feet away, a man stood silently watching the postcard-perfect
cottage. At least a half-mile from the nearest neighbor, it
was secluded enough to be considered 'country', but still
only a quick hop in the car would bring you to the local
7-Eleven and nearest Wal-Mart Supercenter. Perfectly
charming, it was, like out of a perfectly charming fairytale.
Maybe Grimms' *Hansel & Gretel*, the man thought, his cold
eyes once again falling on the swing set. *Yes.* A perfectly
charming, unassuming house in the woods with tasty sugar-
frosted windows and stone walls the color of gingerbread.
From the outside all looked too good to be true. Too
delicious to resist. But tomorrow, when the sun rose on the

clearing and the first police car gently rolled down the dirt driveway, like poor, hungry Hansel and his sweet sister, it would be a house of horrors that the shocked policeman would find awaited him when he turned the knob and stepped inside.

The night air was refreshingly cool and crisp; it tasted of burning wood and smelled of rich compost and sickly-sweet night-blooming jasmine. And, of course, pine. Above him, the towering treetops blocked out even the starlight; their leaves rustling and swaying in the wind like the pompoms of a cheerleader. Strangely enough, though, other than the soft whispers of the trees, not a sound could be heard in the pure black woods. Not the hoot of an owl, or the croak of a frog. Even the two stabled mares were settled and quiet. It was as if everything living had picked up and wisely left for the night.

Framed like a pretty picture in the warm kitchen lights, she washed dishes at the sink, her honey-colored hair pulled back into a soft pony. The window was cracked open and he could hear the running of water, the clinking of dishes, the soft hum of her voice as she attempted Elvis's 'Are You Lonesome Tonight?' It excited him.

The man had watched her for what felt like hours now, as she made dinner and drank a glass of wine and, finally, put the kids to bed after reading them each a story. Now the night was coming to an end. He fought off the flock of anxious butterflies that made his heart pump like it had been shot up with adrenaline. The anticipation was the best part and the worst part of the night; as any hunter worth his weight could tell you, it's the thrill of the hunt that makes the game taste so sweet. She shut the window against the unusual cold that had news shows all over the state of Florida talking, and snapped out the kitchen light. The chimney stopped puffing and the porch went black. Less than a minute later, the bedroom lights came on.

She didn't bother to close the blinds. There was no one around for miles. There was no one who could see in. He watched as she unbuttoned her shirt right in front of him, unhooked her bra and showed him her big, beautiful breasts. She slid off her jeans and folded them neatly, placing them on a bench at the foot of the bed. Wearing only a pair of silky red panties, she lingered for a moment at the window before pulling on a T-shirt and heading into the bathroom.

Poor Charlene. Charley, as she liked to be called. Still wearing her sexy, fire-engine red undies even though there was no one to wear them for anymore. She'd gotten the house in the country; he took the condo in downtown. Heading full speed ahead into the dark middle ages with a few lumps around the tummy and no one but her two little kids to kiss goodnight. No one around to protect her when the forest came alive.

So vulnerable. So lonely.

What she needed was a little company to ring in the New Year with.

It wasn't long before the lights went out in the perfectly charming little cottage. Then the devil emerged from the pitch-black shadows of the woods and crossed the lush lawn, passing the swing set and playhouse, careful not to disturb the nice horses as they slept. At the back door he simply turned the knob and quietly stepped inside.

Of course she hadn't locked it, because it was safe out here in the pretty countryside, where no one was around for miles.

Anxiety:
like metal on metal in my brain
Paranoia: it is making me run
away, away, away
and back again quickly
to see if I've been caught
or lied to
or laughed at
Ha ha ha. The Ferris wheel
in Looney Land is not so funny.

A paranoid schizophrenic
patient

67

'Okay, are we broken up and no one's told me?'

Julia looked up with a start from the *Federal Reporter* she'd been buried in all morning just as an intense Dayanara Vega slipped into the seat next to her in the Graham Building's empty law library. 'I can't believe it's really you,' Day said with a harsh whisper, even though no one else was around. She poked her arm with a fingernail. 'Maybe you're an apparition.'

'Hey there,' Julia replied softly with a surprised, tired smile. It was a picture-perfect Sunday morning and only the workaholics and the lonely were in the office. Smart South Floridians were down at the beach with the tourists, nursing their Saturday night hangovers and working on their tans in February.

Day frowned. 'Where the hell have you been, girl? I've gone through two boyfriends and a vibrator since the last time we went to lunch. We haven't talked in so long, all my good gossip is actually fact now,' she sniped, her clipped, polished fingernails tapping away on the table, while she obviously waited on an answer.

Julia rolled her eyes with an embarrassed smile. 'Uh-oh. I think I can handle your acrobatic escapades with the eligible bachelors of Miami, but I definitely don't want to know about your dalliances with a back massager, Day,' she replied lightly. 'TMI.'

'Oh, so you only want to hear about the good times,'

Dayanara replied with a short laugh, but the pout was still there and despite the sarcasm and tough exterior, it was pretty obvious she was hurt. It'd been more than a few weeks since the competency hearing when the two of them had last spoken. While Julia wouldn't say she'd been avoiding her friend, she hadn't been seeking her out, either. Things had just gotten so complicated since Christmas. Since Andy. Days had slipped into weeks, and weeks into ... well, months, as she tried to adjust to this exhausting, clandestine double life she was now living. A life that included flying – whenever she could afford it and whenever she could manage it – to New York on weekends to see her brother. Everything else and everyone else had from Monday to Friday to fit in. And it didn't always fit. She held back a yawn. If she didn't have to be back for a Marquette meeting this afternoon and to research a motion, she'd still be up there right now, in fact. Instead, she'd caught the 6 a.m. flight out of LaGuardia and had come straight to the Graham Building. Her suitcase was still in the car.

'For someone who is trying a high-profile murder trial, you sure do know how to keep it on the low,' Day groused. 'I've stopped by your office maybe a dozen times; I've called and left messages on your cell, at home, with your secretary. I do have a personality disorder, you know. The next step for me is stalking. So just tell me, is it me, or is it the 'I-have-a-boyfriend-now-so-I'll-just-drop-all-of-my-friends' syndrome? The latter I can hate you for, the former I get to hate myself.'

Julia took off her glasses and rubbed her eyes and wondered how to have this conversation. She'd picked up the phone a dozen times herself to call Day these past few weeks, but ultimately had set it back down each time. No matter how much she wanted to let someone into her life, share the heavy burden of her dark family secrets, she knew that meant telling a frightening story that no one would ever – could ever – possibly begin to understand, no matter how much they might insist they could. Her whole life was a lie – who she was, where she was from, what her family was like, who her family was. Even her name – Julia Valenciano – was only a half-truth. There were too many lies told to too many people, too many secrets kept for too many years to go back and start from the very beginning with a friend who knew her and liked her as a completely different person. From colleagues to best friends to lovers to her damn hairdresser – every single relationship she'd built in her life was grounded in falsehoods and nurtured with more lies. Even if she could somehow explain her parents' brutal murders to Dayanara or Rick – or anyone else for that matter – without them running for the nearest exit in horror, she knew she'd never be able to rationalize still loving their killer. And she just couldn't sit back and accept the silent passing of judgment on her brother that was sure to follow. She would rather be alone with the burden of her past than sacrifice Andrew again. He was back in her life now – suddenly and completely – and she was all he had left. His was the only truly honest relationship she had that was still intact.

'First off, leaving a message with Thelma is about as useful as flossing before the dentist pulls your tooth,' Julia began. 'It's a gesture that takes too much time and is not at all appreciated. Secondly, I haven't even been home to get messages lately – I've been out of town a lot. And third, it's not you and it's not me and it's not anything, Day. Things have come up since Christmas. I've . . . I've just been real busy. I'm sorry I haven't called.' She tried to find her friend's eyes. 'Really.'

Dayanara watched her cautiously for a long moment. 'What things?'

'Trials. Hearings. Pre-files. Arthurs. Meetings.' She looked down at the pile of law books in front of her. 'This case. You know how crazy my judge is, and my DC still has it out for me. I'm beginning to think they've joined forces.'

'Hmmm . . .' Dayanara leaned back in her chair, rocking on the back legs. With her eyes squinted, and her arms folded across her chest, she said, 'There's more to this story than legal research and Judge Farley working you to death. You look like shit.'

'There's more to every story,' Julia replied softly. 'But that's all I can give you right now.'

Day smiled. 'I'm a narcissist. As long as it's not me, I'll move on. For now.'

'I promise it's not you. So why are *you* here on a Sunday?' Julia asked.

Day curled a lip in distaste and plopped forward again in the chair. 'I have a Rule Three with a stupid-assed defendant who unfortunately hired an even more stupid-assed attorney to represent him at his trafficking trial. It's set down for next week and I haven't done shit on it.' She nodded at the *Southern Seconds* and *Federal Reporters* on the table. 'Doctor Death, I presume, is your excuse?'

Julia sighed. 'Marquette's attorneys filed an emergency writ of habeas with the Feds on Friday. Rick's got a hearing in District Court on Tuesday. Farley won't give them a continuance and they're, of course, hoping to delay the trial. Mel Levenson's arguing – with the help of the French government – that the failure of detectives to notify the French Consul General in Miami of Marquette's arrest violates the Vienna Convention.' She blew out a low breath. 'It's a noise-making motion that won't fly in court at this stage of the game, but I do believe my first murder has now *officially* been elevated to the level of international incident. And in a big way.'

'So says the front page of yesterday's *New York Times*. Congratulations. I never even knew there was a World Court till I read that this case might end up in it. I guess this means the paparazzi will be hogging all the good parking spots down at the federal courthouse this week. Better there than here. This trial is gonna be a nightmare when it does happen. I told you your fifteen minutes were just starting.' Day looked suspiciously at the stack of books again. '*Rick's* got a hearing?'

Julia shrugged. 'You know what it's like to be the grunt. You have to pay your dues.'

'I remember the grunt who won a competency hearing all by her lonesome a couple of months back. I think your dues have been paid in full, honey. He should be in here researching for *you*.'

'Thank you for the compliment, but don't be a rebel-rouser. The head of the AG's office will be arguing it with him. I'm not admitted to practice in Federal Court, anyway.'

'So how are things with the invisible man?' Day asked, her fingers back tapping the table. 'Do tell. Or is he one of those "things" that have come up since Christmas, monopolizing all your precious time and taking you away from your friends? Sweeping you out of town on weekends?'

Julia looked down at the statute book in front of her. Rick was another relationship that she knew had to be re-examined, but it was far more difficult and complicated to distance herself from him than Dayanara, or even Aunt Nora and Uncle Jimmy, who she also hadn't seen since Christmas. For one, they were still trying this case together. And secondly, she was still sleeping with him. While it still wasn't a steady Saturday-night date, and she didn't know exactly where she even wanted it to go anymore, she knew she was not ready to give it up just yet. Their relationship had stalled out, but not in a bad neighborhood, and she didn't want to walk home alone. It was as simple as that. So she'd just let them drift aimlessly about in neutral and neither had complained. 'We have our moments. And when we do it's fun. Like I said before, I've been distracted lately. See, Day? I told you it's not just you.'

'Now I definitely feel better. So what's happening with this crazy defendant of yours? Is he *really* crazy, or am I not allowed to ask? Are you sworn to secrecy with the snoots in the Major Crimes Club and exclusives on *The Today Show*?'

Crazy was a strange term in a courtroom. While a defendant had to be *competent* to stand trial, he had to be *sane* to be convicted. And sanity had nothing to do with how well one could behave in front of a judge, or if a defendant knew what the hell his lawyer was standing next to him for. Sanity basically boiled down to one moment – or in this case, moments – when a crime was committed. The moment that David Marquette buried a knife in his young wife's chest. The moment he smothered his infant daughter. The moment he beat his toddler son's head in. The moment he repeatedly stabbed his own little girl as she cowered in a dark corner in her princess gown. *Did he know what he was doing? Did he not know it was wrong?* Those were the questions that needed answers. Answers that no one could seem to agree on.

'You can ask, but I can't tell. I've been gagged. Farley shut everyone down. The press has been getting so out of hand. As a matter of fact,' she said, looking at her watch, 'I have a big pre-trial meeting with the inner sanctum at two. There you go – I just gave up classified information in the name of friendship.'

'Oooh . . . A pow-wow on a Sunday? I thought the Chiefs would all be golfing.'

'I think it's to throw off the paparazzi. No one expects the government to actually work on a weekend, much less on a Sunday.'

Day laughed. 'Very funny.' Then her face grew serious again. 'Listen J, these "things", this case . . . remember, it's just a case. Don't let it wear you thin, is what I'm saying. You don't have to go it alone.'

Julia nodded and bit the inside of her cheek.

Oh yes, Day. Oh yes, I do. And that's the worst part. Where I might be going, no one wants to follow.

Day looked up at the clock then jumped out of her seat. 'It's only noon. We have plenty of time. Grab your purse and close those friggin' books,' she said, slapping down the cover of Julia's *Federal Reporter*.

'What? Where are we going?'

'You owe me a lunch, girlfriend, and, before you hunker down in your pow-wow with all the really important Indians, I'm gonna let you take me, so I can tell you all about the juicy gossip you've been missing out on these past couple of months,' she said as she led Julia out of the empty library by the hand. 'Most of it's about you, anyway.'

68

'He says the voices began right after the baby was born,' Dr Barakat explained, after the coffee was poured and the conference room had settled down. He slipped on reading glasses as he spread out his notes on the oblong cherry conference table, around which sat Julia, John Latarrino, Steve Brill, the Coral Gables Police Chief, Elias Vasquez, Bob Biondilillo, the Director of the Miami-Dade PD, and the Chief of Legal, Penny Levine. Charley Rifkin and Rick flanked Jerry Tigler at the head of the table, and the three senior investigators from the SAO Investigations Unit upstairs were left holding up the back wall.

'Medical records confirm Sophie Marquette had what's known as a strawberry hemangioma on the left side of the skull,' Dr Barakat continued, 'about twenty centimeters above the eyebrow. It's a non-cancerous vascular tumor that looks like the lump on a cartoon character's head after he's been hit with a frying pan. As is typical with hemangiomas, the bump grew and became more discolored in the weeks after her birth. That was when Dr Marquette says he noticed it began to take the shape of a horn.'

'A horn?' asked the State Attorney with a skeptical frown.

'Like the devil, Jerry,' scoffed Rick, holding his two index fingers up behind his ears. The room tittered.

'He claims his wife began to act strange almost immediately after Sophie's birth,' the doctor continued. 'Jennifer stopped going to Mass on Sundays, and he says she wouldn't even drive by the church anymore, going out of her way just to avoid it. Emma and Danny had each gotten a Precious Moments Bible when they were baptized, but he couldn't find either in the house. Same with rosary beads, crucifixes. Not even a dried palm from Palm Sunday. He claims that all religious artifacts had been mysteriously removed from the home. Although their other two kids had had lavish christenings, Jennifer refused to even discuss baptizing Sophie, and he says he became concerned that something was very wrong. Fundamentally wrong.'

'Who is this guy? Jimmy Swaggart?' asked Rifkin, scratching at his head. 'I'm Jewish, so what do I know, but who the hell keeps tabs on where the little woman's been stashing the family Bibles and palm fronds?'

'Delusions with religious undertones or themes are experienced in almost half of all people with schizophrenia,' Dr Barakat explained. 'Most organized religions require a person to believe in things they can't see, taste, hear, smell, feel. Biblical stories speak of heaven and hell, damnation and the devil, God revealing Himself to Moses through a burning bush. It's acceptable in society to believe such things in the name of religion, so when you think about it, it's really not so far a leap for a delusional person to light the rhododendron bush up in an attempt to open a repartee with Jesus.'

'We spoke with over two hundred people about this guy,' Lat said. 'Nobody mentioned Marquette was a zealot.'

'Let's make sure we interview the pastor of the church that Marquette and the missus were regular customers at,' Rick replied, 'just in case you missed something.'

Lat caught the use of pronouns, as he was sure everyone else did. Instead of reaching across the table and rearranging the man's over-bleached whites, though, he decided to take the high road and let it go. For now. It was only a few more weeks until this case and Rick Bellido were far behind him. Then it was time for a long vacation on a small boat somewhere in the Bahamas.

'It was around this time,' Dr Barakat continued after the awkward moment had passed, 'when Sophie was maybe a couple of weeks old, that he says the voices started up, followed soon after by visual disturbances. Dr Marquette claims hearing angry voices, sometimes speaking in rhymes, that would explain in graphic detail just what was happening to his family, both physically and spiritually – what the signs were, what changes were taking place in their souls and in their bodies. He claims that he knew these demons were like tapeworms feeding off a host, sucking the life out from the inside out so that, I think it's important to note, Dr Marquette stressed they were not human beings anymore.'

'So he had no intent to kill a "human being" as it is defined in the homicide statute. Very clever,' Penny remarked.

Dr Barakat smiled. 'That was my thought, yes.'

'This guy has all the right answers,' said Rick, shaking his head. 'He's smart as hell.'

'School records place his IQ at 149,' Dr Barakat replied.

'He's a genius,' said Julia softly.

'Don't be too impressed,' Rick remarked. 'So were Ed Kemper and Nathan Leopold of Leopold and Loeb fame. You know what they say – there's a fine line between genius and madness.'

'The voices would tell him when to look at just the right moment to see his children in their *real* forms, so he would know the voices weren't lying to him. That's when he'd catch the flash of a yellow smile on his toddler son. Glowing red eyes, gone in a blink on Emma. Fangs on his wife.'

'I had a wife like that once,' Brill piped in. 'Sucked the life right out of me, too.' The room laughed again.

'So *he's* not possessed, it was the wife and kids?' Lat asked. 'Is that it?'

'Yes.'

'Usually we hear it the other way around. But that doesn't work in court and our boy knows it,' Rick said. 'Did he tell anyone what he was thinking, Chris? That he was having these thoughts? Of course not.'

Barakat shot him a look. 'I would have been surprised if he did. He claims, of course, that he couldn't discuss his suspicions with anyone, because he says he knew no one would believe him. "I'm a doctor. A surgeon," he said to me, "people would think I'm totally crazy." He reports hearing his own thoughts broadcast over all the radios in the house whenever he was home – night, day, whenever. He says he knew they were always listening to him, that that was a form of intimidation practiced to keep him subservient, to torture him, and make sure he didn't tell anyone outside the home what was happening.'

'Anybody got him acting looney, agitated, speaking to the empty chair next to him in the OR?' Rifkin asked.

'He certainly wasn't speaking in tongues, but we do have that flare-up with the nurse he fired,' Brill replied with a shrug. 'But that was nothing more than an irritating subordinate versus a demigod in the operating room. She talked back and he'd had enough.'

'She's on Marquette's witness list,' said Penny. 'Guaranteed Mel's gonna use her to support his argument that Marquette was losing it.'

'That's friggin' bullshit,' said an exasperated Brill. 'You can't believe this crap might actually work?'

'I haven't met a jury yet that I trusted to do the right thing. Make sure when you cross her, that you play up her incompetence,' Rifkin added with a nod at Rick.

'How does he explain being the only one in his family not possessed?' asked Júlia.

'He doesn't. He says he believes he was spared for one reason and one reason only – to save the souls of his family. Their bodies were devoured already on the inside, so that they were just occupying empty shells of skin. Dr Marquette says he knew he had to intervene, had to stop them, or their souls would be damned for all eternity, like vampires. And "the presence", as he calls it – the demons – would move on to feast on others.'

'So he killed them,' Rick said.

Barakat shook his head. 'That's the interesting part, he doesn't actually admit to killing his family. He stops short of describing what happened on the night of the murders, by claiming he can't remember.'

'Why?' asked Lat. 'Why would he say he can't remember when he's already admitted it by pleading insanity as the reason he did it?'

'Two lines of thinking,' Barakat offered. 'Three, actually. One is he's truly schizophrenic and he can't actually face what he's done yet in his mind. The psychotic break he suffered has effectively enabled him to stay in a deluded state of denial about the actual murders themselves.'

'Or?'

'He's a psychopath and doesn't want to take responsibility yet. He's playing a game with you all. He's in check, but not checkmate, and he doesn't want to give up on a way out. Once he admits to certain facts, the jig is up and he's locked in to a story. Ted Bundy, a classic sociopath, played that cat and mouse game for years with investigators, frustrating them with promises of confessions that never materialized.'

'Obviously you are choosing what's behind door number two,' said Rick.

'Obviously. I already told you he's not schizophrenic and that he was sane,' replied Dr Barakat as he slid his report into a file. 'As a matter of fact, I told you from the moment I first met the guy he's a malingerer. A damn good one. Don't you have Pat Hindlin as a second on this? What did he say?'

'That he's a sane, calculating psycho. The score's tied two-all. Levenson has Koletis and some woman out of California. Margaret Hayes.'

'Hayes? Never heard of her,' Barakat said.

'No one has. But everyone knows that for fifteen or twenty grand a pop, Levenson Grossbach & Associates can buy whatever opinion it wants to hear.'

'And the third?' asked Julia as Christian Barakat stood to leave.

'Third?'

'You said there were three possible reasons for Marquette to not cop to the specifics of what he did on the night of the killings.'

'Well, that one's rather obvious, isn't it?' Dr Barakat replied with a dry smile. 'He didn't do it.'

The room fell silent.

'Excuse me?' asked Lat.

'I'm not saying that's the case. What I am saying is that we have a man who is either schizophrenic, or is smart enough and cunning enough to convincingly *pretend* to be. If he's the latter, he's a complete sociopath. If he's the former, well, he's obviously a very, very sick man. And I'm just advising you what you probably already know, Detectives: mentally ill people make false confessions to crimes all the time. Statistically, schizophrenics top that list.'

'Could be another angle that Mel's gonna spring later, Ricky,' Rifkin added when no one said anything. 'Two theories of the case. The jury can pick and choose their sympathy verdict for our wholesome farm boy: he didn't do it. But if you think he did, then he was sick and didn't know what he was doing.'

'You know, defense attorneys are just pieces of shit,' Brill said after a moment with a bewildered shake of his head. 'So this "the devil made me do it" defense might let this guy actually walk free?'

Again the room stayed quiet.

'The devil made me do it,' Rick scoffed as he tossed his pencil into the middle of the table and stood up. 'I wonder if we'll have to name him in the conspiracy.'

69

'Where are you rushing off to?' Lat asked as the meeting broke and Julia gathered her stack of legal pads and files, car keys already in hand. Small conversations cluttered the room and clogged the doorway, preventing a quick escape. She needed to go, but she didn't want to be remembered as the first one out the door.

'I'm hoping to rescue my dog from the kennel before they close for the night,' she said, glancing at her watch again. 'I've gotta make it there by six.'

Lat laughed. 'The kennel? Don't tell me you're one of those neurotics who leaves their pooch in day care when you have to go to work so they won't be alone.'

She smiled. 'Do I look like I'd own a teacup anything?'

'I pegged you for an Akita, actually.'

'Beagle-mix named Moose.'

'Even better. I had a beagle named Dusty Paws when I was a kid. He loved to howl at the moon. So why's poor Moose locked up?'

'I just flew in this morning from New York and haven't had a chance to go home yet. Hence the mad rush.'

'New York?'

'Family,' was all she said.

'And you came straight here?' He let out a low whistle. 'No wonder you're Bellido's favorite. So what are you and Moose up to tonight?'

She felt her cheeks grow hot and Rick walked up before she could answer. 'Hey there,' he said with a smile, his hand on the small of her back. 'Crazy day, right? Look, we're gonna go grab some dinner at Christy's. You want to join us?'

She figured 'we're' meant sitting sandwiched between Charley Rifkin and the Director of the Miami-Dade PD, who were both looking across the room at them. If the seating arrangements alone weren't enough of a reason to pass up a steak dinner for a peanut-butter sandwich, the sure-to-be subject matter was – she'd had enough of Dr David Marquette for one day. Her head ached with legal issues and creepy thoughts. She needed a break. 'Thanks, but like I was telling Lat,' she started, then saw the detective had already walked away. 'I need to get home,' she finished quietly.

She promised to call Rick later, grabbed her purse and files and hurried to her car. The beautiful Sunday was still beautiful, but it was fading fast as the sun began its slow slip under the horizon. A brilliant idea came to her just as she pulled into the parking lot of the Hollywood Animal Hospital. It would be a shame to miss even one minute of a perfect day – if anything, time spent locked up in a man-made hell with her brother made her appreciate that now. So instead of going home, she had the tech put another rubber ball on the bill and drove straight to the Hollywood boardwalk with a crazed, howling Moose.

The beach was still jamming with joggers, rollerbladers, skateboarders, baby carriages, and sunburned Canadians. For the locals, the impending Monday morning meant back to work as usual, and so they rushed or bladed or strolled about with purpose – sure of where they were going and what they were doing – determined to get it all in before the sun set and the ball came to an end. But for the tourists, a late Sunday afternoon wasn't so desperate. Much to the irritation of the natives, they meandered, flitting from shop to shop or menu to menu like honeybees, stopping abruptly to take a picture or enjoy a view.

It was a blessedly distracting crowd to get lost in, to forget things and names and faces if only for a little while. Julia made her way through the smog of coconut-scented sun-screen to an empty bench just a few yards down from the mammoth Hollywood Beach Resort – a landmark, 1920s hotel that had definitely seen some better days. She loved the boardwalk. It was one of the reasons she'd picked Holly-wood to live. The eclectic old T-shirt shops and fast-food stands, Mom and Pop restaurants and seaside motels that still hung out vacancy signs. It was a place that you just knew had once been great, where you could walk down the boardwalk and still see the ghosts of Al Capone and his boys or follow Rita Hayworth and Jimmy Cagney as they strolled to the sand, flashbulbs popping in their wake, because it hadn't changed. Yet. Of course, like Miami Beach twenty years ago, Hollywood was in the process of redis-covering itself, and the bulldozers and architects were steadily making their way up Ocean Drive and down John-son Street. But until the new and shiny refaced a small slice of history, the boardwalk would still be her favorite place to go for a jog or a long, mind-clearing midnight walk.

Moose was sucking wind from the three-block walk from the car. Although he chased mailmen down the street as if they were carrying satchels of steak bones and still caught his fair share of lizards, the last few weekends of doing not much of anything at the kennel had packed a couple of pounds on him. It was Uncle Jimmy's bikini-watching board-walk expeditions that had kept Moose in top guard-dog form, but it had been a long while since Moose had trolled the beach or frolicked in the dog park. And just as long since Julia had spoken to her aunt and uncle. She closed her eyes. She'd come here this afternoon to *not* think, but the ghosts, they found you wherever you went, didn't they?

'*Sometimes you got to make decisions that people don't like, bella,*' Uncle Jimmy had warned once when she ran against a friend in high school for a spot on Student Council. '*Sometimes they don't like you for making them. They make it personal, which ain't right. You won't be needing those people in your life.*'

His almost prophetic words haunted her now. Julia hadn't wanted to make a choice between her aunt and uncle and Andy, but she obviously had. She didn't want to make it personal, but she also understood that there was no way it couldn't be. For any of them. It was hard to believe so much time had slipped away; it used to be she spoke with Aunt Nora at least once a day. But as the days and weeks continued to pass, the wall between them grew taller and more difficult to scale.

Past the high-rise resort to the west, the setting sun shot translucent beams of gold out from behind puffy clouds, bathing everything it touched in an ethereal, almost holy light – like a Renaissance painting of Deliverance. Even by Florida sunset standards, it was a beautiful sight. The air felt alive, buzzing with people and music. So different from yesterday, when she and Andy had watched the bleak winter twilight descend upon the concrete skyline of Manhattan from behind dirty, steel-checkered windows. She wondered if her brother remembered a sunset any other way. If it was ever beautiful in his mind. Maybe, she thought, maybe one day she could show him this.

Moose began to howl and bark. 'I thought I might find you here,' said the familiar voice behind her. She spun around with a start and there was Uncle Jimmy, crouched beside her petting a completely delirious Moose, who danced around in circles on his hind legs like some foofy circus poodle.

'Uncle Jimmy . . .'

'And you,' he said, standing up with outstretched arms. 'What? You don't give your uncle a hug no more?'

She nodded and hugged him hard.

'Now that's better,' he said gruffly in her ear, patting her back as if she were a baby. 'I missed them hugs. Where you been hiding, bella? I go by your apartment on Saturday on the way to the ponies, no one's there. I stopped by again today – nobody. Your aunt, she's going crazy. She needs her Julia fix. She's got nobody to cook for,' he finished with a smile.

Julia smiled back but said nothing. She hadn't spoken to Nora since that day right before Christmas when everything had changed.

'So she's fattening *me* up. Then she complains I'm too fat.' He rubbed his generous stomach, which was discreetly hidden behind a lime-green Guayabera shirt and black shorts. 'Sometimes there's no pleasing her, is all I'm saying. You just love her for who she is and accept that she ain't gonna change. That she can't. It's too hard for her.'

'I was in New York,' Julia said quietly.

There was a brief, deliberate pause. 'Oh yeah? Just now you got back?'

'I've been going up to see Andy. That's why I haven't been around.'

Jimmy didn't blink. 'Oh yeah? What'cha doing that for?'

'He has nobody, Uncle Jimmy.'

He laughed wryly. 'He brought that on himself, Munch-kin. Can't gun down the kiddies on the playground then bitch there's no one to play with.'

'He's not bitching . . .' She shook her head. 'He's sorry, Uncle Jimmy. If he could change things he would. If he could switch places, I know he would. He was sick.'

'Yeah? Is he better now?'

'Yes. He's much better. He takes his meds. He doesn't have the hallucinations anymore. And the voices, they're softer . . .' It was too much to explain. She knew he didn't want to hear it anyway. That it wouldn't make a difference. 'They're moving him to a different hospital soon. We're just waiting for a bed.'

'*We're* just waiting for a bed . . .' he repeated with a frown. 'So, your brother, he could get out one day?'

'One day,' she replied with an uncomfortable shrug. 'I don't know when.'

Jimmy said nothing for a long, long time. Then he squeezed her arm gently. 'Well, your aunt, she misses you. I miss you, Munchkin. We didn't even get to see you none for the holidays. And I miss my little buddy here, too.' He bent down and scratched Moose's tummy, who was now laid out like a porn star in the sand. 'Yeah, that's right. That's a good boy,' he cooed. 'Where you been putting this guy when you go on your trips to New York?'

'At the kennel.'

'The kennel,' Jimmy repeated thoughtfully. 'Ain't no place for a dog. Surrounded by strangers, all those caged animals. He needs to get his ass home. That's where he belongs, ya know. Where people love him.'

'Uncle Jimmy . . .'

'That's all I'm saying. Ain't no place for him.' He stood back up and set his firm stare again on Julia. 'He needs to be where he belongs. Stop that other business, caging up with them other dogs. Some of 'em, they look real cute, but they're bad. Some of 'em, they're sick, ya see. Remember that, bella,' he said with a menacing shake of his finger. 'You don't know how bad one of those other dogs can be till it rips your fucking throat out. Then it's too late. Remember that now.'

She looked away, her eyes full of tears. 'I will, Uncle Jimmy.'

'Good luck now with your trial. We'll be watching you. And call your aunt,' he shouted over his shoulder as he headed back down the boardwalk.

'She won't pick up the phone.'

'I'll work on that,' he replied, but didn't turn around again.

Julia watched as he plodded slowly past the arepa cart and the sunburned tourists in his black Jesus sandals and white Jox Sox, obviously favoring his bad back, but just as obviously straining not to, so that she wouldn't see he was in pain. Then he disappeared into the Hollywood Beach Resort, the automatic doors closing behind him, just as the sun finally slipped under the horizon and night officially began.

70

'What if he really is insane?' Julia whispered aloud in the dark. Rick lay beside her under the covers, his body pressed up against hers. She could tell by the scratchy sounds of his breathing that he was almost asleep. A gusty wind blew the potted palms around outside on his patio, creating a violent dance of shadows on the ceiling.

There it was, out in the open. She'd finally said it. The night before she was going to pick a jury in the single most important case of her career, she'd finally said aloud what had been quietly gnawing at the back of every thought since David Marquette had pled NGI months ago. Since Andy had come back into her life. Since she'd looked into the eyes of her own brother and instead of seeing a monster, had seen sorrow and frustration, confusion and anger, as he fought with invisible demons that Julia now knew didn't just go away with medication and group therapy. Since she'd witnessed first-hand the effects of an insidious disease that took on many forms. A disease no one seemed to really understand, including the very doctors who treated it. Or diagnosed it.

The same body, two completely different men. The same story, two completely different tales.

Four different forensic psychiatrists had delivered two radically different, irreconcilable diagnoses of the same man. And so it would soon be up to a jury of twelve men and women – none of whom were likely to be an MD or have a degree in psychology or social work – to deliver the ultimate verdict: was Dr David Alain Marquette a brilliant psychopath or a paranoid schizophrenic? Brutal killer or selfless savior?

Dr Jeykll or Mr Hyde?

But Julia knew that those twelve jurors would look to the State to help guide them to the right decision. They would look to the State to present the evidence that David Marquette was the cold and calculated killer they had charged him with being.

Julia Valenciano on behalf of the people of the State of Florida . . .

Even if it was her trial partner who discredited the contrary opinions of other psychiatrists, the jury would look to her because she sat at that table. They would rely on *her* word, *her* arguments, *her* cross-examinations, *her* directs. And that was the problem. That was what kept her up all night, whispering her fears aloud in the dark. You could only play for one team and the sides had long ago been chosen – Julia Valenciano was on Team State.

But what if they were wrong?

'You're kidding me, right?' Rick asked after a long silence. 'I guess not,' he said with a sigh when she didn't respond. He rolled away from her and onto his back.

'What if we're wrong? I mean, what if he really is sick?' she asked. 'Haven't you ever just once wondered that, Rick? Haven't you ever been unsure?'

'Honestly, no. Look, Julia, you've been to the depos. You've read the reports. What's there to wonder about? You've been a lawyer long enough to know that for enough money, you can find an expert to say just about anything for you. And that's just what Mel has bought himself. Listen, honey, I've been at this job for twenty-plus years now, and I've seen some sick crimes and some sick people in that time. But what I've mostly seen is bad people pretending to be sick.'

She was quiet for a long moment. 'So you think most people fake it?'

He almost laughed. 'In the criminal justice system? Yes. I think most people fake it. Wouldn't you? Look at what the man has to lose here.'

'But do you believe that some people *are* mentally ill?' She felt her stomach flip-flop. *Never ask a question you don't want to know the answer to.*

'Jesus,' he said with a yawn looking over at the clock. 'Most women like to cuddle after making love, Julia. Not cross-examine.'

She said nothing.

'Okay, I'll bite.' He propped himself up against the headboard and tried to look at her in the darkness. 'Yes, I do think that a lot of people have mental problems. Serious ones, like schizophrenia and manic depression and maybe even post-partum psychosis. And I think that a lot of those that do, end up, unfortunately, spinning through the revolving doors of the system. It's just a sad fact of life, sweetheart.

'And I feel bad for those people,' he continued when she still hadn't said anything. 'It must really suck to have something wrong with your head. But I don't believe in the "devil made me do it" crap, Julia. I don't. I think that even the mentally ill can control themselves and their actions. And if you do hear voices, I believe you also know that it's wrong and against the law to drown your five children in the family tub, no matter who's telling you to do it.

'Now before you count me in with the Tom Cruise "psychiatry is a fraud and there's no such thing as a chemical imbalance" crowd,' he continued, 'let me just say this: while I may be sympathetic to someone who's mentally ill, most brutal killers in this world know exactly what they're doing when they're doing it. Just because the crime is sick or repulsive or heinous by all definitions normal, doesn't mean the person who committed it is legally insane or, for that matter, mentally ill. People – even prosecutors sometimes – tend to look at those acts, at the crime itself, and think, "Jesus, there must be a *reason* someone turned out this way. He must be *insane* to burn someone alive or torture another human being or lock his own kids in a cage and slowly starve them to death." Then come the psychiatrists, parading about with their DSMs and medical jargon, half of whom are bleeding hearts who *want* to believe everyone has something wrong with them. But the truth is, Julia, BTK knew exactly what he was doing when he broke into women's houses, tied them up, and tortured them for hours before killing them. Just listen to his *Dateline* interview if you're not so sure. Same goes for Cupid, when he drugged and raped and slaughtered those women, and Son of Sam when he trolled the streets of New York looking for couples to execute in the middle of the night, and the Menendez brothers when they blew their parents away with a shotgun to get a head start spending their inheritance. The list goes on, since the beginning of time. Pick up a paper anywhere in the damn country on any day of the week and you'll read about some crime that defies moral comprehension. The crimes are sick, yes, but these are not sick people, Julia. They're evil. A psychiatrist may give them each a medical diagnosis and tell them that they have an antisocial personality or are bipolar, or maybe are even schizophrenic, but we certainly shouldn't give them an excuse.'

'No excuses,' she said softly.

He sighed again. 'You're having pre-trial jitters, that's all. It's totally normal. We're picking a jury tomorrow. The past few months have been draining on both of us, to say the least, and the press coverage has been intense. A million voices on the TV every night – half of whom don't have the wits to comment on the weather, much less a complicated legal case – helping you second-guess your decisions. It's your first homicide and it's an insanity case and we're seeking the death penalty. I wouldn't have thrown all three at you your first time up at bat, but there's no undoing it now.' He paused for a moment before looking over at her. 'Unless you want off.'

'No,' she replied quietly, still watching the shadows dance.

'I hope not. It's kind of late for that.' He rearranged the pillows underneath his head and laid back down, his hand finding her shoulder under the covers and rubbing it gently. 'Look at it this way, maybe they do hear voices, and maybe those voices are mean and tell them to do horrible things, but that doesn't give someone the legal excuse to go out and butcher their family.' He yawned again. 'If I told you to go out and kill your mother right now would you do it? Hell no. I'm just as real a voice. The point is, you still have to make the decision to do the crime, honey. That's why it's not insanity. It's murder.'

Julia bit her cheek hard. For what seemed like an eternity, she watched the shadows and waited until Rick finally rolled over on his side and she could tell by the sounds of his deep breathing that he'd fallen asleep. Then she got out of bed, stumbled into his bathroom, and in the darkness, where she was sure he could not hear her, she began to cry.

71

John Latarrino was so conditioned to his phone ringing in the middle of the night, he sometimes thought he heard it before it actually rang. This was one of those times. He reached over Lilly, his snoring eighty-pound golden retriever who had snuck up on the bed again, and grabbed the cell off the nightstand. He didn't recognize the number. He looked at the clock and rubbed his eyes. It was three in the morning. Maybe it was one of his snitches.

'Hello?' he asked, his voice scratchy with sleep.

'Lat?'

He knew immediately who it was and he sat up with a start. 'Julia?'

'I'm sorry to bother you—' she started.

Maybe it was the connection, but her voice sounded so small and unsure. Vulnerable. Distracted. Lat felt a strange panic, and his chest grew tight. Something was wrong. He knew it. 'No, no, that's fine. I didn't recognize the number, is all.'

'I'm at a pay phone.'

'A pay phone? I didn't even think they made those anymore.' Now he was out of bed, parting the blinds and looking out the window. Looking for her, somewhere out there. He watched as the palms whipped about under the streetlights. A couple of his neighbors' garbage cans had toppled and tumbled out into the street, where they aimlessly rolled about. The wind was nasty tonight. Judging from the small puddles that dotted the sidewalk and the smattering of drops on the window, it had rained, too. He must've been in a pretty deep sleep not to have heard it. 'What's wrong? What's the matter? Are you okay?'

She hesitated. 'I'm okay, but I need another favor, Lat. I . . . I went for a run and I lost track of where I was.'

'A run? Like jogging?'

'Yeah, yeah. I'm in North Beach, at a gas station, but I don't think it's a very safe area,' she said rather breathlessly. 'I . . . I have to get back to my car. I was hoping maybe you could help me.'

72

She stood under the hot shower, her eyes closed, her head resting against the tiled wall. Through the steam that fogged the room, she could hear her favorite morning DJs, Paul Castronovo and Young Ron Brewer, cracking jokes about the Marquette trial and all the 'crazies' that had camped out on the courthouse steps hoping to win an opening-day seat in the clerk's morning lottery. While their producers scrambled to try and get O. J. Simpson on the line, they invited listeners to call in and play the *Name That Nut!* game, offering a 'Paulie's Pick' gift certificate if the nut in question turned out to be French. Changing the station wouldn't change the subject, either. Down the hall in the living room, David Marquette was the top story on the morning news; Doctor Death sure to be the headline on her doorstep outside. For at least the next few weeks, Julia knew that there would be no escape from the madness that had once again descended on Miami as it readied itself for another high-profile murder trial.

She was so exhausted, both physically and mentally. After Lat had picked her up – thankfully without quizzing her as to how she'd come to be in that crappy part of the beach at 3 a.m., jogging in the rain in shorts and an oversized T-shirt, nothing but car keys and five dollars in her pocket – he'd simply taken her back to her car, which was parked on a side street down the block from Rick's condo on SoBe. No questions asked. Maybe he'd figured out who she'd gone home with and didn't want to get into it. Or maybe he'd just correctly assumed she had nothing to talk about – that she was in whatever she was in alone.

She shook her head to get the stream of embarrassing thoughts out of it. She wished she could just redo last night – she wouldn't even have gone out. She wouldn't have had that conversation with Rick. She wouldn't have asked the question that she didn't want to know the answer to. She hadn't wanted to call Lat, but there was no one else and she'd been scared when she'd finally stopped running and realized she was a long way from Kansas. A really long way. Surrounded by a lot of strange faces in a lot of darkened doorways who'd realized the very same thing.

There was no way that she was going to go back up to Rick's apartment, hop back in bed and pretend everything was dandy in the morning. She wasn't that good an actress. So she'd just headed home. And although she'd tried, she hadn't slept more than twenty minutes once she did lay her head down on the pillow. Besides just the nagging worries she'd finally voiced to Rick, there were too many things to think about with the rapid approach of morning. In just a few hours, she'd be picking her first death jury in her first murder trial, and although Rick would be the one asking the prospective jurors questions, she'd still be there in the camera-filled courtroom, helping to ensure that, out of a pool of hundreds, the two of them picked the twelve right ones. Men and women who – in spite of the intense publicity, and the death-penalty protestors and mental-health advocates swinging from the palm trees outside – could set it all aside at the end of the day and cast their vote to flick the switch.

Rick. She blew out a long breath and rinsed away the shampoo that burned her eyes. Today was sure to be awkward. *Was he awake? Did he even know she was gone yet? Would he notice? Would he care?* Just the fact that the last question had crossed her mind was a sad commentary on the state of their affair. Things had maybe not been right for a long time, but still she'd stubbornly plugged along, not willing to pull her finger from the damn just yet. Blaming their growing distance on long hours and exhaustion and closing her eyes and ears the whole time to the real reasons they would never make it.

The water finally began to turn cold, snapping her out of her thoughts. She quickly finished rinsing off, wrapped herself in her oversized purple terry robe and headed for the kitchen with Moose at her heels. The comforting scent of fresh-brewed coffee drifted through the apartment, and she could already taste a cup with a cigarette. The Breakfast of Champions, she thought as she tapped a fresh pack of Parliaments on the counter. It was amazing how quickly she'd let herself get hooked again on a bad habit.

She poured herself a steaming mug, lit a cigarette and opened the kitchen window that looked out on the complex's deserted pool area downstairs. Empty beer cans and a couple of liquor bottles overflowed from one of the garbage receptacles; pizza boxes were left behind on a lounge chair. Someone must have had a heck of a party last night.

She wondered, as she blew a smoke ring out the window, if it was just coincidence that her brother liked to smoke the same brand of cigarettes. Then there was coffee – Andy took two sugars and cream in his, too. No sugar at all in tea. And foods – they both hated tomatoes, but loved pizza. Pepperoni pizza with black olives. Juicy Fruit gum and 3 Musketeers bars. Little stupid, strange peculiarities that she'd only recently found out the two of them shared. Invisible, innocuous ties. She couldn't help but wonder sometimes with a bit of unease, just how many more of those there might be . . .

413

Andrew's transfer to Rockland was now just weeks away from finally happening – which was exciting, but also unnerving. Although it was still a lock-down psychiatric facility, Rockland wasn't maximum security and the rules were sure to be much more relaxed there. Instead of just visiting a few hours every couple of weeks under strict supervision, Andy might actually be able to leave for the day or come home with her on a weekend pass. And, of course, as Dr Mynks had expressed at Christmas, the ultimate goal was for her brother to one day be released back into the community. What an overwhelming, exhilarating, frightening moment that would be for him. And for her. The man hadn't been on the other side of razor wire and barred windows in fifteen years. He hadn't been able to sleep past seven or stay up after ten or make it through the night without bed checks every thirty minutes. He hadn't picked what he wanted to eat or when he wanted to eat it. He hadn't played in a park or eaten in a restaurant or stepped foot in a grocery store. What would freedom feel like for him? What would it sound like, taste like, look like? It made her think of all the defendants that, as an ASA, she'd pled to lengthy prison sentences without much thought at all. After a while, for a prosecutor, years just became numbers; the defendants, just names on a calendar.

The defendant scores thirty years state prison. The offer's twenty, followed by five probation.

The defendant's a habitual. The offer's ten and ten.

He pleads to the charge, does the statutory max with a three-year min-man for the gun.

She closed her eyes. Even in the quiet of her kitchen, with no one else around, she felt this overwhelming, almost debilitating pressure, squeezing her head like a vice. A pressure to please, a pressure to succeed, a pressure to do the right thing, when she wasn't sure just what that was anymore. A pressure that seemed to be growing more intense every-day. She had a sudden urge to call her brother and just hear his voice before she got in her car and drove back down to the circus that was waiting for her at work. She knew the nurses would have him up by now. Even though he didn't know what case it was, or what it was about, he did know she was starting a big trial today and he knew she was anxious about it. Last week he'd confessed to her that before he'd dreamed of playing baseball, he'd wanted to be a lawyer, too. *Another invisible tie.*

A lone pink foam noodle slowly drifted across the blue water and she thought of the empty pool in the back of the Marquette house, the kiddie toys that floated across still water, never to be used again. The elaborate swing set in the backyard and the slip-and-slide in the front. The hopscotch board – the game Emma and Danny had never finished playing – that she'd stepped carefully past, down a brick pathway that led up to the perfect house. But things were never as they seemed, were they? Behind the grand door a real-life horror story had awaited her.

Never pretend to know someone's life, Julia. You'll only know what they want you to know, when it is they want you to know it.

We're talking three little kiddies bludgeoned and stabbed in their sleep by their daddy.

God willing, the little guy never knew what hit him. Just went to sleep with a kiss from Mommy and never woke up.

Look at me, Daddy! Look at what you've done to me!

She shook the creepy thoughts away, crushed out her cigarette and shut the window.

The same body, two completely different men. The same story, two completely different tales.

The same troubling thoughts, going full circle in her head.

Round and round and round. Nothing was black and white anymore; everything was gray and all she wanted was for the disquieting insecurities to just stop. She wanted someone to stop them for her. And everyone else besides Andy seemed to have an agenda.

While she hadn't expected her relationship with her brother to be what it was when they were kids – on many levels they were still strangers – she was surprised by how easy it was to know him again. How comfortable she felt around him, even when there was nothing to say. She'd been very careful not to go near the night their parents died, but maybe, hopefully, they'd never have to. Maybe, she thought, they could just go forward. She didn't want to know the details. Julia understood Andy's illness now. She understood what it had done to him. And she knew she could forgive him. That was enough, wasn't it?

She poured herself another cup of coffee, grabbed a couple of Advil from the cupboard and headed back to the bathroom. Her head hurt from the lack of sleep and from thinking too much. On her way through the living room her eyes caught on the chaos playing out on the TV. A perky blonde *FOX News* reporter stood in front of the Miami courthouse, where news vans from every conceivable station in the country – and even from around the world – already lined the streets. A split-screen aerial view from the helicopters hovering overhead showed clusters of small white tents dotting the parking lot and sidewalks – underneath which ran elaborate mini-command centers for the various media outlets. A large, red BREAKING NEWS banner ran across the bottom of the screen.

'Jamie, the *Miami Herald* is reporting this morning that Marquette is now being named a suspect in the unsolved homicides of *two* other North Florida families in Wakulla and

Santa Rosa counties. In January of 2004, thirty-six-year-old Diane Tebin and her nine-year-old daughter, Lilly Rose Tebin, were found slain in their home in Milton, just outside of Pensacola. Mrs Tebin had been raped and stabbed repeatedly, but no suspect has ever been identified in those murders. Then, the following November, another family and another brutal murder. Forty-three-year-old Sharon Dell of Crawfordville, Florida, her teenage daughter and toddler son were all discovered dead in their home on the outskirts of Tallahassee by Mrs Dell's mother. Ms Dell, a recent widow, had, like Diane Tebin, been raped and then stabbed repeatedly.

'Now, neither Miami-Dade Police nor Coral Gables officials are commenting, but our sources have learned that these murders have been linked somehow back to the slayings here in Miami. Calls to Marquette's defense attorneys have gone unanswered, and Major Crimes lead prosecuting attorney Ricardo Bellido – who, it was also announced this morning, will be succeeding Miami's retiring State Attorney, Jerry Tigler – also wouldn't comment on the latest developments in the case. David Marquette, as you know, Jamie, is the Miami doctor who's pled insanity in the grisly October murders of his wife and three small children in Coral Gables, Florida and is set to begin trial this morning here, at the Miami courthouse behind me. His case, as you can see, has garnered much international attention, sparking an often heated and bitter worldwide debate on capital punishment. Dr Marquette, a dual citizen of both France and the United States, claims he suffers from schizophrenia. Just last week, France filed an official complaint with the International Court of Justice in The Hague against the United States concerning their treatment of Dr Marquette at the time of his arrest. Death-penalty protests in Miami and Washington have . . .'

Julia practically dropped her coffee and ran to the front door. She grabbed the Broward Edition of the *Miami Herald* off her mat, ducking quickly back inside when she spotted the news van in the parking lot.

Jesus, they'd found out where she lived . . .

She slammed the door shut and leaned back against it, breathing heavy. She remembered Charley Rifkin's warning, prophesied months ago.

If Dr David Marquette becomes the next Scott Peterson du jour . . . the press will be camping out in both your backyards until Corrections finally sticks the needle in.

She stared at the headline in her hands in complete disbelief.

DOCTOR A SUSPECT IN OTHER GRISLY UNSOLVED FLA HOMICIDES

'You're right, Jamie. You are so right,' Perky continued excitedly back in the living room. 'This is sure to affect the sympathy factor. Death-penalty opponents and mental-health advocates around the world are also likely to feel the reverberations. And, no matter how you might personally feel about these issues, it's once again *Miami* that's in the unwanted glare of the international spotlight. It was only a few short years ago when the serial killer Cupid was tried and convicted in this very same courthouse for drugging, raping and killing eleven young women. Now here we are again, back in Miami with perhaps another brutal serial killer . . .'

The phone rang. 'Hello?' she asked hesitantly, her eyes glued to the television.

'Julia! Jesus Christ!' Rick shouted. 'Where the hell have you been? I roll over this morning, the phone's ringing off the fucking hook, and you're *gone*. You gave me a damn heart attack!'

She said nothing. She couldn't.

'No note, no phone call – Jesus. What time did you leave? Hello? Are you still there?' he asked when she still hadn't answered him.

'Yes,' she said softly.

'Look, I don't know if you've turned the news on yet,' he finally said with what sounded like an angry, exasperated sigh, 'but you better. Something's happened. Ivonne Ledo called – Farley's JA. The judge wants everyone in chambers asap.'

73

'This is outrageous, Judge! Twenty minutes before we're set to pick a jury and *this* is the story the whole damn pool is reading downstairs!' Mel Levenson bellowed, waving a copy of the *Miami Herald* about in his balloon hands. He looked like he'd just been boiled: his face was as red as a lobster, large beads of sweat dripped from his hook nose and off unruly, gray Elvis sideburns.

'You may be giving some of that pool way too much credit,' Farley replied with a dry chuckle, looking around at the crowd in his chambers from his throne at the head of a long conference table. 'So don't get yourself all worked up now, Mel. But I do agree that it's rather interesting this breaks today.' He looked at John Latarrino for an answer, his eyes narrowing. 'Detective? What's the story here? Is he a suspect in these killings?'

'He has not been named a suspect,' Lat replied carefully. Across from him, Bellido leaned casually back in his chair, almost removing himself from the conversation, long fingers thoughtfully stroking his chin, probably covering up a toothy, smug smile, Lat thought. The longer this case went on, the more intolerable he was finding Ricardo Alejandro Bellido, the name the guy now made sure the press addressed him by. The thought of the man becoming the next State Attorney was enough to make Lat seriously consider moving departments north and over the county line to Broward. 'At this point, I'd have to say he's just a person of interest, Judge. There are certain similarities between the crimes, which, obviously, I'm not at liberty to discuss. We're working with the Florida Department of Law Enforcement and the local authorities in both Wakulla and Santa Rosa counties.'

At the far end of the table he watched as Julia settled into a seat with her coffee, but he noticed she wasn't looking over at him. And she wasn't looking over at him on purpose, he figured. She was probably a little embarrassed about last night's late-night phone call and North Beach rescue mission, which was definitely a little weird, but then again, he'd had his share of weird nights himself over the years. A lot of regrets swallowed along with his morning coffee. Everybody had. And the pressure of this case was sure to get to people in different ways, especially the major players. He just hoped she wasn't worried he'd hold it against her. Whatever she had going on in her life – whoever she had it going on with – he knew she'd figure it out. She was a smart woman.

'There you have it, Mr Levenson,' said Farley with a shrug. 'He's not really a suspect. No harm intended, says the detective.'

'This is bullshit, Your Honor!' Mel yelled, leveling a fat fist on the table. 'The prosecutors and detectives here are just not happy that on the eve of trial, public opinion in this case is not in their favor. They're not happy that their attempts to prosecute and execute a clearly insane man – who, by the way, is being *forced* to take psychotropic meds by this court so he can *stay* sane in front of a jury – have ignited worldwide outrage, and so they will do anything and say anything to change their bloodthirsty image.' He leaned on the table and looked directly at Rick, his eyes narrowing. 'Especially our future State Attorney here, who apparently will be making a permanent run at the job come November. I'm guessing congratulations are in order.'

Rick didn't even blink.

Mel turned back to the judge. 'And that "do anything and say anything" mentality includes making my client look like a psychopathic *serial killer* in the public eye! All it takes is the *allegation* he's involved in another couple of murder investigations to taint the whole pool downstairs. Just the allegation, and Mr Bellido knows it. I'm telling you, Judge, you won't find one prospective juror in that courtroom this morning who hasn't heard this story already and formed an opinion – and if you do, I'm removing him for cause, because he's lying. I can't even move this mess to another county now – hell, even to another *country* – because it's world news. *World* news. And these detectives – and Mr Bellido here, with his hidden smirk – sure as hell know it! The news hounds have up and done it again, Your Honor.'

Lat sat straight up in his chair, his blood boiling, while Brill pushed his back hard from the table.

'Alright. Enough with the name-calling,' the judge said with a sigh, holding up his hands as if to separate the two sides. Mel plunked back down in his seat, breathing heavy, pulling his shirt cuffs back down and out his sleeves. Rick maintained the disinterested stare.

'Well, you just said it, Mel,' Farley continued. 'He's tainted the world. So don't bother asking for a change of venue now to Martin County. I'll be sure to give the pool a curative instruction when they get up here.' The judge turned to Rick. 'While I was very happy to hear on *The Today Show* that you'll have Jerry Tigler's endorsement on county bus benches across Miami-Dade come September, this isn't how we're gonna try this case.' His icy stare drifted back and forth between Rick and Julia now. 'Do you both understand me? Nice try.' He sat back and perused the entire table. 'You've all been gagged. And that includes your detectives and your private investigators. Your mothers and your grandmothers, too. I don't want to hear about another suspected leak unless it's coming from underneath someone's kitchen sink. Got it?'

'Fair enough, Your Honor,' said Rick, rising. He smoothly buttoned his jacket. 'I don't know how the press got a hold of this information, but I certainly won't mention another word about it.'

'Including, I'm sure, the fact that David Marquette is *not* actually a suspect. How convenient,' scoffed Mel, grabbing his file from Stan Grossbach's hands. 'Your Honor, if I'm not going to get a venue change, I think I should at the very least get a continuance charged to the State. We should wait until the press dies down on this and people at least forget what they heard this morning on CNN.'

Farley actually laughed. 'Have you been looking out your window for the past few months, Mr Levenson? The press is going *nowhere*. If anything, a continuance will just encourage a few more diehards to pick up a camera and cross the pond. Or even worse for you, your client could actually be charged as a defendant in the North Florida murders. You want a continuance, it's a defense continuance, so say goodbye to speedies. And you can try this case maybe next March, because I'm sure my docket is pretty full till then.' He shot a look over at the court reporter, who obediently stopped typing. 'And, let's be honest here, Mel, I just don't think your client's daddy is gonna be too happy to hear that. Especially with Junior enjoying the luxurious accommodations of Hotel DCJ across the street. 'Cause that's where he'll sit till we try this thing.'

Mel shook his head. 'I'm between a rock and a hard place on this, Lenny,' he said between gritted teeth.

'Then let me make it easy for you. I'm not giving you a

continuance anyway, even if you want it. There. I just handed you your first issue on appeal.' The judge turned to Jefferson, who stood by the door, fidgeting with his glasses. 'Jefferson!' he said, making the bailiff jump in his skin and drop them to the floor. 'Go bring up the first fifty from downstairs. We're picking this jury in an hour.'

74

'How could I not have known this?' Julia demanded once they were all across the street in Rick's office and away from the boom mikes. Her voice was shaking with anger.

'You did know,' Rick said quietly.

'Bullshit. I knew there were some unsolved homicides that Lat and Brill had looked at a while back, but there's no link here.'

'Apparently Marquette was within a thirty-mile radius on the night each family was murdered, attending medical conferences in Tallahassee and Pensacola Beach,' Rick said with a shrug.

'Jesus Christ, so were a million other people,' she said, looking around the room.

'There was no forced entry in the homes. Mom is raped and killed, posed in a prone sexual position; kids are killed in their beds. A knife from the kitchen cutlery set and a baseball bat are the weapons of choice. There are definitely similarities.'

'You just vaguely described most sexually violent crime scenes. I'm sure there are another fifty unsolved homicides just like this across the country.'

'Perhaps, but *these* two unsolved homicides happen to be in Florida, just a few miles down the road from where our psychopathic defendant was left all alone in some hotel brushing his teeth in the middle of the night.'

'But there's no physical evidence linking him to those murders! No DNA, no semen, no hair, no ID. Nothing.'

'Which is why they're unsolved, Julia. I think there are enough similarities that it's worth looking into,' Rick said slowly, restraint obviously tempering his words.

'Maybe looking into, but the press now thinks it's a hell of a lot more than that.' Julia felt like the only one in the room not in on the joke. She felt them all watching her and it made her angry. 'Mel Levenson is right. All we're doing now is tossing out a frightening serial-killer angle to taint the pool and tip the scales of public opinion back in our favor. We all know that there's nothing to make these murders stick on Marquette, save for him being within a thirty-mile radius when they were committed. So let's not kid ourselves why it is the press even found out about them today.' She turned back and looked at Lat for the first time that morning. 'I want to know, did you leak it?'

'No,' said Lat with a slow shake of his head. 'I didn't leak it, Julia.' And she knew he didn't.

Brill held his hands up. 'Don't look at me, Jules. I don't even watch the news.'

She turned to Rick. 'I don't need to leak anything, Julia,' he said before the question was even asked, his dark eyes narrowing. 'I've got a great case and I know it.'

'Look, you don't need the two of us for jury selection,' Lat finally said when the silence in the room had lasted too long. He tapped Brill on the shoulder and the two of them headed for the door. Lat looked at Julia as he walked past. 'Why don't you give me a call when you're done today?'

She said nothing. The cold silence remained in the room even after the door closed behind them.

'What happened to you last night?' Rick asked coolly.

'I went for a jog.'

'A jog?' He shook his head in disbelief. 'You left clothes at my house.'

'I'll have to pick them up.'

'And your purse.' He opened up his desk drawer and handed her pocketbook to her. 'You still have a couple of things at my apartment.'

'He's never been linked to those cases, Rick,' she insisted again. The thought came out before she could stop it. 'Was all the bad press and The Hague complaint going to hurt your run at State Attorney? Or is convicting Marquette going to give you the winning vote? By the way, I guess congratulations are in order.'

He stared at her for a long time. His dark eyes were cold and indifferent, as if he didn't even know her. As if she were just some stranger standing in his office. A horrible chill ran through her and she wondered if he even remembered that just last night – only hours ago – he'd made love to her in his bed. 'Julia, if you can't handle this, then I think maybe now's the time to get out.'

She said nothing for a long moment, wondering just how he meant that statement and just how she should take it. Thoughts rushed in from every direction, threatening to collide like a dozen freight trains.

Maybe he was right. Maybe now was the time to get out of this case. Head back up to New York and find herself a new profession, a new life. Maybe change focus in her career and do tax work or civil litigation. Or do nothing with the law anymore. She could just waitress if she had to, like she had in college. A nice, stress-free, simple life. She could be near Andy when he went to Rockland. Maybe get a life ready there to bring him home to one day.

She looked past Rick at the skyline behind him, the mirrored windows on the high-rises twinkling like diamonds in the brilliant sunshine. Maybe there was nothing for her in Miami anymore, anyway. She knew Nora and Jimmy could never accept Andrew in their lives, or accept the fact that she'd welcomed him back into hers. Even though Jimmy had promised he'd work on getting Nora to pick up the phone, she still hadn't. Everything was so different now. It would be impossible to get back to the comfort and familiarity of the way things used to be, wouldn't it? There were too many secrets to navigate through. Too many lies to forget. And forgive. And, of course, there was Andy. She couldn't desert him again; she owed him that as his sister. But, for Nora, there could be no future with Andy in it. And while Jimmy might be the calming voice of reason, at the end of the day, it was Nora who he went to bed with. It was Nora who he would grow old with. It was Nora who he'd ultimately have to side with if sides were drawn and ultimatums declared.

Julia stared at the brass nameplate on Rick's desk. *Ricardo A. Bellido, Esq.* In a fleeting moment of happiness weeks back, she'd once actually said the name Bellido aloud after her own, just to hear how it sounded. God, how life could do a complete 360 on you in just the blink of an eye. Again.

She knew in her heart that their relationship was dead. But it was so hard to walk away from something she thought she could've made work, even though right now, with the way he was looking at her, she felt dirty and small and stupid for ever having thought that. The failure of her relationship with her aunt and uncle already rested squarely on her shoulders and she didn't think she could also carry the weight of a failed romance as well right now. She wasn't ready to hear the news yet.

And then there was the one final thought that made it impossible for her to run and hide somewhere. If nothing else, today had proved that.

What if he really was insane? What if they were wrong about him?

Although it certainly wasn't her job to play defense attorney, she couldn't subscribe to the 'win at any cost' mindset of her own teammates. She'd seen even Mel Levenson compromise his arguments to keep his membership in the Good Ol' Boys Club. This case was getting so out of control. No one played by the rules anymore, and she was the only one who could see that. The vice squeezed tighter and tighter.

The choice was hers and she knew it. Her abrupt departure would raise questions that they both knew Rick would not want to have to answer in an election year. Any dissension in the ranks would be a PR nightmare that Mel would be sure to exploit in the press. Office policy sexual harassment violations would be political suicide.

She shook her head and wiped the defiant tears from her eyes before they even fell. She didn't look at him. 'No. I can handle it just fine,' she said, not sure what question she'd answered.

Then she walked out of his office and headed back over to court.

75

It took five full days to finally pick a jury. Like Mel had said, it was unrealistic to think that they could find twelve people in the pool who hadn't heard the name David Marquette. And they didn't. What they did find was twelve people who *said* they hadn't yet formed an opinion on the case, could put aside everything that they had heard, could render a verdict based solely on the evidence presented to them in court, and could vote for the death penalty. Three men, nine women. Six whites, four blacks and two Hispanics. They ranged in professions from a retired college professor to an ex-preacher at the Cowboys for Christ Evangelical Ranch in Homestead.

'We just seated the last one this afternoon,' Julia said to Lat over the phone at her desk. She pulled her hair off her face and swallowed a yawn. 'Farley swore them all in maybe an hour ago.'

'I saw it on the news. You sound tired.'

'It's been a long week. Where are you?' she asked.

'At the Alibi with Brill.' The Alibi Lounge was a favorite haunt of cops, prosecutors, judges, defense attorneys and the occasional defendant. Conveniently located just down the block from the courthouse, the Graham Building, the PD's offices and the jail.

'Rick said he wanted to go over some of your testimony for Tuesday. I think he wants to put you on after Pete Colonna and Demos, the Gables sergeant. Can you come back over?'

'It's six thirty on a Friday night. I'm off the clock. If Ricardo wants me, he can go over my testimony here, while I have a cold one and enjoy the NCAA finals.' His voice softened a little. 'Hey, why don't you join us for a beer, Julia? You've been working so hard lately. Too hard. He doesn't cut you much slack, and,' he paused for a moment, carefully considering how to word his next sentence, 'you can't expect to take care of everybody else if you can't take care of yourself. Didn't your mother ever tell you that?'

She swallowed the lump and ignored the question. She knew she was starting to look like she was feeling – tired and stressed. She'd lost a few pounds, which wasn't necessarily a bad thing, but her clothes weren't fitting right. Her relationship with Rick was obviously looking strained, too. Even in court, they were barely talking. She hadn't agreed with his juror picks; he hadn't really cared. Next week was sure to be even more difficult unless a truce was called. This was not how she envisioned trying her first murder. 'Maybe we'll come over there, then,' she said with a sigh. Maybe a drink or two would help ease the overall tension that everyone was feeling. It was better than spending another night at the office until ten. Moose was getting ready to disown her and she was about to have to take out a loan to pay for his doggy day care, which all too often was turning into an overnight boarding when she couldn't make it home before they closed. She pushed thoughts of her aunt and uncle out of her head. There was no time to go there.

'First round's on me,' Lat said. Then he yelled out, 'Whoa. That's a bullshit call!' Presumably at the TV.

'I have some things I have to finish up here first,' she said quietly, her voice trailing off as she stared at the UCR, NCIC and ViCAP reports from Investigations that Marisol had left on her desk. UCRs were the Feds' Uniform Crime

431

Reports, which assembled nationwide statistics on all types of crimes, including murder and sexual assaults. ViCAP was the more powerful investigative tool. The acronym stood for the FBI's Violent Crime Apprehension Program, a nationwide law enforcement data information center that collected, collated and analyzed violent crimes – specifically murder – and included solved or unsolved homicides or attempts, especially those that involved an abduction, or were apparently random, motiveless or sexually oriented, or were known or suspected to be part of a series. Serial killings.

She hung up the phone and chewed on the tip of a pencil. The long and the short of it was, she just didn't trust Rick anymore. She'd seen first-hand what he could do to the truth for his own benefit. Maybe David Marquette was the inhumane monster everyone said he was. Maybe Rick was right and the signs were all there and she was the only one unable or unwilling to read them for what they were. But she knew it was time to determine the facts for herself, rather than have the information spoon-fed to her by someone with a hidden agenda. So, in addition to asking for UCR statistics on solved and unsolved homicides, she'd had one of the analysts upstairs in Investigations run certain information through both the ViCAP system and the NCIC death files to find Florida homicides connected with either a sexual battery or attempted sexual battery over the past five years. There were a whopping 487. Of those, 72 remained unsolved, with most being either prostitution-related, drug-related or both. But then there were the 17 special ViCAP unsolved case sheets the investigator had set aside that more closely matched the parameters of Julia's requested search. The Tebin and Dell murders were in that pile. But there was one more case sheet that caught her attention.

LEON COUNTY SHERIFF'S DEPARTMENT
INVESTIGATIVE REPORT

Victims: Charlene 'Charley' Handley, age 39; Kaitlyn Handley, age 4; Tyler Handley, age 9.

City/State/Jurisdiction: De Leon Springs, Florida

County: Orange

Cause of Death: Homicide: multiple stab wounds, blunt trauma.

Weapon: Kitchen knife, baseball bat (suspected, still unknown).

Sexual Assault: Probable, Charlene Handley.

Suspects: Unknown.

Investigative Notes: *Unknown subject(s) made entry possibly through first-floor front door of one-story ranch residence. Residence is located in rural community in central Volusia County. No visible sign of forced entry. Body of victim Charlene Handley located in master bedroom. Autopsy determined 22 stab wounds to upper torso and neck area. Weapon found at scene, left inside victim Charlene Handley. Victim had been sexually assaulted with unknown object. No semen, or other DNA sample currently known available. Victim Tyler Handley found in bedroom, northwest side of house. Cause of death: blunt head trauma with unknown weapon resulting in multiple skull fractures and brain swelling. Weapon used: unknown, possible baseball bat, based on diameter of skull indentations. Victim Kaitlyn Handley found in bed, back bedroom, northeast corner of house. Cause of death: blunt trauma to the head with an unknown weapon, same as above. Footprints left at scene were casted, but too distorted for comparison. Victim Charlene Handley is estranged as of 2/05 from husband Ronald Marcus Handley, D/O/B 2–16–67, SS# 126134256, an attorney who currently resides in New York: 2123 West 93rd Street, New York, New York.*

Three women alone in the house with their children. Bludgeoned and stabbed and raped in their beds in the middle of the night while they slept. The Handley murders were almost identical to the Tebin and Dell murders. And except for the presence of David Marquette in the bathroom with a knife stuck in his gut, the facts looked identical to the Marquette murders as well. She searched the case sheet frantically for the date.

Was he a serial killer or a bizarre victim of circumstance?

December 31, 2005.

She closed her eyes as the room started to spin. David Marquette was in jail on that date. There had to be somebody else.

. . . I'm just advising you what you probably already know, Detectives: mentally ill people make false confessions to crimes all the time. Statistically, schizophrenics top that list.

Julia had read enough mental-health treatises, articles and books to know all about the bizarre, but not uncommon, phenomenon of false confessions. Some studies placed the number made in criminal cases to be as high as twenty-two percent. And just a few weeks ago, the State's very own psychiatrist had conceded the possibility in this case.

What if David Marquette really was schizophrenic? What if the delusion that he had killed his family had seemed real in his mind, but what if he didn't do it? What if someone else had been in that house, attacked his family, ejaculated on his wife, and, after being surprised to find Marquette there when he was supposed to be out of town, had stabbed him, too? What if someone else knew the alarm code? What if Marquette had told that person the code himself?

She grabbed the 911 tape from the Marquette file box on the floor and popped it in her boom box. Her mouth was dry, her mind racing with possibilities.

Beep.

'*Police and fire. What's your emergency?*'

Silence buzzed the line.

'*This is the nine-one-one operator. Is there an emergency?*'

Still nothing.

'*This is the nine-one-one operator. Do you have an emergency?*'

'*Help us . . .*'

'Okay, I can help you. What's your name, hon? Can you speak up? 'Cause I can barely hear you.'

'Help us . . . please.'

'I'm going to help you, honey. I need you to stay on the line and tell me exactly what's happened.'

'I think he's coming back.'

'Who's coming? Are you hurt? What's your name?'

'I think he's coming back.'

'Who's that? Has someone been hurt? Do you need an ambulance?'

'Uh-oh. No, no, no. Sshh, sshh, shhh . . .'

'Hello? Hello? Are you still there? Hello? Is there someone on the line? Is there anyone there? This is the emergency operator.'

'No, no . . . Oh, no, no, no . . .'

'Emma?'

'No, no, please . . . no, Daddy!'

It could go either way. Emma never said on the tape that it was her father stabbing her. She only said 'Daddy'. Maybe she was calling out *for* him, not naming her attacker.

Maybe there was someone else in the house.

It was a bit bizarre – definitely a long shot – but stranger things had happened. Julia knew the walls of the PD's office and The Innocence Project were filled with pictures of the mentally ill who had been wrongfully convicted. Marquette had never gone into detail about exactly what had happened that night, stopping short of actually *describing* the murders with all the psychiatrists. Dr Barakat had called that blame deflection, a psychopathic character trait. Even when admitting something, the psychopath won't ever take full responsibility, hedging his bet to see how much you really know. Avoiding responsibility. *I didn't do it. Nobody saw me do it. And if you did see me do something, it wasn't my fault anyway.*

She grabbed her purse off the bookshelf and stuffed her

436

briefcase with the case sheets and files and hurried down to Rick's office to show him what she'd just found out. In spite of all that had happened in the past week, she still wanted to give him the benefit of the doubt. Maybe he didn't know about the Handley murders. It had probably been entered in the ViCAP system *after* Lat and Brill conducted their initial investigation months back, *after* they'd run the profile. There would be no need then to run another report after Marquette was behind bars. No one in De Leon County would have thought of a connection to the Marquette murders, as David Marquette was in custody at the time, seemingly having confessed to his crimes just a few days before Christmas.

The halls were eerily quiet and deserted. On Fridays, the office pretty much cleared out by five. By seven, the only souls still left hanging around were pushing a vacuum or standing around in a uniform and listening to their iPod downstairs in the lobby. Even the crazy press was long gone, having headed back to their hotels as soon as Farley swore in the jury.

On two, she slid her security badge through the access doors and walked down the black hallway. She passed the empty secretarial maze and stopped at Rick's door. For some strange reason, she hesitated for a moment, her hand barely touching the handle. Her eyes focused on a crack in the door. Light was shining through.

She heard the rushed, heavy breathing inside. The familiar, intimate sounds that only a few days earlier she herself had been making in his arms. She saw the blur of body parts through the sliver of open door, but couldn't place who it was, or what exactly they were doing.

No, that was crazy. She knew what they were doing. She knew just who was in there with him.

Julia closed her eyes and let go of the handle, backing away, as if it were electrified. Then she turned and ran back down the hall.

77

The Alibi Lounge was located in the lobby of a Travelodge, just off 11th Street and 11th Avenue. Removed from the glitz of SoBe by more than a few miles, and sitting on the fringe of Liberty City, there were no sun-worshiping Miami tourists holed up in this part of town. People stayed at the Travelodge for one of two reasons: either they were a witness in a criminal trial; or they were visiting a sick relative up the street at Jackson Memorial, Cedars Medical Center, Baskin Palmer or Sylvester Cancer.

Julia had never been to the Alibi before. As she pulled the Honda into the parking lot, she wondered why she was even here. Why she hadn't just gone home to cry with Moose and finally finish off the rest of that bottle of Stoli in the cupboard.

She spotted Lat right away at the bar, talking with Brill and a couple of PDs.

'Hey there,' he said with a grin, motioning her over when she hadn't moved. 'Let's get you a seat.' He turned to Brill, 'Go get another bar stool, man.'

'What the fuck do I look like?' Brill barked.

'Be gracious for once in your life. The lady needs a seat.'

'Give her yours,' Brill grumbled. Then he looked at Julia and sighed. 'Ah, for you, Jules, I'll do it. Mainly 'cause you stood up to that asshole today.'

'Speaking of the devil,' Lat said, looking back at the door after Brill had stomped off. 'Where's Bellido?'

'He's not coming.'

'Why not?'

'I didn't get a chance to actually ask him.' She looked straight at the bar, focusing on a bottle of Hennessy on the top shelf.

'What?'

'He's busy. Or he was. I suspect he's done now.'

'What the —' he started to say, then he finally found her eyes, which picked that moment to swell with tears. 'Oh shit.'

She hung her head. 'I think I need a drink,' she said quietly, her voice catching. She never should've come here tonight.

'It wouldn't be the first time,' Lat said after a moment.

'No?'

'Nah. Ricardo's got quite the reputation with the ladies. Most of it of his own making, though. I haven't heard too many impressive tales from the other side.'

'How did you know?' she finally asked.

'Julia, please. Everyone knew about you two. If it makes you feel any better, everyone also knows he's an asshole.'

She said nothing.

'Who was it?' he asked.

'My DC, I think. It was hard to tell. I never heard her moan before.'

Lat shook his head.

'I feel like a fool. An idiot.' She looked helplessly around the room. 'And I don't know why I'm here . . .'

He pushed himself back from the bar. 'Stop. Enough. Let's go.'

'What?'

'We'll get you that drink, love, but somewhere else.' The bar and pool tables were crowded with private defense attorneys, PDs, correction officers and cops. Odds were that the Travelodge guest list included a few reporters who were mixed in as well. 'There's too many people here who would love to see you cry, Julia, and then spend the next hour or two wondering why. Let's go. I'm out back.'

Brill walked up, bar stool in hand.

'No need, brother. We're out of here,' Lat said, grabbing his leather jacket that hung on the wall. He slapped Steve on the back. 'Thanks.'

'Where we going?' Brill called out.

'I'll call you in the morning,' Lat yelled back.

Julia quietly followed Lat past the pool table and through a back door that led directly to the parking lot. To her surprise, he walked past the police cruisers and a black Taurus over to a polished red and silver Harley.

'Technically, today's my day off. And this is what I ride on my day off. Here,' he said, unsnapping a helmet off the back and handing it to her.

She stayed where she was. 'A motorcycle?' she asked hesitantly.

'I wear one. I'm no idiot,' he said.

'I . . . I don't ride motorcycles,' she stammered.

He stared at her. 'Why not?'

She hesitated again. 'My mother always told me not to. Told me I'd crack my head open.' She anxiously rubbed her thumbs on the helmet's smooth surface.

He climbed on the bike and smiled at her. 'Is your momma here now?'

'Well, no,' she said. Then added, 'She's dead.'

'That sucks. I'm sorry,' he replied and the smile instantly disappeared, replaced with somber silence. 'Have you ever ridden one?' he asked when she still hadn't said anything.

'No.'

'There's nothing to be worried about. You're in good hands.'

She looked about the lot. Her car was parked on the other side of the hotel.

'You could always follow me, I suppose,' he said with a shrug, starting the engine. The bike rumbled to life.

She said nothing. But she didn't move.

'Come on, Julia,' he said over the engine. 'Get on the bike. You've had a real shitty day and mine hasn't been much better. Let's go for a ride.' He held out his hand.

She bit her lip, then nodded slowly and took it, climbing on the back. Good thing she'd picked a pantsuit today.

'Ready?'

She wrapped her arms around his waist and nodded, her head against his back, her eyes shut tight.

'Hold on,' he said. Then he hit the gas and the bike sped out of the Alibi with a loud roar, past the courthouse and the State Attorney's Office, onto the ramp for 195 and out of Miami.

78

The wind whipped at the exposed skin on her hands and neck as they raced north. She finally opened her eyes and watched as cars and trucks moved beside them at seventy miles an hour – so close she could maybe reach out and touch them – but yet she couldn't hear anything over the roar of the bike, which was probably a good thing. The noise and the fear prevented her from thinking.

She wrapped her arms tighter around Lat's waist and buried her face into his leather jacket. Her palms began to sweat, and she feared her fingers might slip through one another and cause her to lose her grip. She had a frightening but funny thought that she might blow off the back of the motorcycle like a cartoon character, and smack straight into the path of a semi, her body splayed like da Vinci's *Medicine Man* across the front grill.

Traffic was light this time of night. They sped over the flyover at the Golden Glades – the concrete clog of ramps and overpasses that connected Miami's four main expressways – and into Broward County. She had no idea where they were going, but as exits streaked by in blurs of green and white – including her own – she found that she didn't really care anymore. The cold wind was invigorating; the deafening roar of the bike strangely soothing. She could feel the distance stretching between her and Rick – physically, emotionally, metaphorically – with every mile marker Lat passed and she didn't want him to stop. She wanted him to keep going until she just couldn't think anymore. Until Rick

Bellido and her feelings for him eventually stretched into nothingness.

At 1595, he headed east, toward signs for the Fort Lauderdale/Hollywood International Airport and the beach. When the interstate finally ended, he turned north onto a quiet, almost deserted stretch of three-lane highway. Closed, no-name car rental agencies and auto repair shops lined the road that led toward downtown Fort Lauderdale. Just to the east, Julia spotted the smoke stacks of Port Everglades, where massive cruise ships from all around the world dropped anchor. She'd been to Fort Lauderdale countless times to see Nora and Jimmy, but strangely enough had never been this way before.

As he pulled up to a light, the engine quieted a bit and Lat turned his head to look at her. 'You okay back there?'

She nodded. Her ears were ringing like she'd just stepped out of a rock concert.

He reached down and took her hands in his. Her fingers felt like blocks of ice. 'Cold?'

She nodded again.

He rubbed her fingers gently, and she felt a tingle run up her spine. When the light turned green, he moved her hands up underneath his jacket, pressing them back together up against his stomach, a signal for her to hold on again.

Her fingers began to defrost and she could feel the rise and fall of his chest under them as he breathed, his strong muscles tightening against her hands through his shirt as he leaned his body into the bike. It was a strangely intimate moment. Lat and she had definitely developed a friendship over the past few months, but Julia suddenly felt embarrassed to be this close to him, her arms wrapped around his waist, her face buried against his back, smelling the leather of his jacket. Embarrassed to be feeling the way she was now feeling.

As they got closer to downtown, fast-food restaurants and drug stores popped up next to Blockbusters and nail salons, and the traffic got a little heavier. He turned down a side street into what at first looked like a quiet, residential neighborhood, but a block or so up, in a small strip mall, Julia spotted a dive shop and a yacht uniform outfitter next to what looked like an unassuming restaurant. The Southport Raw Bar. Hand-painted sea creatures swam across nautical blue wainscoting.

Lat pulled the bike past the cars that packed the parking lot, creating a spot on the sidewalk next to the front door. A sign above the entrance read *Eat Fish – Live Longer. Eat Oysters – Love Longer. Eat Clams – Last Longer.*

She pulled off her helmet, as the sound of silence slowly filled her head again. 'Where are we?' she asked, looking around.

'We're getting you that drink,' he replied, as he got off the bike. He helped her off as well and then watched with a grin as she walked carefully to the door. 'You okay, Counselor?' he asked.

'Just a little stiff,' she replied, with an exaggerated grimace. 'Thanks for breaking me in slowly.'

'I kept it under ninety,' he replied with a laugh, holding the door.

They'd taken maybe two steps inside when a tall guy in retro horn-rimmed glasses wearing an apron and sporting a mop of curly brown hair strode up and slapped Lat hard on the back.

'John-John! What the hell are you doing up here?'

'Hey, Buddy!' Lat said to his friend, shaking his hand hard and slapping his back. 'Just in the 'hood. Thought I'd bring you a new customer. Julia, this is Buddy. Buddy's the owner of this fine establishment and the maker of the best chowder in town. Julia's the prosecutor on a case I'm working.'

'I thought you looked familiar,' was all Buddy said, and for that Julia was relieved. He smiled and said with a laugh, 'This guy's gonna single-handedly double my business this year.'

'Look at this,' Lat said, gesturing around the packed restaurant and bar. TVs blared basketball and hockey games from every corner. 'He's turning them away. Speaking of which, you got a table?'

'Are you kidding me?' Buddy led them outside to a crowded waterfront patio. Boats bobbed up against the dock in every slip and the air smelled like fish and beer. Reggae music played somewhere. Two minutes later Lat and Julia were sitting at a plastic table nursing their own Budweisers.

'A Harley, huh? I never figured you the type,' Julia said after the waitress had taken their order of chowder and Old Bay shrimp.

'There's a life lesson for you, love. Never judge a book by its cover. Guys who ride Harleys aren't all outlaws, you know.'

'Obviously,' she said with a smile. She sipped her beer and looked around the deck. 'We sure are a long way from Kansas, Auntie Em. Do you live around here?'

'Nah. My friend's got a boat off one of the canals, and we take it out fishing sometimes. I got an apartment in Miami Beach, but I wish I was here. I like Fort Lauderdale. It's quiet, more laid-back. I just don't want to do the commute yet.'

'The Beach is nice. MTV seems to like it. So does Paris Hilton,' she said.

'Just my point. I'm not a Puff Daddy guy. I don't do hip-hop. I do Lynyrd Skynyrd. And I don't own black ostrich pants. It's getting a bit too funky on the beach for me.'

'It's just Diddy now. Puff is gone. And I think he took the P with him.'

'There you go,' Lat said with a shrug. 'Where do you live?' he asked.

'In Hollywood. At a complex off of Stirling and 95. I'd love to live near the beach, but it's not in the budget. Not as a state employee. Even the Conquistador is a stretch.'

'Hmmm. Maybe I should have asked you that before I rode you thirty miles away from your car. My bad. I figured you for a Gables girl.'

She shook her head. 'No, no. Thanks for . . .' she hesitated, struggling to say just the right words but not much more, '. . . this.' She looked around the restaurant with a smile. 'This place is great.' Colorful Budweiser and St Pauli Girl umbrellas dotted the tables, and in the center of each was a roll of paper towels, a few plastic well-used menus and an old Corona bottle with a single flower in it. 'And with real flowers, too,' she said absently, gently fingering the petals. 'I love peonies. The cheap man's rose, my mom used to say. But they're still my favorite.' She shook a thought out of her head. 'And the ride was . . .'

'Scary?'

She smiled. 'A little.'

'I thought you were gonna take out a rib.'

'Sorry,' she said, turning red. 'It was only scary at first, though. You're a good driver.'

'I'm glad I didn't crack your head open. I would have hated to have proved your mother right about us outlaws. I'm sorry, by the way.'

She shook her head, not understanding.

'About your mom. I'm sorry. When did she die?'

Julia swallowed the lump in her throat with a long sip of beer. 'A long time ago,' she said finally. 'It's been fifteen years.' It was funny. She'd never even shared that information with Rick. Why had she told him her mother was dead?

447

'What happened?' he asked.

His question took her by surprise. 'It was an accident,' she said softly. 'Her and my father.'

'You must have been young. Damn . . . I'm sorry.'

'It's okay. You didn't do anything.' She smiled again, but it was strained.

'Do you have any brothers and sisters?'

'No,' she answered quickly and took another sip of beer. 'There's just me.' She suddenly remembered the biblical passage between Jesus and Simon Peter after the Last Supper at the Mount of Olives, before Judas's betrayal. *I tell you, Peter, the cock will not crow this day, until you have denied three times that you know me.* She looked away, feeling ashamed.

'Who raised you then?'

'My aunt.' She blew out a short breath and tried to change the subject. 'So are you from Florida?'

'Is anybody actually from Florida? LA. I came to Miami because I learned Spanish in high school and I knew I didn't want to work in the movies. My family is still out there. A mom and two brothers. One is great, the other not so great.'

'Why?'

'Drugs, gangs. Same house, three different results: a lawyer, a cop and a criminal. At least we're all in related professions. And it definitely makes for some lively conversation around the Thanksgiving table.' He shrugged again. 'So how did you end up with Bellido?'

'I don't know,' she said, taken off guard again. She looked out at the water. 'That's the funny thing. Six months later and I still don't know.'

'Six months. Who-hoo . . .'

'Is that a long time?'

'Not for me. I've had some go into the home stretch.'

She knew what he was really saying without actually saying

it and that same stab of pain jabbed her chest. The one the fast motorcycle ride had let her forget. 'It was off and on. I wouldn't say we were always together. I mean tonight shouldn't have been a surprise. I'm sure, as you said, there were others.' She closed her eyes and rubbed them. God she didn't want to have this conversation. She didn't want it to smart so much and she didn't want everyone to have seen it coming. Everyone but her. 'I guess I'm a fool. He was there whenever he wanted to be, and I was there whenever he wanted me to be. It was a destructive cycle. Now we have to finish this case and it's only just begun.'

'Do you love him?'

'Jeesh,' she said, looking at him. His blue eyes didn't waver, so she finally looked away, at a piling on the dock. It was easy to see now how he could work a subject in his custody. 'No. I can't say I love him,' she said quietly, twisting the edge of the paper towel that was on her lap. 'I want to say I did, but I can't. It never even came up between us. I guess that's strange. But I wanted him to want me. I wanted him to love me, I guess. I wanted him to say it . . .' Her voice drifted off and she paused, shaking her head. 'Why am I telling you this? I need more liquor to justify telling you this stuff. A lot more.' She finally looked back over at him. He was still watching her intently. 'Tell me something, John Latarrino. Please. Something I can use against you later on if I need to. I am so embarrassed right now.'

'I'm an insomniac and I don't clean my bathroom.'

She laughed. 'That's helpful. Tell me, why do you pace the floors at night, Detective?' The waiter picked that moment to drop off two more beers, the bowls of chowder and platters of fried seafood, extra obviously sent over by Buddy.

Lat turned and waved a thank-you to his friend who stood by the door. Then he looked back at Julia and smiled.

''Cause I haven't found the right woman yet to keep me in bed.'

Her cheeks went hot. 'Oh,' was all she said.

He shrugged and finished his beer. 'I was married once. Right after I came to homicide from robbery. It lasted a year. It never should have happened, but it did. Thankfully, there were no kids. We never had time to make any, which, according to her, was the root of my problem.'

'Was the divorce amicable?'

'I'd say so. She wound up marrying her attorney. Now they have three kids. I got the dog. Lilly. An overweight, neurotic, cute golden retriever.'

'Ouch. And you . . . now?'

'Like I said, now I pace the floors at night. Just like you.'

As Lat had promised, the food was great, but the company was better. They slipped into lighter conversation that over the course of the next two hours covered every topic from politics to the U2 sweep at the Grammy Awards. Buddy joined them for a drink and a Lat story before hopping off to another table. It had been a long while since Julia could actually remember laughing.

An almost full moon slipped through the fronds of a palm tree, slicing ribbons of light across the black, almost motionless water. It was late. The restaurant had emptied out, and most of the boaters had left. Southport sat in the dead end of a long canal, but T-boning the other end was another waterway. Julia could see an elaborate yacht zigzag by in the distance, all lit up. 'Is that the Atlantic?' she asked.

'Nope. That's the Intracoastal,' he answered. Then he looked at her. 'Were you close?'

She stared at him. 'What?'

He picked the peony out of the Corona bottle and handed it to her. 'To your mother. Were you close?'

The tears started to spill before she could even think to hold them back.

'Oh shit,' Lat said, startled. He began pulling off sheets of paper towels and shoving them at her.

She nodded, her face buried in a paper towel. She felt like such a moron. 'I'm sorry. I'm okay.'

He stood up and slapped money on the table. 'I'm the one who should be sorry. I didn't mean to get you upset.' He looked around the restaurant then reached down and took her by the hand. 'Come on, Julia. Let's get you out of here.'

79

Neither of them said anything as he led her by the hand down the dock, around the back of the restaurant and through the empty parking lot, presumably to avoid having to say goodbye to Buddy and explain why she was crying.

'Put this on,' he said, taking his jacket off as they came up to his bike. 'I think it's gotten colder.'

She nodded, slipping her arms into the sleeves. She couldn't look at him for fear she might break down once again.

He got on the bike and offered her his hand. Without another word, she climbed on behind him, hesitantly wrapping her arms around his waist as he started it back up. The past two hours had been so good, but now everything felt awkward and clumsy. Out of place. Almost as if he'd read her mind, Lat reached down and took her hands once again in his own, rubbing them with his fingers before tucking them up under his shirt, like he had before. Only this time, it was his bare chest that she felt move under her fingertips. She closed her eyes and rested her head against his back, unsure what to make of her feelings again – or his – as he took off out of the parking lot.

Instead of heading to 595 and back down to Miami, like she was sure he would, he passed the airport and turned east onto a deserted Dania Beach Blvd. At A1A – the two-lane beach road that ran down the entire east coast of Florida – he headed south toward Miami. It was well past midnight and the sleepy highway – normally packed with tourists and sun worshippers – was unusually empty and quiet, the beachfront restaurants and T-shirt shops all closed up for the night. If she'd been with anyone else, even Rick, she would have definitely felt a bit anxious – not knowing exactly where she was or where they were going – but with Lat she felt surprisingly relaxed. She thought of that crazy day in court months back – his words to her in those panic-stricken moments right before the competency hearing. *Trust me.*

The same moon from Southport followed them as they drove along the beach, past seaside motels with flashing neon vacancy signs mixed in with the occasional high-rise Holiday Inn. She inhaled the salty sea air that she loved so much, watching the black waves break white against the shore. She could almost hear the waves calling her.

'Can I help?' Julia asked.

Andy looked up at her from his trench in the sand, his eyes squinting against the sun.

'Mom said to tell you I can help.'

He shrugged, but only because he had no choice and he knew it. 'If you want.'

'Whatcha making? A hotel?' she asked.

'The Colosseum.'

'The what?'

'The Colosseum. It's in Italy. It's like a stadium, like a really old baseball stadium.'

Wow. She could see it now. A stadium. That was so cool. 'Can I make the concession stands, like they have at the softball fields in Eisenhower Park?'

'No,' he sighed. He thought for a moment while she stood there. Then he motioned for her to come into the trench with him. He took her hands in his and carefully guided her to where he was carving the

*seats. 'You have little fingers. That's good, Ju-Ju. Real good. You can
make the tunnels . . .'*

Julia closed her eyes. Why had she denied him?

They said nothing along the ride, even at the lights. But
the awkwardness was gone now, replaced by this silent,
scary, electric energy between them. She didn't let go of his
waist, even when she could have, and he didn't move away.
She could feel his heart beat under her fingers. When he
suddenly turned off A1A onto Stirling, she knew where he
was going, even before he pulled into the parking lot of
the Conquistador Apartments.

He shut off the engine and stepped off the bike. She
stared at him. 'My car—' she began to say.

'I'll take you in the morning. I don't want you to have to
drive tonight. It's real late and it's a long way to Miami,
Toto, so don't even think of putting on your running shoes.
It's my bad that you ended up all the way up here, anyway.'
He held his hand out to help her off.

There was no point in arguing with him. And the truth
was, she didn't want to. She nodded and took his hand,
climbing off the bike.

They walked in silence up the stairs of her building to the
second floor, their fingertips still lightly locked. 'Do you
want to come in?' she asked quietly, looking down at the
doorknob after she'd slid the key in. This was how it had
started with Rick. The ill-thought-out invitation. But she'd
never felt like this when Rick touched her.

'I'd love to,' he said.

She turned and looked back at him in surprise. Her heart
pounded furiously.

'But I'd better not.'

'Oh,' she said, hoping she didn't sound disappointed.

Hoping he couldn't read her thoughts, but knowing he probably already had. She felt so exposed with him. He was standing close to her, just a few inches away. She could smell the faint scent of his cologne.

'Look, I'm sorry about before—' he started to say.

She shook her head, not wanting to go there again. 'Don't be. Thanks again for dinner.' She slipped off his jacket and reached over to kiss him goodbye on the cheek, but hesitated, her mouth lingering for a moment against his skin, and neither of them moved. His five-o'clock shadow felt like a fine sandpaper under her lips. She stepped closer, her body touching his, as her lips softly brushed his face, finding his mouth. She felt his warm hands on her shoulders, pulling her even closer, his fingers pressing into her back. His lips were very soft; his tongue tasted like beer. She remembered how her fingers had felt against his chest, how it felt to touch his heartbeat. The kiss lasted just a few seconds before he pulled away.

'Whoa,' he said, backing up slightly. He shook his head. 'I don't do rebounds, Julia. They never work out in my favor.'

She didn't know exactly how to feel right then, but if she could use one word, it would probably be empty. She watched him walk off down the stairs and she wished once again that she could do the impossible: that she could undo time. She listened to his motorcycle start up across the parking lot and then fade away as he drove off. Then she went inside her apartment and cried. But it wasn't over Rick Bellido.

When she woke up the next morning, her car was parked in the lot downstairs and John Latarrino was nowhere to be found.

80

In a criminal case, the burden of proving the defendant's guilt beyond, and to the exclusion of, every reasonable doubt fell on the State. As defense attorneys loved to endlessly remind juries, a defendant was under no obligation to prove anything at trial, and in fact, was under no obligation to even present a case, make an argument, or call a single witness to the stand. And on rare occasions they didn't – choosing to gamble their client's freedom on the argument that the government simply hadn't done its job.

But insanity cases were different. The law in Florida presumed that every man was sane when he committed a criminal act. As such, a plea of insanity was an *affirmative* defense to the crime of murder. Unlike the 'no one saw me do it' defense, the burden of *raising* the defense of insanity and then *proving* it was on the defendant, although the standard of proof was considerably less. Rather than reasonable doubt, the defendant only needed to present 'clear and convincing evidence' that he was insane. So while the State had to prove that the crime of murder was committed and the defendant was the one who'd committed it, the *defendant* then had to prove that he wasn't responsible because he was legally insane at the time of the crime. Then the burden fell back on the State to prove that he was – again, beyond and to the exclusion of every reasonable doubt. A confusing game of legal semantics, perhaps. But the end result was that the State's psychiatric big-guns wouldn't actually get pulled out until the second half of the ballgame, when the defense put on their show and made the defendant's sanity an issue.

Julia's bone for being second seat and for successfully tackling December's competency hearing was the opening statement, which was set for Monday morning. The opening was the first opportunity for both sides to stand up and tell the jury exactly what their case was about – what evidence was going to be presented, what witnesses would be called and, most importantly, what all that meant. With all the juicy, gory, never-before-told details thrown in. Although each side had asked the jurors questions during voir dire, opening arguments were also the first real time that the jurors got to hear from the lawyers themselves. And Julia had tried enough cases in her career to know that first impressions were lasting ones. As fundamentally unfair as it might be, it was oftentimes a personality contest in the court-room and most cases were won or lost before one witness ever took the stand – if the jury liked you, if they felt for your story, if they *trusted* you, then you had them at hello. With one caveat. If you told them that you were going to prove something, then you better damn well have proved it, because back in that jury room, like a scorned girlfriend, those jurors would remember everything you didn't do but said you would, and the all-important trust you had worked so hard to build up would be gone. Then, in their eyes, you'd be nothing but a well-dressed liar.

Since the moment Rick had first pulled his BMW up in front of the house on quaint Sorolla Avenue, Julia had been crafting her opening. It was a prosecutorial habit. As soon as you were assigned a case, skimmed through an A-form, pre-filed a witness, you began to piece together the way you were going to tell the story – what facts and what witnesses brought it to life or moved you to tears. She'd imagined time and again, as her case got closer to trial, how she would bring a jury back to the night of October eighth with just her words; how she would walk them through bloodstained, dark hallways; how she would make them feel the unimaginable horror that had brought veteran police officers to their knees crying. She wanted the jurors to experience the same intense roller coaster of emotions that she'd first felt when she'd stepped into a home that, from the outside, looked so perfect. Disbelief, shock, sadness and, finally, incredible anger. Anger at the thought that a father could do this to his children, a husband to his wife. As the facts developed and the case came together, piece by piece, she'd continued to develop and polish her opening – both in her head and out loud for Rick and the many obnoxious videotaped dress rehearsals he'd had her do a few weeks back. Back when they'd been much more than trial partners and the very idea of her boss actually picking out her outfits for trial somehow hadn't sounded as repulsive and controlling as it did that day in Miami Subs when she'd scoffed at the very notion over burgers with Dayanara.

But now, in the final hours before her performance, before her opportunity to win over the jury, the pieces weren't fitting as perfectly as they once did, and she'd spent the entire weekend holed up in her apartment trying to figure out just how to make them. Trying to figure out how to reassemble a puzzle that, like a Rubik's cube, always seemed to be changing on her. When the yellow side was perfect, the red was out of alignment. When she straightened out red, green was a mess and yellow didn't seem to fit anymore. There was no one solution she could think of to make it all work. To make the facts all easily snap back into place, like everyone else seemed to be able to do without reservation. She didn't know what was right, who was wrong.

Who to trust. And no matter how hard she tried, she couldn't dismiss the unsettling doubts that continued to nibble at her every thought. Doubts she'd never had in any other case.

But, of course, this was not any other case, was it? Even she could recognize that. Aunt Nora had been right all along – David Marquette was too close. Too close to home. And the lines of judgment and reason were blurred beyond distinction.

'It's not about what you *believe,'* her criminal law professor at GW had said once in class, *'it's about what you can get a* jury *to believe. At the end of the day, that's the only thing that's gonna matter, folks.'*

Maybe that was the trick, she thought finally as the sun came up Monday morning and slowly warmed the ceiling. Maybe the sides of the puzzle that were turned away from the audience didn't need to make sense because no one was going to see them anyway. Maybe the jury didn't need to hear the whole story.

So hours later, in a jam-packed courtroom, she stepped up from behind the State's table, said the well-rehearsed lines that she'd committed to memory. She took her choreographed steps in front of the jury box.

'Ladies and gentlemen, I am going to tell you now a tale of rage and brutal murder. A tale that seems to make no sense, which, of course, is what makes it all the more tragic. A tale that will, without question, shock you, horrify you, terrify you, haunt you. A story that will surely bring the strongest among you to tears . . .'

She couldn't help but wonder as she spoke if the twelve men and women could see right through her. If they could see her for the fraud she knew she was. It was almost as though she were watching an operation from the spectator seats above the operating room – she was present, but she wasn't really there, removed somehow from the ugliness of it all while the poor guy below flatlined right in front of her. The poor guy who sat only feet from her now, wearing the same vacant expression that he'd worn when she'd first laid eyes on him. The same faraway gray eyes that had once turned to her in this very same courtroom, pleading for understanding. Her understanding. His team of attorneys had cleaned him up and cut his hair and put him into a neat new suit for trial, but he was still the same empty shell of a man, Julia thought, that he had been in his red Psych Floor jumpsuit.

'"... he's coming," she whispered in the dark to the 911 operator, just as the last person little six-year-old Emma Louise Marquette would ever see on this earth suddenly flicked on the lights. And you will hear little Emma's scared voice, ladies and gentlemen, the very moment her killer finally found her secret hiding spot, tucked behind a box of Barbie dolls and a Hello Kitty chair in her pretty purple bedroom. The moment he came at her, his knife in hand. The precise moment Emma knew she would die. "Oh no, no, no, no ..." you will hear Emma cry out to her killer as he fell upon her.' Julia paused deliberately and looked over at David Marquette. '"No, Daddy!"'

Some jurors broke down in tears while others turned red with anger, gasping and shaking their heads in disgust.

If her argument had lost its emotion or conviction over the past few weeks, that was apparently not what the jury saw, heard or felt. The Perfect Story was told perfectly, and she got the reaction Rick and Charley Rifkin and Jerry Tigler wanted. The reaction the cameras wanted, too. And when she finally finished, an hour and forty-five minutes later, it was no longer curiosity that they stared at David Marquette with. It was pure contempt. She had done her job well. And they hated him for it.

'Great job,' Rick whispered when she sat down next to him, with a nod of his head and a genuine smile that she hadn't seen in a long, long while. 'You nailed it. You really nailed it.'

Julia hadn't told him about the Handley murders. She hadn't shared with him her thoughts about the possibility of another killer. She hadn't reasoned with him about the statistical likelihood of a false confession. The time had passed for arguments and reasoning a long while back. Now the stage was set, the lights were up, the audience was out there and it was on with the show. The show that Ricardo Alejandro Bellido himself – the next State Attorney of the Eleventh Judicial Circuit – had written and casted and directed. There would not be any last-minute changes. Period. She knew that now. Julia watched him smile and nod at her with approval for having followed the script, but for the first time ever, she didn't care that he approved. In fact, it repulsed her that he did.

There was no point in confronting him with what she'd seen and heard on Friday night, either. Their romance was over and she didn't want it back. Even the memories tasted off. And, sadly enough, she knew that at this point he would probably use even just the perception of her jealousy as an excuse to boot her off the case if he could, their relationship was so strained. The case that was supposed to have made her career once upon a lifetime ago, she thought bitterly, as she packed up her briefcase after Farley broke for lunch. Now that promising career teetered precariously on the brink of self-destruction as she grappled with the truth and everyone else's perception of it.

It was funny, though. As she went to duck out the judge's back hallway and avoid the press, she passed her DC and Charley Rifkin, chatting quietly by the door. They were probably waiting on Rick to finish up speaking with the 911 operator, the State's first witness, who was set to testify

461

at one thirty. Rifkin, as usual, nodded uncomfortably and looked away. She knew he still did not care for her. But for the first time in months, Karyn smiled at her. A big, cheerful, toothy grin.

Like they were the very best of friends.

81

'Casamassina, Cirto, Grubb, Morales, Monteleone,' the nurse's disinterested voice crackled to life over the intercom system.

Andy looked up from the picture he was drawing.

'Please report to the nurse's station.'

Outside, the light was almost gone; the skyline of Manhattan was beginning to glow. It was six o'clock. Meds time.

He carefully tucked both his sketchpad and his pencils in the footlocker next to his bed, under the stack of new polo shirts that Julia had given him when she'd been here to see him a couple of weeks ago. Nothing was allowed to actually be locked up at Kirby – including, ironically enough, a locker – and things were known to sometimes just 'disappear' if extra measures weren't taken to hide them away. His sketchpad was his camera and he didn't want his pictures – especially this picture – to go missing like so many others had over the years.

Meds for his ward were dispensed from a rolling cart outside the nurse's station – a white Formica island encased in thick, bulletproof glass that sat right outside the TV/rec room and dining area, directly across from the open dorm sleeping area, and down the hall from the semi-private two-bed dorms, where his room was. Like the center of the Pentagon, it was strategically located right in the middle of all the action, so the nurses and SHTAs could watch everyone all the time. He joined the end of a long line of men that had started to snake its way down the hall toward the semi-private rooms. Even though many of them had been in here as long as him, he had no friends.

'Ladies and gentlemen, I am going to tell you now a tale of rage and brutal murder. A tale that seems to make no sense, which, of course, is what makes it all the more tragic. A tale that will, without question, shock you, horrify you, terrify you, haunt you. A story that will surely bring the strongest among you to tears . . .'

He froze. Just down the hall on the big-screen TV in the rec room there she was. Julia. On the Channel Four news. In a nice blue suit and wearing stylish, chrome glasses, her long hair in a soft, pretty bun. What was she doing? Then it clicked. Her big case. This was it.

'. . . Assistant State Attorney Julia Valenciano started off the State's case this morning in a packed Miami courtroom by doing exactly as she had promised — by bringing many of the jurors to tears. Today we learned for the first time some of the more gruesome details as the prosecutor described just how the bodies of the children were first discovered in the home on . . .'

'Isn't that the woman who was here last Saturday? The one who came to see Andrew Cirto?' Nurse Lonnie asked the other nurse who was filling out med sheets and putting pills in dispensing cups.

The door to the nurse's station was open. He could see them through the thick, scratched plastic. He could hear them as they worked.

'. . . attorney Mel Levenson, in his opening, told the jury that his client is a paranoid schizophrenic who is not responsible for the deaths of his wife and children . . .'

'Sure looks like her,' replied the other nurse, whose name he didn't know, squinting at the TV.

'Yeah. That's his sister,' Samuel said quietly, glancing up from his chart at the screen.

'No friggin' way. I didn't know Cirto even had family left.' The unknown nurse let out a low, *don't-wanna-mess-with-that-none* whistle. 'Thought he whacked 'em all.'

'Guess he missed one,' Samuel replied dryly. 'She's been here a lot lately. Last couple of months I'd say. You just don't work enough weekends is all, Barbara,' he added with a grin and a teasing nudge of his clipboard.

'I don't need to work any more than I already do in this place, thank you very much.'

'What's her business on that doctor case?' Nurse Lonnie asked.

'I think she's the prosecutor,' Samuel replied.

'The prosecutor? No friggin' way!'

'Again with the friggin' . . .' Nurse Lonnie sighed.

'Sorry. So what's she doing showing up here all of a sudden?' Nurse Barbara asked with a shudder as she looked out into the rec room, her eyes scanning the crowd of inmates. 'Research?'

He knew they didn't see him standing there on line. Or maybe they did and just didn't care if he heard them. If anybody heard them. After all, the men in here were not human, anyway. They were the keepers of the monsters.

Andrew stepped off the line and into the rec room. He watched as his little sister stepped out of the courthouse and into a waiting crowd of photographers, like a movie star. Her briefcase in hand, she looked so smart, so confident, so important.

A somebody.

She stood on top of the bed in her pajamas, a pink and red striped scarf wrapped dramatically around her neck, a pair of mismatched mittens on her hands. When she jumped, her long black hair seemed to just float on the air, spreading out around her like a huge parachute.

'I don't want to be a vet anymore, Andy,' she said with unflinching conviction in between jumps. 'I'm gonna be an actress. I want to be in movies and on TV.'

'That's a stupid idea,' he said, watching her.

'No, it's not.'

'Yes, it is. Do you know how hard it is to be an actress?'

'So? I can do it if I want.'

'Fine. Go ahead. You have to take your clothes off if you want to be famous, though, you know. All famous actresses do.'

The jumping slowed. 'Nuh-uh.'

'Yup. Just watch R movies. The girls are all naked. And they curse, too.'

She was silent for a long time and he suddenly felt bad for trying to pop her balloon. Before he could apologize, though, she sullenly asked, 'Whatta you gonna do? Play baseball? Duh.'

'I'm gonna be famous, but you got to have a plan to get there, Ju-Ju. I mean a real plan.'

'Give me a break.' The jumping resumed full speed.

'Playing ball's not enough. Dad says little-league fields are full of dreaming ballplayers. You gotta be special.' He looked down at his right hand and wiggled his index and middle fingers. 'This . . . is the secret weapon. This hand's gonna take me places, Ju-Ju. I'm gonna work on my split till I can get it up to maybe ninety-five. Coach Rich says I have it, too. I got the stuff. If I can throw a split faster than ninety, I'll definitely make the bigs one day. Ya see, you gotta have something special, Ju-Ju. Something nobody else has. And ain't nobody's gonna have a split finger like mine.'

He looked down at his maimed hands, the ones that were supposed to take him places. On his pitching hand, his thumb flopped listlessly back toward the wrist. He couldn't wrap his fingers around a baseball anymore even if he tried. Deep scars sliced haphazardly across his palms, all the way up to his fingertips. That's where they'd implanted the chip so many years ago. Rusted and rotting now, its wires probably frayed and poisonous, he knew it was still in there, somewhere.

He could feel it.

Then he hung his head and started to cry.

82

'The knife was placed almost straight into the umbilicus. There was no tearing, ripping or pulling of the surrounding tissue, like you would expect to find if there was a struggle, or if the target was moving about when stabbed. The tissue below the navel is not vital, unless the blade were to puncture the loop of small intestines, which, as I testified before, didn't happen in this case.' Dr Larry Price, the trauma surgeon from Jackson who'd operated on David Marquette sat on the very edge of his seat in the witness chair, his entire face hovering less than an inch above the microphone. He was more than just a little uncomfortable being a witness; he was a nervous wreck. He'd been in that seat for an hour and twenty minutes already – on direct and then cross and now back on redirect – and that was an hour and nineteen minutes too long. For everyone. He shifted in his seat, wiped the sweat from his lip and cleared his throat. An ear-piercing twang of feedback blasted the courtroom. Judge Farley rubbed his ear and rolled his eyes.

'And, again, if the intestines had been punctured, Dr Price?' Rick asked.

'I would've had to repair it. And, of course, there's a risk, you know, of infection from spillage of the intestinal fluids into the abdominal cavity. So it can be serious, no doubt. But if you know what you're doing, you know there is no vital, life-sustaining organ in that area.' He looked over at the jury, his eyes finding one of the women jurors in the front row. Alice Wade, an elderly retired librarian from

Iowa who lived in Leisure City now. 'That's why when the Japanese samurai would commit *seppuku* – a ritualistic form of suicide, known to the western world as *hara-kiri* – they would actually disembowel themselves by digging the knife in and then dragging it across their belly,' he explained, gesturing with his own hand on his stomach, 'and then pulling sharply upward at the end. More than a knife wound, it pretty much ensured death in the event they didn't have an assistant – a *kaishakunin* – to cut off their heads and finish the job,' he finished with a smile. Alice Wade turned green and looked away.

'Objection,' said Mel, standing. 'Inflammatory and irrelevant.'

'Definitely sustained,' said Farley with a shake of his head. 'Are you done with redirect now, Mr Bellido? I think the jury gets your point. I think we all get your point. It didn't look like a suicide attempt to Dr Price. Let's move this along.' He tapped his watch.

'Thank you, Doctor,' said Rick, sitting down. 'I have nothing further, then.'

'Mr Levenson? Tell me you're done with this witness, please.'

'Yes, Judge. Nothing further,' Mel replied.

Dr Price practically ran for the courtroom doors.

'Alright, then,' said Farley with a sigh. 'State, who's next?'

Rick took a long, deliberate moment to look up from the table. The courtroom had excitedly learned to hang on his every pregnant pause now. He rose and straightened his expensive suit. 'The State rests, Your Honor.'

A loud murmur broke out in the crowded courtroom. To the surprise, maybe, of the reporters, legal analysts and news commentators who were expecting the fourteen-week marathon of a Michael Jackson trial, it had taken just five days to put on the State's case in chief, which included calling twenty-two witnesses to the stand. Leonard Farley might have the biggest docket in the courthouse by far, but when you finally got the man to actually go to trial, he was no nonsense. He'd told the pool during jury selection that if they were picked to serve, the case would take up only two weeks of their time, and he meant it. At whatever cost. So court had started at 10 a.m. – the second he finished his morning calendar – and it had ended most nights well past seven or eight. In the event the jury did find Marquette guilty of first-degree murder, they were told that the penalty phase would be carried out six weeks later, at a separate mini-trial where both sides would present witnesses. Then they would get to recommend whether David Marquette lived his life out in a maximum-security prison cell, or died for his crimes by either lethal injection or in the electric chair. And no matter what, Farley had assured the pool, *that* would take only one week.

It was Rick's case, so he had handled most of the witnesses and the evidence, but Julia had been there beside him every day at the State's table. She'd participated. She'd stood and asked all the right questions of her witnesses on direct. The Coral Gables PD records custodian, the Crime Scene techs who'd shot the video and taken the pictures, the techs who'd dusted the house for prints, the nurse anesthetist from Sinai who ID'd David Marquette's voice on the 911 tape, the Marriott manager who testified that the defendant had been a registered guest at the Orlando World Center on the night of October eighth. She'd re-established those witnesses after Mel Levenson and Stan Grossbach had crossed them. She'd had marked and entered into evidence the hotel bills, lab reports and even the plaster casts of the distorted bloody footprints that had walked the halls of the house on Sorolla. She herself had used the poster-board pictures of the crime scene and the Marquette children to demonstrate where the bodies were found.

But all along, Julia felt as if she were watching someone else acting as her. Someone who was crumbling and slipping away a little piece at a time, day after day, until she feared she might not recognize the person that was left at the end of it all. And it frightened her.

'Alright, then, Mel,' said Farley after he'd dismissed the jury for the weekend. 'Who's on for Monday and what's your time frame?'

'I've got several defense witnesses, Judge. I'm not sure what order I'll be putting them on in.'

'Does your client plan on testifying?' Farley asked doubtfully, looking over at the defense table. His white eyebrows crawled into a frown.

'I'm not sure, yet,' said Mel with a shrug. There was no way he was going to give away his hand in front of Rick Bellido and a courtroom still filled with cameras, but based on the peculiar behavior of his client, it wasn't just Farley who was obviously doubting Marquette would testify. Through jury selection and now five days of oftentimes brutal and graphic testimony, Marquette had sat expressionless, tapping his foot under the table, and staring out into space, rolling his tongue about the inside of his mouth. Julia had often wondered how she would look if she stood accused of murder. She'd observed defendants in court before – defendants she'd brought to trial – and wondered how she would act if she were innocent. How she would act if she were guilty, but trying to look innocent. If there was a difference. Then there was the third category. How she would act if she were crazy . . .

'I want to go to closing by next Friday. Is that going to

happen, gentlemen?' As an afterthought the judge looked at Julia and added, 'Ladies?'

'I know you have a schedule, Judge——' began Mel.

'No. I have a cruise. I'm leaving on the thirty-first. That gives us an extra week if we need it.' He climbed off the bench and headed for the door, which Jefferson held open for him. 'But I'm sure we won't,' he called out gruffly without turning around as he disappeared down the hallway.

83

'I want you to handle Christian Barakat when we put him on,' Rick said to Julia in a low voice as court emptied and they packed up their files. 'You did well at the competency hearing. Even Farley commented on it. Your opening was great, too.'

She just stared at her briefcase.

'You've done well with this whole trial,' he said, hesitating when she hadn't said anything. 'I should tell you that.' A long moment passed. 'Listen, Julia,' he continued, his voice a little softer, 'I know it's been, *difficult* between us, but, you've handled it. It hasn't been easy. I know it definitely hasn't been on me, at least.'

She wondered just what he meant by that, considering she didn't think he knew that she knew the reason why her DC now wore a permanent smile and had an extra spring in her step. She certainly wouldn't put it past him to work the two of them if he could. She suddenly thought of those intimate moments in his apartment, in his bed, his hands on her body, and she wanted to cringe. But still she said nothing.

'I think the jury needs to see you take on this issue,' he continued when she hadn't acknowledged his emotional pain. 'We've clearly made our case here and the only problem is going to be how believable Marquette's shrinks are, starting Monday. We had a couple of liberals, unfortunately, get through on jury selection. So I'll do the cross of Koletis and Hayes, but I think it's a good idea for the jury to see you dismantle the defense with our own psychiatrist. I might even have you handle Pat Hindlin, too, so look over his depo this weekend. It's getting *your* face in front of that jury again before we close. That's one of the reasons I asked you to second-seat in the first place, your demeanor with a jury. Your presence. They can identify with you. With our victims.'

One of the reasons. The other was over now.

'Are you okay with this?'

Julia nodded slowly. 'Yes,' she heard herself say. 'I'll do it.'

'Because they like you,' he said as he headed out the small gallery swing door and down the aisle. Outside in the hall a mob of reporters still waited anxiously for him to make an appearance. Rick might not be allowed to talk to them anymore, but they definitely could take his picture. 'The jury really likes you. And more importantly, they *trust* you. That I can tell,' he said, pushing open the courtroom doors with a serious, but confident smile.

84

When Julia finally got back from court herself – after ducking through the judge's garage in the basement again – there were three new cases on her desk, a dozen phone messages on her voicemail and thirty-two emails in her in-box. She might be a prosecutor in the murder trial of the century, but in the pits of the State Attorney's Office that didn't mean shit. The Chief Felony Assistants who handed out the new cases didn't care she already had 102 of them, and, of course, her DC didn't want to know how she prepped her calendar, as long as it was prepped. She was probably praying nowadays that Julia would slip up.

She felt so overloaded, so out of touch with everything, with everyone. So alone. This double life that she'd been leading was catching up to her, no doubt. The pressure was all around her, pushing her from every direction and no matter how hard she tried to get it all done, no matter how much she withdrew, she couldn't seem to distance herself from it. And that was what worried her so much.

Rick. Karyn. Charley Rifkin. Even the State Attorney himself. There was no one to trust anymore in the office. Even her detractors wore smiles and handed out praise. And there was Nora and Jimmy. God, how she missed them sometimes. She missed having a family, even if it was a mess. But she, like Andrew, was an outcast now. A misfit. A Charley in the Box. She picked up the phone and dialed their number, but got the answering machine instead, like she always seemed to. She hung up without leaving a message and looked at her watch. It was too late to call Andrew, and even if she could speak with him, what could she really say? She was in this by herself.

She put her head in her hands and rubbed her temples. This case. The sneaky press releases, the details no one told her – the details she should have known. The political motives. The underhandedness of it all. She had heard every sleazy lawyer joke in the book while she was in law school, but they were never about prosecutors. That was what had taken her by surprise the most. Maybe she should have seen Rick and Karyn coming. Or Rick and any other female in the office for that matter. Maybe that was her mistake. But she never would have thought he would manipulate a case for his own political benefit. She always thought he was better than that.

It must be like this for other prosecutors who have tried high-profile cases, she told herself. Launched out of obscurity, everyone was watching your every move now, critiquing your every sentence, every hairdo, every outfit. You're constantly in the spotlight and yet you never asked to be a celebrity. The pressure-cooker feeling was to be expected. She just had to get a grip, and leave it at that. It would all be over soon enough, anyway.

It was almost eight o'clock already. Once again, she was sure the building was empty except for her. She checked out the window for signs of either Karyn or Rick's car in the empty parking lot as she quickly packed up her briefcase and file box, because that was the last thing she needed – catching an elevator down with the two of them.

Her eyes caught on the Dade County Jail. While South Beach just got the party started when nighttime descended, this part of the city definitely emptied at the stroke of five. Especially on a Friday. Law firms, medical offices, the courthouse, commercial high-rise offices, the PD's, the Graham Building – all lifeless till Monday morning at eight. That's when you wouldn't be able to find a parking spot if your appointment depended on it. All except for DCJ. Like a Motel 6, the warden always left the lights on for you there. She stared for a long moment at the ninth floor. The Crazy Floor. If she closed her eyes, she could almost hear their shrieks . . .

The screamers.

The phone rang at her desk, pulling her out of her thoughts and making her jump. Out of habit she answered it, although as soon as she did she instantly regretted it, realizing that it was probably a reporter trying to hunt down a quote for tomorrow's headlines.

'State Attorney's. Valenciano,' she said, slinging her purse over her arm and pulling out her car keys.

There was silence.

'Hello? Can I help you?' she asked again, impatiently.

'Julia Valenciano?'

It was a male voice. Deep and scratchy, but yet muffled. There was something very familiar about it. Julia tried to place where she'd heard it before. Maybe it was that reporter from the *Post* who'd called yesterday.

'Yes?' she asked.

'Julia Cirto Valenciano?' he repeated. 'The prosecutor?'

'Yes? This is she.' A strange, uncomfortable feeling washed over her then as she listened to his labored breathing. *In and out. In and out.* Maybe he had asthma, but just his breathing was creeping her out. 'Can I help you with something, sir? I don't mean to be short, but it's late and I—'

'It wasn't him,' whispered the voice. 'Are you listening now, Ms Prosecutor? Do I have your attention? He didn't do it.'

Then he laughed and the line went dead.

Maybe it was a prank, she told herself over and over as she pushed open the glass doors of the Graham Building and hurried across the deserted parking lot to her car. She threw her file box, briefcase and purse into the back seat, quickly climbed in behind the wheel and locked the doors, breathless. She looked around her. Hers was the only car left in the lot.

Maybe it was a reporter. Or a protester. That had to be it. A right-to-lifer messing with her. Reporters had somehow found out the direct line to her office and had been calling her for weeks. Hell, they were like cockroaches, waiting for her everywhere now. Outside her office. Outside her apartment. On the beach when she jogged, she'd spotted a few. And now the protesters that yelled nasty things at her on her way into court every morning had obviously found her too. They would say anything, too, she knew. Anything to draw attention to their cause. Anything to get rid of the death penalty, she told herself as she sped out of the parking lot. They'd do anything.

That had to be it. But questions flew at her as she tried to navigate 195 at eighty miles an hour. Why would they call her and not Rick? He was the lead. Maybe they had. *Or maybe they knew what she'd found out last week about the Handley murders* ... She thought for a moment about when David Marquette had said those three words to her in the courtroom back months ago. *I saved them.* The only words he'd ever said in court and they were *to her.* It was almost as if he knew what she was thinking at that moment when she looked into his white eyes. It was as if he *knew* about her past. As if he knew about Andrew.

And how did they know she was still in her office tonight? Court had gotten out hours ago. Was someone watching her car? Her office window? Was someone watching her right now? Ready to jump out of the bushes with his creepy breathing and anti-death-penalty poster and scare her half to death when she opened the car door at the curb? She looked at the cars all around her to see who might have their eyes on her instead of the road. The flesh on the back of her neck prickled and she sped up.

She thought of a funny comment Andrew had made to her once when she was up at Kirby. *Just because you're paranoid doesn't mean someone's not following you.* Now she *was* paranoid. But now she had a reason. And she was taking no chances. So she got off a couple of exits before Stirling and took the back roads home, careful to keep checking her rear-view mirror to make sure she wasn't being followed. She didn't park in her spot, though, instead parking in the complex across the street and ducking through the walkways of the buildings adjacent to her own.

She wanted to call Lat. She wanted to tell him what had happened, what she'd found out. What the protesters knew now. She wanted him to come check her apartment for her. She wanted to hear his voice tell her it would be okay. But she couldn't. He'd made it clear what their relationship was and she'd have to accept that. And besides, he also knew that Marquette was an unofficial suspect in the North Florida murders and he hadn't told her, either. He, too, had kept secrets.

She locked her apartment door, turned off all the lights and closed the blinds in every room. She wished she had

Moose here with her. He was little, but he was very protective. And he could warn her if someone was out there, watching. Waiting.

It was a protester, she told herself as she locked her bedroom door and slumped down on the floor in the dark with her back against it, both the cordless phone and her cellphone between her legs. *That's all it was.*

There was no reason to be afraid.

86

'It's as if a cataclysmic earthquake has happened inside David's head.'

The courtroom remained perfectly silent as Dr Al Koletis took a long sip of water and looked up from the notes of his psychological evaluation of David Marquette, his reading glasses perched on the tip of his hooked nose.

'That's how I explain schizophrenia to the parents or loved ones of patients I have diagnosed, Mr Levenson,' he explained. 'In the simplest terms I know how. Here we have a normal person. Everything is fine. He or she has friends, a job; they've developed normal, loving relationships. They're functioning, thriving, well-adjusted members of society, oftentimes headed for a bright future, perhaps preparing to leave for college, as the disease tends to historically strike young men in their late teens, women a few years after that. But far below the surface, undetectable seismic changes deep within the brain's structure have already begun. These changes then cause – let's call it a pre-existing fault line – a genetic weakness or genetic predisposition, perhaps, far below that surface to collapse and catastrophically fail. Suddenly and seemingly without warning. Like an earthquake.

'Now, sometimes earthquakes can just jolt you out of bed, or knock a few paintings off the wall. But other times, they can have a far greater effect. They can change the integrity of the structure, so that it might *appear* fine at first glance, but one look inside the walls and you'll see how fragile they are, how they can fail at a moment's notice. And, of course, sometimes an earthquake of a great enough magnitude can change the entire landscape, leveling mountains and relocating seas.

'That is the disease of schizophrenia. The period of this gradual build-up of stress factors and seismic changes in the brain is called the prodromal stage. Looking back on that stage, you might be able to see subtle early-warning signs that something was not right. Depression. Withdrawal. Changes in sleep patterns. The earthquake itself is acute psychosis – when reality has collapsed and catastrophically failed. That is when the hallucinations and paranoia begin. And the aftermath is called, appropriately enough, the recovery period.

'Like an earthquake, the disease strikes every person differently. Some come through psychosis and do fine on medication. Some even without. The very lucky few are fortunate enough to never experience another psychotic episode. But then there are the ones who live on the fault line and are in constant danger of aftershocks and more quakes. These are the victims of the disease who might look fine on the surface – with two arms and two legs and a college degree in their pocket – and yet they can't live by themselves; their foundation is unstable and their walls are cracked. And, finally, there are those whose whole landscape has changed. They are the ones who go into a hospital and don't really ever come out. They cannot function in society. They are almost a completely different person because of their illness.

'David was living on a fault line,' he continued, taking off his glasses and thoughtfully chewing on the tip. 'He had experienced a psychotic break at the age of nineteen. It was a matter of time before he had another, especially since he was not taking preventative medication. It's perhaps a miracle he did as well as he did until that point. But outside stress factors – like the distant forces that work to destabilize the earth in and around a fault zone – such as, perhaps, his new baby and pressures at work and within his marriage, caused that fault line to break once again. This time with truly catastrophic results.'

'You have testified that David Marquette is a paranoid schizophrenic,' Mel began slowly. 'That he suffers from a mental infirmity or disease. You and Dr Hayes have testified that on the night of October eighth, because of this disease, he was psychotic and delusional, hearing voices and experiencing visual hallucinations that told him his family was possessed by demonic spirits, that told him he needed to save the souls of his children and his wife.'

'Objection,' said Rick. 'Is there a question in there somewhere? Or is counsel making his closing argument?'

'Don't be picky, Mr Bellido. I gave you leeway, too,' cautioned Farley. Then he looked at Mel over the brim of his coffee cup. 'Move this along into a question please, Mr Levenson. *Tempus fugit.*'

Mel shrugged. 'I ask you, Doctor, due to this mental infirmity, this mental disease of schizophrenia, did David know that his actions were wrong? Was he able to distinguish right from wrong at the time the crimes were committed?'

Mel was very careful not to label his own client a killer or a murderer. It was a delicate dance with words. He needed to match the language of the law that Judge Farley would instruct the jury on before they headed in for deliberations without further alienating them from his client.

'Objection. Leading.'

Farley shot Rick another dark look.

Dr Koletis didn't wait for a ruling. 'In my opinion, David was indeed legally insane the night his family was killed. He was acutely psychotic and delusional. He still cannot and will not discuss his actions in detail, other than to say he saved his family, because he fears reprisals. From whom, he refuses to say, but I suspect it is the demon spirits he rid his family of. He has buried those intimate facts, because they are too difficult and frightening for him to deal with, given his fragile state of mind. But he saw fangs on his three-year-old and his daughter's eyes glowed yellow. His wife burned a Bible and his baby daughter sprouted a horn. He believed these spirits were hypnotizing him with subliminal messages broadcast over the radio. The visual hallucinations were corroborated by audio hallucinations that continued to tell David his family was not human. That continued to tell David that his own life was now in danger, and that if he, too, became consumed by the devil, there would be no one left who could save his family from damnation. Don't you see?' he asked, looking over at the jury, demanding their attention. 'He didn't kill his family, because he knew that they were already dead. What he did was save their souls from eternal damnation by ridding their bodies of the demonic spirit that had murdered them. It was all part of the paranoid delusion he was suffering from.' Only one member of the jury nodded. The others looked away and down at the floor.

Dr Koletis slowly turned back to Mel, shaking his head. 'So to answer your question, Mr Levenson, no, he did not know that what he was doing was wrong.'

'And now?' asked Mel.

Dr Koletis paused for a moment and then looked over at the defense table, where David Marquette still stared

blankly out in front of him – as he did every day in court –
rolling his tongue and tapping his foot.

'Sadly enough,' he finished, 'in his mind he still thinks
he's done nothing wrong.'

87

The man with the stringy long hair and gladiator sandals sat in the rain on the courthouse steps, dressed in a straitjacket and shorts. Taped to his chest was a sign that read 'Don't Medicate Me Just to Kill Me'. The rain had gotten the sign wet and the words had started to run and drip. He was being interviewed by a reporter.

Julia hustled into the courthouse past them – and the rest of the large, strange crowd of protesters, reporters and trial watchers – obscured thankfully from view by her oversized umbrella. She moved along with the restless herd of defendants, witnesses, attorneys and cops, through the metal detectors and lobby, pushed like cattle onto the escalator. At this time in the morning, waiting for a spot on an elevator might take hours. She could feel people pressed up against her, touching her with their wet clothes and umbrellas, breathing on her. Counting from ten wasn't good enough anymore, so she started at forty, clenching and unclenching her fists, trying hard to breathe through the silk scarf she'd wrapped around her neck and buried her head into.

'Hey there,' a voice whispered in her ear. 'Where've you been hiding?' She felt a hand on her shoulder and it made her jump. She sucked in a breath and turned around to see John Latarrino standing on the step below her in a pair of dress slacks and a crisp white shirt that was dotted with raindrops, his gold detective's badge around his neck, his gun holstered at his side next to his cellphone, a sports jacket casually slung over his shoulder. His hair was wet, and a couple of drops ran down off his neck and into his shirt. He smiled at her.

Mel had invoked the rule of sequestration – better known simply as 'the rule' – the second the jury was sworn, which excluded all prospective witnesses from the courtroom during trial, so that their testimony wouldn't be influenced by listening to someone else tell a different version of events. Since Lat might be called back in rebuttal, he was still considered prospective. Julia hadn't seen him since he'd testified last week.

'I stopped by your apartment this weekend,' he said as they stepped off the escalator on four and into the utter bedlam that waited for them. 'But you weren't in. I was looking to see if you wanted to take a Sunday-afternoon spin with an outlaw.' The smile suddenly melted into a concerned frown when she didn't respond. 'Are you okay?' he asked her in a low voice, gently grabbing her elbow and turning her to face him.

She nodded quickly, but turned away from him. Without uttering a word, she disappeared into the sea of cameras and strangers that waited outside 4–10. A sea held back by a few police and correction officers, a portable metal detector as an extra security precaution, and plastic retractable movie-theater stanchions.

With her head down, she made her way through the crowd and onto the metal-detector line behind those reporters and bystanders who were lucky enough to have won their courtroom seat in Judge Farley's lottery. A couple of signs bobbed up and down in the crowded hallway, as they did outside. Some were handmade by angry people with magic markers and time on their hands, others were supplied and held up by volunteers from organizations like NMHA, the National Mental Health Association, NAMI, the National

Alliance for the Mentally Ill, Human Rights Watch, Amnesty International and, of course, the ACLU. Someone suddenly stuck a sign that read 'The Death Penalty Is Murder!' in her face, hitting her in the forehead. 'You know, you'll be going to hell, too!' its holder sneered as she passed, so close Julia could feel the spray of his spittle on her face.

'Back off, asshole!' she heard Lat shout behind her as she pushed her way past a wide-eyed and amused reporter who had turned to watch the scuffle. 'Take your shit outside. Cormier! Get him out of here! Nobody should be touching her!'

'Let's go, pal,' said another voice. 'You're out. You crossed the line.'

'Freedom of speech, Officer! I can say whatever the fuck I want to a prospective murderer! Does it make you feel important to put an insane man to death, lady?' was the last thing she heard as she made her way down the aisle to the State's table.

. . . 7, 6, 5, 4, 3, 2, 1 . . . breathe.

Until Monday morning, the focus of the trial of the century had been on the murders. On the cold, calculated brutality of the facts. On Jennifer and Emma and Danny and Sophie. On Jennifer and David's marriage. On David Marquette as a vicious psychopath: a cunning, manipulative, abusive and secretive man who wore two different faces – one for the outside world of doctors and patients, friends and colleagues, and a very different one at home behind closed doors. This focus was not just in the courtroom, but also in the press, as news commentators wrapped up the day's events in court, and then speculated about the testimony of tomorrow's witnesses.

But Mel Levenson had changed that focus. At least temporarily. For the past three days, the defense had put on their case. Defense psychiatrists Al Koletis and Margaret Hayes had told the courtroom about David Marquette's bizarre delusions. All about the world he supposedly lived in since he was a teenager. About the voices he heard and the twisted faces he saw. The defense and their witnesses and their doctors had dissected Marquette's childhood, his family life, his marriage and his institutionalized twin brother. Now the topic *du jour* for the international press and around every water cooler in the country was insanity. What it meant legally. What it was medically. And that publicity, in turn, had flooded the streets and the hallways with the curious and the concerned. Legal commentators for CNN and Fox and MSNBC now debated the morality and constitutionality of medicating the mentally ill so that they could stand trial or even be executed, while famous criminal cases of those who'd pled insanity before were discussed ad nauseam on primetime television as the video reels of their trials ran over and over again. Most of those defendants, the legal analysts noted, had failed miserably. David Berkowitz. Jeffrey Dahmer. Ted Bundy. Sirhan Sirhan. Henry Lee Lucas. Charles Manson. John Wayne Gacy. Andrea Yates. Spitting out statistics alongside mug shots, analysts pointed out that insanity was offered as a defense in less than one percent of all criminal proceedings, but was actually successful in only a quarter of those cases where it was pled.

Now was Julia's turn as the State began rebuttal. She hadn't wanted to ever come back to the courtroom. To this circus. After Friday night's strange phone call, she'd spent the weekend again holed up in her apartment with Moose, sorting through her Marquette file boxes, afraid to venture out even if just to get the morning paper, for fear that a hidden reporter might snap her picture and put it on the front page. Then the protesters might be able to find out where she lived. The invisible pressure in her head made it feel as if it were about to explode, and she willed herself not to look behind her at the sea of strange faces who watched her. He could be out there right now. In the rain. In the hallway. In the courtroom. Right behind her with his raspy breathing and creepy laugh. Ironically enough, it was Andrew who'd talked her into coming back, cautioning her about what might happen to the rest of her legal career if she left now and moved back to New York on the next plane out like she wanted to. Andrew's transfer to Rockland was set for this Saturday morning and she was flying up late tomorrow night to be there when it happened. To help him get settled in. No one knew how long he'd be at Rockland. It could be another ten or fifteen years. It could be as little as two. It all depended on his evaluations and what the psychiatrists said. But Julia knew one thing for certain: she wanted to be near her brother. She wanted to support him and his recovery and she wanted to be able to visit every weekend, not just once a month when she could get a decent airfare. He was all she had left, and she was all he had, and she wanted to build a life for him to eventually come home to, be that in two years or twenty. And she wanted it to be far away from Miami.

She looked up from her seat as the door to the hallway opened and watched as David Marquette, flanked on all sides by police and correction officers, was shuffled into the courtroom. The jail had gotten so many death threats after the ME testified last week that, in addition to the standard metal accessories, Marquette now sported an armed entourage and wore a bulletproof vest whenever he stepped foot out of his cell, lest some nut try and take him out with a bullet.

That was what was so funny, Julia thought as Farley took the bench in his usual huff and Jefferson commanded the courtroom to rise. The State would risk the lives of four other men just to keep this one alive long enough so they could kill him themselves. Even Jay Leno had made a joke of it last night on *The Tonight Show*.

What a laugh.

88

'State?' grumbled Farley, leaning back in his throne and gesturing to the witness stand, where Ivonne had just sworn in Christian Barakat. The doctor looked dapper and distinguished in a tailored charcoal suit and silk tie. If this case became a toss-up between the experts, Barakat's dark good looks just might be the deciding factor. At least for the female jurors, every one of which had instantly perked up when he walked through the gallery.

The courtroom sat in silence for maybe thirty seconds, which was thirty seconds too long for Farley. He shot back up in his chair, his eyes narrowing. 'Hello? Ms Valenciano, do you want to actually question this witness, or are we just supposed to look at him all day?'

Julia stared at the notes in front of her. Her lines. She bit the inside of her lip and slowly rose, walking over to the podium without them. She felt the jury's eyes on her, watching her every move. Alice Wade smiled at her.

The jury really likes you . . . they trust *you.*

'Good morning, Doctor. Please state your name and occupation for the record,' she began.

'Christian Barakat. I'm a board-certified forensic psychiatrist in private practice, here in Miami. I have an office over on Brickell in downtown.'

'How long have you been practicing psychiatry?'

'Sixteen years.'

'Please tell the court about your professional qualifications and experience.'

Barakat was a seasoned witness. He'd testified in dozens of high-profile cases and he knew exactly what information he needed to get out on the stand to establish himself as an expert. His impressive list of professional accomplishments alone, including an undergraduate degree from Yale, *summa cum laude*, an MD from the University of Miami Medical School and a prestigious fellowship in psychiatry at NYU, took almost ten minutes to rattle off. Even Alice was drooling.

'Have you had an opportunity to examine the defendant in this case, David Marquette?' Julia finally asked. *Here we go again, Emma.* But Emma wasn't dancing in her bloody Cinderella gown today, demanding justice.

'I have.'

'When was that and under what circumstances?'

She heard Rick's voice, far-off in her head. The day he'd asked her to try this case with him, and then sealed it with a sultry kiss in his car. Now he was the new State Attorney.

'I interviewed Dr David Marquette on two separate occasions,' Barakat replied, taking out his notes and leafing through them. 'The first time was December fifteenth, two thousand five, pursuant to a court order to determine the defendant's competency to stand trial. I then examined him again on January sixth of this year, two thousand six, to determine whether he met the legal definition of insanity when he murdered his wife and three children.'

'Objection!' Mel said, rising. 'The witness is drawing a legal conclusion.'

'Sustained,' said Farley. 'Let's let the jury decide if the defendant is a murderer, shall we?'

Julia looked over at David Marquette, small and unsure, staring vacantly out from his spot at the defense table, oblivious yet again that people were labeling him a murderer.

It was as if he were in his own little world, a million miles away from the courtroom.

This case . . . It's too close, Julia. It can only bring . . . despair.

It wasn't him. Are you listening now, Ms Prosecutor?

I saved them.

She shook the rambling thoughts out of her head and delivered another well-rehearsed line. 'Please tell the court about your evaluation of the defendant on January sixth.'

What was he thinking in that world? Was he frightened? Did he really know that he was facing death? Did he understand yet that he had done something horribly, terribly wrong? Would he be terrified when reality finally came back knocking on his door, demanding entry, like Andy said might happen? Would he be able to live with himself when he discovered the truth?

'It's like you lived this whole other life and then someone pulls the curtain back and says, "Ha, ha! No you didn't! This is your life!" But you don't even recognize it . . . And now, there you are, left with what you've done. All alone. You're left with what you've done. And it doesn't even make any sense. That's when you realize you'd be better off if you'd just stayed crazy, Ju-Ju.'

She suddenly saw her brother, Andrew, in that same chair. Fifteen years ago, in a courtroom filled with photographers and prosecutors and judges pointing at him. Condemning him. A frightened boy with a mop of black curls and pale skin whose mind was trapped in a very different, terrifying world, all alone in a courtroom full of people who hated him. A courtroom full of strangers who didn't understand, who didn't want to understand. At least David Marquette still had his parents sitting in the row behind him. Family that had stuck by his side. Family that recognized what this disease could do. She tried in vain to blink back the tears. There had been no one sitting there for Andrew.

I'm sorry, Ju-Ju. Sorry, sorry, sorry, sorry, sorry . . . I didn't mean for you to hate me. I know what I've done and I wish I didn't do it. I wish I could go back. I wish I wasn't born.

'State? Hello? Is there another question you want to ask the nice doctor or are we done here?' asked Farley, irritated.

She looked around the courtroom. All eyes were on her. Waiting for her next question. She had no idea what Barakat had just said. Or for how long he'd been talking. Or for how long the court had been waiting on her. But it didn't matter anymore, anyway.

She took in a deep breath. 'Doctor, psychiatry isn't an exact science, is it?'

Barakat looked surprised by the question. 'No, it's not,' he answered.

'I mean, there's no test, no *physical* test that can determine if someone is actually suffering from a mental illness, is there?' she asked. 'Like there is for cancer or heart disease?'

'No, there's no blood test or X-ray or MRI used to diagnose mental illness, if that's what you're asking. By its very name, Ms Valenciano, mental illness refers to a sickness in the mind – disturbances in one's thought processes or feelings or emotions, which are not measurable in a blood or urine sample.'

'So how is mental illness diagnosed, then? More particularly, Doctor, how is *schizophrenia* diagnosed?'

'By listening to the patient's complaints, observing their symptoms and their behavior.'

'But basically, by listening to what the patient *tells* you is happening inside their head, correct?'

'Basically, yes.'

She could feel Rick trying to catch her attention behind her at the State's table, but she ignored him. 'Schizophrenia presents with different symptoms in different patients, right,

Dr Barakat? I mean, no two people will ever experience the same exact paranoid delusion?'

'That is correct.'

'And no two people will experience the disease in the same way? For instance, some might have visual hallucinations, others might hear voices, and others might even smell weird smells or have other sensory distortions. Some might withdraw into catatonia. Some might demonstrate a combination of these symptoms. Correct?'

Barakat looked over at Rick. These were leading questions, with the confrontational undertone of a cross-examination. Technically, Mel could object because leading questions were not allowed on direct, but he certainly wasn't going to do that. The courtroom sat in tense, excited silence. 'Yes. It can be a difficult disease to correctly diagnose and treat, but there are hallmark symptoms that a psychiatrist looks for.'

'Did David Marquette have any of those hallmark symptoms?'

'Yes,' Barakat replied slowly. 'Again, he *said* he did. He claimed to be hearing voices, and having visual hallucinations as part of the elaborate paranoid delusion that his family was demonically possessed.'

'But you don't believe he's telling the truth about his experiences?'

'That is correct. I believe he is malingering. As I testified, I believe he's manufacturing the symptoms of schizophrenia to avoid criminal responsibility.'

'But his case, this was a tough call for you, wasn't it?'

Dr Barakat stared at her for a long moment, but Julia didn't even blink. He'd suddenly figured out what she was doing and where she was going. 'Pardon me?' he asked, shifting uncomfortably in his chair.

'Even though David Marquette presented with all of the hallmark symptoms of schizophrenia, symptoms that you admit are not readily faked or manufactured by most malingerers – blunted affect, flattening of emotions, catatonia, severe withdrawal – in the end, it was simply your *gut* that told you he must be malingering, correct?'

There was no way to escape his own words and Barakat knew it. 'Yes, sometimes as a psychiatrist I must rely on my instincts.'

'And if those instincts are wrong?'

'I don't believe they are.'

'You don't believe they are, but there's no medical test to confirm that, now is there? Let me ask you, Doctor, *if* David Marquette is a paranoid schizophrenic, *if* he did suffer the persecutory delusion exactly as he claims to have suffered it, *if* he did actually believe his family was already dead when he stabbed them and bludgeoned them, *if* your gut instinct was wrong, would he be criminally responsible for the murders of his wife and children?'

'Objection!' Rick finally sprang to his feet.

Farley looked at him, his brow furrowed. 'You can't object to your own witness, Mr Bellido. This is direct examination.' He raised his eyebrows, and with the hint of a smile, added, 'Maybe you forgot, but Ms Valenciano is your co-counsel. She's on *your* side.'

Julia pressed on, her back to Rick. 'Yes or no, Dr Barakat. If David Marquette suffered this delusion, if it was all real in his head, would you say he was insane under the definition of Florida law?'

Barakat looked at Rick and then over at the judge, as if he didn't want to say what Julia was about to make him say.

Farley shrugged his shoulders. 'Answer the question, please.'

'Yes. I would have to say that *if* Dr Marquette did in fact act under the delusion he reported, that he would have been unable to discern right from wrong at the time. He would be legally insane.'

A frenzied murmur swelled in the crowd, threatening to explode. Julia finally looked over at Rick and met his icy stare with one of her own.

'I have nothing further,' she said flatly and walked back to her seat.

89

She held her hand up before her and moved quickly past the press that tried to block her exit with their microphones and cameras. Their lights blinded her; their questions made her head spin. She just wanted her fifteen minutes to finally be over.

'*Do you believe that Dr Marquette is being wrongly prosecuted?*'

'*Is David insane? Do you believe he really is insane?*'

'*Do you think the State Attorney is harboring a hidden agenda here? What about Rick Bellido?*'

'*Is this a political persecution?*'

'*Murderer!*' someone shouted out, but Julia didn't turn to see who it was. '*He's a murderer! A butcher! You're the one responsible! You're letting him get away with murder!*'

'*How could you do this?*' another cackled. '*He's the devil!*'

'*Off to hell you'll go!*'

'Order! I want order in this court!' Farley bellowed.

She pushed open the heavy mahogany courtroom doors and hurried into the hallway. The doors slammed shut behind her with a dull thud, silencing the questions and the shouts and the screams, but only for a moment. Panicked, her eyes darted about for a quick escape, but the hallway suddenly looked completely unfamiliar. Like in Wonderland, the many doors that sprouted off were all the same now, and she couldn't remember which one led to where.

Liaison had moved the crazy morning crowd back outside, but people still milled about in front of the courtrooms, rocking baby strollers and waiting for their lawyers or their family on the graffiti-carved wooden benches. They eyed her strangely as she ran to the escalator on shaking legs. At the far end of the hall, she spotted a couple of cameramen, who threw down their coffee cups and reached for their cameras, quickly figuring out that they must have missed something.

She felt physically ill. She would probably lose her job today. No she *would* lose her job. That was a given. She probably would never get another job as a lawyer in this city – Rick and Karyn and Charley Rifkin and Jerry Tigler would make sure of that. She ran her hands through her hair. Or any other city, for that matter. Any evaluation of her job performance over the past three years had just been sabotaged by the last thirty minutes she'd spent in court.

Even with the impending crash and burn of her career, it was a strange sense of calm that began to settle over her as soon as she reached the escalator. 'I didn't raise you to go along with the crowd,' her mother had said to her sternly once, after she skipped class in junior high with a girlfriend. 'I raised you to do what's right. Listen hard enough to the voice inside your head and you'll know just what that is.' *I did it, Momma. I did it.* Although it might not make a difference in the end, even if a jury chose to ignore all that they'd just heard – she'd done what she knew was right today.

'Julia! Wait up!'

She heard Lat call out her name and she moved quicker, pushing past people and rushing down the escalator, two steps at a time. She couldn't look at anyone right now. She couldn't face their questions or their disappointment. Especially his. She got off on two to grab an elevator down to the basement and head off the press, who she knew had their satellite trucks just waiting outside. They were probably looking for her right now as the news spread about what she'd just done in the courtroom.

The cellphone in her purse rang. Her heart skipped a beat. She reached down and grabbed it with trembling hands. Maybe it was Rick, calling her to fire her himself before she even cleared the building. Or maybe Lat looking to see where she'd gone. Or Friday night's protester calling to maybe comment on what a fine job she'd just done. Or the hecklers from the court to call her a murderer and damn her to hell. But it was a 212 exchange.

'Hello?' she whispered, as she waited with the crowd, looking over her shoulder for a sign of Lat or a reporter.

'Ms Valenciano? It's Mary Zlocki at Kirby Forensic.'

'Hello, Mary. I'm just getting out of court.' She moved onto the elevator and hit the basement button.

'It's about your brother,' Mary continued.

'Yes. I'm, I'm coming up on Saturday. I'll be there for his transfer.' The line grew thick with static as a bunch of people got off on one. Julia pressed herself up against the far side of the car, out of the direct line of sight of anyone looking for her in the lobby. 'Look, I'm in an elevator, Mary. I may lose you.'

The people around her shot her an annoyed look as the doors closed again. Everyone had a cellphone nowadays, but no one ever seemed to like it when you actually used yours in public.

'I need to speak with you about Andrew,' Mary repeated. Then there was silence.

Shit. 'Mary? Mary? Are you there?' she asked softly. The doors opened into the dark basement garage finally and Julia stepped out alone. 'Mary?'

'Ms Valenciano?' said a stern voice over the line that Julia immediately recognized belonged to Dr Mynks. Mary was gone. She headed for the glimpse of light and the ramp that led back up to 13th. 'This is Dr Mynks, Ms Valenciano. I have to speak with you about Andrew.'

'I just told Mary, Dr Mynks. I'll definitely be there Saturday. My plane comes—'

'Ms Valenciano,' the doctor interrupted in a soft, but firm voice, 'Andrew is dead.'

Julia dropped the phone, watching it shatter on the garage floor. And beneath the circus that was David Marquette's lynching, she began to scream.

90

She sat on the same ripped vinyl bench, staring at the same *People* magazine on the chipped end table that she had almost three months before. How different life was now. She looked around the waiting room, empty once again on a Saturday morning.

The guards in the bulletproof booth wouldn't even look at her, once they figured out why she was here. 'That's Cirto's sister,' had quickly spread among the MH Police, like the panic of an infectious disease. And she was the leper.

The door next to the booth opened and Dr Mynks suddenly appeared. Julia gathered her purse and rose to follow him back to his office, but he stepped into the reception area, letting the door close behind him this time. In his hand he held a large brown paper bag, like one that you might get at a supermarket. It was clear that their meeting was going to take place here.

'Ms Valenciano,' he began in that same soft, yet cold and impersonal voice he had used on the phone. 'On behalf of the staff here at Kirby, allow me to say that we are sorry for your loss. This is a tragedy and we will, of course, be looking into all the circumstances surrounding your brother's death.' He handed her the bag. 'The nurses on Andrew's ward thought you would like to have this. These were his belongings. Most of it is just clothing, but there are some drawings he was keeping on his wall, as well as a journal he was writing, his wallet and a high-school graduation ring. All the things he came in here with.'

Dr Mynks's words were spoken so quickly and so matter-of-factly that Julia knew he didn't mean them. He didn't mean any of them. For him, Andrew Cirto's death wasn't a tragedy; it was simply a statistic. An unfortunate statistic that had unfortunately happened on *his* watch, and would now be a blemish on *his* record. To him, Andy was a patient number, an inmate, a murderer, and his death was otherwise insignificant. She was waiting for Mynks to look down at his watch in annoyance. Maybe tap his foot impatiently just to give her the hint to get lost.

She took the bag, which felt too light to contain all of someone's worldly belongings, and stood there for a few moments, not sure what to do. Not ready to leave. Not ready for any of this to be real. 'What happened?' she finally managed in a squeaky voice that sounded nothing like her own, as she looked around the waiting room. She felt the guards watching them. She looked and saw one of them was laughing.

Dr Mynks didn't even blink. 'Suicide. Like I told you on the phone, Ms Valenciano.'

She didn't look away. She didn't nod. She didn't shake her head. She just stood there with that profoundly blank look on her face until he finished.

'He hung himself. In the shower,' he finally added. *Now* he looked at his watch. 'Look, once again, I am sorry for your loss, but depression is a byproduct – for lack of a better word – of schizophrenia. Your brother had come to terms with his illness and, eventually, the crimes that he'd committed. That was one of the reasons he was being transferred to Rockland. Sometimes, unfortunately, those realizations are just too overwhelming for a person to emotionally handle. Once the medication has worked its magic many patients cannot deal emotionally with the crimes they committed when they were ill. And then with all the recent changes in Andrew's life . . .' His voice trailed off. He held up his hand in front of him. 'I am not saying that's the reason Andrew took his own life. There was no note and he told no one what he was going to do, so this is all, of course, conjecture.'

There was nothing else to say. Dr Mynks had said it all without saying a thing. Julia had been the recent change in Andrew's life. The reminder from his past that he could not cope with.

'Now, if you'll excuse me,' he started to say, but Julia didn't hear the rest. She'd already turned, and with all of Andrew's belongings clutched tightly in her hand, she headed back out the security doors and into the cold New York City sunshine.

91

The Barnes and Sorrentino Funeral Home on the corner of McKinley Street and Hempstead Avenue was still painted that same unremarkable yellow that she remembered. Set slightly back from the road by a small patch of lawn, blooming flower beds lined a cement walkway that led to a dark wood front door. Julia had biked past it maybe a million times while she was growing up, on her way to the library or the bagel store, and she'd always thought it was a doctor or dentist's office. It wasn't until her parents were waked there that she realized it was a funeral home.

A light drizzle had begun to fall and she stood for a moment outside in the empty parking lot next to her rental car as memories rushed her. The gas station on the corner she and Andy would fill their bikes up with air at had closed, but the Venus Café was still across the street. Every Sunday after church her dad would take the family there for brunch and the best pancakes Julia had ever tasted. In fact, she'd had them the last time she was here in West Hempstead, when Nora and Jimmy had taken everyone in the family for a bite to eat in between the afternoon and evening wake services for her parents. She hadn't had pancakes since.

Come on, Julia, honey. We can't be late now. People will be waiting.

An older lady with a stack of teased snow-white hair and ruby lips greeted her as soon as she opened the door, appearing seemingly out of nowhere. 'Oh my,' she said, looking past Julia at the parking lot behind her as the door closed. 'Looks like it's starting to rain again. Maybe that means spring is coming soon.' She smiled. 'Can I help you?'

Julia looked around the dark lobby. 'I called yesterday. I'm . . . My name is Julia Cirto. I called about my brother, Andrew Cirto.'

'Yes. I'm terribly sorry for your loss. I'm Evelyn. Why don't you come into my office?'

Julia followed Evelyn past a gas-burning fireplace and down the worn red-carpeted hall. What an odd color for a funeral home, she thought. A red carpet. Maybe it was meant to be symbolic. A grand exit from life. *You, too, were a somebody!* Inside a modest office, Julia took a seat in one of the two paisley wing chairs that were posed perfectly in front of an antique desk. Eveyln took the other.

'We received the body today from the Medical Examiner's Office in New York County. We just needed to meet with you to . . .' Evelyn hesitated for a second, searching for, Julia assumed, the most delicate word possible, '. . . go over a few things. We have a catalogue that you can look through, or we have—'

Julia shook her head. 'I, I can't afford much, Evelyn. There was no insurance, and my brother didn't, well, he didn't have any money. But I want him to have something nice. I can spend about five thousand dollars. Can you pick something nice for me?' She didn't want to see all the prettier caskets she could have picked, or all the extras she could have had. Just take her money and get this done. She wanted to believe Andy had the best.

Evelyn nodded. She reached over and lightly touched Julia's knee. 'Of course. We'll handle everything.' She paused for a moment. 'I'm curious. You're from Florida, and your brother died in Manhattan. Why did you choose Barnes and Sorrentino? Are there other relatives here in West

Hempstead or on the Island? Is there any bulletin you would like us to notify?'

Julia looked around the tiny office. One small window faced the parking lot. She could see that the rain was coming down harder now, forming deep puddles on the uneven asphalt. She remembered trick-or-treating up the block, and walking to Echo Park Pool. 'I used to live in West Hempstead. My brother and I both did. We grew up here, a couple of blocks away, on Maple. It was the only funeral home I knew,' she said absently. She looked down at her lap. 'My parents both had their services here.'

'Oh my,' said Eveyln. 'When was that?'

Julia shook her head. 'A long time ago,' was all she offered.

'Oh,' Evelyn said again. 'Well, we'll make sure that everything is taken care of. Now, about the wake. When would you like to have the services, over one day or two?'

'No, I don't need a wake. There's just me,' she replied quickly, her voice a whisper. 'There won't be anyone else. No one here knows my brother anymore.'

'Oh,' said Evelyn again. She looked out the door down the hall. 'I'm not so sure about that. We did get a flower delivery today. We put them in Chapel A.'

'That must have been mine.' She bit her lip. 'Everyone deserves flowers, Evelyn.'

'Okay,' replied Evelyn, slowly. She rose from her seat. 'Let me show you the room, then, for the service, if you decide to have it here.'

'We're Catholic. I think I'm going to have it at St Thomas.'

They walked down the hall in silence. Outside the room designated as Chapel A, a black magnetic board encased in glass read 'Andrew J. Cirto' in small, white letters. In two days or so, Julia knew the letters would be switched around to read someone else's name. Evelyn opened one of the double doors and Julia closed her eyes.

You don't have to look if you don't want to, Munch. The caskets will be closed.

Please, don't honey. Don't look, little one. That's something you don't need to see. You don't want to remember her that way.

'As you can see, it was a rather large delivery. We had to put them all in here,' Evelyn said.

Julia opened her eyes. The room was filled with hundreds and hundreds of white peonies.

92

The massive church was eerily quiet on Monday morning. Just the patter of rain slapping against the stained-glass windows could be heard echoing across the marble and through the towering stone-columned halls. Julia sat by herself in the front pew. Directly in front of her, draped in a white cloth and the funeral spray she'd ordered, was Andrew's casket, propped on a metal transport gurney. The white peonies from the funeral home filled the altar. She hoped Evelyn had selected a nice casket. She hoped it was lined with satin and maybe a soft pillow. She hoped he looked peaceful inside.

You don't have to look if you don't want to. The casket will be closed.

And so she hadn't.

The parish of St Thomas the Apostle ran two churches in West Hempstead – the main church and the much smaller chapel on the other side of town by the Southern State Parkway. Her dad had always liked the chapel, so that was where her family usually went on Sunday mornings when she was a kid. But if given the choice, Julia herself always liked the main church. Especially for midnight Mass on Christmas Eve. Besides her parents' funerals, that was one of the only times she could remember the huge church being filled to capacity, with every row filled and spilling out into the vestibule and onto the front steps. The choir would sing in the loft above, accompanied by the old organ and the folk guitars. Most of the choir members were the older brothers and sisters of her classmates at St Thomas's elementary school next door – juniors and seniors at Sacred Heart Academy or Chaminade High School in Mineola. Julia could remember there was a time when she'd wanted to join the choir, too.

The door to the sacristy opened and a young priest walked out, his heels softly clicking on the polished marble floor. He fashioned a long stole around his neck and kissed it, genuflecting in front of the altar. He looked down the center aisle of the empty church. The two pallbearers from Barnes and Sorrentino stood in the far back by the doors, off to a side hall. 'Do you want me to wait a little bit longer?' Father Tom asked, softly. He looked like a young, balding George Clooney.

Julia shook her head. She didn't look behind her. She didn't need to. 'No, Father.'

Aunt Nora had hung the phone up on her last night, the second she mentioned Andy's name. She hadn't even gotten to tell her he'd died. The line had stayed busy after that, all night long. Besides her and Uncle Jimmy, there was no one else to call. There would be no one else who even cared.

In her hand she held the folded-up drawing that Andrew had almost finished sketching. She'd found it in the paper bag of belongings that Dr Mynks had given her. It was a picture of her. Sitting at the table in the visiting room, smiling, framed by stars and moons.

'Okay, then,' Father Tom said. 'I suppose this will be very intimate.' He smiled a gentle smile and, instead of moving behind the pulpit, he stepped down off the altar and walked over to where she sat, sliding into the pew right beside her. To her surprise, he found her hand and held it softly in his. 'We are here today to say goodbye to Andrew Cirto, a loving son and brother,' he began in a mild voice that matched his smile and his touch. 'A lost soul who will be missed by all who knew him, by his family and, most of all, by his sister.'

Julia did not correct him. She bowed her head and listened while Father Tom held her hand and went on for ten minutes about all the things Julia had told him last night when they met over coffee at the rectory. About ice-skating with Andy in Hall's Pond Park, and movie nights at the Elmont Theater with their mom. About how it was Andrew who always held her head over the toilet whenever she threw up, and who shared his sandwich at school when she had forgotten hers – even though that meant being made fun of by the older kids. About how he'd shoved the first boy who had said something nasty to her. About how he would wait for her when she missed the bus at school so they could walk home together. About what a great listener he was and what a great friend he had been. All about the gentle, misunderstood man with the sheepish grin of a boy that she had just come to know again after too long of an absence. And while she listened, she was relieved to hear that Father Tom never once mentioned that Andrew was a murderer. Or a crazy. Or sick.

'Let us now pray,' Father Tom said and Julia got down on her knees and prayed hard to a God she thought was cruel sometimes. A God she had long stopped believing in. A God who now beckoned her back with his soft whispers. She closed her eyes and saw Andrew's face as she wanted to always remember it, before the sickness sucked the life out of him. Swinging a baseball bat with a smile at sixteen. The tears slipped out of her eyes as Father Tom led an empty church in prayer.

'Hail Mary, full of Grace,' he began softly. 'The Lord is with thee. Blessed art thou amongst women, and blessed is the fruit of thy womb, Jesus.'

'Holy Mary, Mother of God, pray for us sinners,' Julia said, joining him. 'Now, and at the hour of our death.' She cast her eyes up to the Sanctuary, to the crucifix suspended above the altar. She saw Jesus smile down at her. He was whispering the words along with her.

'Amen,' she whispered back.

93

A Home Sweet Home mat greeted visitors outside her front door on the second-floor landing; a wreath of dried flowers blocked the peephole. He'd have to talk to her about that. That wasn't safe. Lat rang the bell again and waited, tapping his palm impatiently against the door.

'Julia,' he said in a quiet voice, 'It's me, Lat. Come on, I know you're home.'

Still no answer. Then he started to knock. Hard. A few dried petals fluttered to the cement floor.

'Listen, I saw your car across the street. I know you're in. I need to talk to you. Come on, open up.'

Still nothing. He walked back down the stairs a bit to see the window in her apartment that faced the parking lot. He didn't see any lights on whatsoever. And that's when John Latarrino started to worry. He'd checked JetBlue and knew she'd come back on her flight this afternoon. Her car was parked across the street in another apartment-complex lot, but she wasn't answering her phone and she wasn't answering her door. She'd been acting so strange lately, and after what he'd found out this past week, he knew that anything was possible. Even the worst anything.

'Julia,' he said again, louder this time. To hell with her neighbors. He banged on the door now. He hoped his voice sounded steady, devoid of the raw fear that he now felt gripping his belly. Graphic, horrifying images popped into his head and he pushed them aside. 'I'm going to take the door if you don't open—' he started, but the knob suddenly twisted in his hand.

She stood in the front hall of her pitch-black apartment. The moonlight that filtered in through the living-room windows behind her backlit her petite frame in silhouette. He couldn't make out the features of her face.

'You scared me,' Lat said, feeling the relief wash over him.

She said nothing and she didn't move.

'Julia,' Lat said, ignoring her body language and instead moving past her, into the dark apartment. He looked around the living room. He could make out the shadows of clothes and boxes that were strewn everywhere. 'Are you okay?' he asked after a moment, reaching out to touch her shoulder.

She pulled away from his touch. 'You checked up on me.'

He took a deep breath and looked straight at her. God, he wished he could see her eyes. Did she hate him? Maybe he shouldn't have sent the flowers.

'Yes. I checked up on you,' he said finally, because there was nothing else he could say. He looked around the hall for a light switch. 'Why are you sitting in the dark? Where are the lights in this place? 'Cause we have to talk—'

'I don't want the lights on and I don't want to talk. I want you to go. That's what I want.'

'Julia, I'm sorry about your brother. I'm really sorry. I wish you had told me—'

'Told you what?'

'Told me about him.'

'I don't know exactly what you know, Lat, so I don't know what it is you'd wished I'd told you. That my brother was a murderer but he couldn't help himself? That he was just sick and inside he was really a great person and a warm human being who was misunderstood by everyone, including me?' She turned her head away, crying.

'I want to see you, Julia. Where the hell are the lights?' That feeling of panic was grabbing at his throat once again.

She didn't want him to see her like this. When things were fracturing right in front of her, slipping out of reach. 'No, just go, please,' she pleaded.

He grasped her hand in his and moved her further into the apartment with him, closing the door behind him with his foot. He felt along the wall until his fingers finally found a switch. A living-room light snapped on.

She had her head down, her long black hair draped over her face. Her whole body was shaking, and he knew she was trying to control the sobs. He didn't know exactly what to say, but he knew bullshit wouldn't work on her.

'Listen, Julia, I've read the newspaper articles. I ... I talked to the DA in New York. He read me the file. I know what happened to your mom and dad that night.' He paused, wondering how far he should go. 'Dr Mynks told me about Andy. And I'm sorry, Julia. I'm so sorry for your loss – your losses.' He blew out another breath and looked around the apartment. He wasn't very good at these things. He sucked at funerals and awkward moments. 'You were acting really strange. Things weren't adding up and then, well, you burned Dr Barakat in court and ... you just took off in the middle of trial. And you haven't been back. It all makes sense now ... I just ... Why didn't you tell me? Maybe I could've done something.'

She turned again toward the wall, wiping her eyes with the palms of her hands. 'What is it you wanted me to tell you? And when? Maybe over a motorcycle ride on the beach I could whisper in your ear that my brother's a schizophrenic? Oh, and by the way, he killed my family one night while I was at a sleepover? What do you really think you would have done with that information, Lat? But that's not all. There's more to the story,' she said, her voice rising with anger. 'See, it wasn't actually his fault because he was *made* that way.'

'What are you talking about?'

'That wasn't in the court file, Lat? It *must* have been. 'Cause it turns out my dad was sick, too. And my grandfather, we think. We *think*, 'cause no one wants to talk about these things. No one should've ever thought about having a kid. They knew what it was like. My mother, she knew, too. She *watched* him struggle with it. They both knew hell, right here on earth. My dad lived it.' She struggled to find her breath, backing up further against the wall, 'They knew the odds, that we could get it. Like blond hair or a cleft chin. They knew they could *give* it to us. But they did it anyway. They still had us, Lat. It was the most selfish thing in the world they could have done – to bring us into it. But they did it anyway . . .'

He moved toward her. 'Julia . . .'

But she held her arms up in front of her, keeping him away. 'I don't want your pity, John. I don't want anyone's pity. No, no, no, no. No pity.'

'Is that why you never said anything?' he said, his voice rising in frustration. 'You're so damn strong you think you can handle all this alone? You're gonna prove yourself to everyone watching? That you can take on bad judges, and you can take on the criminals and you can take on the system? This case – Marquette – it's so close . . . I can see that now. It's unreasonable to think it wouldn't have gotten to you.'

'I read the paper this morning on the plane. The *New York Post*. A little girl watched her momma's boyfriend kill her and then kill himself. Then this little girl, she sat in the house for two days next to the bodies before someone finally came and rang the bell and found her. And I felt bad, Lat. I felt *pity* for her – for what her life is now, and for what it will be like for her, growing up, so different from everyone else. But tomorrow there'll be another tragedy to read about. Maybe it will even be worse. And in a week or two, I'll forget all about the little girl who was found with the dead bodies. Right? I mean, we all do. We forget about the tragedies that are bad enough to make the paper. There's too many of them, and they always happen to someone else, don't they?

'But the headline makers, you know, they grow up, John. They ride the bus next to you, they work in the next cubicle over. They're people whose tragedies define who they are to everyone who meets them. You're not the nice girl in algebra anymore – you're the girl whose parents were murdered by her crazy brother. You're not the secretary with the terrific laugh – you're the chick whose family died in a house fire. And I'm . . . I'm just so tired of being defined. I'm tired of being different. Of being the girl in the headlines.'

'Julia . . .'

'So I don't tell anyone, and maybe I do try and prove myself everyday. Maybe I have to. Prove that I can get through life, that I won't be swallowed up by my tragedy, by memories that never, ever go away, no matter how much I wish them or lie about them.'

He was next to her now, his arms wrapped around her shaking body. She tried to break out, but he just held her until the fight was finally gone and she collapsed crying against his chest. He smoothed her hair back off her face, stroking it, his fingers running against her wet cheek and down her neck.

A long, long while passed until he finally spoke. 'I still think you're the hot prosecutor with the great laugh and the nice chest,' he whispered softly in her ear.

He felt her body shake up against his and he knew she was laughing. He moved his hand gently under her chin, cupping it in his hand. She tried to move away, not wanting him to look at her. 'Sshh, sshh,' he said, bringing her face up toward his own.

Her fiery green eyes were red and swollen. She must have been crying for days. Longer, maybe. He wiped her cheeks with his thumbs. Funny, she looked so beautiful. So defiant. So vulnerable. So strong. So scared. He bent down, close to her face.

'You said no rebounds,' she whispered. But she didn't move away.

'This,' he said, pulling her even closer to him, '*this* is no rebound.' Then he did what his body and soul had ached to do for so long, and he kissed her.

I Felt a Cleaving in my Mind

I felt a Cleaving in my Mind –
As if my Brain had split –
I tried to match it – Seam by Seam –
But could not make it fit

The thought behind, I strove to join
Unto the thought before –
But Sequence raveled out of Sound
Like Balls – upon a Floor.

Emily Dickinson

94

'Mr Bellido?' Farley grumbled as he swept to the bench on Tuesday morning. Jefferson had once again missed his cue but this time the judge didn't care. He waved off the bailiff and motioned for the packed courtroom to sit. He was already three days past his promise and his deadline, and only four short days away from missing his boat to the Caribbean. The antics and delays of the past few days had worn him thin. 'Are you ready to proceed with closing?'

'I am, Your Honor,' said Rick, as he rose from his seat at the State's table. He carefully buttoned his jacket and walked over to the jury box. 'David Marquette is a murderer. On October eighth, two thousand five, at approximately four thirty a.m., the man who had taken an oath to save lives, the man who had made a promise to love, honor and cherish his wife and their children, grabbed a baseball bat and crept into the bedroom where his wife, Jennifer, slept peacefully in their bed. Then he struck her over the head with that bat so forcefully, she was *probably* rendered unconscious after the first blow. I stress probably, ladies and gentlemen, because the ME can't say for certain and we don't really know. We all *hope* that she was, though. Because that's when Dr David Marquette took out his knife and he stabbed her. Not once. Not twice, but *thirty-seven times.* Over and over and over again. With such force, he went through her body and into the mattress.' He paused again for a long moment, not taking his eyes off Marquette, who still sat expressionless. 'Make no mistake, ladies and gentlemen of the jury – he *is* a murderer.'

Rick walked slowly over to where the smiling portraits of the Marquette victims had been mounted on easels across from the jury box. Beside each portrait was a graphic crime-scene photo of each victim. He knew that the jury hated looking at the pictures. He had watched them cringe when he had first introduced them at trial. Even for him, they were disturbing and difficult to look at, and he knew that particularly the women wanted to turn away. But they could not. He would not let them. Like a skilled hypnotist, he held them there – fast in their seats while he took them back in time.

'David Marquette then left his wife, dead on their bed in the master bedroom, and he walked down the hall to the rooms where his three children lay sleeping. Little Danny, baby Sophie, big-girl Emma. And with that same bloodied baseball bat and that same knife, he *intended* to deliver that very same fate to his own small children.

'But something went wrong. Something David Marquette had not anticipated, ladies and gentlemen. His daughter woke up. What woke her, we will never know – maybe it was the cry of the baby or the screams of her brother – but she woke up and she found Danny, either dead or dying in his bed. And that little girl – who was all of six – was smart enough to call nine-one-one for help. Smart enough to make sure she named the man who would go on to murder her with that knife. "Oh no, no," we know she cried out in terror when he called her name in that dark bedroom. "No, Daddy!" was what she said.'

Rick stepped aside and let the jury look over at the defendant. He let them take the image he had so artfully and vividly painted for them and put the expressionless man with the new suit just ten feet across from them into the disturbing picture. The courtroom was completely still. It was almost as if people were afraid to breathe, lest they miss something.

'That's when the plans changed, ladies and gentlemen,' he continued. 'That's when David Marquette – who had been smart enough to plan his own alibi – realized there would be no escape back to a comfy hotel room in Disney World, where he could feign surprise and shock in the morning when someone called with the horrible news about his family. That's when David Marquette needed to think of a way out. And he needed to think fast, because he now knew that within a matter of minutes the police would be knocking on his front door downstairs. The plans *had* to change.' He paused. 'There was someone else. An intruder.

'He had driven down from Orlando earlier that night to be with his family because he missed them so. He had been away for a couple of days already at this medical conference and he just couldn't wait another night to spend time with Jennifer, to hold the baby and kiss the kids. Because he was such a great father, a great husband, just like everybody always said he was. One of the many faces we know David Marquette wore.

'At four thirty in the morning, he was in the bathroom taking a shower, getting ready to head back up to his conference, when his wife – his beautiful wife, Jennifer – was murdered in her sleep by an intruder. A would-be rapist. An intruder, or maybe even intruders for all he knew, who then took a bat and a knife and slaughtered his whole family, like Charles Manson. He stepped out of the bathroom into a dark bedroom to find his wife dead, and his daughter, Emma, screaming his name. He ran to her room, *to her aid*, surprising this intruder, and that's when he had been attacked himself, stabbed brutally in the stomach.

'The reason he wasn't stabbed thirty-seven times, like his

wife, or twenty times, like his daughter? The reason he was still alive? The intruder didn't have the time. Thanks to Emma, he knew the police were coming now, and he fled out into the night, leaving his murder weapon behind, carefully placed right in our poor, destroyed defendant's stomach. Carefully, I say, because, as you all know, the very knife that had butchered David Marquette's entire family somehow missed all of his vital organs. Conveniently, loaded with only the good doctor's prints, because, of course, this intruder must have worn gloves. It was a horrible, dramatic wound that the defendant knew would bleed a lot and would seem serious and life-threatening on scene, but wouldn't be if you knew how to place it – if you'd had the surgical training – if you got the proper medical attention right away. Medical training, of course, we know David Marquette did have. Medical attention he knew was on the way, because he'd heard his daughter make that call.'

The jury stared at David Marquette. One woman shook her head and looked down at her lap, crying.

'A perfect back-up plan, wasn't it, folks?' Rick continued. 'Not so bad for thinking on the spot. For someone who had only minutes to rinse off all his family's blood in the shower and then delicately perform surgery on himself with the very same murder weapon. Not bad at all. In fact, some might say thought processes made under such pressure were brilliant, not disorganized. Cunning, not illogical. Maybe even genius. But there was one problem. Dr David Marquette had forgotten one minor detail in that perfect plan, or we might not be here today as he enjoyed the proceeds of his wife's multi-million-dollar life insurance policy and a life free of kids and responsibilities. Free to do what he wants, when he wants, with any one of the many girlfriends colleagues have testified he'd been fond of entertaining.'

Rick paused again. 'He forgot to unset the alarm, ladies and gentlemen.'

The courtroom murmured.

'Objection!' Mel Levenson said, rising to his feet. He knew the way this was turning out. He could smell it in the courtroom, the change in the air. He had to break the spell. 'This is all conjecture, Your Honor.'

'This is closing argument. Overruled,' said Farley, motioning with his hand for Mel to sit back down.

'The damn alarm,' Rick continued, shaking his head. 'Out of habit, David Marquette had unset it and then reset it when he snuck home that night. When he came home to murder his family and begin his new life. But you know what they say about the best-laid plans . . .

'When David Marquette lay on the floor of his bathroom – the knife already in his stomach, the plan already in motion – he heard the alarm go off as the officers made entry into his house. As he listened to them race up the stairs and scream at the sight of the dead bodies of his wife and three children – he was smart enough to realize that there had to be some other explanation. The plans had to change once again.

'So in a hospital bed in Jackson Memorial, he turned to the familiar. The only disease that could offer an explanation for the unimaginable carnage he could no longer deny he had committed. Schizophrenia. His own identical twin suffers from it. Mimicking the bizarre symptoms he had watched unfold in a mirror image of himself over the years would not be that difficult a task. Especially not when you're a doctor and you've done a rotation on a psych ward. Let's face it, ladies and gentlemen, Dr David Marquette knew the symptoms to manifest, the voices to offer up to the psychiatrists that would examine him. He knew enough not to claim it was little green men he saw, but the devil. He knew enough to flatten his emotions, to feign catatonia. He even knew how to compensate for the physical and mental effects of the antipsychotic drugs they would be sure to give him. The stint he'd done in a private rehab for *cocaine psychosis* during his second year in college could now be considered his first misdiagnosed psychotic "break." The young man whom a caseworker had noted during that *very stay* as, and I quote, "manipulative and deceitful, superficial in thought and speech, with egocentric and grandiose ideals that are not grounded in current reality". The man who had demonstrated, as far back as fifteen years ago, evidence of a psychopathic personality, was really a misdiagnosed schizophrenic. Just like his twin brother.

'It was this horrible disease that had corrupted his brain with sick thoughts. That had made him believe his family would be forever damned if he did not save their souls. That had made him try to kill himself, to save himself from possession, too. That knife wound was a half-hearted attempt at *hara-kiri*, he wants us to believe. A horrible suicide attempt so that he could join his family in the hereafter.

'Don't buy it, ladies and gentlemen. Don't believe any of it. Dr Barakat, a forensic psychiatrist with sixteen years of experience in the field, didn't. Neither did Dr Hindlin. See the cunning pattern of behavior. See the brilliant thought processes that are actually involved here.' He looked over at the defendant once again. 'Truly brilliant, I have to admit.' But Marquette did not look up.

Rick turned back to face the jury. He waited a few moments until all of their eyes were focused back on him. Even the criers. 'David Marquette has fooled some people with his story and his act, but he hasn't fooled us all. The facts are the facts. They speak for themselves, and he can't get out of them. David Marquette hasn't fooled the seasoned homicide detectives or the State's psychiatrists, and he hasn't fooled me. Don't let him fool you. He's not a man whose illness manipulated him to commit murder; he's a man who's using an illness to manipulate the system into exonerating him. He's not a schizophrenic, ladies and gentlemen. He's a cold-blooded psychopath. And he needs to pay for what he's done.'

95

The courtroom was completely quiet as Rick sat down by himself at the State's table, which everyone could notice had a conspicuously empty seat at it. Her absence this morning had been the talk of all the papers, all the tabloids, all the talk shows, all the news programs. All morning, all over the world.

After the hush of stunned silence finally broke into excited whispers, Farley declared it was time for lunch and recessed court till 2 p.m.

Julia sat on her living-room couch chewing on what remained of her thumbnail, in her pajamas and slippers. She stared blankly at the TV as the commentators quickly took to the air to analyze what Rick Bellido had said, and what it meant, and what the jury must be thinking, and what this must mean for the defense. The consensus among all, she saw as she flipped through the channels, was that Rick had delivered a brilliant closing argument.

As she watched, one by one, the parade of well-coiffed, smiling analysts disparaged her name, seemingly disregarding everything that had transpired just last week. Rick had exacted his revenge on her. He had discredited her and her direct exam of Barakat as much as he could without discrediting his case. She was the inexperienced, naïve fool here.

She finally walked into the kitchen and made herself a pot of coffee for lunch. She opened another pack of cigarettes and sat at the kitchen table, her head buried in her hands.

And she didn't answer the phone, no matter how many times it rang.

96

At 61 years of age, 6'2" and 310 pounds, Mel Levenson might not be a match for Rick Bellido's looks or his suave Spanish charm in a courtroom, but he certainly had more experience with a jury. Thirty-six years of it. And that was a hell of a lot more than what Bellido and his Cupcake of the Month had. He rose slowly from his seat and lumbered over to the jury. He could tell from the jurors' faces – those that would look at him, anyways – that he was down a point or two. So he knew he'd better make every word count if there was any hope of keeping his client off of death row.

'I've been doing this a long time, folks,' Mel began with a smile in a friendly, conversational tone. 'A long time. And I always like to remind the jury that whatever the prosecutor or I say in closing arguments is not evidence. No matter how we say it, no matter what we say, and no matter how convinced we may look while we're saying it. Closing arguments are just an opportunity for the State and the defense to sum up the case, and what *they* think the evidence presented during the trial. But it's not evidence. That's not always easy to remember when you have someone as well-dressed and good-looking and convincing as Mr Bellido up here telling you how it is you should see things,' he said, throwing his smile in the direction of the State's table. The courtroom tittered and a couple of female jurors looked sheepishly down at their shoes for a moment.

'The prosecutor has offered us a, to use his own term, "brilliant" theory of the case to consider. But it's his theory, and it's just that — a *theory*. It's what *he* thinks the evidence showed, not what it did. And Mr Bellido has a very active imagination. He has concocted a far-off convoluted tale — three different tales, actually — of what he says my client *really* meant to do that night. But he's no psychic. He's no mindreader, folks. And none of this theory he's expounded is grounded in any facts that we heard here during this trial. Remember that. He's built you a huge castle out of nothing but buckets and buckets of sloppy mud, but it has no factual foundation and so it doesn't stand up. It can't be supported. His story doesn't work.'

He rested his big hands casually against the railing. For such a large man, he displayed a very laid-back, down-to-earth, intimate persona. 'The law in Florida is this, plain and simple: if, at the time he committed the crime charged, the defendant suffered from a mental infirmity or disease, and because of this condition, either he didn't know what he was doing, or he didn't know what he was doing was wrong, then he is legally insane. It's really as simple as that. And,' Mel said, holding up a finger and suspending the moment, 'it doesn't matter if he was sane last year or last night, or even if he is sane right now as we look at him — what only matters is if he was legally sane at the moment he committed the crime. That's all.' He paused for a long moment as everyone looked over at the defense table.

'Mr Bellido doesn't want you to believe my client is a paranoid schizophrenic. He doesn't want you to believe he hears voices in his head, or that he has disorganized thoughts, or that he suffers from paranoid delusions. He doesn't want you to believe that the voices — which never let up, ladies and gentlemen, as Dr Koletis and Dr Hayes both testified — that these voices told David his family was possessed by demonic spirits. He doesn't want you to believe that these voices told him he was not killing his wife and children, but that he was saving their souls. Saving their souls from a damned eternal existence in hell. Mr Bellido doesn't want you to believe that in David's mind – in David's reality – he did not know what he was doing was wrong, because in this reality, his wife and children were already dead. He wasn't killing them – he was exorcizing the devil that possessed the shell of their dead bodies. The devil that was soon to consume his soul as well. Then no one would be left to save his family. And no matter what a prosecutor or a seasoned homicide detective or even his own attorney might tell him, David knows this was true. There is absolutely no reasoning with him, even if you could reach him, because *that is David's reality*. And he knows he did the right thing. And, I'll tell you this much folks, that in his reality – he *did* do the right thing!' He slapped the railing and turned around to face the rest of the courtroom. It was as if he were addressing not just the twelve-member panel, but the world.

'And it's easy to not believe, isn't it? It's easy to question how could someone actually think these crazy things. So, folks, I want you to imagine for a moment you are in the delusion that David was living with. And then I want you to imagine it's not a delusion. That it's *really* happening. I want you to imagine what it's like to constantly hear different voices chattering and screaming and whispering away in your head. Voices that sound just as real, to you, as I do or Judge Farley or Mr Bellido does. Voices that talk to you constantly, even when you're sleeping. And you don't know that you're ill, folks. You can't recognize something's wrong because that's part of the disease, after all. So close your eyes, if you would, and imagine the terror that David lives with every day.'

'Objection!' said Rick, rising to his feet as the jury members closed their eyes. 'This is a Golden Rule violation. He's asking the jury to place themselves in the position of the defendant!'

'I'm asking them to step into a delusion and imagine that that is real. I'm not asking them to imagine they are the defendant.'

'Mr Levenson is splitting hairs,' barked Rick.

Farley raised a skeptical white eyebrow. 'Maybe. But he makes a good argument. Overruled.'

'The voices whispered to him – all day, all night, every day, every night – that his children were slowly being possessed by Satan,' Mel continued. 'He *saw* the signs of possession – the mark of the beast – in the growths on their skin and head. He *saw* the signs of the devil's presence in the way they chewed their food, and grasped at their toys. He *saw* the signs when his wife cut her finger on a kitchen knife, but it didn't bleed.' Mel paused. He needed to tread cautiously, or else risk disparaging the reputation of the victim. 'We know from the semen stain on her shirt, that Jennifer had engaged in relations with someone else,' he said softly. 'But to David her infidelity was twisted into a sign that his wife was sleeping with the devil himself. It was these signs that confirmed for him what the voices had been saying all along.

'Okay, so now David knows he's not paranoid – *he's right*. Now the voices can truly be trusted. And these voices that have befriended him with their prophetic whispers, they tell him that his children's souls will be consumed – forever condemned to burn in hell if they are not saved by the father who spawned them. He looks at his children from across the breakfast table and now he suddenly sees the red flash of demon eyes before they look away, or the dark yellow teeth when they smile at him. When he kisses his wife, he feels a piece of rotting skin slip off her cheeks. The devil has just shown his face to David Marquette. And the voices are right once again. Satan is in his house, he has possessed his family, and only David Marquette knows it. Only David Marquette can see it. Only he can stop it. Think about it, folks. It's like being trapped in a horror movie, but for David, there's no theater to run out of. No one to tell him, "Whew! It's only a movie!" There is no escape. For him, *this is reality.*

'I ask you, folks – no, no,' Mel said, shaking his head, 'I *implore* you – put yourself *into* the delusion and imagine that *that is your reality now.* This is your reality. This is what you see, and smell and taste and hear and believe. And maybe now you can imagine the frightening hell that is my client's everyday existence. That is the disease of schizophrenia. And that is what David Marquette suffers from.

'The law recognizes that someone who is insane is not responsible for his actions, no matter how brutal those actions might be.' Mel looked over in Rick Bellido's direction. 'Sure, it would make us feel better to blame someone for the deaths of four people. It would be neater to wrap it all up and call David Marquette an evil SOB. A cold-hearted psychopath, as Mr Bellido contends, that didn't care about his family and only wanted a carefree life to spend his newfound millions. But that's not what the facts showed. We heard from all different witnesses, including Jennifer's own family, who told us that David was a great father, a great husband. Yes, he had a couple of affairs over the years, but that doesn't mean he wanted to kill his wife. It doesn't mean he wanted to kill his children. And the State has offered no witness to testify that he did. But the prosecutor knows that by calling David Marquette a psychopath, it actually makes the whole nasty, brutal crime easier to explain to the voters of Miami.'

'Objection!' Rick said, jumping defiantly to his feet once again.

'Sustained,' Farley said, looking down over his glasses at Rick with a coy smile. He motioned for him to sit back down. 'Try not to characterize Mr Bellido as pandering his case to the good people of Miami in hopes of getting them to vote for him in his election bid next November.'

The courtroom tittered. Rick sank back in his seat red-faced.

Mel looked back at the jury. 'Let's face it. It would be easier for us all to hate David if he is a psychopath. There would be no pity in that instance, only loathing. And it would be a lot less frightening than the truth – that a debilitating mental illness could actually drive a once-brilliant surgeon, a loving father, a wonderful husband to commit the crime of murder without even any provocation. It would be a lot less frightening than finding out that there is no one we can blame.'

Mel waited a moment then continued, almost thought-fully, 'Schizophrenics, as Dr Koletis and Dr Hayes and Dr Barakat and Dr Hindlin explained, don't all suffer from the same delusion. They don't all hear the same voices, and they don't all see the same hallucinations. As it is with any mental illness, the disease manifests itself in the mind, and so it affects each victim in a horrifyingly unique way, so there is no standard universal psychiatric litmus test. There's no rash that erupts on the skin, or wayward cell that can be examined under a microscope to identify it, to verify that what the patient is telling them is the truth. Dr Barakat, the State's own psychiatrist, called David Marquette a malingerer. A fraud. A liar, basically. And yet we all heard Dr Barakat in this courtroom last week when he finally conceded to the Assistant State Attorney herself that he cannot say with any medical certainty that David Marquette does not suffer from schizophrenia. We all heard Mr Bellido try to object and prevent his own witness from speaking the truth. We all heard Dr Barakat then testify that *if* the delusion David reported to him was in fact accurate; *if* that was what David *saw, heard, believed, thought,* when he picked up that knife and that bat and he killed the devil and saved his family's souls, then David Marquette is not legally responsible for his actions. He is, in fact, insane. Even the State agrees.

'That brings us full circle, folks, to my final comment,' Mel said, making sure he made eye contact with every jury member. Making sure they all heard him, that each was listening. 'We have become a society of "I'll believe it when I see it" people. Church attendance around the world has fallen off, people are suing to have "In God We Trust" removed from our dollar bills.' He held up his hands defensively in front of him. 'Don't get me wrong, this is not about religion, folks. I'm only making a point. And that point is, we *know* schizophrenia is a real disease, even though we can't "see it" on a microscope slide or in a blood test. We *know* that this disease makes people who have it suffer from horrible auditory hallucinations, terrifying paranoia, and sometimes even vivid, twisted visions that can make them legally incapable of knowing what they are doing or the consequences of their actions. That can affect their ability to distinguish right from wrong. We *know* that inside the brain of a schizophrenic, reality – as *we* all know it exists – is actually seen completely differently by one who is afflicted with this disease. We know this, even though we ourselves cannot see it. Even though we cannot hear it. In this instance, we can only close our eyes and thank God, or whoever else you want; we can only imagine.

'My job during this trial was to prove to you that my client, David Alain Marquette, was legally insane at the time he committed those murders. I have done that. The only way Mr Bellido's theory works – the only way that my client can be found guilty of murder – is if you do not accept that David suffers from schizophrenia.'

Mel looked over at the defense table, but his client just stared down, rolling his tongue around in his mouth. It was as if he'd been in another room with a set of earphones on, and hadn't heard what everyone had just been saying about him. His eyes remained as ghostly gray and lifeless as they had since the first day he had stepped foot in a courtroom.

Mel shook his head sadly as he headed back to his seat. 'The man has already been sentenced to a lifetime in hell,' he said softly. 'Please don't sentence him to death.'

97

The damage was already done before Rick's feet managed to find the floor again. 'Objection!' he yelled. 'The jury is only determining guilt at this phase of the proceedings, Your Honor. Mr Levenson's comment leads them to believe that if they find the defendant guilty he's going to be sentenced to death!'

The eyebrow went up again. 'That is what the State is seeking, right?' asked Farley.

'As Your Honor is aware, sentencing is separate and apart from a finding of guilt. That is determined only after the penalty phase. And in any event, sentencing is imposed by Your Honor, not by the jury.'

'But you are seeking the death penalty, right, Mr Bellido?' Judge Farley's back was arched and he clearly was annoyed. He hated being challenged, especially in front of cameras. 'Isn't that correct?'

Rick gritted his teeth. 'Yes, Judge, but—'

'I thought so,' said the judge. Then he looked over at the jury. 'If you find the defendant guilty, then we'll proceed to the penalty phase, where you all get to decide if the defendant should be put to death. However, I'll be the one who actually sentences him.' He turned back to Rick, his eyes narrowed. 'Anything further, Mr Levenson?'

Mel settled in his seat again and gently patted his client's back. 'No, Your Honor. I think we're done here.' The courtroom was perfectly quiet, but there was an electric charge in the air. Everyone knew the end was near.

'Mr Bellido, will you be giving a rebuttal?' asked Farley with what sounded a lot like a sigh.

Rick thought for a moment. The judge was obviously pissed at him now and, knowing how vindictive Farley could be, he knew that that fact would surely be further communicated to the jury should he give another closing. He looked at the men and women in the jury box and saw that they were getting a bit restless, as well. It had been a long couple of weeks, and an overwhelming, draining day. Giving a rebuttal meant he would risk boring the jury, further confusing them with psychiatric terms, or worse – pissing them off. And that could translate into unintended sympathy for the defendant. The biggest problem for most lawyers, he'd observed over the years, was not knowing when to just shut the hell up and sit back down. Thankfully, as he watched the jury, he saw that no one on the panel was looking over at the defendant, and that was definitely a good sign. An inability to make eye contact with either Marquette or his attorney meant that they were siding with the State. It meant they felt guilty for condemning him.

There was no reason to push it just because he could. 'No, Your Honor,' Rick said finally. 'There's no need. The State will rely on its closing and the jury's own recollection of the evidence in this case.'

'Alright folks, then that concludes closing arguments in this matter,' Farley finally said when the frenzied murmurs began again. He said nothing for a long while, his white brow furrowed, his face turning a deeper red with each passing second, until his silence finally had once again commanded everyone's attention. Now he was pissed at the whole courtroom. 'It's late in the day,' he finally said. 'Let's break here. I'm going to release the alternates and charge the panel on the law in the morning. They should be ready to go into deliberations around lunchtime tomorrow.' Then he climbed down off the bench before so much as another whisper broke out, and stormed into the back hallway, letting the door slam behind him.

'All rise!' barked Jefferson, once again, just seconds too late.

98

The phone call came maybe an hour or so after court had recessed for the day. She knew right away from the 305 area code and the 547 exchange on the caller ID that it was the State Attorney's Office. The last four digits told her it was someone in Major Crimes.

Julia didn't bother picking up the phone and hearing the news that she was being fired directly, so she just let the answering machine get it, while she sat on her kitchen counter, listening with her eyes closed. She didn't want to have to defend herself or banter back and forth about what had happened in court last week. She didn't want to explain what had happened with her brother or why she'd suddenly disappeared from sight for the last five days. She knew that a desperate attempt to try and save her job at the last minute would sound just like that – desperate. And she didn't want to give anyone, especially not Rick Bellido if it was him on the other end of the line, the satisfaction of hearing her cry or break down over the phone.

Please leave a message after the tone.

'Ms Valenciano, this is Charley Rifkin over at the State Attorney's Office. I was hoping to speak with you this evening. I have Colleen Kay in my office from Human Resources . . . Your behavior in trial last week was completely inappropriate, clearly rising to the level of insubordination . . . unprofessional and unbecoming . . . in such a hostile and aggressive manner . . . I am shocked and discouraged . . . Mr Bellido has commented that . . . Further, your failure to show up . . . necessary to terminate your employment . . . it is expected that your office will be cleaned out within the next forty-eight hours . . .'

At some point she just turned off the machine. When she flipped it back on again, she hit the delete button. There would be no need to ever replay that message. She'd heard all she needed to hear. She'd been fired over her answering machine. And if that wasn't bad enough, Rifkin hadn't even bothered to take her off of speakerphone while he did it. She was glad she hadn't picked up. She knew Rick was in there, probably snickering with his buddy over what a good bang she'd been and how right Rifkin had been about her from the beginning.

She'd expected the call, she supposed, but it was still a blow. Being a prosecutor was the only thing she knew. And it was over. Her entire career had just crashed and burned right in front of her, and she'd piloted the plane. Only a couple of months ago her future had looked so promising.

She wiped the tears and looked around her messy kitchen. She couldn't stay in this stifling apartment a second longer or she'd surely go crazy. She'd retreated into her tiny cave to lick her wounds, but now they'd found her and were shooting their bullets in here, too. She could feel the walls moving in, crushing her wherever she turned, and in the living room, the TV beckoned her to come back in and watch as the commentators talked about her in a dozen different languages. She ran into the bedroom and threw on a pair of running shorts and a T-shirt, pulled her hair back into a pony and headed out the front door.

She'd done her job. The protesters wouldn't even be looking for her anymore. She blasted her MP3 player as she ran, hoping to drone out the voices of Charley Rifkin, Judge Farley, Rick, Karyn, Dr Mynks. Everyone who'd wanted to see her fall now had themselves a front-row seat on national television. As the miles dragged on, and she hit her runner's high, she saw Andrew, sitting in the visiting room at Kirby, waiting for her to come see him, his carved, bloody hands outstretched across the chipped pressboard table, his lips blue and swollen.

And then with all the recent changes in Andrew's life . . .

She thought of all the ways she could have saved him from himself. All the things she should have done. All the ways she had failed him.

'Look at me now, Ju-Ju! Look at what you've done to me!'

She thought about David Marquette and how she had failed him too, not recognizing his sickness from the beginning. How she'd helped bring him to this point. How she would be responsible when they stuck the needle in his arm. The tears slipped from her eyes, but she never actually felt them run over her cheeks. Instead, they trickled past her temples as she ran even faster, brushed off-course by the wind in her face, like a raindrop on a windshield, finally disappearing with her sweat into her hair. She ran and ran and ran until they stopped coming. Until she didn't see Andy anymore. Until it was just the music that she finally heard in her head. Then she turned around and ran back home. It took over ten miles today to clear her head, and she wondered if there would come a point when she couldn't outrun the demons anymore. She wondered if that would be the end, or if, like Andrew and David Marquette, she wouldn't even realize it.

She slowed to a walk as she approached her parking lot. The first thing she noticed was the red and silver Harley in guest parking. She stopped dead in her tracks and stared at it for a second.

'Hey there!' Lat called out from where he sat on the stairs

that led up to her apartment, some fifty feet away. He got up and started toward her, but she didn't move.

'Hey,' she answered, trying to find the right words. She hadn't expected to see him today. Deep down, she supposed part of her hadn't expected to see John Latarrino ever again. She'd spent the day preparing for that reality, by not allowing herself to even think about what had happened last night. And now here he was, waiting for her.

'You look like you need someone to take you to dinner,' he said with a smile as he walked up.

'Yeah?' she asked.

'Yeah.' He paused for a second, while she looked down at the ground, and with her hands on her hips, pretended to catch her breath. 'I tried to call first, but you didn't seem to want to pick up the phone today. So I figured I'd come over and make the invitation in person.'

She felt her face flush, and she hoped it was still red from running, so he wouldn't notice. There were so many emotions running through her head, so many things she had said, so many things he had heard her say last night. She hated feeling so *exposed*. No matter how intimate she'd been with Rick, there was always a part of herself that she knew she held back from him. And after all that had happened, after how he had betrayed her, she was so very thankful for always exercising that emotional discretion. But last night . . . she'd been so damn vulnerable. So needy when Lat had shown up at her door unannounced. So she'd said things – too many things. John Latarrino knew everything about her now. Everything.

Tangled against his body, his heartbeat pulsing in her ears, his touch had made her quiver in a way Rick's never could. When he had finally kissed her, there was a completion of this *connection* that she had not felt before with

546

any man – and she had just let herself give in completely to the overwhelming feeling. For fifteen years she'd been hiding behind a made-up past of well-spun lies – lies that sometimes she even believed were true – and now, for the very first time since her parents were murdered, someone finally knew what her life really was all about. And he hadn't run away in fright. That was what was so beautiful. So peaceful. He hadn't judged her. He hadn't judged Andrew. He knew who she was, and it was like this enormous burden had been lifted off her shoulders, carried with someone else's help now.

He had made love to her for what seemed like hours, slow and sweet and incredibly gentle, but their first kiss had never ended. His mouth had never left hers. It was as if John was as hungry for her as she was for him, and neither could bear to let the connection go for even a split second, for fear it might end. So he had moved with her into the bedroom, his body pressed tightly against hers on the bed, as they danced and writhed as one to soundless, frenzied music – but he'd never once broken the kiss. When he had moaned, it was with her. Even their voice was as one. Afterwards they lay facing each other, their mouths only a few inches apart, so that she breathed his breath, and he hers. They lay like that for the longest time, and that was when she told him things she never should have told him. And he had listened until she was finally empty. His soft blue eyes never even looked away. Not even for a second. She had not wanted to fall asleep for fear of losing the moment, because she knew she would. As any drunk will tell you, daylight changes everything. And even through the sweet, euphoric stupor she was in, she knew that when the sun rose, she'd probably come to regret too many moments from this night.

He was gone when she woke up.

She finally looked up and smiled softly. 'Dinner, huh? I guess a burger would be nice.'

'A burger?' he replied incredulously, heading back with her across the parking lot. 'You are a cheap date. I was going to suggest stone crabs and a bottle of wine. Oh, well,' he shrugged, kicking a stone. 'A burger and a beer it is, then. My type of woman. I know just the place.'

'Stone crabs? Wow. You do know how to impress a girl. Uh-oh, what have I done?'

'Only the best, sweetheart,' he said. 'Only the best.' He reached out and gently touched her hand, as she stepped onto the staircase. He hesitated for a second before he asked his question. 'You doing okay today?'

She could tell by the worried look on his face that it was the first thing he'd probably wanted to ask her and she looked away again, totally embarrassed. Maybe he already knew from Rick that she'd been fired. Maybe that's why he was here, to pick her up yet again after she'd tripped on her face. *Poor, fragile Julia with the awful past had just had another bad day.* But there was no way she was going to lean on him again. She would not allow herself to be a pity call, or worse, a pity fuck. She'd rather be alone with the demons.

'Yesterday was . . .' Her voice trailed off. 'Look, I'm sorry about last night, Lat,' she said finally.

'Don't be sorry.'

'I said some things—' she began.

'That I hope you meant.'

'And I did some things—' she started.

'That I also hope you meant.' He smiled.

She pictured his warm body pressed on top of hers, his hands moving over her, and she looked away, to a spot of peeling paint on the staircase railing. 'I'm so embarrassed right now,' she said softly.

'Don't be. If it was too heavy, Julia, I wouldn't be here.'

'Okay,' she finally said, nodding. 'Let me just go change.' She started up the stairs.

'I was called out at seven, or else I wouldn't have left,' he said.

She didn't turn around. 'Good,' was all she said before disappearing inside her apartment.

99

Dinner had been just that – dinner. Cheeseburgers and fries with gravy and lots of coffee in a corner booth at an empty diner. He asked about Andrew – who he was, what he'd been like – and so she told him. But only about the Andrew she knew from childhood, before schizophrenia ravaged his mind. It was just too painful to go into the recent past. It was too hard to admit yet that things could have been different; that for the past fifteen years, she could have made them different. He asked about her dad and mom, too, but Julia couldn't put her whole family in the same picture, into the same conversation, yet. So she couldn't give him that and she didn't answer him. She knew the pieces were not all there, and the ones that were, were not always fitting together, no matter how much she wanted to force them. Without the help of Nora or Jimmy, some pieces of the past would never be found; the picture never really complete.

No matter how nice it might have felt to finally share the burden of her life with someone, she made sure that that Julia was from the night before. The emotional wall was back up in its place, although she feared it would be far too easy for John Latarrino to knock it back down if he really wanted to try. He'd discovered all her weak spots now and she wasn't very strong anymore.

But he didn't try, and he didn't push her, he accepted her silence and understood her distance. Instead, he changed the subject to talk about his own family. And about fishing. And the Marlins trading Juan Pierre. And places in Europe they both hoped to travel to one day. Completely innocuous, unremarkable subjects that over a couple of hours and a few cups of coffee slowly revealed they had a lot more in common than Julia would have thought a few months ago. And to her relief, he never once mentioned work, or cases, or defendants, or crime, or the trial of Dr David Marquette – which was funny, since they were probably the only two people in America who were *not* speculating about what the verdict was going to be or how long it might take the jury to reach one. If he knew she'd been fired, he never said a word about that either. He let her body language lead the conversation, and after a while, when he sensed she didn't want to talk anymore, he took her by the hand, slipped his jacket around her, and put her on the back of his bike. They rode once again along A1A, this time heading north, and once again, she thought about Andrew as she looked out at the black waves. God, she missed him. She didn't know where they were, or for how long they'd been driving when he finally turned around and headed back, but a part of her wished he didn't. A part of her wished he'd kept going – with her arms wrapped around his waist, the cold wind breaking in her face – until Miami was just a distant blur behind both of them. A tiny, tiny dot on a big map. The night had ended when it was almost morning, with a sweet, soft kiss at her door, but she hadn't invited him in, and he hadn't pressed her for an invitation.

Sleep had not come at all after that, but even so, she'd spent most of the morning toying with the idea of just staying put in bed, buried under the covers until the jury came back with a verdict and the Marquette case finally disappeared from the headlines. Until she could finally figure out what she was going to do with the rest of her life, where she was going to do it, and who might be in it. Rifkin's foreboding forty-eight-hour cleanout deadline kept ticking away anxiously in her head. While she definitely didn't want to see anyone at the State – especially not Rick or Rifkin or Karyn – and she didn't want to be seen, she feared putting off cleaning out her office even until tomorrow, lest she have to consider reordering her diploma from the microfiche archives of GW. Because she certainly wouldn't put it past anyone in that office – including the State Attorney himself – to order everything of hers to be tossed out in the dumpster. And just the thought of Rick Bellido going through her things and touching them made her cringe with anger and revulsion. She thought of calling Dayanara, but didn't want to get her involved. Day still had a career to look after. She knew she had to go back in.

From her parking spot across the street in the Kristy House lot, she spent maybe an hour late that afternoon just watching the strangers she used to work with walk in and out of the Graham Building. Strangers who she'd once thought of like her other family, laughing and joking and chatting with one another. Strangers who she knew she would probably never see or hear from again after today. As the clock finally hit four thirty, she watched as they poured out the front doors, running to their cars or the Tri-Rail. That was when she knew it was time to go in.

While she would have preferred doing this at, say, two in the morning, she'd figured that the first thing Colleen Kay from Personnel probably had done was deactivate her security card. As it was, she feared she might have to endure the embarrassment of an escort or two from Investigations standing over her while she cleaned out her desk, making sure she didn't slip an extra paperclip into her moving box.

But it was after five and the lobby was pretty dead when she walked in, and no one paid any attention to her, including the bored guard who simply motioned her through the metal detectors. Dressed down in a T-shirt, blue jeans and sneakers, her hair pulled in a pony, and hid under a ball cap, recognizing her out of her everyday attire of a suit and heels would probably require a double-take. With the two cardboard boxes she'd picked up from Publix folded under her arm, she quickly ducked into the stairwell, taking the stairs up to three, because she knew no one else ever did. Most of the secretaries and support staff were already long gone. As for prosecutors, she could only hope that a good lot of them were either heading home via the elevator right now, or were otherwise buried under mounds of paperwork in their own offices.

The hallway was clear, and she quickly slid her card through the security access doors. She 'prayed neither Personnel nor Rifkin were as smart as she gave them credit for, lest she have to wait for someone to come open the door, or the escort she feared to head down from Investigations. When she heard the familiar click, she breathed a heavy sigh of relief, and, with her head back and her shoulders straight, she made sure she walked through that hallway as her mother said — like she still belonged in it.

She felt the eyes of a few straggling prosecutors who were working in their offices look up and follow her as she passed. The hallway stretched longer and longer before her, like a rubber room, until she finally reached her open office door, stepped in and quickly closed it behind her. She leaned back against the door, breathless. *Please God, just get me through this.*

She looked around the small, cluttered office that she'd called home for over two years now, complete with its own coffee pot, radio and TV. Hell, she'd probably spent more time here than she had at her apartment. Since she'd come to felonies from County Court, she'd moved around in divisions, but she'd always managed to keep the same office, and she'd liked that. A pink gift bag sat on top of her desk calendar, which was still turned to the month of February. 'The boss is always a ass' Marisol had written on the enclosed piece of pink notepaper. 'Remember that. Good luck. I'll miss you.' Inside the bag was a white T-shirt embroidered with pink rhinestones. Julia bit her lip.

She was probably the talk of the whole office today, from administration to the boys down in the mailroom. Everyone knew she'd managed to get herself fired, a feat which was about as rare for a state employee as a solar eclipse. She imagined the crowd of curious co-workers waiting all day long to hear through the grapevine when she finally showed up to collect her things. Maybe peeking their heads in every so often to see if she'd been escorted back by security yet, wanting to discreetly watch to make sure she left the screws in the wall when she took down her diplomas. *No one ever wanted you here, anyway. You know that. You know that's true. They're glad you're gone. Now they want to watch you fall.*

She wiped her eyes with the back of her hand. *No, no, no, don't think like that. Please don't think like that.*

She switched on the small portable TV that sat on top of her file cabinet for company and set out to finish the task ahead. Of course, the coverage was all about the trial. One of the jurors had had a babysitting issue, so court had not reconvened until eleven thirty this morning. Farley had not sent the jury in to deliberate until almost two, and since everyone had ordered lunch right after that, discussions hadn't actually started until three. The judge had told them to go for a couple of hours, then he would dismiss them around six, and they could start fresh in the morning. Given the length of the jury instructions alone, it was expected that the jury would be sifting through the legal wording, maybe going over the testimony, and any notes they took during the trial, and taking an initial vote to see where everyone stood. Tomorrow was when the true deliberations were expected to start, and because of the sheer volume of the case, most analysts predicted they would carry over to at least Monday. Judge Farley would miss his cruise. Good.

Julia began to dump the contents of her drawers into the cardboard boxes, sifting through old pens and old pictures and old messages that she knew at one time were real important. She couldn't afford too long of a stroll down memory lane, lest Rifkin or Colleen Kay figure out she was here and missing an escort, so she moved quickly.

The sudden rush of excited voices in the hall outside made her look up from what she was doing. At the sound of footsteps, she held her breath. There were at least several sets. Then they hurried past her door, fading down the hallway. She let out a breath.

She looked around her office and instinctively turned back to the TV. Channel Six's Michelle Korant was standing in the hallway outside 4–8 chattering excitedly and motioning with her hands as people poured into the courtroom behind her. Julia raised the volume.

'This was completely unexpected, Tony,' Michelle was saying. 'Completely unexpected. Judge Farley is waiting on Corrections now to bring David Marquette back over from the Dade County Jail, which may take—'

Julia sucked in a quick breath at the news prompt that flashed underneath the pretty reporter.

THE JURY HAS REACHED A VERDICT

100

Anyone who'd still been in the Graham Building was now heading over across the street to the courthouse. TV trucks from every station with their forty-foot antennas lined the streets and circled the block. MDPD cars and City of Miami cruisers completely blocked off 14th Street, and more were busy setting up a perimeter around the building, their blue and red lights spinning. On the courthouse steps, a large, frenzied crowd of reporters swarmed around Rick Bellido as he tried to make his way across the street and into the building. Of course, Rick never took the entrance under the courthouse. And, of course, he never turned down an opportunity for an impromptu press conference. She heard his voice on the TV as she watched him out her window.

Julia had gotten dozens of verdicts back in her career as a prosecutor. Even when it was just a simple County Court misdemeanor jury she was waiting on, there was always this incredible, sickening, exciting rush of adrenaline that filled her whole stomach the second the phone rang in her office and she heard the clerk's voice tell her to head over, because her jury was back. The feeling wasn't unique to just Julia, either; she knew every prosecutor felt it. Getting a verdict was probably the most thrilling, nerve-wracking part of the job. The excitement would build on the elevator ride downstairs, the walk across the street, through the court-house. It was always a bit contagious, too, as word spread to others. Like little children blindly following the Pied Piper through town, people who didn't know you or your case would fall in behind as you made your way to the courtroom. Even if the case wasn't important or newsworthy, *the jury had a verdict.*

Julia had that sickening, exciting feeling now. She looked at her watch. It was only 5:18. They'd been out officially only three hours. A quick verdict couldn't be good for the defense in an insanity case, not with all the issues they had to consider. She paced her office for a long while, feeling her heart race, as that familiar shot of adrenaline hit her bloodstream. Now would be a good time to throw the rest of her desk in a box, she thought. Take her diplomas and her Bic pens and hightail it the hell out of Dodge while everyone was busy looking the other way.

But she couldn't.

She looked out her window again and across the street. The steps of the courthouse were virtually empty now. Everyone had already gone in.

This was her case. Her last verdict. She wanted to take that walk across the street one last time. And she wanted to see the faces of the jury she had picked. She wanted to look in their eyes and know what they were going to do before the clerk announced it to the world. And perhaps, most importantly, she wanted those three men and nine women to see her there, too. She wanted them all to know it was not just another case for her. It never was. She left her boxes on her desk and headed across the street.

No one paid any attention as she slid in the very back of the packed courtroom, because everyone – every correction officer, every police officer, every camera, every microphone – was trained on the somber-faced jury that was filing back into the box from the jury room. None of the jurors looked up from the floor or out at the crowd. None of them, she noticed, looked over at the defendant.

Lat came from somewhere and stood next to her in the back of the courtroom. Without a word, his hand found hers, grasping a pinky and rubbing it gently. Her palms were drenched in perspiration.

'Ladies and gentlemen of the jury, I understand you've reached a verdict,' said Judge Farley, folding up the verdict form he'd just read to himself. He passed it back to the clerk.

'We have, Your Honor,' said the red-faced foreman, swallowing the back half of his words as he finally looked up and spotted the wall of cameras trained on him from every angle in the courtroom.

'Will the defendant please rise,' said Farley, looking over at David Marquette.

'Want to get out of here?' Lat whispered in her ear. 'We don't have to stay . . .'

'I want to hear,' she whispered. She swallowed hard. 'I want to hear them say it.' She never took her eyes off the foreman.

A somber-faced Mel leaned in and whispered something into his client's ear before they both stood. Mel straightened his jacket and buttoned it, but David stared straight ahead, his hands held behind him. Julia noticed they were shaking ever so slightly.

'Will the clerk please publish the verdict, then,' said the judge.

Ivonne nodded and stood herself. She put on her reading glasses and opened the verdict form. 'We the jury,' she began, 'in the county of Miami-Dade, Florida, on this the twenty-fourth day of March, two thousand and six, as to count one of the indictment, to wit, the death of Jennifer Leigh Marquette, find the defendant, David Alain Marquette—'

The clerk gasped just a little as her eyes rolled over the

words before her mouth spoke them. She looked up into the cameras, her eyes wide. She finally stammered out what the entire world was waiting to hear.

'We find the defendant not guilty by reason of insanity . . .'

101

The courtroom exploded as a stunned Ivonne continued to read all four verdicts. One after the other, not guilty by reason of insanity. Judge Farley had known what was coming, and he'd wisely hit the Liaison security button under the bench as soon as he'd handed the form over to Ivonne. Liaison was the division of MDPD on the third floor of the courthouse that provided contact services between most of the County's police departments and the criminal courts. More than just making sure officers received subpoenas and showed up for court, Liaison also provided armed plain-clothes police for the courts. Because correction officers didn't carry firearms, as a security precaution, Liaison had already sent a few officers over to Farley's courtroom to help the judge maintain order. Judge Farley's emergency under-the-table buzz had tipped them off as to just what the verdict was going to be, though. Ten more Liaison officers were already through the door before Ivonne got the final verdict out of her mouth.

'Oh my God!' shouted one reporter into a camera, breaking the courtroom code of conduct. 'Not Guilty! He's Not Guilty! All counts!' That started the rest of them as Farley's rules got chucked out the window. Reporters began to air directly from the courtroom, not wanting to be beaten out in the hall in the ratings department by the shouts and screams of the competition.

Farley was yelling at Jefferson. Jefferson was yelling, 'Be quiet! Court is still in session!' at everyone. And no one was paying any attention. Julia had never seen anything like it. It was bedlam.

Rick Bellido sat alone at the State's table, stunned, staring out at the jury, who were now unable to look at *him*. Reporters snapped pictures and shoved microphones over the gallery railing in his face, demanding comment. For once, though, Ricardo Alejandro Bellido had nothing to say.

David Marquette hung his head on the table as Mel slapped his back. Alain pushed his way up to the railing and hugged his son's attorney, tears streaming down his face. Julia scanned the crowd for David's mother, but she wasn't at her husband's side, where she had been every day since the start of trial. She finally spotted her a few moments later, further back in the crowd. While the whole room surged forward to the gallery, Nina Marquette – dressed in a conservative navy suit, her white-blonde hair pulled into a classic chignon – slipped further and further back to the door. Reporters shouted questions at her, but she held her hand up, turned and walked out of the courtroom without her husband. Her eyes met Julia's for a simple moment as she pushed open the mahogany doors, but Julia could see that she wasn't crying today. And she wasn't smiling. Her skin was ashen, matching her hair, and she looked physically ill.

A reporter finally noticed Julia, pointed his microphone at her and began to scream her name. An army of cameras spun in her direction, their lights blinding her, while another set attacked Lat. She pulled her hand away from his.

'Ms Valenciano, are you happy with the verdict?' 'Was justice done?' 'Have you spoken to David Marquette?' 'Can you confirm that you have been fired by the State Attorney's Office?' 'Were you prepared to testify for the defense in the penalty phase?' 'Should the death penalty be abolished?' 'Do you have anything you'd like to say to the jury?'

'*Detective, are you angry with the State?*' '*Do you believe Ms Valenciano is responsible for the verdict?*' '*Are you continuing to try and link Marquette to the North Florida murders?*' '*Is there any further evidence that you can now reveal to the public?*' '*Will he be charged in those, even if you do have enough evidence, now that he's been found insane?*' '*Is he a serial killer?*'

The questions came so fast, it was almost as if the reporters shouting them didn't really want answers. Julia just kept shaking her head as the world began to spin and the cameras and faces closed in on her. She didn't know how she *should* feel, what she *should* say. It was all so surreal. So unexpected. And there were so many emotions. Part of her, she supposed, felt vindicated – the jury had heard her, and they'd listened. They had placed the blame where it should be – on the disease, not the man. Part of her felt unfathomable guilt and sorrow for Jennifer, Danny, Sophie and, especially, Emma, who knew only terror in the final minutes of her life, and would never understand why. Julia hoped that, in their eyes, she had done right by them. They all were consequential victims of madness. And, finally, part of her felt ashamed – as if she'd betrayed her office and her oath as a prosecutor. Justice was never as black and white as it seemed in the case law and statutes.

The judge finally found something heavy to slam on his desk and, with the help of Liaison, finally brought the courtroom back under control. He was done making nice with the cameras. The love affair was over. Let them write what they wanted.

'So help me, I will find everyone in this courtroom in contempt if I don't get quiet in the next five seconds,' he barked into the microphone. 'The defendant might be the only one here who I *don't* sentence to jail tonight.' His eye caught on the crowd of reporters in the back. 'There will be no interviews in this courtroom while court is in session! And even when it's not, do you hear me? Do that in the hall or on the front lawn for all I care,' he said, his eyes flickering with surprise when he saw it was Julia they were trying to talk to, 'do it with whoever you want, but you will not do it here.' He threw an icy stare in the direction of an exasperated Jefferson. 'Next time, do your job and make sure these people are kept under control. This is a courtroom, not a damn rock concert.' Finally he looked out with general disgust at everyone else. 'Now let's get this over with,' he grumbled. 'There's no sense in putting it off another day and keeping the circus here in town.'

The judge turned to the jury, while motioning to Jefferson to escort them out. His face and his body language instantly told them he was not pleased with them or their verdict. 'Ladies and gentlemen, thank you for your service,' he said abruptly. 'It is no longer needed. Jefferson will show you back out through the jury room. If you want to speak with the press, you may do so, because God knows they want to speak with you. If you don't, you can remain in the jury room and Jefferson will eventually escort you out to your cars, although I can't guarantee when that will be.'

As Jefferson began to usher the jury out, Julia saw some of the men and women cast a final, halting glance over at the defense table. The expression shared on their faces was one she had seen before, but not here in a courtroom, and she swallowed hard at the sight. It was the same look strangers would afford some disheveled, crazy, babbling bum on a street corner that they'd reluctantly just given a dollar to. It was a look of pity. Of contempt. And of unmistakable fright. But there was a flicker of something else, too. As they dashed to safety on the other side of the street to gossip with their friends, as they filed back into the comfortable security of their jury room, it was the look of self-righteous pride that Julia recognized. Pride at their own generosity and understanding.

As soon as the jury was gone, Judge Farley turned to the defendant, who was still standing. 'Mr Marquette, the jury has found you not guilty by reason of insanity on all counts of the indictment. I think we can agree – Mr Levenson, Mr Bellido – that the evidence has shown that you are indeed mentally ill and, further, that you are manifestly dangerous to yourself and to others. Can we dispense, then, with the need for an evidentiary hearing on that issue, gentlemen?'

Both Rick and Mel nodded. 'Yes, Your Honor,' said a visibly emotional Mel. It was clear that even he had not expected the jury's verdict. Rick's 'yes' was almost inaudible.

'As such, pursuant to section 916.15 of the Florida Statutes, and any applicable sections of the Florida Rules of Criminal Procedure,' the judge quickly continued, 'I find that the defendant most definitely meets the criteria for involuntary commitment, and as such, am hereby committing him to the custody of the.Department of Children and Families. The department shall decide what is the appropriate maximum-security state facility the defendant shall be sent to for treatment, but this court will continue to retain jurisdiction. Ivonne, set this down for report status in six months. At that time, Mr Levenson, I will review the hospital's report on your client's progress and we will proceed from there with any further extended commitment that I may then order.' Farley looked at the gaggle of press in revulsion. 'That's it, court's concluded. We are done here.'

Julia knew the judge had seen her in the back of the court, and she waited for him to maybe say one final thing to her before he stormed off the bench, but he didn't. The door to the back hallway slammed shut behind him and she never saw Judge Farley again.

Lat attempted to lead her toward the doors, his hand held protectively against the small of her back, as the questions and shouts started back up again now that Farley was gone. The crowd had thinned, as some of the cameras hurried after reporters into the hallway to grab the jurors before they left the building, and others went to hunt down Rick Bellido, who'd apparently ducked out the back hallway after the judge. Julia turned to look one last time around the courtroom where her career had abruptly, unfortunately ended. It was not lost on her that she might never be in another one again.

In the gallery, David Marquette held his hands out patiently in front of him for Corrections to cuff them. Another CO knelt at his feet, busy locking the shackles that held his feet in chains. She watched him for a second, his shoulders slumped, his arms and legs bound, as the remaining spectators talked excitedly about him, and the cameras continued to shoot him. That was when David Marquette suddenly turned his head and looked behind him.

Maybe he was searching for his father to say goodbye. Or maybe his mother. Maybe he was even searching for her. Or maybe, she would come to wonder later, he was actually looking for the cameras that filmed him. Whatever the reason, in a courtroom full of people, his ghostly gray eyes found hers once again, just like at the competency hearing. Across a room full of chaos, he locked in on them and held them fast as Corrections clicked his chains in place.

She couldn't look away. She couldn't move, even with Lat and the press that surrounded them pushing her gently to the door. Sound swirled in a vacuum, everyone, everything moved in slow motion. And as Corrections finally began to lead David Marquette across the gallery to the door that would take him to the bridge and DCJ, he did something Julia had never seen him do before. Not even once. Something that made her heart stop and her blood suddenly turn to ice water.

He smiled at her.

102

Ladies and gentlemen of the jury, I understand you've reached a verdict.

The judge's words sounded thick, as if they'd been dipped in molasses. All around him, he noticed, time had somehow suddenly slowed to a virtual stop. Seconds had stretched into hours, like a bad movie with too much slow motion in its direction. He heard the restless crowd around him suck in a collective breath and then hold it as the judge spoke. The moment seemed so fragile, as if he had just watched someone drop an expensive glass vase and was just waiting for it to shatter into a thousand pieces. He imagined, as he looked straight ahead at nothing, that if they did sentence him to die, this might be what his final moments alive would feel like. The last few hours lasting as long as days; final seconds becoming an eternity, until, he suspected, there'd come a point he'd actually be anxious for it to just end. His body was physically tingling, from both the terror and the excitement, as a million little fingers delicately crawled across his skin under the ill-fitting, cheap black suit his attorney had made him wear. The prickly feeling was at once euphoric and also insatiably itchy and uncomfortable, and he resisted the urge to claw himself out of his restless skin. It was imperative that he remain here, in the moment, no matter how anxious he might be. The end was almost here.

Will the defendant please rise . . .

They were all here for *him*, he knew as his eyes took in the room without ever moving. Not for his brilliant father or his cold, society mother or his sorry-ass, tragedy of a brother. This time it was for *him*. They had traveled from as far away as China and France and Germany – all around the world – to see *him*. To hear *him*. To watch *him* with their cameras. And as he sat there, waiting to rise up and hear his fate, suspended in this fragile moment, he knew that in dozens of countries, millions of people, right now, were talking about and shedding tears over *him*. Of course, the attention was never his intention, yet he couldn't help but find it funny how things worked out sometimes. And he couldn't help but be more than a bit proud of himself at how far he'd come with this. At how far he'd made it. But, of course, it was not time for smugness. The vase was still out there in mid-air.

His attorney gripped his arm and leaned into his ear. 'David, David, listen to me,' he whispered sternly, hoping to get through. 'If the verdict is guilty, say nothing. Do nothing. Everything you say and do can be used against you. I will come see you across the street as soon as they complete the booking and the paperwork, and I will try to have you placed back on nine, so you can continue your meds. The penalty phase will not be for a few weeks, probably.' Mel lifted him by the elbow, encouraging him to stand up now. 'So say nothing, that's very important to remember.'

He stood.

Will the clerk please publish the verdict . . .

The judge kept up his angry stare as the clerk rose, unfolded the paper and finally put on her reading glasses. Sitting up stiffly in his seat, he moved closer to the bench, tapping his wrinkled fingers impatiently on the wood, and surveying his courtroom with a suspicious, anxious stare.

And that was when he saw the judge blink.

It had happened so fast, he was sure no one else had noticed. But he'd played enough poker in his life to know a tell when he saw one. Judge Farley, with the flicker of panic in his cold, angry eyes, had just choked right in front of him and given away his hand. And in that brief, fragile instant, he knew what the clerk was about to say.

He felt everything inside of him relax, and he bit his cheeks as the clerk began to read aloud the words he already knew were coming. He bit them hard until they bled. The pain kept him from moving. From cheering. From sighing. From smiling. From laughing.

We find the defendant not guilty by reason of insanity . . .

He'd wanted to scream, or jump. Even hug his attorney back. He'd wanted to reach over the gallery rail behind him and hug his crying father, too, before he finally smacked that pitiful, profound look of despair and disappointment off the old man's face. It was the same familiar look his face slipped into whenever he got within ten feet of Darrell after he'd been diagnosed. That's why he wanted to remove it. His mother had always been far more discreet, reserving her looks of disappointment and shame and despair for more private moments, when the cameras were off and the guests had gone home, but there was no need to look behind him to know that she was gone already. There was no way she could handle the failure of being the mother of two schizo sons, the mother of an insane murderer, no matter how well she'd played the supportive role these past few months. The label alone would probably kill her. Good.

The men and women who judged him were still sitting in the box, shifting uncomfortably in their seats, the cameras were still set upon him. So, of course, he didn't slap his father. Or yell at his mother's shadow. And he didn't hug anyone. He didn't do anything. He just swallowed the blood from the chewed wall of his cheek and he stared straight ahead.

The shouts and screams erupted everywhere, all around him. He heard the cheers of those who had made him their cause. The Pro-Life poster boy. The champion of the Treat People With Mental Illness In A Fair And Decent Way groups. And he heard the cynical jeers of those who thought him the devil incarnate. Of those who believed him a malingerer. A faker. A murderer.

Amidst all the noise and shouts and clutter, from somewhere behind him, he heard them call her name.

'Ms Valenciano, are you happy with the verdict?' 'Was justice done?' 'Have you spoken to David Marquette?'

His miracle worker. His Anne Sullivan. She who had made the blind see his illness; who had made the deaf hear the voices only he heard. Assistant State Attorney Julia Valenciano. They continued to shout their questions, but she never answered them. He didn't hear her sweet, defiant voice. Even so, he *knew* she was there, somewhere behind him, waiting. He could feel her. He could even smell her perfume. Their electric *connection* was still there, as it had been since the beginning, and he knew she would not leave him until it was all over.

I find that the defendant most definitely meets the criteria for involuntary commitment, and as such, am hereby committing him to the custody of the Department of Children and Families . . . I will review the hospital's report on your client's progress and we will proceed from there with any further extended commitment . . .

He owed her big-time. He owed her, perhaps, his life. And it was time to let her know just how thankful he was to have it. It was time to let the world in on the proud little secret that he had been keeping all to himself. Well, maybe not all to himself, he thought with a chuckle. There was one other out there who was very good at keeping secrets.

As they came for him with their shackles and chains and

handcuffs, he patiently held out his arms, because he knew it would not be long before he was free of them. Before God miraculously healed the sick and he would be well again and they would have to regrettably let him out. The time was sure to quickly fly . . .

He let them lead him away, but he knew she still waited. Until the last second, she waited for him. So he turned around and he made sure he thanked her for all she'd done for him with a big, friendly smile.

Damn, she sure was pretty.

To God

Why have you made life so intolerable
And set me between four walls, where I am able
Not to escape meals without prayer, for that is possible
Only by annoying an attendant. And tonight a sensual
Hell has been put upon me, so that all has deserted me
And I am merely crying and trembling in heart
For Death, and cannot get it. And gone out is part
Of sanity. And there is dreadful Hell within me.

Ivor Gurney – English composer, poet and patient,
The City of London Mental Hospital

103

It was strange, she thought, to hear the birds chirp and sing outside. From her window, all Julia could see across the neverending empty field that stretched past the parking lot was a blanket of white snow. And looming in the not-so-far distance, underneath a veil of gray clouds, the majestic chocolate mountains were still wearing white caps. It looked cold and abandoned and desolate. But right next to the window, in a naked Honeylocust tree sprinkled with snow and crusted with ice, a pair of cardinals was busy building a nest for their babies. Even snow in May couldn't stop the tiny green buds from pushing through the snow dust, or the birds from building their family a new home. It was a sign of spring, John had told her.

'The positive thing that we can look to here, if it can be said that there is anything positive about your condition, Julia,' Dr Ryan was slowly saying, 'is that you actually recognize the signs of your illness. And, as you know, that is a good sign indeed, in terms of predicting an outcome here.' A badge clip on her white jacket said Marie G. Ryan, MD Psychiatric Services. 'And, of course, there is the possibility this is an isolated psychotic episode, although given the family history, I am not holding out much hope that's going to be the diagnosis.'

She knew she should be listening harder, but she couldn't focus. The birds were chirping so loudly, it was almost as if they didn't want her to hear anything but them. Their chirping seemed to fill her brain, so that there was no space left for anything else to be heard. She picked certain words that the doctor was saying to concentrate on, thinking that might make it easier. *Positive. Condition. Predicting.* She couldn't let herself lose the words. They were the only rope she could cling to now and she couldn't let them go, no matter how loud the chirping became. No matter how hard it was to focus. She knew what would happen to her if she got tired and let them go. That was what was so . . . *positive. She knew what would happen to her, and that was a positive predictor.* It all suddenly snapped into place and made sense. She breathed a silent sigh of relief.

'There are other positive factors to consider as well. You're female. Statistically, females have a more favorable outcome – one, five, ten years down the road – than men. You're first showing signs of the disease at the age of twenty-eight, which is also good. The older the age at onset is positive. Prior to only a few weeks ago, your behavior, your thinking, as you and John have both related to me, and as your medical history presents, was considered to be relatively normal. You did not suffer from bizarre thinking or associations as a child. No delusions, or hallucinations, no prior psychiatric hospitalizations. That, too, is good for a couple of reasons.' Dr Ryan looked over at Lat. 'Individuals who have led a normal childhood,' she said, holding her fingers up like quotation marks when she said the word normal, 'and who then have a rapid, sudden onset of the disease, as opposed to one that develops slowly over months or years – well, statistically speaking, those patients have a better long-term prognosis. Of course, everyone is different, and I do have to stress that that is only statistically speaking.'

'But what about what happened with her brother? Her parents?'

'The murders were definitely a traumatic event, no doubt,

but by normal childhood, I mean that her development – emotionally, socially, behaviorally – was normal. There were no emotional-development issues reported. And given just how traumatic and stressful that event was, it is remarkable that she did not have a psychiatric history after that. While stress is no longer considered to be the cause of schizophrenia, it may be the proverbial straw that breaks the camel's back in individuals who may be genetically predispositioned. In other words, the fact that Julia did not develop schizophrenic or psychotic symptoms long before this suggests she's very strong.'

It's as if a cataclysmic earthquake has happened inside her head. The mountains are falling, the seas are opening. The landscape will never be the same.

Julia's eyes darted to the window again. She watched as the male cardinal, with his brilliant red feathers and black crest, suddenly flew off by himself into all that white. She followed him until he became a small red dot and finally disappeared out of sight. The female stayed back in the branches, next to the window. Julia noticed that she stopped chirping.

'But we do have your family history to consider, Julia, and that, unfortunately, is not so good.' The doctor's soft, tan face changed a bit. It grew more intense and serious, almost as if it were brittle. 'Again, as you already know, statistically speaking, the more relatives in the family tree with the disease, the poorer the outcome tends to be. You have a father and a brother, both in your direct line of consanguinity, who have developed the disease. And we don't know about the rest of your lineage, as there's no one left on either side who can relay that history. But you are responding to the medication nicely, and that *is* positive, and you are no longer hearing the voices, is that correct?'

The female looked around anxiously for her mate now. She started to chirp again, but it was a different type of chirp, Julia thought. It was a 'Hey, where'd you go?' chirp, and it grew a little more insistent. Finally, she left her nest-building behind and began hopping from branch to branch in the sprawling tree.

'Julia?'

Dr Ryan was looking at her. For how long, she didn't know. How long had she been gone this time?

'Julia? Are you still hearing the voices?' Her voice was slow, but the tone was raised, as if she'd asked the question a few times already.

Hold on to the words. *Medication. Positive. Voices.* She shook her head. 'No. They've stopped, I think. Sometimes . . .' Her voice drifted off. The room was very hot.

'They stop sometimes?' Dr Ryan tried not to frown. 'I thought you weren't hearing them anymore.'

Julia shook her head again. 'No. I don't. I don't, I don't hear them anymore. Sometimes I get, ah, I get nervous again, like they . . .' She took a deep breath. The room was so hot now. And the words felt thick as they came out of her mouth. She could feel both of them watching her, studying her, analyzing what she was doing and saying and comparing it to normal reactions, sentences, emotions. To be sure, Dr Ryan was more clinical in her observations, comparing her to her other psych patients, or maybe to a textbook. But John was more personal. She assumed he was comparing her to the 'old' Julia that he used to know. The Julia that didn't babble sentences which made no sense or hold her head like it hurt. Or drift off somewhere where no one could find her. She looked at the floor, embarrassed that he had to hear her say these things. 'Like they might come back. Like I won't know it if they do.'

Like a cancer patient in remission or an MS patient in between episodes, everything now related back to her disease, as, she suspected, it always would. Was she exhausted because she hadn't slept well or was her brain throwing another white spot? Did her back hurt because she'd pulled a muscle, or was it the cancer cells back, building another complex tumor somewhere in her body? She had to analyze every thought now to see if it was indeed normal, or if she was being tricked by her own mind. Would she know if the voices came back? Would she be *aware* next time that something was horribly wrong in her head? Or would madness consume her completely on her next go-round and she would be too sick to help fend it off again?

She knew all about the disease, all about the prognosis. She'd studied it for months. From how she remembered it, the odds weren't looking so good. And unfortunately, her awareness of being sick was the one reality she hadn't lost yet. It was the one thing she clung to. Like a drowning pathologist lost in the middle of the Atlantic without a lifeboat, she would know the clinical experience of her own tragic demise before it took her under.

Almost as if he had read her mind, Lat leaned over and grasped her hand, rubbing it gently. 'People beat this, you know.'

'John is right, Julia,' Dr Ryan said slowly. 'With the help of medication, some people do go into full remission. I know you've had a horrible experience with your own family, and I know that you're familiar with the disease in a negative, forensic setting. But more than two million people *live* with schizophrenia in the United States, Julia. With treatment, some of them fare quite well. They have jobs and families. They don't all live on the streets or commit homicide. Forget what you've seen in a courtroom, or watched on TV. They're not all violent and they're not all homeless. There is hope.' She finally smiled and then looked over at Lat. 'You have many positive predictors for a good outcome. And, perhaps more importantly, I can see you have a wonderful support system. I think you're more than ready to continue treatment on an out-patient basis.'

She smiled and stood up from the seat that she'd pulled up next to Julia's. 'The most important thing will be for you to continue to make sure you take the medication. Even when you're feeling completely normal again, for lack of a better description.'

'I get very tired,' Julia said.

'Yes, well, the Mellaril seems to be working for you right now, and I'm hesitant to change that. The other antipsychotic drugs can have some very serious side effects, including the second-generation antipsychotics. I don't think we should change what's working. And the Elavil will help with anxiety and depression. That takes a bit longer to see results.' She headed to the door, opened it and turned back to Julia with a final, soft smile. 'I'll see you in three days in my office and we'll look at how things are going for you. Good luck to you.' Then she disappeared out the door and they were alone.

The chirping and singing started again. Julia looked back out the window. The male was back, his beak filled with twigs and brush.

'When can we go home?' she asked softly. 'I . . .' she tried to finish the thought, but it got stuck somewhere, so she just stopped.

'I've rented a house in Anaconda,' he said, his eyes following hers out the window. 'It's only a few miles away. It's laid-back and ultra-quiet, so don't expect South Beach and the hootchie mommas.' He smiled. ''Cause I didn't pack your leopard pants. Or mine.'

She finally smiled and laughed a little.

'I think we're going to stay out here for a while, though,' he said quietly.

'Lay low,' she whispered, growing serious again.

'That's what the cowboys and criminals do. Welcome to the Wild West. Everyone lays low out here, separated by a few hundred acres of land.' He followed her gaze out the window. 'It's beautiful, isn't it, though?'

She nodded, but his words slipped off and she blanked out yet again. Her mind kept doing that. Taking short cat-naps without telling her. When it woke up, everyone and everything seemed to have moved on without her.

'What do you think?' he asked softly, trying to find her again. He waited a few moments before trying once more. 'What do you think? Isn't it pretty country?'

'Yes,' she said, biting her lip and looking at the cardinals building their nest together in all that snow. 'Is it really cold?'

'Everyone says this was just a late-season storm. Spring's here, that's for sure,' he said, tapping on the window. The birds ignored him. 'It's so peaceful out here. I think that's what you need right now, Julia. That's what I know I need. Get away from all that craziness and get you better.'

All that craziness. The last few weeks were a blur. Maybe that was a good thing. She couldn't remember exactly when she'd figured out her head was not working right anymore. Even with all the medicine, and the whispers in her head now gone, she couldn't figure out what *had* been real. The phone calls, the protesters, the reporters following her . . . It wasn't like she now saw the past clearly and lucidly. It was still deceptively foggy. David Marquette's smiling face flashed in her mind too many times. Over and over. Had she been wrong all along about him? Had that really happened? Had the devil really smiled at her? It was the one thing she was afraid to ask John about. So she lived with it.

He insisted no one else knew what had happened with her. He'd told her there was no public breakdown. Nothing made the papers. In the days after the trial had ended, she'd gotten progressively worse – strange and reclusive – and he'd known something was going really wrong. When he'd finally sat her down and asked her, she could remember telling him that something was not right in her head. That her thoughts were not sounding like they used to. That they sounded like they belonged to someone else. That they sounded like they were coming from the TV sometimes. It was probably the hardest thing she'd ever had to say to someone, much less someone she knew she was falling in love with – but she'd wanted it to stop so bad. She'd wanted to be normal again. And she was so scared. She didn't know where to start or what to do. And she didn't want anyone to know.

That very night, he'd gotten on a plane with her and taken her here – far, far away from the spotlight of Miami. She hadn't known where they were going. She hadn't known where they were for a few days. She'd signed whatever papers he put in front of her; she'd taken whatever medicines he fed her. She remembered crying when they pulled past the sign for Montana State Hospital. Here, in the middle of the Rocky Mountains and the snow and the quietness, finally no one knew her name. That's what he'd told her.

'. . . before I plunk down any money, I want to make sure I actually like it out here. Real estate's always a good investment, I think, even if retirement is a long while off. I've been thinking of looking at Bozeman. That's where Montana State University is. One of the Robbery guys went there. Talks it up all the time. Nice college town. Not too far from Helena. Or maybe Jackson Hole, Wyoming. You'd be a cute ski-bunny, I bet.' He turned away from the window and took her hand. 'So what do you think, pretty lady? Would you like to raise some horses out here with me someday?'

'What about work?' she asked. 'Don't you have cases?'

'Miami's not going nowhere. They'll live without me for a little while. A long while, if that's what it takes.' He laughed. 'I just got a cell message from Brill. Apparently some of the boys are hoping I don't ever come home.' He looked at her for a long moment. 'Look, I got a ton of time saved up. I haven't taken a vacation in years. Haven't had a need to. This is good for me.'

She hung her head and closed her eyes, hoping to hold back the tears.

'Hey, hey, hey,' he said, reaching over to touch her face. 'We're gonna get you better. We're gonna relax. We're gonna go fishing and walking and hiking. And then maybe we'll go back. Maybe. But right now, let's take this one day at a time.'

She looked at him. He was smiling, but she could see how tired he looked. And incredibly worried. 'I don't want you to do this for me,' she started, the tears falling once again.

'Listen to me, Julia. I love you. And that's real. I've known it for a long time. I love how strong you are. I love how unpredictable you can be. I love how determined you are. No matter how crazy life may become, I've never been so sure of anyone or anything before. And this,' he said squeezing her hand, '*this* is reality. *We* are reality. In the Rockies or in Miami, wherever you want, wherever works, I'll help you get through this. You'll beat the statistics and you'll be fine. And if you doubt it, if you slip backwards, if you relapse, just remember that *we are reality*. And I will still love you. And I'll be there to help bring you back.'

She nodded and closed her eyes. 'I love you, too,' she said. She just wished their relationship didn't have to start like this. It wasn't fair. 'Thank you,' she said.

'Your aunt's been calling, too,' he said softly. 'I didn't tell her anything, but she wants to talk to you. She says she's been trying you for weeks . . .' his voice trailed off. 'She told me to tell you she misses you.'

The tears started. There was no way to hold them back. *Where had everything gone? What was real?*

He smiled again, wiped her tears with his thumb and kissed her softly on the lips. 'Now let's get you out of here and back into all that beautiful, cold sunshine. I got a log cabin I want to take a look at with you.'

Epilogue

'Excuse me?' *Tap, tap, tap.* 'Hello there? Is anybody home?'

Julia looked up from the stack of accordion files, notices, motions and A-forms she'd been trying to sort through on her overcrowded desk. She still wasn't quite sure where everything was, or where it should go, and judging by the size of the mess in front of her, she was beginning to realize that might take weeks. What a homecoming. Now, standing in the doorway, leaning against the doorframe, with one hand resting on an oversized hip, was her new secretary, and she didn't look very happy. With her free hand, she impatiently tapped long red fingernails against the open door.

'Hey,' Julia answered back slowly, smiling. She thought her name was Linda or Lurinda. Maybe Lucinda. But there had been so many new faces to remember these past few days that she couldn't be certain, and she was well past the point of being able to ask again. Judging from the recent exchange of pleasantries, she was guessing her new secretary might have no idea what her name was either. There was an awkward momentary pause.

'There's a lady here to see you,' the Unknown Secretary finally said.

'Is she my one o'clock?'

'No. She's set for a pre-file on Wednesday upstairs with Tessie Savastano.'

'I'm sorry,' Julia said, shaking her head. 'I don't know Tessie. Who's she?' She felt embarrassed. Again. She'd been gone less than a year, but the players were all different now.

Besides the usual lightning-quick ASA turnover rate, the new State Attorney, Steve Besson, had cleaned house. Even the support staff had changed places and faces. Funny how he'd managed to find the same personality quirks in the new ones, Julia thought.

'Tessie's the C in Spivac, which is Leonard Farley's old division. The lady outside said you got her case, though.'

'I was in Judge Farley's division before I left the office. Can you tell her that I'm not in that division anymore and that Tessie Savas —' she attempted, then cleared her throat, 'tell her that another attorney will be handling her case?'

'I did. I told her she had to see the attorney who's doin' her pre-file. She still wants to see you, though, and she don't wanna leave.' Lurinda or Lucinda rubbed her nose with one of her ultra-long nails and raised her eyes up to heaven. The zillion gold bracelets on her arm chimed. 'She looks like one of our victims, anyway,' she said, her lip curling in distaste.

Our victims. Welcome to the Domestic Crimes Unit. The only specialized unit at the State Attorney's Office with readily identifiable victims. You couldn't spot a robbery or fraud victim from a mile off, but an abused woman gave off more than a few signs.

Julia shrugged and nodded. 'Okay, then. I guess you can bring her in. I'll see if I can help her.'

The Unknown Secretary let out an exasperated sigh and walked off. 'Whatever,' she mumbled, flashing Julia the back of her hand. Julia wasn't quite sure what she was mad about, but her attitude was strangely comforting. After all, she'd worried for weeks when she decided to come back that people might coddle her or treat her differently. That was the last thing she wanted. So rudeness and unprofessional indifference was somehow refreshing.

She sipped at her coffee and looked around at the bare

industrial-gray walls of her new office, pockmarked and nicked with holes and scratches and screws left behind by its many previous occupants. It had probably been years since the walls had seen a new coat of paint. It would probably be a few more before they would again. Still stacked on the floor against the file cabinet were her framed law-school and undergraduate diplomas, her license to practice law from the Florida Supreme Court and her original Oath of Office from when she was first sworn in as an Assistant State Attorney in 2002 under Jerry Tigler. She had yet to frame the new one.

Next to her diplomas, in two cardboard boxes, was everything else she had once used to turn four walls and a desk into her own slice of home. Her coffee machine, pictures, knick-knacks, books, more pictures, a clock, her small TV and a radio. The boxes and diplomas had sat there going on a week now, and she wasn't sure now if she'd ever actually hang them up. Only a couple of pictures had so far made it out of the box. One was of Andrew. The other was her and Lat at the entrance to Yellowstone National Park a couple of months back. That sat on top of her desk, in front of all the mess. It reminded her what she was lucky enough to go home to every night.

John hadn't wanted her to go back. Ever. He'd made that clear from the second they'd gotten back to Miami, when his vacation time was finally up. He made that clear every hour or so when he called to see how she was doing. Even though Rick Bellido was long gone – along with Charley Rifkin and most of the rest of the office after the elections – Lat knew better than anyone that it definitely didn't mean the stress was. The cases still were what they were. The defendants were still criminals. The system was still irretrievably broken. And while she'd responded very well to medication and was faithful, so far, in taking all of her pills everyday, she knew he was worried. Worried about a relapse. Worried she would stop being compliant for some reason and it would be even worse than before. Worried she would become a negative, hopeless statistic, and he wouldn't be able to reach her next time. Worried, maybe, that their time together might be limited.

He'd begged her to reconsider, but she couldn't stay home and collect disability, even if the law and the doctors said she could. She would always be running from her illness – always have to – hoping to be three steps ahead of it. Hoping to maybe outsmart it, if there was such a thing. She knew that to have come this far in recovery, she was already one of the lucky ones. If she gave in to the idea that she was sick – that she was broken or didn't work right – she knew it would consume her. Totally consume her. And if she tried selling flowers on the side of the road or answering phones for a living just to live an okay, stress-free life, for her, that would also mean that it had won. *It. Schizophrenia.* Even another field of law was out of the question. She'd only ever wanted to be a prosecutor.

Lat had suggested, and she'd considered, another county, like Broward or Palm Beach, or maybe even the Keys, where she could be back in a criminal courtroom, but with a third of the caseload and no drama or office history to cart along as baggage, but she'd chosen to come back to Miami. When the new State Attorney – an ex-Miami-Dade cop-turned-lawyer-turned-prosecutor-turned-judge who was a personal friend of John's – afforded her that opportunity, she took it. But now, with a pile of new cases in front of her, a new boss and a bunch of new judges to familiarize herself with, she suddenly wasn't so sure about the decision she'd once been so sure about.

A few minutes later, there was another tap at the door. A young, slim black woman stood just outside in the hall, a baby balanced on her hip, and a whining toddler wrapped around her legs. Julia sucked in a breath, but hoped she didn't actually make a sound.

Even from ten feet or so away, she could see the ugly white and pink lines that criss-crossed the woman's face. Keloids had formed over the jagged scars, creating a grotesque network of white, raised lines that looked like termite mud tubes. It was impossible to say if she had once been a pretty woman. Julia noticed that one of her eyes was swollen shut as well.

'Pamela,' Julia said quietly, before the woman could say anything. 'Pamela Johnson.'

'You remember me?' she asked.

Julia nodded, rising from her seat. 'Come in, sit. Did Letray do that, too?' she asked, motioning to the woman's eye.

'Yeah. He got mad again. He always gits mad. But this time was worse. He tried to kill me. Said I was too ugly to touch no mo'. Said he was gonna do the job right this time. He just lost his job again.'

Julia said nothing for a moment. 'What was he charged with?'

'Aggravated battery, I think. He hit me with my momma's iron skillet.'

'Is he in custody?'

'Just made bond last night, I heard. I'm stayin' at my sista's house. Till he comes lookin'. She can't keep me there if that happens, though.'

'I think the case is upstairs with another prosecutor, Pamela. Her name is Tessie—'

Pamela shook her head. 'I been thinking 'bout what you

said last time. You know, the last time Letray went off.' She paused. 'You kept him in jail last time.'

There was no sense in sugar-coating the reason why. 'But you didn't help me. He got out, Pamela.'

'I know, I know,' Pamela finally said, shaking her head, and wiping tears from her good eye. 'And, well, you're the only one who made any sense, miss. I shoulda listened to ya. I got babies to take care of and the man's gonna kill me. I know it. You were right. My momma says I ain't got no one to complain to. Says I should have left him long ago. Says no one's gonna want me now, anyways. That I might as well put up with Letray beatin' on me, 'cause I ain't gonna do no better.' The toddler at her knee pulled on her skirt, trying to climb up on her lap. The baby pushed him away with a palm to the face. That started everyone crying.

'Don't believe that.'

'Look at me,' Pamela said quietly, putting the little one over her shoulder. She hushed the toddler with her free hand, rubbing his head.

There was a long silence.

'I know you fought for me last time and, well, I want you to fight for me 'gain,' Pamela said finally, wiping the tears defiantly from her face. 'I don't want to do this no mo'. I want him to pay.'

Julia looked hard at Pamela Johnson. At twenty-three she had two kids, no job, no future and a face full of ugly scars. She was being hunted by the devil disguised as a man and shunned not just by a cruel society who didn't understand, but by her own family. It was hard to imagine life getting much worse than that. For Julia, it put her own daily challenges in perspective.

She looked at the smiling picture of Andrew on her desk, the one she had taken at Kirby one afternoon in the late-winter sun. Beside it was the picture he'd drawn of her. She'd looked at them every single day since he'd died – even in the hospital – and she vowed to never again forget. No matter how frightened she might be of the future.

She nodded at Pamela Johnson. 'We'll need to start with your statement,' she said quietly, looking down at the blank notepad in front of her, blinking back tears herself. 'And remember,' she said, softly. 'This isn't going to be easy.'

Author's Epilogue and Acknowledgements

She wondered if the voices did come for her, would she know
they weren't real? Would she know the difference between a DJ
on the radio and a phantom?

In my second year of law school a good friend's brother
was diagnosed paranoid schizophrenic. 'Mark' was twenty-
six when he started hearing voices in his head. Voices that
whispered of violent mob conspiracies and warned of
treachery and collusion everywhere, even among family and
friends. Voices that never quieted, that got louder and more
desperate once the sun went down. According to my girlfriend, there was no bizarre childhood to report, no telltale
warning signs of mental illness that had always plagued her
brother, made him a misfit or labeled him as odd. He was
just an ordinary, affable guy trying to finish college, with a
bright future, a girlfriend, and a baby on the way. For anyone
who knew him, news of Mark's illness was as shocking as a
diagnosis of lung cancer in a young man his age.

Fortunately, Mark himself was able to recognize that
something had gone terribly wrong inside his head and, with
the help of his family, voluntarily checked himself into a
psychiatric hospital. Although the onset of his psychotic
symptoms was relatively quick, the initial long-term prognosis was good for him. Mark was discharged a couple of
weeks later and sent home on antipsychotic medication.

Sadly, though, my friend's story didn't end there. In fact,

for 'Tina', a real life nightmare was only just beginning. Like a scene from a twisted soap opera, as her brother lay medicated in a hospital psych ward, surrounded by psychiatrists and protected by padded walls, Tina was just outside the door being let in on a dark family secret: Mark wasn't the only one in the family with schizophrenia.

The news was devastating. Throughout our last year of law school, Tina struggled to learn all she could about the debilitating mental disorder that had seemingly ravaged her family. A mental disorder that no one wants to talk about. That good families just like hers strive to keep hidden and out of sight, stashed away with the other skeletons and dirty linen in the proverbial family closet. And that was when Tina first discovered the terrifying facts about schizophrenia. There is no known cause. There is no clinical test, like an MRI or a CAT scan or a blood test, which can definitively diagnose the disease. There is no cure. But there was one consistent statistical anomaly that my friend just could not ignore.

Although doctors don't know why, and scientists have not yet identified a 'schizophrenia gene', schizophrenia runs in families. And with each family member afflicted, the risk of another relative developing the disease rises dramatically. So at the age of twenty-four, with her whole life in front of her, my friend had to cope with the very real possibility that she, too, might one day develop schizophrenia. That she, too, might one day 'go insane'. And there was nothing she could do to stop it. I couldn't imagine anything more terrifying.

Except for a friend who'd struggled with anorexia in her teens, before Tina told me her family story I'd never known anyone with a serious mental illness — at least, no one who would admit it. And I'd definitely never known anyone who had schizophrenia – the Mother of All Bad Mental Illnesses. Russell Crowe hadn't yet played the brilliant John Nash in *A Beautiful Mind*. And Geoffrey Rush hadn't yet mastered Rachmaninov's third piano concerto as Australian pianist David Helfgott in *Shine*. Unlike alcoholism or drug addiction – or even depression, as of late – schizophrenia is not, and will never be, a 'vogue' mental illness. No one talks about it. No one wants to talk about it. The social stigma associated with the disease is still far too heavy and damaging to careers and relationships. In fact, when Tina first told me about her brother, the only people who came to mind that I *had* heard of with schizophrenia were far more infamous and deadly than any gifted musician or mathematician catapulted to celebrity by brilliant screenwriters and talented actors. Like most people, I was ignorant of the facts.

I didn't know schizophrenia affects one percent of the world's population. I didn't know 2.2 million Americans have the disease. I didn't know that that's more than those afflicted with AIDS, multiple sclerosis and ALS (motor neurone disease) *combined*. I didn't know that schizophrenia is an organic brain disease. And, perhaps most important, I didn't know that schizophrenics are not *always* psychotic and they're not *always* aggressive or dangerous.

After graduation, I left New York to begin my career as a prosecutor with the State Attorney's Office in Miami. Not less than five minutes after stepping through the courthouse doors, like it or not, my eyes were forced open to the very real, sad fact that mental illness – in varying degrees and with differing diagnoses – goes with the criminal justice system like pickle relish on a sub. It's a condiment that's not on every slice of bread, but it's on a lot more sandwiches than you'd think. And I came to understand that for those who suffer from severe mental disorders such as schizo-phrenia and manic depression, and for their distraught families, that system can seem like a cruel revolving door, particularly for those whose illnesses cause them to resist help and refuse medication. Many self-medicate with drugs or alcohol. Many end up homeless.

As I hope I made clear in *Plea of Insanity*, not every violent crime is committed by someone who is mentally ill. And not every mentally ill person commits violent crimes. As a former prosecutor and police attorney, I can tell you that there are some unbelievably heinous or atrocious crimes that simply defy explanation, that leave victims and cops and relatives screaming for an answer to the question, 'Why?' So I must impress here that there's a definite distinction from the thought disorders in a schizophrenic that may cause him or her to act violently, and the evil acts of a psychopath simply devoid of conscience. The latter is far more dangerous and unpredictable.

A little over a year after his initial hospitalization, as is typical for many schizophrenics, Mark stopped taking his meds and suffered a second psychotic break. While caught up in the terrifying web of the same bizarre delusion that had sent him to the hospital before, he slit his wrists and then drowned his baby in the bathtub. Mark lived, but his son did not. To understand the insidious disease that infected a young father's mind and chewed away at his thinking till it was frayed like an electrical cord was to know that Mark never intended to murder his child. He was truly a sick man who was not responsible for his actions. And after lengthy discovery and consultation with the family, the State agreed as well. Mark was found not responsible and sent to a maximum-security forensic psychiatric hospital to get the help he needed.

My friend's tragic story haunted me for years until I finally decided to write *Plea of Insanity*. I wanted to pen a courtroom novel that was psychologically thrilling, and yet, at the same time, sympathetic to those who suffer from this frightening disease and their families. I wanted to entertain, but I also wanted to educate, because that's the real key to understanding and eradicating the ignorance that fuels the stigmas associated with mental illness. To accomplish that goal, I needed to make sure that the fictional tale I told was medically and legally accurate, which, of course, demanded tremendous amounts of research as well as the generous assistance of many people who donated their time, wisdom and insight to this project, and to all of whom I owe a great deal of thanks, especially, in no particular order, to Dr Jim Hicks, MD, Director of Psychiatric Services at Kirby Forensic Hospital, and the entire staff at Kirby, including former Chief of Safety and Security, James C. Gilbride, and Chief of Secure Hospital Therapy Assistants, Anthony E. Rouse; Dr Thomas Macaluso, MD, Medical Director of Psychiatric Services, Memorial Health System; Mr Dean Mynks, Director of Case Management, Henderson Mental Health Clinic; Dr Reinhard Motte, Assistant Medical Examiner, Broward County Medical Examiner's Office; Kathleen Hoague, Chief Assistant, Felony Division, Miami-Dade State Attorney's Office and Gail Levine, Senior Trial Attorney, Miami-Dade State Attorney's Office, the SAO's resident experts on insanity pleas; Janet Gleeson, Assistant District Attorney, Brooklyn County District Attorney's Office, New York; Special Agents Eddie Royal, Larry Masterson and Chris Vastine with the Florida Department of Law Enforcement, who *always* answer the phone for me; Greg Cowsert, Esq., Regional Legal Advisor, Florida Department of Law Enforcement, Tampa Regional Operations Center; Anita

Gay, Assistant United States Attorney, Legal Advisor for the Professional Responsibility Advisory Office; Douglas Donoho, Esq., Professor of Law, Nova Southeastern School of Law; Esther Jacobo, Division Chief, Domestic Crimes Unit, Miami-Dade State Attorney's Office; Priscilla Stroze, Division Chief, Miami-Dade State Attorney's Office; Julie Hogan, Assistant State Attorney, Office of Statewide Prosecution; Marie Perikles, Esq., Office of the Inspector General; Mr Tyrone Dean and Mr Richard Gagnon for their precious insight; Marta Marquez, Police Complaint Officer, Miami-Dade Police Department for a great tour of the Communications Bureau; and, finally, of course, to my amazing friend Tina for having the strength to share her story. Extra special thanks go to great friends Marie Ryan, Esq., Assistant Commissioner, New York City Police Department, and Joanne Marchionne, MSW, who offered up their time, comments and encouragement without hesitation when I know they had a zillion other things to do, and for my unbelievably supportive husband, Rich, who not only read the same sentences phrased a dozen different ways, but always listened. Over and over and over again. Last, but not least, thanks go out to my mom, Thea Pellman – my human thesaurus and recollector of strange trivia and odd facts – and, of course, my dad, John Pellman, who's always the very first to offer to read a work in progress and always says it's perfect.

I hope you enjoyed the read and I hope you indeed found it thrilling. Although part of the storyline for *Plea of Insanity* was inspired by Tina and Mark, I am happy to say that the story is not Mark's. Nor is it Tina's. Released from a state psychiatric facility several years ago, Mark continues to take his medication and is fortunately doing quite well. He lives on his own, supports himself and has a job. He is not a violent man. Tina, who thankfully never developed schizophrenia herself, has had a successful career and is busy raising a family of her own. Brother and sister remain extremely close. They pray daily for a cure.

For more information on schizophrenia or other mental illnesses, please contact the National Alliance for the Mentally Ill (NAMI), Colonial Place Three, 2107 Wilson Blvd, Suite 300, Arlington, VA 22201–3042, or to find a local NAMI chapter, call 1-800-950-NAMI or visit their website at *www.nami.org.* Or contact NARSAD, the National Alliance for Research on Schizophrenia and Affective Disorders, at 60 Cutter Mill Road, Suite 404, Great Neck, New York 11021, (800) 829-8289 or visit their website at *www.narsad.org.* Other helpful websites that offer information about schizophrenia, including symptoms, treatment and support groups, include *www.schizophrenia.com* and *www.support4hope.com* and *www.webMD.com.*

Bibliography

Bruni, Frank. 'Behind the Jokes, A Life of Pain and Delusion; For Letterman Stalker, Mental Illness Was Family Curse and Scarring Legacy.' *The New York Times*, 22 Nov. 1998.

Halleck, Seymour L. M. D. (1967). *Psychiatry and the Dilemmas of Crime*. New York: Harper.

Hare, Robert, PhD. (1995). *Without Conscience: The Disturbing World of Psychopaths Among U*s. New York: The Guilford Press.

Hicks, James Whitney, MD. (2005). *50 Signs of Mental Illness*. New York: Yale University Press.

Hoague, Kathleen G., Esq., 'To Proceed or Not to Proceed . . . The Basic Rules of Competency.' 1999.

Hooper, James F., MD, and McLearen, Alix M., MS. 'Does the Insanity Defense Have a Legitimate Role?' *Psychiatric Times*, Vol. XIX, Issue 4, April 2002.

Kaye, Neil S., MD. 'Feigned Insanity in Nineteenth Century Legal Cases', www.courtpsychiatrist.com.

Redlich, Allison D., PhD. 'Law & Psychiatry: Mental Illness, Police Interrogations, and the Potential for False Confessions.' *Psychiatric Services*, 55:19–21, Jan. 2004 (http://ps.psychiatryonline.org/cgi/content/full/55/1/19).

Resnick, Phillip J., M. D. 'The Detection of Malingered Psychosis.' *Forensic Psychiatry*,Vol. 22, No. 1, Mar. 1999.

O'Malley, Suzanne (2004). *Are You There Alone? The Unspeakable Crime of Andrea Yates*. New York: Simon & Schuster.

Torrey, E. Fuller, MD. (2001). *Surviving Schizophrenia (Fourth Edition)*. New York: HarperCollins Publishers.

He just wanted a decent book to read ...

Not too much to ask, is it? It was in 1935 when Allen Lane, Managing Director of Bodley Head Publishers, stood on a platform at Exeter railway station looking for something good to read on his journey back to London. His choice was limited to popular magazines and poor-quality paperbacks – the same choice faced every day by the vast majority of readers, few of whom could afford hardbacks. Lane's disappointment and subsequent anger at the range of books generally available led him to found a company – and change the world.

'We believed in the existence in this country of a vast reading public for intelligent books at a low price, and staked everything on it'
Sir Allen Lane, 1902–1970, founder of Penguin Books

The quality paperback had arrived – and not just in bookshops. Lane was adamant that his Penguins should appear in chain stores and tobacconists, and should cost no more than a packet of cigarettes.

Reading habits (and cigarette prices) have changed since 1935, but Penguin still believes in publishing the best books for everybody to enjoy. We still believe that good design costs no more than bad design, and we still believe that quality books published passionately and responsibly make the world a better place.

So wherever you see the little bird – whether it's on a piece of prize-winning literary fiction or a celebrity autobiography, political tour de force or historical masterpiece, a serial-killer thriller, reference book, world classic or a piece of pure escapism – you can bet that it represents the very best that the genre has to offer.

Whatever you like to read – trust Penguin.